ALSO BY CECIL FOSTER

No Man in the House

Sleep On, Beloved

Caribana: The Greatest Celebration

A Place Called Heaven:
The Meaning of Being Black in Canada

SLAMMIN' TAR

SLAMMIN' TAR

a novel

Cecil Foster

Random House of Canada

Many thanks to the Ontario Arts Council
for its generous financial assistance, which
bought me some time to write.

Copyright © 1998 by Cecil Foster

All rights reserved under International and Pan-American
Copyright Conventions. No part of this book may be reproduced in
any form or by any electronic or mechanical means, including information
storage and retrieval systems, without permission in writing from the publisher, except by a reviewer, who may quote brief passages in a review.
Published in 1998 by Random House of Canada Limited, Toronto.

Canadian Cataloguing in Publication Data

Foster, Cecil, 1954-
Slammin' tar

ISBN 0-679-30879-2

I.Title.

PS8561.O7727S52 1998   C813'.54   C97-932289-8
PR9199.3.F572S52 1998

Printed and bound in the United States of America

10 9 8 7 6 5 4 3 2 1

To Donna Goffe for caring,
friendship and understanding

———

For Sharon Beckford, who offered
new horizons and inspiration.

chapter one

Elongated rays from the waning sun nudge through the tall casuarina trees as Grantley Adams International Airport comes into view. I know this scene well, recognize all the landmarks. With eyes closed, I can tell you how, like time, the narrow road snakes through the villages of Providence and Friar Pilgrim. How the sun deceptively bathes them in a thin layer of gold. Many travel this road, or dream of travelling it, many times. In the calm of the evening, the airport first appears on the eastern tip of the island as a mere reflection, beckoning in the distance, the perfect embodiment of this paradise. An enticement nobody, especially not the weak and ambitious, can ignore. A promise only fools will not consider. I know where this road leads. More importantly, I understand from whence it emanates. I know the full story, millions of stories, actually, for stories are my life and calling. Simply put, I am the champion storyteller, the darn best around. It's me alone who can truly boast without fear of challenge:

A riddle, a riddle, a ree
No man can tell this riddle unto me
Except he is better than me.

Look for yourself! There it stands. Grantley Adams International Airport, the beginning and ending of so many journeys and dreams. The same old story. There it is, just an arm's length from the dark blue ocean, standing imperially, arrogantly, in the open field — the last bulwark. You must forgive me, for suddenly I am feeling a little queasy and a tiny bit claustrophobic, you know, just a smattering, nothing too much to worry about. To continue with the task of recording these scenes, I must shift my position, must get a bit more blood flowing to my head, must avoid being crushed. Excuse me for digressing while I make myself comfortable...

As I was saying, even though I know this land as well as you know the back of your hand, I *must* record every event of this day, this hour, this very minute. For we storytellers know one thing: we must take nothing for granted. No matter how well we know someone, a scene, a place, anything — there is always the chance of a slight change occurring just when we let down our guard. And it is that one change, the unexpected development that goes unnoticed to all but the trained eye and ear, that could make the difference. Breaking the familiar, this is what makes the story we are born to tell different from all others before, what makes it unique from all stories to come. So, I must continue to put myself through the paces. Must be on guard. I *must*, even though this story is now boring as shit. Experience tells me not to trust the beauty of this evening, not for one minute. And yes, if I am a bit nervous, it's because I know I can never make a mistake of judgement again. Ever.

I am sure you listeners can detect the apprehension in my voice. I always feel a little shaky when I travel, especially when I see the airport for the first time. Just the early jitters. But don't worry; I'll struggle on and grow stronger. Still, I hope Mother Nyame has not tuned in to this story just yet. Something, and I don't know quite what, tells me the great warrior mother has a special interest in this story; she the very one that owns all stories and decides which gems to share; she whose main purpose in life is to ensure the fidelity of all stories. Mother Nyame likes strong, forceful stories that are well expounded, or so she says. Yes, they can be graphic, but they must be objective. They must be enunciated in a loud, clear voice and with conviction. So, of course, I hate to concede that there are times when I no longer feel in control, when even my voice rebels and takes on those unsteady, staccato tones. How I hate the sound of my voice cracking up. A real storyteller, a true professional, always has control over the voice, the most powerful of weapons, the ultimate tool. Spurring us on, Mother Nyame will ask: What is there to the story if the tones and emotional levels are too hot, if they are all over the place? Isn't that like a prophet going dumb at the crucial moment? In my case, she would scream, keep the damn thing focused! Stick to the point and stop all this meandering! Just tell the story straight up. But you know me, I like to talk, and when you can tell a good story, when you are a seasoned old hand at the job, you can afford to take a few liberties.

"Damn lucky devils, all o' you so," the rumbling voice repeats. By now, I am finally accustomed to the presence and drone of this man. Yet I have no interest in him. Someone else is telling his story — someone, poor soul, in this very car. Another storyteller who doesn't even bother to acknowledge my presence, let alone to demonstrate the good manners and professional courtesies that come with a simple hello. I don't mind this snub. I am too big to worry my head about petty feelings. As storytellers, we have always had common courtesies, and good manners too. If we don't possess them ourselves, how can we spot them in others? At least that is what Mother Nyame constantly drummed into our heads. But I've been out of the classroom a long time now — it is hard to know for sure what she is telling the younger generation, or whether these young bloods even bother listening to her ageless advice. And I often wonder what will become of us. Especially now in this so-called age of enlightenment where it appears that just about anybody can become a storyteller, even, I dare say, those totally unsuited for the job. Must be true that times are indeed changing.

Sometimes, we storytellers get so close to our subjects we, as they say in Barbados, take up their fire rage. When they get angry, so do we. If there are animosities and even jealousy, as I am beginning to suspect there are between these two, we experience them too. I'd like to think I am above such an obvious lack of professionalism. I am an objective reporter, properly trained by Mother Nyame herself and damn-well courteous. But I also know my limits and my few faults. And I have my loyalties, too, just like anybody else. That is why I will not even try listening in on the recordings of that other so-called storyteller. To hear that yarn would be as easy as tuning in to the wind, locating the right channel and listening to the chronicling of raw history. History as it is made, we like to say about our jobs. (For the record, that is how anyone can hear my story: just find the right channel and tune in. Simple as that. Listen for the male voice, hopefully, heh, heh, heh, the one without too many shakes.) But, as I was saying, I cannot be bothered with the unimportant. If there is something of consequence that I am overlooking, something someone else is picking up on in some unauthorized report, I am sure Mother Nyame will signal me. At least, I hope she will. After all, I am the official chronicler on this trip, the one with the seniority, the experience and the status. Twenty-five frigging years on the job. But I am feeling too anxious about the future to be agitated by anything else, too apprehensive to be concerned about someone else's diatribe, especially if that someone else is so ill-mannered as to not even recognize my seniority, not even with a *kiss-me-arse* hello. You tell me: how much time and effort would it have taken anyone to extend such a simple courtesy? Tell me! Makes me want to laugh, these young people of today. *Rass hole* upstarts, if you ask me. No sense of or appreciation for the very history they profess to be recording, for the traditions and professionalism they claim to follow and practise.

"If all o' you only know how lucky yuh all must be, eh,

Johnny," the man mumbles on, oblivious to the fact that nobody cares to listen.

Around us, as I had started to say earlier, the signs are ominous. Finally, the ferocious sun is beginning to give up the fight. But even now, it cannot just surrender. It must follow a centuries-old ritual, dancing and prancing in full battle gear, disappearing behind clouds only to reappear fleetingly with a mask of fury, banging its drum, mouthing off about achieving at the very first opportunity what it couldn't today. For an entire day it relentlessly sapped the windswept island of its energy and patience. Now, its glory gone, the sun is reduced to reflecting tantalizingly off the galvanized tin roof of the airport. It toys with the islanders by refusing to disappear as quickly as they wish. With this lingering act of defiance, the sun provides the harbinger of yet another tomorrow, something a real storyteller must always take care to mention, alerting listeners to any promising developments or trends. For every hope and dream, the essence of believing, needs a tomorrow. The sun, like the dreamer, does too. It needs that hope and it needs an enemy, too. Reinvigorated, and in a few short hours, it will return in full fury to the never-ending battle. Tomorrow: when dreams and hopes rise in the morning and, like the sun, perish by dusk. Between the rising and setting, millions of new stories will have started, millions will have ended and millions more will continue drifting direction-less from one day to the next, most of little note or significance. But among all those millions of half-baked stories, one, maybe two or three, will have that one key element that provides the uniqueness, the ingredient, the royal jelly that makes the difference, forever inscribing it in the history books, in the mythological lore. And so is born an everlasting story with its hero or two.

"Someday, I'll get a chance too," the droning continues. I tell yuh, can't you hear the self pity in his tone? "Damn right, I will.

And then I'll have lots o' money, foreign money like *rass*, lining my two pockets. I'll be a somebody too, *godblindmuh*."

In the distance, the blinding reflection of the sun's rays becomes more powerful as our big blue and white Toyota rounds the steep bend and slowly negotiates the final incline of Highway 7. The pot-bellied driver sprawls in front of the steering wheel, dark glasses hiding his eyes. He doesn't even bother trying to avoid the gaping potholes that grow wider with every tropical downpour any more, although every one of the really big drops induces a loud sucking of his teeth.

The driver changes the topic of his discourse and spices up his talks with a stream of colourful profanities. These damn roads are only *mashing up* his shocks and tires, he says, destroying the very soul-case of his car. This is so typical of his bad luck — the destruction of the car that provides his daily bread. This, he says, only compounds the dishonour of having a fading dream that someday he, too, will be a passenger in one of these airport taxis. Someday, he claims, his dream will not die at the airport at the end of the day — like the sun. His incessant talking drives me crazy. I wonder how his life companion puts up with such relentless complaining. My god, this has all the makings of a really awful and boring story. One, I am sure, that hasn't got a snowcone's chance in hell of making it into the folklore, not even as gossip.

"Damn lucky, all o' you, if you ask me," he grumbles on. "Every last one of you going overseas and making something o' yuh life. Just me, like some *kiss-me-arse* idiot, left behind with nothing but a taxi driver job to do all year 'round. Then this blasted road, that the government won't even fix up, knocking the stuffing out o' the blooming car. Only expensing me at the motor mechanic shop. And it ain't even like I'm one of you lucky boys going up north, where you can buy car parts and everything else cheap, cheap, cheap. But, *godblindmuh*, mark my word, my luck will change, man. 'Cause I ain't a fool from birth, I ain't born behind my mother's back."

The Toyota passes between an imposing outcrop of weather-beaten limestone that temporarily blocks the view of the airport. It lingers briefly in the shadows of the tall, majestic mahogany trees lining the highway, finally emerging into flat rolling terrain — some of the richest plantation land on the island — of peanuts, onions, sweet potatoes, sugar cane, corn and green grass. Across the fields of black dirt is the airport, with heat waves shimmering above the building and tarmac. You can't miss it. Undoubtedly, this is the most important building on the island. All roads lead to it. Even nature crowns it as such. The heat waves form a halo above it and even the clouds have parted to pay homage. Unimpeded at this moment, the sun makes a point by surgically spotting a concentrated beam on the only possible refuge from its daily attacks.

Johnny Franklin's heart drops as the airport comes into full view. I feel the thump as strongly as if it is my own heart. No, he is not sad, he tells himself, he just couldn't be. The flutter of his heart is merely from excitement, he thinks, setting off those vibrations that transmit even his most secret thoughts to me. And if you don't mind my letting you in on a secret, this is how I can pick up even the most private thoughts of anyone in my area of influence, just by feeling those vibrations and tremors, and I tell yuh plain, man, sometimes it really doesn't pay to know what some people are really thinking. It can be a real curse, for true. Trust me on that one; I don't think you would want the gift of being able to read minds! Not in a million years, rasta. But here I go again digressing and losing muh focus. Lord, me hope Mother Nyame ain't listening yet.

Johnny is thinking, if I may continue, that it has been a long two months at home, if that is what he can still call this island where he was born. At times, the wait was so unbearable, he just had to get away. Yet even while these thoughts run through his head, I know Johnny doesn't really believe what he is thinking. I only have to look at him to realize that Johnny understands that whenever he's leaving this so-called home he just can't wait to come back. But when he's here, well, that's a totally different matter. I know.

So, why then, you may rightfully ask, is his heart fluttering so bad? Well, listen for yourself. Hear it without me acting as a filter; feel the vibrations from an agitated heart. Maybe it is an indication of the ambivalence gripping him these past weeks, making him both sad and anxious to be leaving. Sometimes Johnny Franklin is his own worst enemy, always keeping himself under control, showing no emotion. Always a brave face. Nobody must know of the battle raging inside him. Nobody must know what he really thinks or, for that matter, what the other men he is rejoining in a few minutes are thinking. Such thoughts must always be kept secret (except from me, of course, and to anyone listening to yours truly, the storyteller), although they are the same experiences passed down from one generation to the next. I want to say these men are better at keeping secrets than members of any masonic lodge and then I remember that the original founder of the now thriving Black masonic lodges in North America was a Bajan, born and bred on this little island, just like these men. Secrets: this is their bond, secured in the knowledge that it is better to suffer in silence than to admit the truth. For truth, like the full glare of sunlight, would only destroy the dreams. And what would men be if they didn't have their little stories, their tales of conquest and achievements, to boast about? They would not consider themselves men. They would be nothing more than mere crybabies, not men.

"One o' these days, *be Christ,* I too will be making the trip," the driver pours forth. "Every damn year, I go down like some idiot to the Ministry of Labour there in Fontabelle and put down my name. And every year they overlook me. It's politics, man. Pure politics. Just because I don't support this government, they're fucking me up."

A gust of wind rushes across the island, buffeting the car and escaping just as quickly. I can safely report, without fear of contradiction, that there is something that Johnny honestly likes about his homeland: the cool moist winds. I like them too. You can always rely on a breeze to wash away the pent-up heat. Every day of the year. Perhaps every hour, even. The cool, salty breezes off the sea are so refreshingly familiar, so dependable, and contain such surety. Just when the island gets too hot, when the temperature rises frustratingly to the boil, a sea breeze suddenly flits across the island, cooling and refreshing. So nice. It's magic, a balm on the wounds, on the blisters and callouses. As if a giant hand is sweeping all the stress and frustrations off the island. Not like up in Canada where the hazy humid days and nights linger unbearably during the harvest. Most summer nights up in Canada Johnny falls asleep only because he is too tired to stay awake. The heat up there isn't the same as down here. With all that humidity, it's suffocating. For the next nine months, if nothing else, he will miss those special winds.

The suddenness of the breeze causes Johnny's heart to flutter some more. He watches as the invisible hand makes a path across the island. He notices how it tussles the tops of trees and wobbles the grass. How it causes everything to rock forward and backward like a throng of defiant people forced to bow before a conqueror. Johnny closes his eyes. Even then, his mind's eye sees the action through to the end: the swaying and bending of the trees, canes, grass and sometimes even people. Despite all the time spent away, the landscape of the island is torturously and painfully ingrained in our minds, in his and mine.

Without daring to look, he knows that on the northern side of the island, for as far as the eyes can roam, are the green fields of sugar cane. The fragrance they give off is so sweet and natural, the strong scents spicing the wind, the unmistakably comforting smells and memories of childhood. At this point, I must point out to you the broad smile on Johnny's face, as he tilts his head back and inhales, shutting out the grumbling of the man next to him. It is the canes that bring back the memories, that started everything really. Yes, I could tell you many a story about the sugar cane — how it is responsible for Johnny's presence on this island in the first place — for my presence, too, as millions of storytellers were dragged out of Africa as well. Barbados, the first land you reach sailing west with a cargo of human, the first land we all saw after Benin and the Door of No Return. You can draw a straight line across the Atlantic from Benin or Senegal, beginning at the Door and ending at Grantley Adams International Airport so many centuries later. A route so many of us travelled, before dispersing to Brazil, Jamaica, the Carolinas and even now to places like Canada. But that's another story for another time. I dare say it's not, as some argue so vehemently, the same story.

For now, it is enough to note the effect even the pollinating smell of growing sugar cane has on this descendant of slaves. At this time of the year, some canes bloom with tall white stalks like flowers, indicating they're full of sweet sticky juice. They are ready for harvesting, for the hacking of the razor-sharp machetes swung by the men who, in the last minutes of sunlight, have gone home to rest for another day's battle. The same men who now envy people like Johnny Franklin and wish they too were driving off into the soft sunset, heading for the airport and a land of opportunity. Little do they know, Johnny thinks. At least, at the end of the day, no matter how tired, those cane-cutters go home to a family. That is enough to fortify the spirits of anyone. Enough to make even the most badly wounded, those who ache spiritually and pain physically, anticipate the rising sun. They should count their blessings.

Had it not been for these annual trips to the airport, Johnny might well have been just another cane-cutter, perhaps even envious of those who labour elsewhere. Rising early in the morning when the cocks were still crowing, leaving for the fields and coming back home as the sun was disappearing, the body salts from sweating under the sun stuck to his skin, on his back, underarms and hands, on wherever there were the telltale stains. He would return home to a quick shower and a meal, perhaps of boiled potatoes, yams, bananas and salt fish in a butter sauce, another chapter in a life with no hope for economic advancement — no future for Maude and the children. Only the monotonous promise that tomorrow would be another day to try to outlast the sun, with only the reliable breezes to dry his clothes when they became dripping wet from his body fluids and clung to his skin. On Saturday afternoons, after sixty hours of chopping, bending, stacking and lifting the canes onto the trucks, of having his exposed arms and face cut by the sharp edges of the cane blades, the lacerations stinging and itching as the salt, leaching from the sweat, reentered him through the abrasions, he would receive a brown packet with his name scribbled across it. The pay cheque probably so small his family would hardly survive on it, let alone save anything for the new home they were building. In the sunset of his life, for that is how tired he feels, he might have been no different from this taxi driver whining next to him. Truly, it is the canes that define everything, going back to when they first tossed so many on us onto ships for the crossing, for the free labour in the worship of this thing, that in earlier recordings even storytellers like me called King Sugar. King Sugar and the Sun, what a controlling combination for these Bajans.

Only the airport makes a real difference in their lives. Juxtaposed between the rich black soil that grows the peanuts, onions and the sweet potatoes and the navy blue Atlantic Ocean in the distance, Grantley Adams International Airport stands like a colossus astride the land. A beacon in the storm, a fort in times of war. It demands respect and, in return, offers hope. And it also promises escape, if only from the relentless sun.

Johnny smiles to himself and hugs the travelling bag closer to his chest. I have to scramble to avoid being crushed, for he doesn't know I'm in that bag. Actually, he doesn't even know I exist. And now he doesn't care for anything. Except the beauty of the land around him. What beautiful and scenic landscape, he muses. Why do I have to give this up? This ambivalence shit really gets to me. So Caribbean, I tell yuh. Now, here is where the real internal struggle begins. Let's listen in. Listen to his thoughts, as the waves take over, listen to how he is trying to convince himself that the Program is still so much better than cutting canes. That no matter how often the strange rebellious thoughts enter his head, he has to discard them. The taxi driver is right, he tells himself. People like him, Johnny Franklin, are definitely lucky to be among the chosen. For proof, he has only to think about the men in the cane fields or sitting jobless in the rum shops or playing draughts and dominoes under the tamarind trees. He has only to remember the four walls rising on the spot of land he is buying with money from the Program. Proof enough, he says.

I'll leave you to decide whether to believe him, if his argument is convincing.

"And once you get up there," the driver is saying, "I hear there's so much woman. White women at that, all of them anxious for you to put the black brute on them. I hear, eh, Johnny, that you guys, maybe not you because you got *you* own people back home down here, but I hear that all you fellas can't wait for the Friday nights to come when you can go into town with all them restaurants and clubs and have one whale of a good time, eh, Johnny. I hear some of you guys does lick out every cent you work for during the week, spending every penny on the women and having a good time, eh, Johnny."

Johnny breathes hard, trying to stop the palpitations. He glances around, hoping the greenery will calm him. Further in the distance he can see the tops of several palm trees. He recalls that the trees line the sides of the roads to the north and northeast of the island, two of the main arteries leading away from the airport. These trees are swaying gently in the evening breeze, as if they, like the occupants in the car, or the people on the island, are lethargically fanning themselves at the end of such a bruising day. Palm trees — the eternal symbols of hope in even the most arid conditions.

Over the tops of the trees, the blackbirds and wood doves circle, readying themselves for nesting, probably in the palms themselves. These are the homers, the reliable followers of the cane-cutters, the birds that pick the worms from the fields. Unfortunately for some of us, they feast on spiders, too. Doves are known as symbols of peace, but in our introductory stories to the young, we are always reminding them how the dove never learned to make a complete home. That story comes from those days of the great Brer Dove, you know, back to the time when there was only one of every species on this earth.

Once upon a time, a very long time,
A monkey beat a rabbit till he fart white lime.

That's what mischievous children say when they want to hear a story dating back to the oral annals, almost to the beginning of time, before the earliest man roamed Africa. The birds of the air and the land held a conference to discuss building homes so their eggs could hatch in warmth and comfort. Brer Dove believed he knew everything and would not listen to the advice of Brer Blackbird, a master builder if ever there was one. When the nest they were building had only a flooring and a few twigs for sides, Brer Dove declared he knew how to finish the job and kicked out his instructor. To this day all descendants of Brer Dove get soaked when it rains, all because — the Brer Anancy curse as we like to call it, because every story we narrate must end with some wider truth — all because their original ancestor did not have the patience to let someone else show him how to put a roof over his head.

With their cooing songs, the doves remind us of the need to celebrate every day's victory over the sun, of going to bed in contentment, assured that the world is resting and the morning will bring new strengths for the battles, or that sometimes it pays to have patience and not be too hot-headed. But their cooing also prophesies that someday the sun will win and its victory will be complete. One day the sun will not set and Brer Dove, like everyone else, will have to sleep in a half-built home, exposed to the blistering sun, with no roof for refuge. Even at the height of the sun's glory, our darkness will be permanent. Such is the prophecy even for those of us who are sons and daughters of Africa, for there can be no escaping that day of reckoning, a day when our children might very well ask why we did not build strong houses or put roofs over their heads. Though the arrival of that day seems inevitable, the doves also assure us in their cooing that, at least for now, it has not yet arrived. There is still hope. Still time to put a roof on the bare walls. Time to figure out what will become of the Black man. And if you are Johnny, I must say, time for at least one more year on the Program.

To be honest, I don't have much respect for those damn birds. It's personal. For centuries these birds have done enormous damage. Check the record and you'll hear all the sudden blips. One of those birds has swept down and swallowed another storyteller. Yes, someone always steps in immediately to continue the narrative, but that does not account for the toll these birds take on all of us. And think of the cost to Mother Nyame, always having to have someone on permanent standby, just in case a bird swoops down. (But who cares about one or two storytellers? We are so dispensable.) Neither does it justify the damage they have done to an entire people with their prophecy of doom. When I think of it, I am grateful not to be as gifted as these birds to know the future. Otherwise, I would not hide from any of them. In fact, and I know it sounds harsh, I might even be tempted to kill myself in the hope of ending the story there and then. For who wants the drudgery of living a life laid out hour by hour, minute by minute, like the approved script from some damn play, with not even the remotest chance for improvisation? So I praise my God every day that while she alone sees time endlessly as the past merging with the present and future, I'm not so lucky. I know the past. All the great storytellers, the *griots*, must. My main task is to record the present. The future I must leave to others, including these birds.

From a crack in the bag, I can see other birds flying speedily in a v-shape across the hazy sky, heading out over the bluish tropical seas. They look in a hurry to get home, or to reach another promised land, somewhere over the waters, before darkness falls. Could they be thinking of Benin? These birds obviously don't pretend to hold out any hope for the future in this land. They do not believe the doves and their promise that all is well for another day and that tomorrow provides new hopes and potentials. But from their actions, they are certainly familiar with the past. They, too, are fleeing the island and the inevitable defeat. Johnny squeezes the bag. He understands the urges of the birds. After two months at home, he wants to fly away so badly. So he squeezes the bag and nearly smothers me.

"Billions of dollars," the taxi driver drones on. Johnny glances at him, for a moment forgetting the birds and the airport and easing the pressure on me. It doesn't seem to bother the driver that nobody has replied to him for the entire journey. "I just wish somebody'd give me one percent o' all that money. No, just a half of one percent, 'cause I ain't so greedy to want it all. Just a few million bucks would fix me up real sweet. Billions of dollars." The chewing gum snaps in his mouth. From the corner of his eye, Johnny notices the dried white saliva in the creases of the man's mouth. He observes how his hands hold tightly onto the steering wheel and how he stares straight ahead through his dark glasses.

Since we left Lodge Road, the driver has been the only one to break the silence the other occupants of his car so willingly embrace. He intrudes on our thoughts with his brusque words or with the loud chomping on the pinkish and now probably tasteless wad of gum. Let me describe him in a bit more detail.

Cuthbert Moore, driver and owner of this taxi, is tallish and fat for his height, probably from spending so many hours sprawled behind this steering wheel with the fancy imitation leather cover. Even as I speak, he is pushing to the back of his head the navy blue cap that is part of the uniform from the Taxi Co-op. Now, as is his habit, he's raising the cap by the peak, scratching the top of his head and, oh god, look at him hawking up spittle from somewhere deep down in his chest and spitting it through the open window. Johnny's wife, Maude, sitting in the back, shifts uncomfortably, avoiding its return on the breeze, into the car through the back window. She partially rolls up the glass and, without saying a word, immediately returns to staring out the window. Something is tempting me to say serves she bloody-well right. But, like Johnny, I must not show emotions. I must remain objective, can't pick sides. Which means, no matter how much I would like to, I shouldn't abuse my position by rubbing lessons from earlier times in Maude's face.

I know Johnny is silently wishing Cuthbert would shut up. He would like him to concentrate completely on driving on these narrow roads with the threatening potholes. And he is wondering why Cuthbert is taking the longer, more scenic route.

Perhaps he is treating Johnny like one of those tourists taxi drivers like himself rip off by extending the trip and then bragging about it later. There is no reason for not zipping along the newly built highway. No reason, unless Cuthbert maliciously wants to dangle all this beauty in front of him, reminding Johnny of what he is trading in, what he is bound to miss.

And this guy should watch his speed, his recklessness. After all, he isn't driving on a four-lane highway like the ones Johnny knows up north. They are on a narrow two-lane road, the vehicles apparently coming at them straight-on, or speeding past only inches away.

Every time a vehicle approaches, Johnny cringes, reinforcing his spine for the expected collision. It is hard for him to believe he once thought this road was actually a highway. Before he went to North America and saw real highways, where one lane is as big as this entire road. He could never be at ease on these roads again. And speeding too? He has changed too much. This kind of driving on these damn roads never bothered him, at least it didn't used to.

"That's what the magazine said: billions of dollars," Cuthbert goes on. "It was one o' them magazines, *Time* or *Newsweek*, I can't remember which one right now. A tourist fella bring it off the plane and left it in my taxi. I read it later and my head almost turned upside down when I come across where it said that the work all o' you leave down here and go to Canada and the U.S. of A. to do is worth *billions* of dollars. You know what's a billion dollars, man, and in U.S. and Canadian money, too? The other day I find myself thinking that people like you, Johnny, people that spend almost a whole year working on the contract up there in Canada got to be corning real *kiss-me-arse* money when the year come. Must be living off the hog, in style up there in Canada, if you ask me. Not like me suffering down here."

Johnny doesn't answer. He continues to look straight ahead through the windscreen with TAXI in big yellow letters in the top left-hand corner. His eyes are fixed on the airport building, his mind on the men gathering there. And in me, I feel the same tension rising in my guts.

With the sun sinking further below the horizon, the ocean beyond the airport is looking more ominous. The colours of the water are changing almost by the minute to a darker blue, washing out the lingering bits of green tenaciously fighting against the inevitability of time for any semblance of permanence. Time, a few hours airborne, Johnny is thinking, will have the same effect on the men. It will bring them down to the reality of life in another country and climate. It is bound to wring everything from them. Everything, unless they're lucky, but a few hollow dreams and their bond with one another.

In the distance, Johnny and I see the white foam riding the crests of the surging waves. At programmed intervals they bash against the rugged and barren coast. Anyone can hear these collisions up to five miles away, as the waves pound the exposed rocks, sending out their warnings in a timeless refrain. If you check the archives you will come across those wonderful stories about the call of the sea, such as the time Brer Fish warned Brer Donkey that the sea had no back door and that Brer Donkey should get back to what he knew best: terra firma. But the foolish ass continued swimming until exhaustion overcame him. Whatever was pulling him across the Middle Passage, the thing that was forcing him to try to pass back through that Door of No Return, was just too strong to resist. It drove him crazy with desire. He drowned before reaching the promised land. That's why to this day we still hear Brer Donkey's anguished cries, the waves still trying to return his bones to the land but succeeding only in bashing and breaking them against the jagged rocks, creating the beautiful white sand. The echoes of this interminable struggle will be the last sounds of the island we will carry onto that plane. The white sandy beaches will be the last sight we see, as the plane departs this island for the ocean. As we follow Brer Donkey's legacy.

Today, even the ocean seems unable to contain its rage. It is banging against the craggy shore like a possessed man punching on a bag to rid his soul of pent-up frustration. The way Johnny felt many days as he sat in the half-finished house with Maude, when he got up in the morning and simply counted the days until he could take this trip. Until he could flee, find a back door, any door, before drowning. In those times, especially when he remained transfixed at the table, imprisoned by the eerie silence, as Maude sat across from him in silence and pretended to be picking rice, I lost my ability to remain detached and felt genuinely sorry for Johnny. As sorry as earlier chroniclers felt for Brer Dove and Brer Donkey, but because of their professionalism, or simply because they could not be heard, they could do nothing to ease the situation. As someone once said, the moving hand writes, and having written, moves on. The consequences should not be our concern. *Just the facts, ma'am. Just the facts.* Particularly, I don't like the fighting, the pain and suffering, the helplessness and torment in that house. I can't stomach it. I, too, wanted him to flee, if only so I could tell a more positive story.

Johnny squeezes the travelling bag even tighter, his fingers digging deeply into the canvas but still keeping the bag between himself and Cuthbert on the seat they are sharing. Nobody knows the frustration boiling inside him, Johnny thinks, not even Maude and the three children he is leaving for almost another year. Perhaps if Johnny knew about me, he might think differently. But his not knowing is one of the crosses I have to bear. Perhaps that is the master's plan to keep Johnny and me from having any real contact. For what kind of storyteller would I be if Johnny and I were best friends? I often think of that, and hope that even the very thought of such things does not affect my sole task in life to remain honest in my pronouncements.

But the remoteness does have its price. I mean, I could only stand by and watch as Johnny counted down the days to his departure. To make time go by faster, I saw him resorting to thinking of how many more hours were left. At that point, I felt like hauling his ass off to a library. I felt like digging up some old tapes and letting him hear storytellers commenting on how it feels to be some convict sent home for a few days for good behaviour. You know, a story about the convict who has been away so long he is uncertain whether the freedom and torment at home are not worse than the prison's solitude. I felt like saying to Johnny, "Are you some kind of prisoner, or a black man with a free will? Make up your mind and stop being so wishy-washy. Stop sulking and moping around the friggin' house. Take charge and, for goodness' sake, be a man!'" Even now, he still puts off deciding what Edgecliff really means to him: is it a prison or his real home? I guess that for him, poor soul, the ambivalence will never end.

As the taxi comes out of the bend, a silver and grey airplane touches down as effortlessly as a bird on the long runway. It kicks up clouds of black smoke and rubber as the wheels slam into the asphalt and concrete strips. Johnny, sitting beside the still-talking Cuthbert, tries to block out everything around him. He tries to suppress the passing images of his homeland by picturing in his mind what is happening inside the plane as it taxies the mile or so to the concrete airport building, where some of the men are already waiting.

As clearly as if he were on the plane, Johnny can hear the hostess announcing they have arrived safely in Bridgetown,

Barbados. For their safety, everyone must remain seated until the captain switches off the fasten-your-seat-belt signs. And, of course, there is always the obligatory thanks to all the passengers, including the hundreds of Canadians arriving on the island for their annual two weeks of sunning on the bones of Brer Donkey, for choosing to fly this airline. Then everyone gathers their belongings, including the heavy winter coats they need for the return trip, and heads for the exit. They're anxious to begin worshipping the god everyone else is fighting and fleeing.

Or, if they are returning nationals, they pause ever so briefly on the top of the stairs, trying to spot relatives on the balcony overlooking the tarmac. The joy of coming home. As a rule, Johnny is always the last off the plane. It isn't that he doesn't like coming home, Johnny tells himself. It is that he hates the shoving in the mad excitement to get to the exit.

Jonathan Decourcy O'Brian Franklin has heard the airline's arrival announcement and has felt this strange foreboding before his departure twenty-four separate times.

Once for every one of the years he has gone to Edgecliff Farm near Arkona in southwestern Ontario, Canada, very near the U.S. border. He has felt that misgiving every time Cuthbert's taxi brought him to the airport. There is a feeling of trepidation on coming home and there is the same apprehension when he is leaving, even after all these years.

This is his twenty-fifth year and already he is considered an old man for the Program, or the contract, as everyone calls it. In his life, he hasn't known anybody anywhere who has worked that long at just one job, or for one employer. They had either been fired or moved on to something else. They did not have the dedication or, as in his case, the lack of opportunities, to go elsewhere. Once he heard some official sounding woman talking on the radio about how, in these changing times, people must be ready to change jobs frequently. Over a lifetime, he remembers her saying, people will have to learn to do many different jobs, and to be always trying their hands at other things. He turned off the radio. The woman was frightening him. Johnny could not bring himself to even think of what he could do next, not at his age, not with his skills.

Two weeks after Johnny's return this last time, Maude had taken him to a party at the Great House on the sugar plantation near their home. It was a retirement party for Oswald Applewheit, the man who had taught Johnny, Maude and many of their age in Sunday school. Johnny remembers how strict Oswald had been, how proud he was of his watchman's job, how he had chased them when as boys they stole canes or potatoes from the plantation. Now, Oswald was too old for the job and the plantation was honouring him with a retirement party. At the end of the evening, an official photographer showed up and took numerous pictures of Oswald receiving a watch and a rocking chair from the plantation's manager. The young woman accompanying the photographer spent a few minutes talking to Oswald and scribbling notes on a pad. Johnny knew such things did not happen on the Program. People did not retire, let alone have parties thrown for them — one day they were simply told they weren't chosen or picked any more. They were like any of the thousands of apples he left hanging on the trees every season, apples that one quick glance told him were unfit. Now rejected, the one-time pickers remained at home to get by as best they could, until they fell to the ground like unwanted apples.

Johnny doesn't want to think about what will become of him. He is only forty-two years old, still young, he tells himself. More than that, the men need him. He has to be there for them. He is the veteran and the leader of the twenty-one men that make the trip every year to Edgecliff. This year, more than any other, the men would definitely need him if his hunches were right. From the time they arrived at the airport, they would be beginning to realize changes were coming and would turn to him for explanations.

"Like she come in just on time, eh, Johnny," Cuthbert says, as we watch the airplane stop in front of the airport building. From the corner of his eye, Johnny sees the driver exchanging glances in the rearview mirror with Maude. Johnny pretends not to notice by staring through the window, concentrating on the activities at the airport and taking in a last view of the scenery.

The car is now so close to the airport, we can hear the still screaming airplane engines. We see the doors to the front and back of the craft open. Two trucks, with what look like ladders, race across the tarmac and park in front of the doors. Two flight attendants in blue and white uniforms, red scarves around their necks, the ends blowing in the wind, wave the trucks closer. In their excitement, the passengers rush down the ramps. Some with coats over their shoulders.

"One thing 'bout these airlines from Canada, if you ask me," Cuthbert says, turning off Highway 7 for the roundabout in front of the terminal. The airplane is now out of sight, except for the very tip of its tail, visible over the building. "They're always on time. And I can bet yuh one thing too: they're going to be leaving right on time when it's ready to take you and them boys back up to Canada, eh, Johnny. Right on time. If you ain't ready when they're leaving, yuh bust luck."

Johnny doesn't answer. He doesn't have to. We are now at the airport — for his twenty-fifth time. As he steps out of the car, the clouds close the window to the last of the sun rays, turning out the lights — and perhaps the halo too — on even the airport.

chapter two

Cuthbert adeptly squeezes the big car into a parking spot reserved for taxis, but usually much smaller ones. "This should be good enough," he says, switching off the ignition and pocketing the keys. Before getting out, he adjusts the air freshener hanging from the rearview mirror among the feathers. And when he thinks no one is looking, he steals another glance at Maude and winks.

Johnny doesn't notice what is happening behind his back. For some unexplainable reason, at this very moment the air freshener hanging from the mirror fascinates him and holds his attention. For the life of me, I can't understand why. Every damn taxi on this island, every car really, has one of these bags. So why act as if he's never seen one before? And they all look alike, and smell the same, too. So what's the big thing about an oblong-shaped bag stinking up the place?

Johnny squints and twists his face. Now it's coming back to me. That look on Johnny's face is all I need to remember, to realize what is on his mind this very moment. He has to be thinking about the first time Cuthbert placed one of these bags in his car. It was Johnny who had given it to him. I remember the occasion, too. Back then they were so close, the two of them, real good friends, like brothers. Johnny was bringing back a gift for him, something for the car that Cuthbert and Maude had written so much about in their letters. I remember clearly now. Back then, everyone still hoped Cuthbert would make it on the contract, that someone higher up would smile on him. Yes, I remember vividly how Johnny handed over the bag with its contents, a year's supply, actually. How Johnny turned to Cuthbert and didn't say anything. Not this man of so few words. Only the look on his face, a look very different from what I am seeing now, told what was in his heart. That he was giving Cuthbert a token of appreciation for looking after the family while he was away. For being his best man, his stand-in, his *step-knee,* as the men affectionately called it. Since then, when the first fall chill nips the air, Maude has always written to ask for another year's supply of air fresheners. Of course, she also asks for gum. Supposedly for the children. Truly, life is made up of so many stories.

"It's only a short distance to walk to the Air Canada counter," Cuthbert says. He again toys with the paraphernalia on the mirror. He watches Maude as she stiffens and opens the door. I feel like vomiting. The way these two are carrying on. So many stories in their body language. If only Johnny would use the two good eyes that God gave him.

Johnny gets out of the car, taking me with him. Somewhat mechanically, he throws the heavy grey coat over his left shoulder. But then gently, ever so considerately, he pushes the car door shut. If it were me, and, of course, seeing what I just saw, I would slam the friggin' door, loud and hard: *BLAM!* shattering the damn glass, if I could, thereby tugging at Cuthbert's heartstrings by damaging his precious car. That's how I would deal with a betrayer. Kick him right in the balls. And he would deserve every ounce of it. Then, I would turn on Maude and deal with her ass real good. But not our Johnny. He's too thoughtful and soft-hearted. Too naive and trusting, if you ask me. Instead, he adjusts the coat that had spent the entire trip on the front seat of the car. The coat that sat there like an unnatural barrier, a tumorous growth of some kind, between two old friends now unsure of their relationship. As if it were covering a gaping hole, or a large block of ice. *Gree-ough!* The chills that man gives me. *Gree-ough!* And Maude, too. *Brrr-uh.*

Johnny takes up the travelling bag and strings it over his other shoulder. The weights of the handles instantly form deep creases in his heavy woollen sweater and I have to scramble for my life as the books in the bag tumble in my direction. Friggin' books! What will he do with these books? When will he find time to read these things that nearly shut out my lights? I tell yuh, it's only because of my amazing agility that you are not now hearing a blip in this story.

Walking around the car, Johnny stops in front of the opened trunk. Cuthbert places the last of the large suitcases on the pavement beside the car, not noticing that it is tipping over the edge. As soon as he lets go, the damn suitcase topples over, with a heavy thud, into the flower gardens, crushing a million plants.

"Hey, you there!" an angry voice calls from behind us. "You mean to tell me you couldn't put down that valise there no better, man? You mean to tell me you hadda let that big able valise topple over and kill off the few half-dead plants the government does pay me to grow? You taxi men really doing a lot o' shit these days, yuh know."

"Ah, haul yuh arse," Cuthbert says, straightening to his full six-foot-two. "What you're gonna do 'bout it? Go ahead, call the police fuh me, see if they'll score you. You's only a kiss-me-arse gardener, Frankie. Begging the damn government for a job watering plants when the day come. Tell the police I say that and see what they'll do."

"What'd you just say?" Frankie asks.

"You heard me right: a kiss-me-arse gardener, watering plants morning 'til night, like you kill a priest or something. This is what you come to: watering plants and pulling up weeds. After you done spend all yuh life working on the contract, like these fellas you see here now. Watering plants! You must be kill a priest and getting punish with so much bad luck."

"At least I was better than you," Frankie retorts acidly. Even as the older man fights back, I know how much Cuthbert's remarks sting him. "You could never get pick. Everybody know you ain't no damn use. Too damn lazy, like hard work do you something."

"Don't bother with me," Cuthbert shouts. "Going on the contract didn't do one *shite* for you, if you ask me. You could as well did stay home like everybody else. And you know what, Frankie? I'd kill myself first if I had was to spend all them years on the contract and end up like you, watering a few dried-up flowers."

Having embarrassed the older man, Cuthbert spreads his broad shoulders and adjusts the cap on his head. Lifting it by the peak, he hawks deep from within and spits into the garden. Then he does it again, and again and again, each time more slowly and deliberately than the last. Each time letting the spit remain longer in the air as he projects the glob farther into the garden. Frankie Devonish, the gardener, in dirty khaki clothes and torn canvas shoes, his face weather beaten, sucks loudly on his few remaining teeth. He is a beaten man. I've seen that look before — on the faces of the discarded. There are a million stories gathering dust in the archives that end this way. I can drag out a few for you, but take my word, these stories are brutal. There is no real response to Cuthbert's ridicule, no refuge among the stares and glares of the onlookers; nowhere to hide. Cuthbert's remarks have drawn blood. Frankie can only search his mind for the appropriate response, for what he should have said to deflate Cuthbert. But at that crucial instant, words failed him. And it is a damn good thing, a retort would only prolong a fight he cannot win.

Even in defeat there is a stark reality. His mind is not fast enough, no longer quick and spontaneous. Just as his body has lost the spring, the elasticity, the resilience and zest for life, lost the strength and youth that would have kept him on the contract. So, dejected, he stoops and raises the head of a crushed plant. He waters it from a green hose and from his eyes. He mutters to himself in the loneliness of knowing everyone is staring at him. I avert my eyes, if you can believe it. A big man crying over a plant and so openly. Crying because of the wounds caused by sharp words. Who says that foolishness about sticks and stones breaking bones but words never hurting? Who still believes that old story? I hope Mother Nyame has purged that one from the system. It would have been better if Cuthbert had punched Frankie, had inflicted physical pain. But no, Frankie's crying because of the truth in those words. I still think it is such a shame when men cry. Isn't it a cardinal rule that if we must, nobody should know? Isn't this the essence of being a man, the testosterone running free in our balls?

Stooping at the edge of the garden, in the afterglow of a sun that has set, Frankie is a sorry sight. He gently fingers the plant. Not much he can do for this plant, or for a broken heart. Not much anyone can say about a dream now putrid. I know that much. Obviously, this gardener is proud of the flowers that sweetly scent the air around the airport. Especially the ones that give off such tantalizing fragrances in celebration of the sun's departure. Hibiscuses, roses, ladies of the night, bougainvillaeas. The men had brought back some as mementos for him from various countries, another symbol of their bond, of the attachment between all men on contract. Such sweet smells and beauty but such benign uselessness — aren't flowers also our final gift to the dead? Usually, nothing makes Frankie happier than seeing a family huddling in front of the gardens for a picture. Now, nothing hides his unhappiness. He does not like Cuthbert, a brute who dares to trample on the flower beds, who crushes life itself and rips out the heart of the gardener. This isn't the first time, but yet another example of the disrespect that the Cuthberts of this world have for the men on the contract. We know how jealousy for these men can be translated into hard, dark hatred, when the envious pounce on these men in unlit alleys, when they are in an alcoholic haze and even more confused and helpless. We know how the resentful take out their frustration on the weak. But Frankie also does not like Cuthbert for other reasons, matters that only this taxi driver and Maude can clarify. Just as the men on the contract do not like Cuthbert for the way he treats their leader.

Picking up from what I started earlier, let me say a few more words about this man, Cuthbert. Apart from his spreading waist, he is about the same height and build as Johnny, although a careful look would actually reveal that he is older. Underneath the cap from the Taxi Co-op, grey hair appears, and in his scraggly beard. As a young man, he caught a mild case of polio, enough to kill any chance of getting on the contract to work overseas. Only strong and healthy bodies qualify for the Program, but Cuthbert never got this message, never killed his own dream. So he misplaces his frustration. He hurls his anger at and hurts the men he envies. What a stupid person this Cuthbert! Forgive me for saying so. What have these men done to harm him? A fool and bully this Cuthbert! I know, the true followers of Mother Nyame might feel I am not being objective here, but am I not entitled to state the obvious from time to time? An idiot, an ignoramus for a man, I tell yuh!

"You carrying in these things by yuhself or you want me to call a red cap for yuh?" It's Cuthbert talking to Johnny. Now, do you see what I mean about the stupidity of this man? Johnny bends over to get a good grip on the handle of a suitcase. "They could use the few dollars, yuh know. The red caps could. They don't work on no contract like you." There is an unmistakable sneer in the taxi driver's voice, something I hope you heard for yourself. Tell me, why would he say a thing like that? And to a man with only a few dollars in his pocket. An ignorant and arrogant beast, I tell yuh. Take my word for it.

"No," Maude says softly. She acts in that guilty way, the

product of an unsettled conscience. Her actions suggest she thinks Cuthbert is getting a bit beside himself, making things too obvious. "We can carry these few things in by we own self. The Lord will give we the strength."

She picks up a bag and, walking ahead of Johnny, heads to the check-in counter. Cuthbert watches her for a moment, lifts his cap by the peak and spits in the garden. From the grin on his face, everyone can tell what he is thinking. I know he is watching the sensuous movements of Maude's firm, protruding bottom under the white sweater and tight-fitting jeans — clothes, I dare say, Johnny brought back for her. He shakes his head and smiles to himself, just like the cat that ate the cheese in that old story. Finally, Cuthbert picks up a suitcase. He drags it noisily to the end of the long line of migrant workers.

"Sixty dollars, Johnny muh boy," he demands and collects his money.

"I'll come and get you when the plane done take off," he says to Maude. "Otherwise, if you want me before then, you can always find me in the taxi stand, wetting my whistle, firing a few beers with the boys over there."

Turning to Johnny, he extends a hand. They shake. I keep thinking Johnny is such a gentleman, such an idiot. Anybody can take him for a fool. Imagine, shaking hands with such a hypocrite. Pontius Pilate at least had the good taste of washing his hands first.

"I gone now," this buffoon says. "Have a safe trip up. Maude will give me good enough notice when you coming back down so that I can come and get yuh. And if you don't mind, you know I does still drop 'round the house now and then, just to see how the construction coming on and keeping an eye on everything for yuh. You know, with you gone for so long, somebody gotta keep an eye on them carpenters and masons. Otherwise, they'd steal yuh blind, man."

At this point, I feel like saying that's exactly what you are doing to Johnny, you bastard. A thief watching another thief, if you ask me. But of course, nobody would hear me.

"I know you don't mind me dropping around," Cuthbert continues. He is unsure what to say or do at this awkward moment. Silence can be such a weapon. Johnny uses it so well. Except, in most cases, Johnny doesn't even know the power of his silence. Most times, I think it's just a case of not having anything to say. So Cuthbert, in the throes of defeat, mumbles on, trying to extricate himself, digging a deeper hole. Such ecstasy this causes me. "It's just that I sometimes wonder what the malicious people around Lodge Road does write and tell yuh." Are these words another sign of another unsettled conscience? The silence hangs heavy. Unknowingly, Johnny offers no absolution. Maude drops her head. I hope in shame. Cuthbert walks away, leaving an awkward and painful silence between Johnny and his woman, Maude.

Johnny looks at the long queue ahead of him and listens for familiar voices. I follow his eyes, searching just like him for signs. There are no strange faces in the line. Not even among the workers for the other farms or those headed for the United States. Another sign the Program can't provide as much work as before. The anti-smoking crusades are ripping the guts out of the tobacco industry, reducing the demand for labourers. In its heyday, not so long ago, there would have been scores of excited first-timers. They would be fumbling with travel documents and immigration papers, eager young men surrounded by girlfriends and relatives. The looks on their faces were the same as anyone on the island getting a civil service job, a coveted lifetime appointment. Such was the time when, once selected, just about anyone looked forward with certainty to several years' work. Back then bankers and shopkeepers advanced credit without question to the family left behind. I remember those heady times.

It was good for me too, for who doesn't like telling a positive and bright story? Not the dreary stuff of today. Back then, a new farm was joining the Program almost every year. Not these days. Nothing is certain nowadays. Everything has changed. Only the old faces remain, minus the fire long extinguished from their eyes.

The line moves slowly. Often, the perspiring men stoop to lift, or simply push ahead with their feet, the big heavy boxes. Almost uniformly, the boxes are wrapped with brown cord and tape. Boxes, bulging valises and handbags — all containing renewed hope and dying dreams. Some owners of the boxes and the dreams are clutching heavy sweaters and coats under their arms, or their women hold them apart from the queue. Others sling the coats over the luggage at their feet. These sweaters and coats are still status symbols: signs the wearer or her man, son or brother is fortunate to have been selected by the Barbados government to work in Canada or the United States, where there is still work and money for everyone.

Along with these sweaters and coats, and all the tropical fruits and foods, Johnny knows that every man carries additional baggage with him. Invisible luggage, only in the head. The fears, hopes and frustrations, but more so the commitment of never betraying the dreams of the people back home. These secrets, as I mentioned before, create a great bond between the men of the Program. The same kind of covenant that binds Caribbean men of one generation to the next. Men who laboured in Panama, Cuba, England, the United States, Ascension Island. The archives are brimming with those stories. People from these islands have gone to work in the hope of giving their girlfriends, wives, children, parents and even friends a better living at home. This is their sacrifice and their secret. An unwritten pact renewed every time one of them brings back a new plant species or flower for Frankie. A trust rejuvenated every time a flower blooms under his care. People like Cuthbert can never know what men on the contract experience. Cuthbert will remain among the uninitiated, never among the chosen but also the cursed. This is why, and I must emphasize this point, in the eyes of the men on contract, someone like Cuthbert, with a better standard of living, could never generate the same respect from them as they have for someone as lowly paid and destitute as Frankie, the gardener. It's too bad the people who could make the most use of, and have the greatest need for, our stories never get to hear them. Life would probably be so different if they did.

Johnny looks around, making mental checks. At the top of the line is Preacher Man, perhaps the most religious of all the people at Edgecliff. Whatever goes wrong or right, Preacher Man can always explain it with passages from his Bible. Every Sunday, no matter how tired, he is always at the Church of the Nazarene, fifteen miles from the farm, worshipping. Preacher Man claims his religion helps him to save money. He doesn't smoke, drink or womanize like the men who go into town on Friday nights. Johnny wonders how much money all these men owe Preacher Man. They always descend like locusts upon poor Preacher in the final week before coming home, when they realize they have no money left for gifts. I can only say it is a good thing Preacher Man's religion teaches forgiveness. Such clemency, whether he likes it or not, would definitely have to be extended to those loans. The same way that I can hear him telling Frankie he should forgive Cuthbert, for the Bible tells him you forgive seven hundred times seven. That's a lot of forgiveness, my brother, so I guess it's okay for him to squander one on Cuthbert, so long as he saves all the others for the right people.

Johnny's eyes move further down the line. For a moment, they seem to sparkle anew, settling on Timothy Hackett, or Timmy, as everyone calls him. Nobody argues as much as Timmy; nobody apparently hates the Program as much; nobody talks about history and black pride as much as Timmy; nobody finds as many faults with the state of this world. Yet, every year without fail, he is the first man at the airport. As soon as he arrives in the barracks on the farm, he starts cursing the place, swearing he will never ever return for another season. And, of course, don't even bother thinking about borrowing a cent from him. Yuh na get none; not one blind cent. Not even if yuh cry blood.

Johnny wonders what Edgecliff would be like without Preacher Man and Timmy, two fanatics in different ways. For me, it's not something I want to think about. I couldn't take all those months in isolation with too many people like Johnny. Silent and thoughtful, no fun really. I like life, conflict, discussion, energy — all the things I find in these two men. Somehow, I feel Johnny likes this cast of characters too, although he is not mouthy like me to say so.

I mean just watch him glancing over at those groups of men standing in front of the check-in counter for American Airlines. He is comparing the groups, the same way a coach preens with pride at the beginning of any new season. He is noticing how the men over there react to one another. He knows there must be people like Timmy and Preacher Man in those groups. Maybe there is even someone like our silent hero in those groups heading for the New England states. Maybe, if he looks hard enough, Johnny will recognize one or two of the workers. Perhaps someone with whom he went to school or, in his youth, played cricket with in the local league on Saturdays. That is if he could remember their names and faces after all these years.

At the head of the line at the Air Canada counter, two men in khaki overalls are straining to throw the heavy luggage onto a conveyor belt that disappears through a hole to the back of the building. Two women are frantically trying to process the travel documents and, with pen and paper, slowly calculate the charges for overweight. The looks on the women's faces are sour. They seem pressed for time, hating every minute of their work. Above their heads is a digital clock. Its red numbers read 16:19. Underneath is another sign of brown cardboard: *Flight AC 961. Departing for Toronto 18:00.* ON TIME, someone has scribbled with a black felt-tipped pen.

To the right of the line, the bronze-skinned Canadians with much less luggage zip through the process. Their line is moving almost twice as fast as ours. The people checking their travel documents seem so much happier. I guess they prefer to deal with people that look sophisticated. But they can kiss my black arse. This is what you get inside this airport terminal, inside this building garlanded only a short while ago with a halo from the sun. This is what you get when you find out the value of fool's gold. I can hear the excited conversation from the nearby line. Johnny and everyone else can, too, if they want to listen. We can hear the visitor's regrets and sorrows, real and professed, for having to leave this land of sun, sand, sea and even sex. Yes, sex. Their conversations drift over to us, informing us that at least some people in this world have lots of fun. Their long faces also betray their feelings. Obviously, none of the visitors is anxious to flee this scorching sun; none is looking forward to returning to a frigid home; and certainly none would even entertain the indignity of picking the apples they eat or the tobacco they smoke. They cannot stomach the prospect of two more harsh months of snow and sleet. Bear in mind that these people are talking about their home, a place where the sun is an ally, a harbinger of hope and life, especially in the awakening after the months of winter's death. Life has its ironies, don't yuh think?

Johnny's eyes move down the line again, worried, searching for other members of his group. Henry. Delbert. Rat Face. Henderson. Oscar. They are all there. As is Tommy, Adrian and...

"Move up there, Johnny, man. You holding back the line," a voice says behind us, interrupting Johnny's thoughts. The queue has moved ever so slightly. But there is a gap, nonetheless, between Johnny and the man in front of him. Anxiousness demands it be filled. So the men shuffle their feet, kick along the boxes and bags. Move a precious inch or two. This void is caused by a man, passport in hand, walking away from the front of the line. He is immediately surrounded by a woman, two young girls and a toddling boy in little white shoes. It is Albert Jones, one of our boys from Edgecliff Farm. Johnny smiles. We know Albert. Of all of us, Albert is the one to steadfastly abide by the rules. As you know, there is always someone like Albert in any group, the one that will never cross against the lights, even when the streets are clear. Sometimes we joke about it. Like recalling how Albert is the only one from Edgecliff, really from all the farms in Canada or the States, to arrive at the airport the full two hours before departure, as stipulated by the airline and the government-appointed Liaison Officer. Most likely, he is also the only one to show up with the specified maximum of three suitcases and a handbag that, as recommended, actually fits under the seat in front of him. Mr. Canada or Canadian, the men have nicknamed him. But, as Albert always tells us, he expects to have the last laugh. He believes he is the only one of the men to have any hope of being rewarded by Canadians for his dedication.

"This year might be different," Maude is whispering. She is standing beside Johnny in the queue. I am right between them, in the bag hanging from Johnny's shoulder, another barrier between these two. "I mean, when you get up there, don't forget that me and you make a big commitment with the bank this off-season. We got to try and finish the house. The children getting big, now. And you can never tell what…"

"I know," Johnny says softly, his lips hardly moving. I hate to be around when they try to make small talk. It's like…like… I don't really know. All I know is that hearing them makes me feel creepy, makes me glad that the creatures of my kingdom are not supposed to have permanent relationships. In fact, some of us don't even need one another to build a home or to procreate.

"Remember to make the arrangements with the farmer as soon as you can." Maude is speaking under her breath. She does not want the words to travel to ears nearby. "Talk to him right away 'cause you got to send back the money every month, to finish paying off the bank so we can get the house done. As Cuthbert tell yuh, we might have enough money to get it up to the ring beam. But not for a roof."

"Okay."

"As you know, a house ain't a house when it ain't got a roof," she whispers. "You need a roof to protect yuh from the sun by day and the dew by night. And from the rain. You got to have a roof over your head."

They lapse into a heavy silence, having nothing to say, unable to reach out to each other spiritually. Mercifully, the line inches forward giving them a chance to hide their embarrassing uneasiness. Now they can pretend to be concentrating on pushing the luggage along. Already they are in different worlds. But I still feel squeezed, claustrophobic. I glance outside the airport, where the sun is finally gone. The island is now in darkness. But the sun's legacy remains in the sweltering heat and the sea breezes battling for dominance. In the sound of the sea waves frantically pounding the rocks in the distance. In the birds asleep in their nests. At a moment like this, I wish someone would rush outside and pick a handful of flowers from Frankie's garden. They could give a wreath to Maude and Johnny, a symbol, I think, of this relationship. Yes, I know such an act would be cruel, but like Cuthbert's words to Frankie, at least the gesture would ring true. But, I am only a storyteller and nobody listens to me. My corner dark, I tell yuh.

chapter three

"*All like now, eh Johnny,* poor Grafton, God bless his soul, would be nervous, nervous as shite wondering what the hell will happen when the damn plane takes off."

Mouther-man, Tommy, is the one you hear talking. That's what I call him, mouther-man, because his mouth is always in gear. Thomas St. Clair Greaves is the tall, slim man in the circle. The one pausing to wipe his nose every minute, with the voice you can always hear from a mile away. A real mouther. The men, armed with their boarding passes, their women smiling on them, are standing around in the corner. Since they gathered, Tommy hasn't put away that snot rag. Neither has he stopped jabbering, actually trying to talk coherently between those hacking, rasping sounds. He holds the folded handkerchief in the palm of his hand as if it is a ball. The Tommy I know keeps the kerchief in his side pocket. But because of the constant coughing, he has not returned the cloth to his pocket. Occasionally he wipes his watery eyes and nose. Or, he raises the handkerchief to his mouth and coughs into it. Then he takes another long drag on his cigarette, says a few words, and coughs again.

Nobody could doubt Tommy is sick. Every cough bores into my heart. There's no way on this God's green earth a man should leave a warm country like this in such a condition. Not to head for a land of almost permanent winter, not with such a wracking cough. But for some people life offers no choices, I suppose. I don't like this coughing or what it portends. Trust me, you know the cough has to be really bad when it can stop Tommy from talking even for a few moments.

"In all my born days, I never did know a man so frightened for a' airplane." See, what I'm telling you. Nothing can stop this man when he is ready to lick his mouth on a good story. To tell the truth, that is one of the things I admire about Tommy. And sometimes I am glad that he is a different type of storyteller, his job the rather simplistic one of just regaling his friends, so I'm not in competition with him; his is not really serious work, recorded workmanship for posterity. Not like mine. Good thing, 'cause he would give me a good run for my money. "That's Grafton fuh yuh. Just start tellin' him 'bout a plane and he'd start getting real frightened."

"What Anancy story you telling we now, Tommy?" Delbert interjects. My heart stops: Oh, my Lord! *Anancy story*. Did my ears hear right? Why would he say a thing like that? Does this mean that they are becoming aware of me, the storyteller? Maybe I have revealed myself in some way. Remember that old-time song?

Anancy is a spider
Anancy is a man;
Anancy's West Indian
And West African.

Otherwise, why would Delbert make such a poignant reference to me, to all my brothers, sisters, to our foreparents? I hope I'm not getting too jumpy. But statements like this, coming on the heels of all these menacing signals of late, put me on edge. I don't know what to believe. So much has changed, and without any prior notice. Sometimes I wonder if Mother Nyame is still in control, if she has not decided to make the storehouse of all her stories, and the storytellers, available to the fish of the sea, the fowl of the air, the animals on land and our human charges. From the beginning of time, we have been the chroniclers of the trials and achievements of African people. You know, sometimes people, especially the brethren in the southern states, even refer to us as the Signifying Monkey, the trickster, at times human, other times animal, but never fooled. But what's in a name? Wherever an African — and here I am not only talking about those born on the continent — can be found, for sure one of us is nearby recording history, whether of an individual or a group like this one heading for Edgecliff. Still, it is truly a rarity when a grown man allows the words *Anancy story* to fall so casually from his lips. I have heard it from children, all those eager saplings drawing from Mother Nyame's storehouse. But once they hit their teenage years, they hardly ever have a need for calling up these stories from the collective memory. No longer do they need bedtime stories to teach them morals of life; after all, they are now grown, chasing girls or boys, planning for children, knowing it all. No longer do you hear them saying with glee such things as *Once upon a time, a very long time.* Or *Crick-crack! Crapaud broke yuh heart.* Or *Tim Tim* to get the story going. I don't like this reference by Delbert. Anancy story, he says. It bothers me.

"Don't make joke, man," Tommy rebukes him sternly. "This ain't no foolish Anancy story. You think I's a comedian or something? At a time like this, I ain't got no time for joking with no 'Nancy story."

Now the blood is truly rushing to my head. This is even worse. What the hell Tommy means by that statement? There is nothing funny about our work. It really pisses me off when I hear people refer to my occupation in the same way they would to the performance of some comedian in a nightclub, a teller of stories whose aim is merely to entertain, to titillate and to elicit a few giggles before the darn yarn, and the moral too, is forgotten. Nothing so with me and the work of all those millions of professional storytellers carrying out their duty, labouring in obscurity, never complaining, never expecting anyone to joke about them. I won't have it. I am a professional. And I'll go further and say this: If people, like this motor-mouth man, Tommy, only knew the true Anancy story, then perhaps they could know and possess their own history. If only he, and all the others listening, could find a way to tune in to what we are reporting, what we have narrated all these centuries, everybody would be wiser and better off generally. But I must control my temper. I cannot afford to get too vexed with these ungrateful vipers. It would only cause me to record the wrong things. I might be a bit touchy about some things, but that is me. How dare he talk so disparagingly about my work? Some people damn well have nerve, eh.

"As I was saying," Tommy resumes talking and coughing, "all like now, like how you see we waiting for the announcement to go on the plane, he'd be frightened, frightened, off to a side over there or somewhere, not even wanting to talk to any of us."

The smoke from their cigarette curls around their heads. It is heavy enough to strangle a horse and every last one of them. My skin burns with each intake of air and my eyes feel dry. What can you expect? These are men who make a living growing and reaping tobacco. To tell them not to smoke is like asking the baker not to eat his own bread. I guess I'll have to put up with this toxic substance. But to talk about telling *funny* Anancy stories, how dare he say that? It still vex me no end, man.

"He uses to be praying," says Barbara, standing beside Tommy. She is wearing a white long-sleeved dress with imitation lace around the neck. I remember when Tommy brought that dress for her. Now, talking about a really funny Anancy story, this one is right up there with the classics, like the ones about the brier patch or Brer Rabbit and the tar baby. It was on the last day on the last tour that Tommy decided to buy this dress. The last thing he bought at that boutique on the way to the Toronto airport. Everybody told Tommy that boutiques only rip people off. He could get a better and cheaper dress elsewhere. Did he listen to anybody? Not Tommy. He had his mind set on that white dress, only because he had seen it in the glossy advertisements. When we got on the plane, the first thing the men saw in the sales magazine was the very same dress at about a quarter of the price Tommy paid. Foolish man, wasting his money. Now, Barbara is wearing it. And proudly, too. Standing in that dress right beside that she-devil they call Maude. I like the pride and appreciation Barbara is showing. It makes my heart feel good to see such gratitude.

But look closer at these women. Above her left breast, Barbara is also wearing a black button. It is auspiciously placed close enough to her heart for everyone to know she is mourning. All of us are grieving, actually. But it is the women who do it openly. The men show their sorrow by talking, by reminiscing. Tommy, the bowlegged man with a few specks of white in his hair, continues coughing loudly, uncontrollably, but still managing to lead the remembrance of our dearly departed. As you can tell, he is doing so rather cavalierly, on purpose, as if this is not too serious, just another funny story. Men, I tell yuh, they must always be pretending, especially when they are together.

Barbara casts a suspicious look at Tommy. Only her eyes show the deep concern for her husband. Because she doesn't want to draw attention to him, she says nothing. She doesn't want people to notice too much the lingering cold that didn't get better even after two full months in the sun. Still, I can read the concern on her face. When you are in my business you learn to go behind the disguises, beyond the laughs and make-believe, the modern hallmark of most African people. I know what she is thinking. This is not the usual cold, nothing like any of those influenzas Tommy had brought back from the cold in North America — viruses, no matter how stubborn, the sun, some strong bush tea, a couple shots of good white rum along with regular early morning sea baths always licked out of him in no time. This one has survived everything she's thrown at it. To her, the rattling in Tommy's chest sounds worse by the minute, and I agree.

"You know what I mean, eh, Johnny. Grafton was one character, eh," Tommy says between his coughs and puffs of smoke. He looks directly at Johnny, seeking approval from the more senior and respected colleague. To me, Tommy appears a possessed man, someone determined to finish his mission, including the story about Grafton, no matter what. No matter how hoarse and husky the coughing makes his voice. No matter how much the show of sickness makes the men feel queasy. Tommy has to prove that a little sickness will never get in his way, will never lay him low. All these are traits of a born storyteller.

"True," Johnny agrees in that soft voice. He, too, is concerned, but doesn't want to appear unmanly by betraying his apprehension. The concern shows in a whisper softer than usual. I know these signs. The intimate group of Edgecliff workers and their women strain to hear the words escaping from lips that hardly move. Only the upper muscles in his square jaw, firming and relaxing, betray it is Johnny talking and not the work of some mischievous ventriloquist so far in the distance the trickster's voice does not carry strong enough for everyone to hear.

"All the same, no matter how I try, and I's a big man with children and know the facts of life, I can't help thinking how Grafton did look when I lean'd over and looked at his face in that pine box. I does think about that morning, noon and night. Shit, man. First thing in the morning, last thing at night. In my waking and in my sleep. When I think of Grafton stretched out there in that pine box, looking so small and bony, but dead as a...a..." Tommy chokes on the words, causing him to cough even more violently, his body shaking and his eyes running. Barbara's eyes do not leave his face.

Nobody says anything. They wait for Tommy to compose himself. In any case, he is adequately expressing their feelings, emotions every one of them had kept buried deep within. They must always act like men. Grafton's death still shocks all the men. What horrifies most is the realization that Grafton died just one month before they were to reassemble at the airport. Less than a month after all the families in the group had gathered at Tommy's bungalow in the countryside, a mammoth house built with money from the Program. The truth be known, Tommy's house is the envy of every man, woman and child in the group. Just between you and me, among themselves, the men pretend these things don't really matter. But with their women, it's a different story. In the quiet of the night, the women do find a way to get the men to buy into their dreams, or to at least feel guilty for falling behind the others. I never underestimate the power of words from a woman's mouth late at night. When domesticated, man is mere putty, to be fashioned one way or the other.

At the Christmas gathering Grafton had said he was feeling a lot better. The doctors had given him the all-clear to go back up. I heard him with my own two ears saying to Johnny how much he was looking forward to returning to Canada. "In any case, Johnny muh boy, this kiss-me-arse man Tommy put me in bare trouble with this house he got up here. Ever since Pearlie set she eyes on what Tommy and Barbara build up here, she's on my arse to do the same for she and the children. She says she's tired o' renting all she life and the children getting big and want their own rooms. So, it's like I ain't got no choice, brother man. I got to stake out my arse on the people farm for another year. Although I was planning to take a year off to rest up and catch myself after the winter that almost knocked the stuffing outta me. But I better now, ready to go back up next month. Still, I hope this is the last time that I got to go back up there so soon. I really hope so." Neither he nor Pearl let on that anything was too wrong. We saw nothing suspicious. Women are always sharing things, discussing their fears and preparing one another for any eventuality. Women talk about everything; maybe they even talk too much at times. Men are different. What's happening to them is never anybody else's business. Not even a best friend can swear he knows everything and, funny enough, a man's best buddy doesn't really expect to know everything. That's how men have operated over the centuries, or that's what I have observed.

Despite Tommy's attempt to make light of the situation, for many of us, Grafton's death is an evil omen for the coming year. His death and the not knowing if he would be replaced on the Program. For many of the men, the way Grafton died is also a potent indicator that they all have to start getting serious about life. A death so sudden is the clearest indicator possible that all those who joined the Program with Grafton are not getting any younger. No longer can they expect to exact from their bodies eighteen hours of backbreaking labour six days a week, in rain, hot sun and in the cold without severe consequences. Sometimes they even work on the seventh day, when even God in her wisdom rested, and if I may make this obvious point, unlike these human beasts of burden, God is immortal. Seven days a week, that's how flexible they have to be. They have to be ready to go to the field whenever called. That one or the two of them will break down from time to time should come as no surprise. Not too many of them could continue working at this break-neck pace without it taking a heavy toll on their bodies. But a death, that is different. Grafton's is the first death on the Program for most of the Edgecliff group. It still frightens every last one of them.

With Grafton gone, Tommy automatically became second in seniority and responsibility on the farm. He is a perfect contrast to Johnny. At times, he even appears to read Johnny's mind with one quick glance. But let me tell you one important thing about

Tommy. It's something he has more in common with me. He has a sharp, acidic tongue. Most times, he isn't afraid to speak his mind. In this way, he is very different from our long suffering friend. It's something I really like about this man.

Tommy drops the butt of his cigarette on the floor and steps on it. "As I was just saying," he continues, still wiping his nose, "when I'd see Grafton laying there dead as a doornail, I had was to turn to my wife, Barbara, who was standing right beside me with a black handbag in she hand, and I had was to say that it was only a year ago, just one short year ago, that Grafton was a strong strapping man. He would be the first in the field on mornings and the last back home at night. Then he would put away a whole lot of food, 'cause he did love his belly. Smokie, when he gets here, can back me up on the food question. Then the old boy would be ready to go back in the field bright and early the next day, working from sunrise to sunset without complaining. The man was a real machine — on his knees picking up apples off the ground; bending over to pick the ripe tobacco leaves or reaching up to pick a pear off a tree without a word. Then, he would come back to the camp, bathe heself, eat a piece o' food, and then spend the night slamming dominoes, a real hard seed domino player, the hardest we ever had in the camp. He'd have the guys up 'til late in the night, until everybody had was to say they were too tired to play any more and they want to get some sleep so they could work the next day. Then, all of a sudden so, without sign or warning, without rhyme or reason, Grafton start saying he got a pain here," Tommy points to parts of his own body, "a pain there. Somewhere else hurting him. He can't swallow. The next thing we know, the man crying out in pain real bad. He can't work. He's in hospital and the doctors poking at him and soring up his body. And then he come back home down here and dead off, just when everything like it's turning around."

"Just the same," Barbara says, giving Tommy the chance

to light another cigarette, "instead o' Grafton, it could just as well be any o' the boys that we mourning fo' today. Just that it's poor Grafton."

"Poor Grafton, my foot," Maude answers. The irritation rises in her voice. Such stridency catches everybody off guard. "What so poor about a man that's dead and gone? Grafton, God bless his soul, is all right, if yuh don't mind me saying so. I keep telling all of you the same thing: I don't know what everybody so sad 'bout. The good Book say that we should cry when somebody's born and rejoice, listen to me good now, rejoice when somebody's gone from this world of sin and sorrow. Grafton's resting in Christ, in the bosom of Abraham. No more pains to worry about. It's we, the ones that left behind, it's we that we gotta be sorry fo'. 'Cause none o' we ain't know what tomorrow brings. Remember the hymn we does sing in the church:

Many things about tomorrow, she starts to sing in a clear crisp voice,

> *I don't seem to understand*
> *But I know who holds tomorrow*
> *And I know who holds my hand.*

Everyone stares at Maude, as if she's mad. Part of her outburst stems from her knowing that none of the women really likes her. She knows what else, besides the need for a home, the women have whispered in their men's ears about she and Cuthbert. Secrets the men have been debating whether to share with Johnny. Is it better, realizing that he is home for only two months in the entire year, for him not to know the truth? That's the debate for them. Maude knows this. Individually, the men have all taken the weak-kneed easy way out, instead of seeking confrontation and clearing their consciences. They chose to resort to the old Barbadian adage that what a man doesn't know can't hurt him. But that doesn't mean they like Maude, or that they are ready to forgive her. I can sense the deep resentment from the way they glance at her, at the coldness in their voices when talking to her. I know the women are thinking what a bad example this Maude is and are hoping that their men won't believe that they are doing to them what Maude is dishing out to Johnny. But they can never be sure. They know that men can hide their true feelings, disguise them for a month or two, until they are all back together. Then they'll say things like all women are alike and that you should never trust them. And it's all because of people like Maude. If I can sense this hostility, what do you think Maude is feeling in her isolation?

"Don't get me wrong," Maude fights back. She is trying to take the edge off her words. "I say what I had to say, not because I ain't feeling sorry for Grafton. After all, he's flesh and blood like any o' we. All I want to do is to emphasize that it is the ones that left behind that we have to worry about. Let me try to show you as clear as I can what I mean. The other day, I was out shopping for one or two things for Johnny to carry back up to Canada with him."

She shifts nervously from one foot to the other. Maude is pausing long enough to send a message to all those who know her secret. She is counterattacking by showing that at least, despite what she does in his absence, she still takes good care of Johnny while he is on the island. His clothes are washed and ironed and he gets a well-cooked meal every day, a meal blessed with the touch of a woman's hand. And she makes sure Johnny heads back to Canada with boxes containing all the things he needs to make life a bit more comfortable.

"And guess who I should I run into, but the self same Pearl. Pearlie, poor thing, is taking the loss real hard. She's really looking thin and bony these day, like she fall off, lost a lot o' weight. And we all know that Pearl didn't have too much fat on she bones in the first place." Maude pauses again, this time to underline that she is still an informal leader of the group. She wants to show that, while others gossip about her, only she keeps in touch with Pearl. "And she still got four young children to raise. All by sheself. Poor Pearlie. Who's going to help she now? That is what I talking 'bout when I say it's the ones that left behind. I had to remind she, and I don't think any one o' we women need reminding about this, but I had was to tell she nevertheless what we think personally 'bout one another, that I am here, and always willing, to stretch out a lending hand to any o' we girls that left behind. But beyond that, who'd help poor Pearlie?"

"She'll get the insurance," Barbara says acidly.

"Insurance. Don't make me laugh, gal." Maude snarls just as scornfully without losing all politeness. I am enjoying this. It's true, I might not like a battle; but I love a war. That's me. These women are showing me a good *bassa-bassa*, a real fight. And you know who I want to win! You know how bad I want to see Barbara put some good licks on Maude. That is why I think the men are wrong for not levelling with Johnny. I would, if it were me. Have the confrontation and clear the air of all the pent-up resentment and hard feelings. That's what I'd do. For this is where Tommy and me part company on the question of being frank and outspoken. I don't bite my tongue for anyone.

In fairness to Maude, she's up to the fight and can give as good as she receives. The look on her face, the timbre in her voice, shows she's ready to rumble. She is happy to confront Barbara. If only because Maude is tired of everyone comparing her to Barbara. She is fed up with people saying it is Barbara that is more thrifty. I, personally, think the people are right. After all, Barbara has completed a wall-house for Tommy. A house, I must say, with a roof. In a longer time and apparently with more money passing through her hands, Maude has managed to raise only four basic walls. No roof here. You be the wise bird and form your own opinion. Furthermore, I ask you, what is she doing with Johnny's money? Is she buying ice and frying it? That's a question I would like to put to her. But, hey, I'm only the storyteller and, besides, nobody really listens to me.

"You better talk to Pearlie," Maude says. "The insurance ain't worth a thing. First it's taking forever to get the money approved and out of the hands o' the government. Pearlie say that when it comes through, when the government finished with it, the money won't even be able to put clothes on the children's back, far less buy food and shelter too. She say it would've make a world o' difference if Grafton did dead up there in Canada on the Program and not home. That way, the money would come straight to she and the children without the government down here interfering and taking out a big cut."

"Christ, I won't want that for a dog," Barbara fights back. "You mean to tell me it's better dropping down dead on some musty farm up there. I mean, and the Lord knows what is in everybody's heart, he knows I ain't washing my mouth on anybody to blight them, but if my dear husband, Tommy, if he was to have, and God forbid, anything happen to him like that, I would prefer for it to happen right here at home, on this little island where his navel string's buried, among his own people. Among people that love him and could close his eyes for him. Not up on somebody's blasted farm where you gotta work like some slave and does get treat like a blasted animal just for a few rare-mouth dollars to help yuh family! Not to die up there and yuh ain't even got nobody to close yuh eyes fo' yuh. Christ, I won't want that for a dog o' mine, let alone a human being that I say I love."

"I ain't talking 'bout wishing or wanting anything for anybody," Maude responds. "Just the facts 'bout the said same insurance you just ask me 'bout a minute ago. That's all I'm trying to do, so don't go off saying I mean what I ain't mean."

"Think they sending up anybody to replace Grafton, Johnny?" Tommy finally asks the question that is on all the men's minds. At this point, he will say anything to change the conversation. For one, he doesn't want Barbara to get carried away and give out too much of the information he has shared with her. The men wouldn't like that. As far as I can tell, they have not broken their bond about life on the Program and would prefer to tell their women themselves rather than have them hear it secondhand. Obviously, Barbara, in her anger, let slip some of the information Tommy had confided in her about life on the farm.

But there is an even more important reason. Tommy knows that Maude has hit one of Barbara's exposed nerves. It isn't often that he sees his wife so angry. As if she is rebelling against someone like Maude hinting at her deepest fears. As if she can't come to terms with a strange idea. I know what that idea is. I suspect Maude does too and purposely drives at it. I mean, you don't look at a woman's sickly husband and not have certain thoughts. If you really want to be mean, to get even, you might even hint darkly at them. As I said earlier, Maude is a fighter. She can take care of herself. And, of course, Barbara has many things on her mind. The long months Tommy spends away from home and, more importantly, the nagging doubts racing through her mind. Especially the doubts that rise up every time she hears the government announcements on the radio. They make her nervous. Particularly the public information spots about people getting tested if they have colds that won't go away, if they can't sleep, if they are losing too much weight without a good reason, if they get the shakes at night. In better times, Barbara would have found someone with whom to share her concerns. Once, it was Maude. They used to talk about every possible thing. They are the two oldest of the women left behind. Their men are best of friends and probably share deep secrets. Why couldn't these two women be close any more? Barbara would love to take a bus ride over to Maude's place occasionally, or to invite Maude over to her new house from time to time. But she no longer feels that closeness. She feels just as betrayed. So she spends her nights in the village church just down from her home. There, on her knees, she prays. And that's where she plans to spend the time waiting for Tommy. Maude knows this. Barbara also knows Maude is aware of her fears, which is why Maude's remark about being there for any of the women cut so deeply.

"I don't know," Johnny says, in answer to Tommy's question.

"Liaison Officer ain't tell you nothing? No hints?"

Johnny shakes his head. He stares straight ahead. Mechanically, he hits his right thigh with his passport and travel documents. He's thinking.

"I run into him the other day and he ain't tell me nothing, neither," Tommy continues. He throws away the last of a cigarette and lights another. "I don't know why they like to keep these things such secrets, as if they're some state secret that everybody can't know." Now, he is puffing and coughing. The sound echoes through the cavernous airport. "But I guess I can't really blame them 'cause all o' we done know what it means if they don't send up a replacement. They don't have to spell out everything."

"What it means?" Maude asks. Oh, how the pendulum of life swings at such short notice. Now it is Maude's turn to be concerned. The pronounced squeak in her voice betrays inner doubts and fears. Barbara looks at her. Both have their fears and need each other. But they are divided by a gulf as deep as the strength of their men's love. Even in asking this question, Maude is commenting on the state of the relationship between her and Johnny. Otherwise, how could it be that the leader of this group has not told his partner about the precariousness of the Program? He has not treated her with the same trust and closeness that Tommy shows Barbara.

"Only that the crops might not be too good this year and some o' we might not last the full season," Tommy blurts out. He is angry because he thinks Maude is trying to show him up. He thinks she is transferring her anger toward Barbara to him. Otherwise, why would she ask this question? Even Tommy doesn't believe that Johnny hasn't mentioned anything about the Program. "As you done know, last year they even thought o' sending some o' we back or shortening the season. The problem is, as Mr. Stewart, the owner of Edgecliff tell we, is that nobody ain't buying the blasted tobacco any more. Everybody done know that's the problem. He can grow as much tobacco as he likes; nobody ain't buying it. People like me getting only trouble when we light up in Canada, you know that!"

"You mean you could come back home before the season's over?" Maude puts the expression in words she understands, all the time figuring out in her head the implications of Johnny's returning home unexpectedly, of what she would do if he were under her feet for more than two months a year, in a house without a roof. "That all of you might not work for all of it, the season, I mean?"

"Damn right too. At a time like this, the tobacco crop getting smaller and smaller, the apple prices real low and lots o' farms in trouble, anything can happen. Look who's coming now. Mighty."

We all look in the direction Tommy indicates with a brisk movement of his head. Mighty is strolling toward us with the usual collection of bags. "Three hundred blasted dollars in overweight," he says. "All of you will have to chip in and pay me back, 'cause all this stuff is really for all o' you. Good afternoon, mistresses," he says. "Don't think I forget my manners, ladies." He smiles and bows to the women. In his hand is a round parcel, wrapped neatly in newspaper and taped.

"What's that you got there?" Albert asks.

"What I got here, my man," Mighty says proudly, "is one

sweet-arse soprano steel pan that I'm taking up north with me. When the nights get too cold, or we feel a little restless, me and Smokie, with Smokie on the guitar, can play a couple of calypsos and lively up things at the camp. What you think?" He taps the rim of the parcel with his fingers. A melodious sound escapes.

"What's that you got there by yuh foot, Johnny?" Mighty points to the odd-looking bag at Johnny's feet. Once again, I hold my breath, just in case they discover me.

"Diaries." My heart skips a beat at the mention of the word. *Diaries.* I didn't know that these damn books that nearly killed me were somebody's journals. Now I am so frightened because those things are such powerful weapons. Just to think of them gives me an extra dose of the willies. I feel a return of the foreboding that first visited me when Johnny packed away those musty-smelling books that I now discover to be personal logs of some dead person. The same books that almost squashed me. But there are other reasons why I don't trust diaries. A well-recorded diary with all the right entries can be almost as good as one of my narratives. That's how powerful those damn things can be. They can put me out of work. There will be no need for people to tune in to our stories. Then what would be the use of our reports? Why would Mother Nyame need a school of us out in the field making recordings that nobody listens to?

Diaries can educate and arm. A poorly maintained diary, and I know of so many, can be a weapon of a different kind, especially when you get a writer who cannot put an entry in its context. Context, the right place for every story, the correct placement of every fact, every item in a simple tale, is so crucial to everything in life. Otherwise, it spoils everything. Believe me, I know what I am talking about. I have seen first hand the effects of such diaries. I have seen both the good and bad. I see people using their own history to drown themselves. Let me tell you, for every good one, there are usually four or five bad experiences. Forgive me if I seem leery of diaries. And excuse me for getting carried away — let's pick up on what these guys are saying about those journals.

"What the hell I hearing," Mighty says. "You plan to keep diaries now? After all these years. You don't know a diary is a hard thing to keep? Lots o' men tried it before but had to give up. It's too much work after a hard day in the field to then sit down and write in a diary every night. I mean, as it now stands, some of we can't even find the time to write a letter to the ones we love and miss so much. Right, ladies?"

"These diaries different. To read, not write," Johnny says. I want to jump in and say what's the difference, really? They are weapons nonetheless. Sometimes, the teacher is just as harmful as what he or she is teaching. "My father dead in Panama. Both he and his father did keep diaries."

"By the way," Mighty says, "what happen'd to yuh eye, man?"

Johnny brushes his left eye. He feels with the tips of his fingers the scar underneath it.

"I okay," he says in almost a whisper.

"Look to me like somebody been trying to lick out yuh damn eye or something, if you ask me. What happen'd?" Mighty's persistence causes all eyes to focus on Johnny, who is trying to force a smile. Maude, feeling uncomfortable, resumes shifting from one foot to the other. "You've been fighting with somebody or something? Maude had to put a hand on yuh or something?"

"Left the man 'lone!" Tommy shouts. "Sometimes you like to ask too much questions. Mind your own business, man."

"Anybody see my man Smokie yet?" Mighty asks. Tommy's rebuke has the desired effect. But it's like water off a duck's back when it comes to scolding Mighty. "It's getting close to the time for boarding. Smokie should be here by now. I hope he ain't planning no foolishness like playing he ain't going back up. You know how he does talk."

"Don't worry," Barbara says. If you listen carefully, you will still hear the shakes in her voice. She is covering it well. "Smokie will show up. Even so, the Liaison Officer ain't give his speech yet. So you still got a little time left."

"Yeah, everybody knows Smokie," Tommy says. He is fighting off another heavy coughing fit. "When he's in Canada, he don't want to come back home — always talking o' running off the contract and living illegally in Toronto or heading for New York or some other place. When he comes back home, he's always saying he ain't going back up, especially if he can find a new woman to spend his money on."

"That's Smokie for yuh," Mighty says. "So much talk, but all o' we know he'll never run away to Toronto or the States. What for? And talking about Toronto, Johnny, think we'll still put up a team in the domino competition this year? I mean with Grafton gone, and he was the best we had, think it make sense even trying? I mean, I know all o' we would like to win the tournament and get to go to Toronto for the Jazz festival and a few baseball games, but, realistically, Grafton on the side did worth four men."

"We'll see." Johnny is noncommittal. In the distance, we see the Liaison Officer making his rounds, stopping to talk to the workers. We also notice that he is alone, with no sign of a replacement. We all make mental notes, but say nothing. And we watch the red numbers above the Air Canada counter steadily march toward the appointed hour with still no sign of Smokie.

For a moment, I try to step back and look at this group. These same men had gathered on the very same spot for the last six years. The same group of men except for two. One of them will never join the group again and, apparently, will not be replaced in the men's hearts or on the Program. The other is the only one probably brave enough, perhaps, crazy enough even, to stop putting up with this annual hassle. Crazy enough to start running after his own dreams.

But these men are assembled at this airport for a reason. Life must go on and the man whose task it is to inspire all of them is making his way to the clearing in the centre of the building. It is the Liaison Officer. He is about to give his usual speech. Let's listen in, but let me warn you early, this ain't no Martin Luther King Jr. you'll be hearing. You would not believe how much I hate these boring speeches, especially from a young politician like this one who really thinks he is God's gift to humanity. But at least the speech will put things in perspective — as Brer Wasp likes to caution, before you sting a man, you better know why you're stinging him, or you could lose your stinger, and your life to boot.

Let me show you what I mean. The highlight of this talk is always a solemn reminder of some sort to the workers, as if the Officer is a father sending a bunch of thoughtless boys off to school. You know, all that yak, yak, yakity stuff about how these poor souls are ambassadors for their country. I mean, where have I heard that before? How can this guy be so boldfaced when he lies like that? He doesn't have any shame, none whatsoever.

Well, the only redeeming thing is that this Officer isn't fooling anyone. Just take a quick glance at the bemused looks on the faces of Johnny and his colleagues: *Goddamn, this Officer can't be for real. No way, man. He got to be joking his head off.* I know for certain that is what my man Johnny is thinking in his quiet, unassuming way. The field of tranquillity around Johnny is still there. And who can blame the men for thinking this way? They have heard this lecture countless times, at the airport and on the farms in Canada. I think they are right to treat all this hot air with the disdain it deserves. Nobody has to tell them that the Officer, a true politician, is speaking for the benefit of the local journalists rather than the farm workers. Quite frankly, I find this man quite insulting, damn malicious, really. Worse, this man calling himself a Liaison Officer doesn't seem to realize he's just a relic from a less than glorious era, his job a leftover from the days when people like Johnny and his colleagues were neither slaves nor free men, but so-called apprentices and the government needed officials to go from plantation to plantation to make sure everybody was happy. The same way the damn magistrates did more than one hundred and fifty years ago. Well, in Canada these guys just go from farm to farm. Same job.

Anyway, there is one good thing about the speech: it is the surest sign the time for boarding is arriving. The long wait is all but over. It's time for the final goodbyes and hugs.

"I don't want to hear any foolishness 'bout anybody doing anything to place this Program in jeopardy," bellows the Officer, who is tall and slim, about thirty-five years old, although he looks younger. A trickster and deceiver, if I ever did see one. Obviously he relishes this stage. Notice he is the only person wearing a full suit and tie in this heat. What does that tell you about him?

Johnny knows the men are wondering, as is he, why all the Officers have always seemed so aggressive when addressing them. He has seen it happen repeatedly over the years. Talk tough at home and to the men. But when it matters, they are quick to lose composure and toughness. Especially when representing the men before the farmers. In the end, the men always turn to Johnny to solve whatever problems they may have. That is why Johnny reluctantly became their leader, a role that was forced upon him. The men simply do not trust young politicians like this one whose aspirations rest so much on maintaining the employment levels on the Program. So the men turn to Johnny. They know Johnny is familiar with the system, perhaps better than any Officer. They realize that in his quiet but dependable way, Johnny will always intercede with the farmer for them. Johnny has the respect of both sides. He is fair in his dealings. He will just as quickly, and with just as few words, tell the men when they are wrong, as he will stand up for them when they are right. The men don't feel the same way about the Officer.

"Don't forget we got lots of young people back here on this island just aching for the opportunity," the Officer continues. "For generations we've been sending men, emissaries if you like, to Panama, America, Cuba, Aruba, Canada and even England to make a living. And a good few of them have prospered. They have gone beyond just helping to put food on the table for their family, or a roof over their heads at night."

The men, these modern-day diplomats, if you know what I mean, exchange winks and mocking nods. They are too... umm...ah...*diplomatic*? From the looks on their faces, Johnny knows most of them are already lost in their thoughts. They are trying to imagine the year that awaits us. In their half-glazed eyes, Johnny can see what they are keeping bottled up inside. He knows because he too feels the nervousness gnawing, like undigested meat, in his stomach. The bitterness from not knowing what to expect. From not knowing how much life is going to change at home with their families, by the time they return. From not knowing if they will ever fit back in again on this island.

"One other point I must take the trouble to explain." The Officer raises his voice even louder. The sweat running down his face and neck is even more apparent, soaking the underarms of his suit. "I want each and every one of you to understand that every man we send up to Canada or the United States means one less job we're got to try and create on this island. Think of that. Another thing. In the years I've been in charge, nobody has run off this Program. Nobody living illegally in Canada or the United States. Nobody taking off and living like some rat in a hole. So let me remind you, if anybody is foolish enough to even think of trying to run, just bear in mind that when they catch you, as they will eventually, and they send your backside back home with only the clothes on your back, then *we'll* deal with you."

Oops, he is catching our attention. A loud, sharp sigh escapes from the crowd. I, too, cannot believe my ears. We are all listening up now. This is the first time we have heard this threat so openly, so tactlessly. And all the while, we have been thinking the government doesn't really care two shits if anybody runs off. In fact, we've been thinking these government people actually encourage people to run, so they can then send up a replacement, another, shall we say, *diplomat*. I look at Johnny. There is no change on his face, not even an extra blink. I don't think Johnny has ever thought, not for the slightest moment, of running away from the Program. Obviously, he's too smart for that. So no need to threaten him.

"We are not sending you to a foreign country to make bad for your fellow countrymen." The Officer soldiers on. At least he has our full attention now. What does Brer Bear say in that story? You can ignore me until I stand up on my hind legs and growl. 'Cause when I growl, you bound fuh tek me serious, 'cause then you know I mean business. That's what Brer Bear says, and you know the story. And here I hope those that have ears are hearing. I don't often agree with the Officer, but his warning makes some sense. Only fools try running. "This year, all the Caribbean islands on the Program had a meeting because we had was to plan strategy to deal with the Mexicans. They horning in more and more on *our* Program. They want to take food out of *your* mouth, out of all *our* mouths, looking to send up more of their people and them Mexicans are damn dependable. They don't run or complain. They work hard and do whatever they are told without as much as one question from them. So we had this meeting. And let me tell all o' you what we decided." Now he's really growling, isn't he? "We agreed that we will have zero tolerance, I repeat, zero tolerance, none whatsoever, for anybody running off the contract." Can't you see him strutting, standing up on his hind legs? "And, after we punish anyone running, we'll also hit back at the area of the island that person that runs comes from. Be Christ, it's licks in the policeman if anybody go and try any foolishness."

This time there is no audible sigh. But you should see the expressions on the faces. I, too, can't believe it. See what I mean about a storyteller always being prepared? This new policy is the news, my friend, and am I glad I didn't drop my guard. Reaching this point is worth the wait and the tedium of this speech.

"So there will be no more people from that area getting a chance, only to disappoint us, only to threaten our livelihood, to give what we have worked so hard for all these years to the Mexicans, who don't run off no contract. So tell that to your friends and family living in Canada and United States. Tell it to all who would encourage you to break the law and run away." Mercifully, the speech is over. One or two people applaud, but there is no enthusiasm. Most are still recovering from the shock.

The Liaison Officer's arrival at Johnny's group coincides with a flurry of activities at the Air Canada counter. Smokie, wearing a big straw hat, cowboy boots and jeans, makes his entry, and in style, as usual. At his side is a young woman of about twenty years. Smokie leaves the luggage in front of the counter and races over to the group. The two men loading the suitcases onto the conveyor belt swear loud enough for everyone in the terminal to hear. Obviously, they thought they had finished working for the day.

And surprise, surprise. With the Officer is a replacement for Grafton, which only proves that I, too, can get things wrong. Not too often, though. The replacement is a tall, gangling, smooth-faced youth of about seventeen. I feel like kicking myself for not realizing who the youngster was earlier. I was the first, the only one really, to notice the Liaison Officer pointing us out to the youth when they arrived at the airport. But even then I didn't make much of this fellow. There is something about him that is so deceptive, that says he isn't the type to be on no farm labour program. There is something strange and unexplainable about him, something that strikes me in the guts, but which I don't have the time right now to analyse. That is why I overlooked him as a replacement. I thought the Officer was simply asking the youngster, probably just another government hanger-on, I thought, to listen to his speech, to learn, as I like to say, how politicians con people. For this youth has more of a politician's — dare I say, perhaps even a leader's — cut about him than even the Officer himself.

"So what you think about your new trainee?" the Officer says to Johnny. "Have you had a chance to talk to one another?" he asks, turning to the young man. "Introduce yourself to the fellows!"

"Winston Lashley," the youth says assertively. "I'm from the Pine, St. Michaels." The words rush out like a blast of hot air. This guy is something else.

"Stick with this man, Johnny here," the Officer says. "He won't set you wrong. He's the best trainer you can get."

Johnny looks inquisitively at the stranger. I can see the thoughts going through his head. He too is taken aback by this youth who just glares at him. When the aura of two strong men meet and clash, one just has to give, has to step aside and submit. When it is clear, as the old women like to say in their stories, that two smart rats can't live in the same hole. Or two men under the same roof. Not only does Johnny think this trainee looks too young for the Program, but from the way Winston is dressed he thinks he could just as easily be one of the many sons coming to the airport to see his father off. And Johnny is right. Winston is dressed too casually, too tropical, in tight narrow-bottomed blue pants, red running shoes reaching up above his ankles and a white shirt with the neck opened to display a heavy gold chain. It is almost as if this guy marches to his own drum, hears his own music and follows nobody. Trouble self, if what we suspect is true. And for these reasons, I hate his guts. One look at him and I know he is trouble self.

Winston smiles at Johnny, as if in triumph. But Johnny doesn't return the gesture. For some reason, he can't look this youngster in the face, eye to eye. A chill runs down my spine. I have to caution myself not to read too much into this little incident. Perhaps it's just because Johnny's thoughts are elsewhere. I know Johnny well; he can't be intimidated that easily. Especially not by a little boy who, despite any future potential, can't even piss straight yet. And Johnny felt the softness of the young man's palm when they shook hands. Obviously, this guy is not used to hard manual labour. This is not someone accustomed to the rough and tumble of rural, agricultural life. The hands are too soft, the fingernails too long and clean. Winston reminds Johnny of his eldest child, who at most is probably only a year younger than this boy claiming to be Grafton's replacement. We are all thinking that he must have been chosen as a political favour to someone.

My concern, however, is more personal. There appears to be something special about this boy, so much so that a storyteller has been assigned to him, the same way I was commissioned to trail the Prophet and now Johnny. I don't like this move and I might have to send a note to Mother Nyame asking her what's up. But I will have to wait and see whether this storyteller will give way to me or follow us to Canada. After all, there is no need for two stories about Edgecliff. The place isn't that important, the story isn't that big that I need help, especially when I didn't ask for any assistance. Unless someone is checking up on me, someone's *pimping* behind my back. If the storyteller doesn't give way, there could be trouble, something I must be ready to deal with. Another thing that bothers me — the voice sounds a lot like that storyteller, the unmannerly one, we met in Cuthbert's car. The one that never did say hi to me. I will be even angrier if the voices are one and the same. Why doesn't this simpleton, this mere minstrel if you ask me, get lost and leave me to do my job?

"You guys better start boarding the plane now," the Officer says.

"We waiting for Smokie to come back," Mighty answers.

"How you getting through with your plans, Jones?" The Officer asks, casting a quick glance over his shoulder to monitor Smokie at the counter.

"You mean getting the immigration papers to stay in Canada for good?" replies Albert Jones. His wife and children standing at his side smile broadly. You can see on their faces how much they dream of immigrating to Canada. "Well, they're coming through real soon. Things really lookin' promising."

"Good. Good. Keep me informed. I'll be up north when it's a bit warmer up there. We might want to bring up someone to take your place if things working out for you so soon."

"The people at the Canadian Immigration, sir, say everything lookin' okay." Albert is so proud of himself. He is bubbling over with information that he just has to share. "In my heart, I really got this strong feeling that this is definitely the last time I'm leaving Barbados on the farm-worker program. I can really feel it in my heart, the Lord knows. I know that the sixteen years I've been going up on the Program has to count for something when they come to deciding if I'll get my landed status. It just has to."

"Sure it will," the Officer confirms. "Just goes to show what

I've just said: it doesn't make sense doing anything illegal." At this point he raises his voice, as if he is shouting across the waiting area. "Always go through the front door when it comes to immigration matters, to seeking permanent residency. You're a good example for all the men, Jonesie."

"There is something I also got to talk to you 'bout, sir." Rat Face Simpson speaks up. "Something that's bothering quite a few o' we the boys. It's this situation with the taxes, how the Canadian government making all o' we pay them income taxes as if we's Canadians, sir."

"Oh yeah," the Officer says. "I won't worry too much about that. As you know, everybody got to pay taxes. And you should look on the fact that you're paying taxes as a good thing — it means that, for all intents and purposes, you are working full time in Canada every year. It's them that only working three or four months that don't pay taxes. But then how much money can you make in three or four months? Not as much as in nine or ten, right? And don't forget something else that happens when you pay taxes, it means you and all the others are what is deemed Canadian residents. You know what that mean?"

"I think so," Rat Face says. "What you think?"

"Well, it means that anyone spending at least six months a year in Canada, anyone like most of you here spending more than one hundred and eighty days working in the country, all o' you for all intents and purposes are Canadians. You are deemed to be Canadians. That means in Canada you are treated like any other Canadian and, unfortunately, that means paying taxes like any other Canadian."

"But the taxes heavy, heavy, heavy, sir," Oscar says. "You think we'll get back any o' this money we paying all the time? And what about the unemployment insurance and the workers compensations and the health levy and this Canadian Pension Plan thing? By the time the government done rake off them own bit, nothing ain't left. Then come the cut o' we own government on top o' everything."

"Everybody pays taxes," the Officer says. "I have to pay taxes too, just like everybody else."

"But why we gotta be paying all them things when we don't get any benefit from them?" Oscar says, sucking his teeth loudly. "I mean, all the fellas here can understand why the Barbados government saving some o' we money fuh we. That's we own government, we're talking 'bout, and we eventually get some of the money back. But it different with these Canadian pensions and levies. And yuh know, I don't know one person that ever get one penny o' this Canadian pension that we all gotta keep paying into. Not one blind cent."

"It's the Canadian way," the Officer repeats. "You are deemed a Canadian. You have the same rights and privileges as any Canadian."

"That's what I keep telling them," Albert interjects. "That why I keep telling them that my case for my immigration papers look so good. All this time I spending in Canada, as a deemed Canadian, paying my taxes every year, not claiming anything from the Canadian government or getting in trouble with the police or nothing so, just working quietly and doing what I gotta do, I know all that time I spend in Canada just gotta count for something. It just gotta count."

"Definitely," the Officer says. "And let me tell all o' you something else while we're talking about these things." He lowers his voice as if in a conspiratorial whisper. I hate it when he acts like this, as if he is so important. "I didn't say it when I was up there talking a few minutes ago. But because I like you guys, I'll tell you what the government is planning to do for all the workers. I know some o' you fellows own property at home, or planning to buy a house or two with the money from the Program. Well, the government is planning to pass a bill in Parliament in the next few weeks to take out insurance on the houses and the mortgage and loan payments for all the workers. If you can't pay for the house, you know, the mortgage and thing, then the government will step in and make the payments through the insurance. What you guys think, a good thing, eh?"

"Sounds good," Johnny says, glancing at Maude.

"That's what a government is supposed to do: look out for its own people. So that hard-working people like you, Johnny, and all of you," he pauses and looks around the semicircle, "you people can all do your work and not worry about anything."

"I like it," Tommy says. "Only a few minutes ago we was talking about Grafton and the insurance..."

"But because the bill ain't pass yet," the Officer cuts him off, "I didn't make the announcement to everyone. I'm only sharing the good news with you guys, because you guys from Edgecliff are my favourite people. So don't go running off your mouths now." This time he looks directly at the women. "I'll have more to say when I come up. I will have more information like what the premiums for the insurance will be, but they shouldn't be too much. By then the government should have something to say officially to you women still at home. Okay!"

The Officer walks off. The men gather up the coats and handbags in preparation for Smokie's return. When he does come back, the young woman is still clinging to his arm.

"Christ, we thought you weren't coming, Smokie, man," Mighty says. "Either that, or you know how to get away from all these windbag speeches." He flicks his head in the direction of the departing Officer.

"You all know Angie, right?" Smokie says. "She was with me at Grafton's funeral. She's the one that keeps delayin' me all this time. You should see how she's cryin' her little eyes out now that I gotta go back up."

"That ain't true," Angie says shyly. Playfully, she slaps Smokie on his arm and looks at the other women.

"But be Christ, let me tell everybody somethin' right now — this is definitely the last time I goin' up on any contract, you hear me? I swear to that," Smokie says. He places a big arm around Angie's narrow waist and pulls her to him. "Tell them, Angie, tell them. Tell them what me and you plannin'."

He looks at Angie. Contagious smiles fill the two lovers' faces and also infect the bemused onlookers. Turning to his colleagues, Smokie announces: "Me and Angie plannin' to open this restaurant when I come down. In case any of you bad-minded people wonderin' what I'm talkin' about: Angie's father is a big civil servant in the ministry and got connections with the government, you know, so gettin' the restaurant licence in a government hotel shouldn't be too hard. In fact, we already apply for it, to get the ball rollin', so that when I get back down here everythin' would be fixed up already."

"What you got there in them bags, Smokie, man?" Tommy says. The coughing has stopped temporarily. He is sucking loudly on a mint candy.

"Food. Good food to cook," Smokie answers. "Food that you can't get in Canada for no amount of money."

"As long as it ain't that goddamn salt meat that you try to make last year. Christ, you almost poison everybody with that rancid stuff, man," Mighty says. "Everybody had the shittings for weeks."

"Was the brine, man," Smokie explains, a sheepish smile on his face. "I didn't have enough salt. Was the brine. Not enough. So the meat turned a little bad. That's what happened, man."

"And what about the year before when you carried up all them bags and bags of curry? Just because you'd find a little Indian thing for a girlfriend and she'd get you into Indian foods," Delbert interjects. "And how you used to cook curry morning, noon and night to get rid of all that damn curry? So much kiss-me-arse curry to eat. Christ, I didn't realize you could mix curry with so many things!"

"You see why nobody shouldn't do nothin' for these ungrateful brutes?" Smokie asks. He is addressing the women in pretend disgust as if he expects the females to empathize with him, but also to bring the women back into the picture and ease the pressure on him. It's a telling move that dampens the bonding of the men, an intervention that forces every one of them to instantly put back in place the mask that had slipped, that hides their real persona from their women. "I mean, here I am tryin' my level best to give these sons o' bitches somethin' good and hot to eat when the day ends. Somethin' to break the gas in their stomach when they come home late and too tired and hungry to cook. And they still complainin' all the time. That's the thanks I get. That is why, when I come back down for good, when me and Angie open the restaurant, all like you so," now he is addressing the men and waving a finger in front of them, "all like you so will have to pay for what you now get free." Smokie's inclusion of the women has robbed the men of that last special moment together. The easy rapport and unquestioning camaraderie is gone.

"Enough of that," Johnny says. "Let's board." He is smiling for the first time this day. I feel good for Johnny. I know how sweet it feels to be back among people who really understand. I cannot wait for us to be all together, back on familiar turf, away from prying eyes, in just a few hours. That is something to look forward to, when the men can be men.

"You got a coat?" Johnny angrily asks Winston. He is annoyed the youngster is staying behind, unwittingly watching the final awkward moments between Maude and Johnny. They try to embrace, like other couples, but it just doesn't work. It is too wooden. Their actions too leaden. In this final private moment, they are unable to overcome the harshness and estrangement of the past two months. "Tell the missus on the farm that I might write she to keep in touch," Maude says. "'Cause you know you and me when it comes to writing letters."

They coldly pull apart, dropping their eyes to their feet. When Johnny looks up, who is standing there gazing at him, but this Winston Lashley with a funny grin on his face.

"Coat! What for?" he responds.

"You're going to Canada, aren't you?" Johnny snaps. He takes this chance to let go of Maude's hand and to begin walking away, Maude still following.

"Yeah! What do you mean?"

"You know what the weather is like this time of the year, right?" Johnny asks. "In Canada." He emphasizes the two words.

After a moment's hesitation, the implication of the question dawns on Winston. To Johnny, his answer is irritatingly slow in coming.

"Oh. I see what you mean. Nobody didn't tell me nothing 'bout no coat. I thought they'd give us coats up there," he says. "I guess I can buy a good cheap one at the airport. No big deal."

Johnny takes the faded grey coat from over his shoulder. "Here, take this." Winston catches it with both hands. "Use it 'til you get one."

My man is his old self again. He has regained his composure. The strident tone of voice is disappearing. "I don't know about them sneakers on your foot, though."

"Thank you," Winston says softly. We are in front of the door that leads out to the aircraft waiting in the darkness.

"Wait," Johnny says. "I want to buy a couple bottles of rum in the duty free."

Winston follows Johnny into the shop. That makes the three of us the last to board the plane, and Johnny and Winston have to sit together. That should make for a great trip. But I don't care about anyone's seating arrangements. I am starting to hear that other storyteller even louder now, and I don't like it one bit. There is still no need for two of us, certainly no need for anyone as different as this interloper. I don't plan to let this issue drop quietly. No bloody way.

chapter four

Listen! There's that distinctive noise. For me, that sound is the most powerful clue we're no longer in the Caribbean. The best I can describe it is as the jangling of something splintering. Not breaking cleanly, but with tiny bits of ice crashing randomly and fracturing even further. Nothing like the clamouring voices, the sweet, erratic cacophony of tropical noises: the ocean, the breezes, the expressiveness of people arguing, the sting of the sun and the quiet of the night, the croaking of frogs and the chirping of crickets — none of those typical battleground sounds we left behind only hours ago and, perhaps, which we miss already.

We all know what we are hearing is really the noise of frozen rain pounding rhythmically on the frosted glass. But in that noise there is so much more. Like a real good piece of jazz, or a calypso where the words and music relay more than is apparent at first notice. But the noise makes me queasy. Especially against the background of such darkness, with only the occasional light along the highway, with now and then the outline of a building or a tree slipping by eerily like in some macabre dream.

From what I can tell, some sprinkles are melting quickly on the other side of this clouded glass. They are forming trickles that eventually become ice again. In no time, the ice flows will merge with the bank of frozen rain and snow building at the bottom of the window. Soon, ice and sleet will cover the entire window. Folks, this is obviously not Barbados, no Caribbean sun or warm breezes to fight with, just ice and cold, and *Canada*.

We are heading overland for the farm. The silence in this

school bus is so oppressive — every man seeking refuge in his own thoughts, battling his own dreams, like a prisoner heading down some highway to some undisclosed rendezvous. All of us are thinking about life in this country. We dread the start of a new season and we usually fear the ending. In my case, I am always wishing someone would tell me at the outset what to expect, that someone would predict in broad stroke what will happen by the end of the season. In the Caribbean, we know the enemy is the sun. The doves remind us every evening. But in this country it is hard to tell exactly who we are fighting, indeed if it isn't our own selves. We just don't know the lay of the land, the hidden minefields, no Brer Dove to counsel us. In this country, there is nobody, nothing really, to tell the future. Nothing except for the sounds around us.

Only one man who arrived on that plane knows for certain where his future lies. Bright and early tomorrow, he will be back at the airport making the return trip. I wonder what he will tell his friends and family when they see him returning with just the clothes on his back. What a fool! Just wait 'til the government back home gets through with him: he'll be saying his own mother is a man when they're done with him. Hardly in Canada for a good half hour and he is ready to break the people's laws. He made arrangements with a friend to pick him up at the airport and for him to disappear. No farm work for him. He was running off the contract, despite what anybody said, and he was going to live in the big city. Make his future there, fool that he is. If you are going to run, at least be smart enough to know the lay of the land, know what you are getting into. Obviously, neither he nor his friend had thought the weather might intervene. No sooner did he get into the car than it ended up in a snow bank. The immigration people had only to walk over, clap the handcuffs on him and bundle him off to the overnight cell. From then on, none of the men could even go to the washroom to fire a pee without someone following them; those guards are just watching everybody and ready to pounce. All because of this one man. What a fool! A real Brer Idiot if ever there was one. From now on, he's done suck salt, as far as any talk about his future goes. Thank goodness he is not one of our men from Edgecliff, for he would only give us all a bad name. Johnny would have had a fit. Now, here in this bus, all we can hear is the screams of this poor idiot as they lead him away. Screams that are now imbedded in our memory, as much as the Canadian landscape. Clearly the sight of this guy being led off in handcuffs still rattles the men, making them more silent than they usually are at this point in the piece.

But something else is also causing this silence. When we left the airport, there was a team of eighteen men from some farm or the other still waiting for some word about their future. Indeed, nobody seemed to know what was going on. From what little I gleaned, apparently these unfortunate souls arrived in this country to the sad news that they no longer had an employer. So unexpectedly comes the word that yet another farm has bitten the dust, so quickly that the information does not arrive in Barbados before these men leave. Now they are huddling at the airport, awaiting word from on high, not sure if tomorrow will bring them a new employer, or maybe employers as the team splits up, or if all of them will be heading back home. God, I hope their women are now as prepared as Maude or Barbara.

So you can understand the cold mood on this school bus. With so many rumours of financial hardships, nobody knows what will happen to any of the teams; nobody is quite sure if these so-called bankruptcies aren't also blatant attempts by the farmers to discard their responsibilities to these men. Everybody knows that these days you don't trust nobody. And with nobody in authority on hand at the airport to explain anything, it's hard for anyone to know what is the truth. So you understand the uncertainty gripping these men. Who will be next, they are asking themselves, for whether they stay or run away, the outcome might be just the same. Long bus trips like these can result in a lot of soul-searching with every single fellow travelling his personal road to Damascus, hoping for some voice to speak and tell him about the future. Even Johnny.

In this quietness, I am picking up other sounds too. Some of them are the same noises as the frozen rain beating on the glass panes of this bus. Except that they are a bit muffled. It is the distance that gives them this characteristic. But these sounds also grab me by the guts. They force me to close my eyes, and then, magically, I can take in the vibes coming from the kitchen of the family home at Edgecliff Farm. I can still hear the snores of the men in the bus, but I can also hear the distinguishable silence in this room that strikes me as colder than anything the men have experienced on any of their countless trips.

There is something compelling about this house. It is in the silence that is so heavy and it is in the look on the face of Mary Elizabeth Stewart. On her face is the same concern I first noticed toward the end of the last season. Look at the way she stands staring through the window into the darkness. She, too, is watching the rivers of ice form on the glass in front of her eyes. She, too, wishes someone would predict her future. It's a scene worth describing.

Every time she breathes, a light film of mist forms on the window pane. I can see it expanding into odd shapes. Just as quickly, the shapes, some of them looking like characters from any Brer Anancy story, disappear. Mary Stewart, the heavy window curtains partly wrapped around her slender body, stares as though hypnotized through the ice-coated window. She is squinting into the darkness for the first sign of the headlights. She knows that somewhere in the frozen rain, and in the worst snowstorm in years, is a bus loaded with frightened men. At any moment she expects the light to appear up the road, signalling that the men are home. Mary is like that; she worries a lot. Only when the men are safe in their beds can she go to sleep.

In the background, above the anxious din of a piano elsewhere in the house, a radio announcer is reading the ever-growing list of closed roads. In the solemn voice normally reserved for emergencies, he is warning everyone to remain indoors. Mary shudders. She notices that he has not said anything about the closing of Pearson International Airport in Toronto, so she assumes it is still open. But even if flights are still landing, she thinks, there is still the problem of negotiating the treacherous roads into the farm.

"I wouldn't want to be out on a night like this," Mary mouths silently to herself. Not with the fierce winds causing the trees in the distance to bend until their tops appear to touch their roots. Even the strongest trees in the apple orchards now look like stiff giants exercising and stretching. These are the same sturdy trees that have been the mainstay of this farm, that have to contend with the strong winds that are now rattling the roof over her head and sending one or two shingles flying. No, she wouldn't want to be outside, with the wind whipping the blanket of snow on the fields into a frenzy, the same fields that, hopefully, should be ready for the young tobacco plants in a few short weeks. But on this night the fields look desolate in the darkness. Underneath the blanket of snow is the cold hard earth that must nurture the plants that George, the banker and the men will rely on so desperately this year.

Her mind returns to that letter from the banker. The same letter with the final accounts for last year, with most balances circled in red. It contains the warning that the new season is a make or break one for the Edgecliff. Those are the exact words: *make or break*. She repeats them to herself, watching how the hot air from her mouth causes frightening shapes to appear on the glass.

Make or break. Words etched in her brain. Another year of losses is unacceptable, the banker says, unless the Stewarts can find some way to inject new equity in this business. George stubbornly refuses to open the letter. Mary understands why.

As usual, George is avoiding discussing anything about the farm with her. Farming is a man's job, he says repeatedly, and if I may give a personal opinion, I kind o' agree with him. Some jobs are just right for men. For I can tell you that even I hear the farmers and their wives saying one thing when they get together to talk about the future: how if they have a choice they'll always want for a son, 'cause daughters do not help out much on the farm, especially when you are old. A daughter grows up to marry someone off the farm. Or she gets an education and runs off to live in some city. A son grows up with the farm in his blood and he marries and brings a wife onto the farm, even if she is educated. That's what they say. So I understand George's thinking — a farm is a prized possession for a man to pass on to his son. The same way George had inherited Edgecliff from Old Man Stewart, now dead eighteen years. So despite Mary's protests, George refuses to read the letter, maintaining adamantly that even without reading it, he knows what the letter says. It would only confirm the gist of his last conversation at the bank.

Mary remembers what happened after that meeting. She is glad she didn't accompany George for the encounter. But she remembers George coming home angry, swearing on his father's grave never to visit the bank again. Mary pulls the curtains tighter around her. She knows this is a critical year because she had seen the letter lying on the sidetable over the Christmas holidays. In the new year, when thoughts turned to the men's arrival, when she couldn't take the suspense any longer, she decided to open the letter. She knows George will see this as another moment of defiance when he finds out. But it was her only way of avoiding death through anticipation.

No, she definitely wouldn't want to be out on a night like this. For all that is happening outside, on the farm and beyond, the Stewart's home seems the safest, even if a bit chilly, place in the world. Mary knows that's another reason George is so concerned of late. Obviously, he, too, cannot accept that they might be forced out into the cold world beyond Edgecliff. Such could be their fate if they did not pull off some miracle this year. They'd seen it happening many a time. In the late fall, they might see the auctioneer's vans drive up to a neighbour's farm. A few weeks later the movers' trucks follow. The night before, the owners slip out, not even letting lifelong friends know where to find them. Then there would be silence, not even the sound of an animal, on the piece of land that used to be a farm. George and Mary never discussed it, but both knew the other was always wondering how long it would be before it was their turn for the visits.

She cannot pull herself away from the window. Her thoughts are jumbled, undisciplined, flitting from the farm, to the men, to the bank, to a future unknown. She wonders how the men are reacting to such dreadful weather. "Must be awful," she mutters. She knows that even the most experienced of them have probably never encountered anything like this. None of them could be thinking too kindly of such weather as a welcome. She wonders why young, strong men would leave their homes in the sunshine for a place like this. Then she remembers the banker and those dreaded vans and feels grateful to the men and to whatever reasons that keep bringing them back.

The announcer finishes reading the latest weather report. He ends with the assurance that snowploughs are still battling to keep the main highways open. The strains of easy listening music, that sound even quieter on a night like this, that make the room feel colder, lifeless and still, resume on the radio. One indistinguishable song follows another. The broadcaster does not bother naming the tune or the band. The music seems to compete for attention with the sound of the piano in the other room. It's the type George likes listening to as he works on the books. The type of background music that he doesn't like her to interrupt, not even when he is in the best of moods. These thoughts send a chill up her back. They are drawing out of her the heat that she has been conserving with the green and white wool sweater and the curtains. Even inside the shelter of the spacious kitchen, she feels cold. She pulls the curtains tighter again. She hears a thread or two snap.

"Maybe we should put another log on the fire," Mary says. She doesn't bother turning her head in George's direction. Without looking, she knows his reaction. How offended he is at this intrusion. But she has to talk to get rid of the nervousness and foreboding inside her. The risk of starting a conversation and offending her husband also holds the chance of overcoming the coldness in the living room. Of trying, even if vainly, to get an exchange of thoughts on how they — *for it will take the two of them working together* — can overcome the seemingly insurmountable problems threatening their livelihood.

When no audible response comes, she continues to run her slim fingers along the flared edges of the curtains and to stare out into the darkness. Neither she nor her husband makes a move to put another log on the fire. She doesn't really expect him to get up, but she feels compelled to continue to stare out the window, her eyes glued to the darkness, looking for those first rays of lights.

"What we need to do is to get that daughter of ours to stop pounding on that damn piano," George says. He picks up the conversation several minutes later, as if it has been hanging in the air waiting for him to latch on. "Maybe we can get her to do something more meaningful with her time."

"What do you want the girl to do?" Mary asks, hardly raising her voice. It is neither a real question nor a statement, but, like the log she will eventually have to throw on the hearth to save the dying flames, a bid to keep the faint glimmer of conversation alive. "And on a night like this, too. We are all anxious for the men to arrive, given the weather."

"If she must play the piano, she can at least learn to play something with a damn melody," he says. "I don't need any more aggravation when I'm trying to balance these damn books. The bank already got me aggravated enough."

She turns to look at him, sitting at the table in the dim light. George is forty-seven years old, slightly balding with a bushy moustache. On the table in front of him is a curled pipe. He picks it up and strikes a match, all the time keeping his eyes on the books spread open in front of him. Not once does he look in the direction of the woman, three years his junior. After seventeen years of marriage, there is nothing new to talk about. Looking at them, how can I not think about Johnny and Maude? Really, I would like all these men snoring in this bus, all of them who think differently, to see and hear what I am witnessing. It would surprise quite a few of them, especially those who believe that it is all wine and roses in the farmhouse. Obviously, marital spats are not just an African thing, as some people like to make out, you know all the endless talk about how Black men and Black women just can't get along; that the Black man doesn't know how to treat his woman; that the Black woman is too headstrong. Obviously, this is just a man and woman thing, pure and simple, colour doesn't matter, perhaps more proof for my theory that marriage should be outlawed. Or forcibly dissolved in five or six years, after one or two children. But that's just my view, you don't have to share it.

"Have you decided if you're going to see the man at the bank?" Mary asks, again not bothering to turn her head. She hears George sucking loudly on the pipe, usually a sign that the lit tobacco has gone out.

"It's all these bills I have to keep worrying about instead of spending my time farming. That's the problem: the paperwork. I was trained at the University of Guelph to be a farmer. Not some damn paper-shuffler." He flips the book closed and pushes back the chair.

"You should still go and see the man at the bank, George. What's his name?"

"The University of Guelph is now the best agricultural training college in this country, if not in all North America," he says. "It trains farmers, not bookkeepers and accountants."

"Hinkson!" Mary shouts aloud. "That's it. Hinkson. Now I remember. You should go and talk with him, George."

"What for?" he growls. Score a point for Mary — as is usual in these cases, the woman always wins in the battle of topics for conversations. Look how with persistence she got George, no matter how he tried to spar and deflect, to come around to talking about the bank!

"He's already sent you two letters," she continues. "I don't think it looks too good if you continue to ignore him. It will give him a chance to do something, anything. You should go and hear what the man has to say."

"I don't have to go into his bank to know what he'll want to talk about," George retorts, the edge caused by the sting of defeat just a minute ago rising in his voice. "He'll be asking me, not about how much land I'll be planting under tobacco or tomatoes this year, but if I'll be able to pay off any of the loan from the bank. What you expect me to tell him?"

George again sucks heavily on his pipe. No smoke comes. The fire has definitely gone out. But at least he is talking to her, Mary tells herself, and given enough time she might yet get him to talk about the letter. George reaches across the table for the small bronze lighter beside the half-opened box of matches. He flicks a flame. He puffs on the pipe and a small stream of smoke escapes from his mouth. But the pipe still won't light. He takes it out of his mouth. Into the palm of his hand, he knocks the top of the pipe. All the time he is wondering why Mary wants to talk to him at this very moment, why she doesn't just go to sleep, leaving him to sit in the dark alone with his thoughts and his pipe. How he wishes he had the strength, the guts really, to tell her to go to bed. But she would misunderstand as usual and that would only cause another argument. He shakes the pipe and knocks it in his palm again. A black and grey ball of ashes and tobacco comes out. George dumps it in the trash can and knocks the pipe against the metal bin.

"But I guess Mr. Hinkson's right," George says. He pauses to put the pipe in the corner of his mouth. With the tip of his index finger, he forces a new set of tobacco into the hole. "Mr. Hinkson's bloody well right. I should be cutting down on these damn expenses." He lights up the pipe again — it's been a long time since he's talked to her about the farm. He knows this and he also realizes that now that she has suckered him in, he can't stop talking. "But how can I do anything when every time I ask the Barbados government to let us sit down and talk about cutting back on the number of men on the farm, they end up asking me to take more?" He hates feeling that she always gets her way, that she knows how to manipulate him. Why is he even discussing anything about the farm with her, he asks himself, when she doesn't even like farming?

He puffs several times on the pipe, each time louder and longer. *"Take more, they say. Everything will work out."* George is well aware that Mary doesn't like it when he mimics for fun the flat Caribbean dialect of the men, but George does it nonetheless. He's a man and does what he bloody well likes, imitates whomever he feels like. *"You want three more, four more men, Mr. Stewart.* That's all they'll talk about. I mean, this very evening I find out they're sending up another man. Even when I told them not to send anyone." George is still steaming. How he hates being manipulated; by the bank, by the governments, by Mary and later, for sure, by the men who will start coming to him with all their problems. Everybody manipulates him. Maybe he is not firm enough. Maybe there is a sign on his forehead saying he is a soft touch, that he doesn't have two balls like any other man.

"A replacement for the one that died?" Mary asks.

"All I know is what they told me on the telephone."

"When did they call you?" Mary asks, hoping to hide her surprise that George hadn't even told her that the plane carrying the men had arrived. She didn't want to raise this issue and have him accuse her of nagging, of trying to start a fight. Not now. Now, she had only to worry about the school bus surviving the treacherous roads. "I don't remember hearing the phone ring."

"Oh, that was a few... what is it?" he checks his watch. "Hours ago! Shit. Time flies. Well, all I know is that they phoned from the airport, saying they ain't got no winter clothes for some new fellow in Canada for the first time. What am I supposed to do? Buy winter clothes for everybody every year? The bank would definitely take away the farm. So I told them to contact the Travellers Help office at the airport and see if they can help them out."

"What a night to come to Canada, too."

"You mean, what a season," George says, puffing away. "And I still got the tax people and all them bloody audits to deal with, wanting all my records to show what I paying the men every year. They even saying I should show the men how to fill out their taxes like Canadians. I had to tell them that's the job for the Liaison Officer and his people, not for me. I'm a farmer, not some accountant. I have enough trouble just paying the men, let alone becoming a tax collector too." Now, he really can't stop jabbering, now that she has him going. All this talking can't be because he is concerned for the men, anxious to see Johnny after all these weeks, but just more evidence of how easily Mary can always get her way with him. So, helplessly, like a wound-up doll, he must keep talking. "I'm the one that will have to find money to pay them. I'm the one that will have to face the damn bank manager and explain everything, every number."

The smoke curls above his head and spreads into the room, slowly dissipating in the air. Mary sniffs loudly, blows her nose and sneezes into the curtains. George looks at her and frowns. He expects her to say something derisive about the smoke. She always does when she blows her nose that way. When she doesn't, he continues. "Any more coffee, Mary? I could use a fresh cup. Warm it this time."

Mary doesn't answer. The first lights from the school bus coming down the road bring a smile to her face. Instinctively, she looks at the clock over the green and chrome fridge. It is 4:35 in the morning. The men were due to arrive at the farm five hours earlier. But at least they have arrived, she tells herself. And, apparently, safely. She also notices the relative silence in the house now that the piano music has stopped. Maybe Jessica also is watching the lights.

"Any coffee, Mary?" George raises his voice. Obviously, he is the one person not to realize the men are arriving. "And I haven't even told you anything about the calls from the Mexican government, how they're badgering me to take at least one or two workers. It's like they'll even give you the men for free just to get a toehold. Any more coffee?"

"I'll check and see," she says, walking away from the window. Abruptly, she stops, just long enough to take one last look at the bus. It is turning off the road onto the pathway leading to the darkened cabin. In a moment the lights in the cabin will be turned on. She will see the lights from the kitchen window. She will know the occupants are safe.

Mary blows her nose again. "Do you have to smoke so much

in the house?" she asks, passing the table. "You smoke too much, George. It's not good for you and you know Jessie doesn't like it. Not to say anything about my allergies."

George stares at his wife and shakes his head sadly. That is why he doesn't like talking to her, doesn't like opening himself up only for Mary to trample him. He doesn't bother saying this time that it is his house, his lungs and his tobacco. Or, that if he couldn't smoke the tobacco he grows and sells, how could he expect anyone to buy it, to help him save *their* farm. Other men at the co-op and in the doughnut shops across from the bank in town say the same thing about their wives. Say that is why they'd rather meet for a talk and a smoke rather than try explaining the facts of life to their wives, rather than admitting to them how helpless and unprotected they'd become, how castrated they feel, something a woman could never understand.

"I've put on the kettle, listen for when it's boiling," he hears Mary shouting from the kitchen. "So you can make your coffee. I'm going up to bed now."

Another reason he doesn't like talking to her, George tells himself. Not only doesn't she listen to him but she never does anything for him any more. I tell you, sometimes these two are as bad as Maude and Johnny, with one big difference: they have to put up with each other every damn day of the year. Obviously, in my books, they are not like Barbara and Tommy. Not by a long shot. But one thing is clear from all this — no matter how you look at it, all these people, workers and employers, men and women, are facing the same uncertainties. And the outlook, on a night like this, doesn't look too good for any of them.

chapter five

This new guy, Winston, still rubbing his eyes, walks briskly into the cold, wooden building. From the way he moves, it is easy to tell something is wrong. To someone like me, who has been on this program so long, spotting those signs is as easy as recognizing snow, or sand on a beach for that matter. Still, there is something special in the way he walks, in his energy as he bounds up the steps and disappears into the darkness. Inside the building there is no light, except for the bright glow from the headlights of the school bus. It's just drab.

Winston places the heavy suitcase and bag on the floor in the middle of the room. For a moment, I think I hear the storyteller inside his bag shudder. All I can say is that it serves *her* right that the cold is also busting her arse. For in case you don't know, this damn storyteller is, how can I put it, a female, one of these new entrants into the profession. Until now, storytellers were male, always were. This departure, this experimentation really, worries me. And, of course, there is still the fact that, despite anyone's gender, there is definitely no need for a second one of us on this trip, certainly not for a woman to be talking about men and their doings. How would she understand anything? And, as I said, I still got enough vim to handle a two-bit story all by myself. If Mother Nyame sincerely thinks she must send me help, unsolicited if I may add, why not someone who actually knows the lay of the land, someone who can contribute and not be a burden, someone who would have an affinity for and understand the subjects of her so-called calling? Why not a traditionalist? One thing I know for sure is that I certainly don't need the help of anyone lacking the good sense to prepare for the cold weather in this country. As far as I know, there is no Travellers Help for storytellers, so take that. I hope Mother Nyame makes a note of this unfortunate situation, notices the shivers and trembling in the voice of this upstart, and quickly remedies this situation.

But, as I was saying, this youngster Winston joins Johnny and Tommy standing inside the doorway. Not once does he remain still. He just paces around, the snow from his shoes forming slippery streaks on the wooden floor. He has to keep moving, for obviously he is still freezing, even though he is wearing Johnny's heaviest coat. To be honest, none of this surprises me. Or Johnny either. My gut feelings tell me we should prepare for even bigger problems from this youngster.

The three of them watch the others coming off the bus and making their way into the building. Most of the men, their winter coats open to the front because of missing buttons, the ends flapping in the strong wind, look like eerie spectres. They tramp through the snow, the top layers of ice crunching noisily under their feet. Several trails in the snow lead to the narrow door. Before entering, the men stop briefly to stomp their feet loudly, knocking the snow from their pant folds and boots.

Winston is imagining how their feet must feel. In his sneakers, his toes are numb and burning. His bottom is already sore from the torturous ride from the airport. Because he was sitting over the back wheels, he felt every bump along the way. This is the usual mistake of a rookie. The old hands would never sit over the wheels. Not in a bus with poor shocks. They know better. Status on the Program gives them first chance at the choice positions in just about everything. And you know how much of a stickler I am for status, seniority and respecting your elders. I am old-fashioned like that, as you must have gathered by now, and I make no apologies. It appears that Winston is not only cold and sore, but starving. I had wondered about this when I noticed he was not eating anything. His last meal was on the plane more than eight hours ago. As his stomach rumbles, he has to be wishing he had not refused the insipid coffee and doughnuts they served us at the airport. Another mistake of a novice, I guess. Part of the heavy price we must all pay in becoming seasoned, I guess.

The men pass the three of them standing inside the door. They hasten into a room through another narrow entrance at the far end of the building. From inside that room, Winston hears a loud click. A light comes on, some of it spilling through the half-opened door linking the two rooms. He also hears the heavy thudding sound of suitcases falling on the floor and the creaking noises as the men sit on what must be their beds.

"Your new home," Johnny says.

"This! My God," Winston's voice cracks. The long ride, the cold, the hunger and now this latest disappointment is too much for him. He can't contain himself any longer. The words blurt out, as if, simultaneously, he has lost control of his tongue and brain. As if the rest of his body is finally rebelling against his better senses. There are times when people get so mad that I don't even have to read their brain waves, but just watch them, feel the anger oozing out of their pores. This is clearly the case with Winston.

Winston looks around the long darkened room in bewilderment. He still cannot believe his eyes. It is nothing like what he expected. In a corner by the door are several broken chairs stacked in a pile. With them are a few long benches, the type that each easily sits six or seven grown men, the type of benches Winston would expect to see in a park or classroom. That is the full extent of the cabin's furniture.

"This is it?" Winston repeats, almost choking in exasperation.

"For the next nine, ten months," Johnny says.

"God! I mean this is a...a...a..."

"Cabin?" Tommy finishes the sentence. The cold air has stopped his coughing and he says he is feeling better. But, obviously, he is growing tired of Winston.

"Yeah. That's it. A cabin. A damn cabin. Like what you'd put soldiers or boy scouts in," Winston explains. He walks away from Johnny and Tommy, stumbling over a box someone has left in the shadows. Winston moves gingerly into the little kitchen off to the side of the building. He walks as if expecting the creaky flooring to suddenly give way under his weight.

Notice the look on Johnny's face as he watches the pitiful sight of Winston surveying all that is before him and dying a bit more with every glance. Winston pauses inside the kitchen and looks at the blackened stove and the big army-like pots on top. Farther on is a washroom with its door hanging on one hinge. Above the bowl, a rusting chain for flushing, the same type of system he has seen in the smelly public washrooms at home. To the side is a shower stall, with a dingy piece of transparent plastic serving as a curtain.

"Not even a phone," Winston says when he returns to join the two men. "And you say that we're how far from Toronto? One hundred and fifty to two hundred miles? We gotta spend all the time in this place, and without even a phone!"

"In a couple o' days the men will put up a few pictures. It will look more liveable then," Johnny says.

"I don't know," Winston is almost beside himself with disappointment. "'Cause this ain't what I left home for. I can imagine what my mother'll say when I write and tell she 'bout this place."

"You'll get used to it," Johnny says. "Everybody does eventually."

"Not even a phone," Winston says. "How can I call home and tell my mother I arrived okay? I got five minds to turn 'round and just go back home."

He continues to look around the bleak room as he speaks, perhaps expecting a phone to appear. With his eyes now used to the darkness, Winston sees a small seventeen-inch television on a box. A rusty wire hanger substitutes for the TV's antenna.

"Well, you can still call home, if that's what you want so badly," Tommy says angrily. "But you gotta realize that the nearest phone is thirty miles down *that* road." He points in the direction the bus is now heading. "In the *next* town. Sarnia, not Toronto. You can walk there if yuh feel like, if yuh gotta call home that bad."

"What about emergencies? What if somebody takes in sick out here?"

"Sometimes they let us use the phone on the farm," Johnny explains. "But we try not to overdo it."

"The heat ain't on," someone shouts from inside the bedroom. "Somebody turn on the blasted heat before all o' we freeze off we balls in here."

Johnny walks in the direction of the kitchen and washroom. He reaches for a small faucet on the wall and twists it sharply. Then, he stoops to feel the old radiator with his hand. Standing up straight, he throws a switch and a small red light flickers on above the radiator. Johnny feels the radiator again. It starts to hum, a sign that perhaps Stewart has fixed the heating since it gave out in one of the earliest cold snaps of the previous season.

"Hot water on, too," he shouts, walking back to join Tommy and Winston. "Give it time to warm up if you want to bathe."

"And remember," Tommy picks up shouting from Johnny, "turn off the blasted hot water when you're finished bathing. You know how mad Mr. Stewart gets when yuh leave the hot water dripping. So don't let we give him something to get mad at so early in the season."

"Bathe!" the voice shouts back from the bedroom. "Bathe! Who the hell you expect to be bathing on a night like this, unless they want a good dose o' pneumonia? Especially when everybody still got all that heat from the island in we bodies."

"Let's put away our things," Johnny says. He takes a couple of steps in the direction of the bedroom. "Tommy, close the door to stop the cold wind from blowing in."

"One more thing," Winston says, his voice calmer. "Tell me, though, when will we get a chance to go into Toronto? I got a list o' things people want me to buy and send back home for them."

"Look, man!" Tommy shouts. He drops his luggage and looks straight at the youngster, his fists clenched. "Look, let me tell you something right now. We're on a blasted farm, yuh hear me good. A farm. That's where we is. In cold-arse Canada. When you left home earlier today, you did know where the arse you was going. To work. Not to dance. Not to party. Not to shop. Not to live in Toronto. Not to live across the kiss-me-arse border in Michigan in the U.S. of A. You left to work whenever *that* bossman out there in *that* house tells you to work. So you better get them stupid-arse ideas out of yuh head, otherwise you'll be in big trouble. Real big trouble. Yuh hear me?"

"But I didn't expect anything like this," Winston whimpers. He sounds close to tears, like a puppy. "Not even a phone. Out here behind God's back. And all this snow and cold. Nobody never did tell me it would be like this. That it could ever be this...this...*cold*."

"Well, what can I tell yuh but that they lie to you," Tommy says angrily. "'Cause everybody coming up here year after year gotta lie when they get back home. You got to lie even to yourself to remain up here, to stop yourself from just running 'way, to keep believing that what you're doing is really important or that things will eventually get better. So yuh better open yuh eyes real soon, you hear me?"

"It's okay," Johnny says, stepping between Winston and Tommy. Ugh, it's not often that I see Tommy so short-tempered.

But this youngster really got Tommy's goat. "Tommy is right — it's tough. But this is also your chance to make a life for yourself."

"But that's different, man, from what they told me," Winston says. "And everybody at home expects me to…"

"Let's try to get some sleep," Johnny says, curtly cutting him short. "It's been a long day. Things will look different in the morning."

Tommy closes the door and fastens the bolt against the howling winds. He returns to the group and starts coughing again as he and Johnny pick up their bags and suitcases. They walk off leaving Winston transfixed, as if too scared to even risk another disappointment by finding out what is behind the bedroom door. As if his life and dreams have come to a grinding halt. These are the pathetic sights that nobody likes to witness, far less record. But such is my job. The only good outcome of this experience is that the damn storyteller in Winston's bag has finally gone silent. A side of me hopes she's frozen to death. Yes, I'm that chauvinistic type of a guy, especially when I start to feel threatened. Still, it's funny how a bout of silence, like a breath of fresh air, can turn out to be the best news in an otherwise rather long and dreary day. But boy, isn't Tommy still steamed?

Now, I saw that look on your face a few minutes ago when I said that I might be feeling a bit threatened by this newcomer. You are wondering why. Would it surprise you if I were to admit that I can appreciate some of Winston's disappointments? It's true. Perhaps I should use this opportunity, with the men settling down for the night, to tell you a little story about a certain someone.

chapter six

Once upon a time, there was this, well, let's just call him a guy, assigned to a task that he really thought was beneath him. In fact, he still does, but that is neither here nor there for the purpose of this story. I still remember how much this fellow cried and begged to stay at home when the assignment first came down. Nothing anyone could say changed his conviction that the Program was not the place for him. This is such a terrible and demeaning assignment, he kept protesting, that it must be punishment for his earlier failures. It has to be proof, he kept insisting, that he is not good enough for a major assignment. Obviously, death has not redeemed him, because, despite his objections, Mother Nyame and her tribe did not hesitate in shipping him off to the farm to which he had been assigned. And it was damn well unfair. They didn't have to treat him that way.

Even today, a quarter century later, a part of this guy still thinks it was punishment. Some might say it was his guilty conscience over-reacting, still expecting some retribution all these decades later, but he can never be sure. A real loss of self-confidence. After all, previous to this, he had had the plum assignment of the century and had screwed up in the worst way. When he thinks back to that time, he can only shake his head in disbelief. How did it happen? It must have been his youth, he surmises. For here was a chance for he and the great man he was shadowing to set the tone for everything that would occur for the rest of this century. But they dropped the ball.

Even now, he doesn't have answers that make sense, not even to himself. He doesn't know why they fumbled so badly, condemning so many generations to life in darkness, so that as a new century begins, storytellers and their charges are still talking about doing and achieving the very things that were within their grasp back then. It's just amazing. To this day, this guy just doesn't know what went wrong. Of course, as I am sure you've guessed, that storyteller is your humble servant.

I can still remember so vividly the envy other storytellers had of me. That was a story in itself. Come with me to back then. See how my good fortune is all my international colleagues are talking about when we take a break from covering the mammoth gatherings of those Pan-African Congresses, those International Conventions of the Negro Peoples of the World, to be precise. Even to this day, I cannot think of a larger gathering of storytellers in any one city. Imagine all the Brer Anancy stories that are pouring forth. And I'm talking about serious, top-notched storytellers with an obvious mission, their charges going on to take pride of place in our people's history and mythology. And all of them envious as *shite* of me. "Shit, you're so lucky, man. You get to report on the *Prophet*," the Ethiopian leader's storyteller says to me. "You're with the *Black Moses,* the true true prophet." Notice the reverence in his voice when he mentions the Prophet. All the others just nodding their heads in approval. For this prophet is the only man in all creation to rally around the same banner millions of black and African men and women from around the world. The only prophet who had a real plan, who took the world by storm, who showed us how to make it into the Promised Land. Africa. Unlike Brer Donkey, he knew the right way back. I remember it so well. "I hope you still speak to us in ten, twenty years from now, when the Prophet has set up his kingdom on the Mother Continent and you are riding high," the storyteller says. Mother Nyame can tell you how many not-too-pleasant complaints about me she received from these colleagues, praising me to my face but cutting my arse behind my back.

Every one of them felt that he, for as I said it was only males in those days, could do a better job and was just plain envious of me.

After all, they knew I was narrating real, pertinent, history. A story with kings and queens and principalities of the most high. A story of our people going before the League of Nations in places like Geneva and speaking with the one voice of a single African government in exile. Our people summoning foreign ministers from European countries to our conventions. A real story about a time and places. Not like being on a goddamn farm in the middle of nowhere. A story of a people on the move. I challenge anyone to disagree that this was indeed the one time the entire universe was taking careful notice of Africans the world over. The New Negro Era, they called it, the Negro on the threshold of a new attitude toward other peoples. We were more than just sons and daughters of slaves, more than cane-cutters, cotton-pickers, pimps, con men or even heavyweight boxing champions. Everything seemed so bountiful then. The arts, theatre, the Harlem Renaissance, jazz and calypso music — all contributing to that feeling that a long-suffering people's time had come. We even had an army, a serious black army ready to fight for a United Africa and we had solid plans to set up a liberated colony in Liberia. Next was to be freedom for the entire African continent. We had a song to inspire us, the Universal Ethiopian Anthem, and we had a flag too — the immortal red, black and green - colours that to this day our youth still wear with pride around the world. The old story of no more Massa was finally ringing true, *buckra* days done, a genuine awakening for my people after three, four centuries of slumber in the New World. A resurrecting of a sleeping giant that had been raped of its peoples and jewels through that Door of No Return. It is no longer just a dream; the mental and physical chains are broken.

Rise up ye mighty people — that is the incantation of

resurrection, this mantra coming straight from the mouth of the Black Moses, and now the refrain of millions of eager voices on every continent, in every sea and ocean. An invocation no different from when an earlier prophet spoke to those dry bones and told them the Word of God.

It felt good to be alive during these times. No longer would anyone dare to suggest to Africans that *the opportunity to earn a dollar in a factory just now is worth infinitely more than the opportunity to spend a dollar in an opera house*. Hell, these were modern times and old house-nigger philosophies were finally and permanently discredited. We not only wanted to work in the factories, the Prophet was showing us how to *own* the damn plants through the Negro Factories Corporation, as well as the chain of restaurants, grocery stores, laundries and even a hotel. We not only wanted to patronize theatres and opera houses, he had a plan for us to take over and control an entertainment industry that in the coming decades would borrow so much from our culture and folk ways. This man was so far-sighted, I tell yuh! Even the sun seemed to be shining brighter and friendlier. Even the pigeons and gulls were lining the parade routes to admire us; the doves would coo in Central Park and surrounding areas, and they would be happy and respectful. And I was the official chronicler. The top flight Brer Anancy, the king of Signifying Monkeys. The entire world, and all generations to come, was depending on me to get the story right, to capture the essence of a very special time.

I still remember the boisterous cry as we were riding through Harlem on horseback. **Africa for the Africans.** Such sweet music. **Africa Must Be Free.** Trumpets blaring, drums beating, people dancing and jiving. Such verve. Such unity and respect.

> *Africa calls now more than ever. She calls because the attempt is now being made by the combined Caucasian*

forces of Europe to subjugate her, to overrun her and to reduce her to that state of alien control that will mean in another one hundred years the complete extermination of the native African.

So spoke this man who, in recognition of his universal appeal, had conferred on him the glorious title of Provisional President of Africa. But even then he knew his fight wasn't only for the liberation of those on the continent. Hear him again:

I hear the unhappy reports of the delegates from Zululand, from Nigeria, from Nyasaland, and from the Congo in Africa. In the same echo methinks I hear also the sad tales of sufferings in Trinidad, in Jamaica, in Antigua and other British West Indian Islands.

You had to have been there to fully appreciate what I am getting at. This wasn't no dreary bus ride from an airport to some farm in the middle of a snowstorm. Nothing so. I can still see the Prophet regally adorned and adored by millions of his people. Prophet Marcus in all his splendour, dressed in the black, red and green colours of a United Africa, leading the procession of all the hundreds of delegates from around the world, emissaries from the larger cities of the American Union and Canada, from Cuba, Haiti, the West Indies, Central and South America, from Europe, Australia, Abyssinia, from Liberia and Ethiopia. Never once did it occur to me to think of this procession as a kind of Palm Sunday celebration, the time-honoured ritual of praising or *bigging-up* the Deliverer one day and crucifying him by the end of the week.

Never once did it occur to me that the very people he came to help deliver would eat him raw, without salt for taste. For the century is young, the people ready for deliverance. And I, also young and unseasoned, have the privilege of recording history in the making, basking in the personal glow from the praise, honour and envy of my professional colleagues. What a time!

Africa for the Africans, the Prophet still shouts in my ears to this day. When I close my eyes, throngs of people are gathering in Madison Square Garden in New York just to hear him speak. Newsreels record his every movement and flash the pictures in cinemas and opera houses around the world. Millions of people in every corner of the globe read his words in his own newspaper, *The Negro World*, and in so many languages — a newspaper, I should say, that was banned in just about every country in Africa and Latin America, but which the colonial masters could not keep out of the hands of the eager millions of readers. They also devoured his magazines, took to heart his rallying calls and at those month-long Pan-African Congresses discussed with heated passion and vision how to free Africans the world over from their sleep.

Then, everything collapsed. Good Friday came as quickly as the batting of an eye. Among the betrayers are those well-known eight prominent middle-class black men, conspiring with the government, joining with that J. Edgar Hoover in the Bureau of Investigation to destroy the first of the many black leaders whose blood rests on his hands eternally. To this day, I still blame myself for not seeing the destruction coming. Any good storyteller always looks for the trends, anticipates developments so that very little will catch him off guard. Anticipating is as close as we can get to predicting the future. I didn't. I had a one-track mind. I had become too close to my charge, too trusting in my belief that the goodness of a man always wins out in the end.

That mistake haunts me still. Whenever I start to spin even the simplest yarn, or even the most noxious anecdote, I always remember my failure back then in the first three decades of this century. What could I have done or said to make a difference?

What should I have done? Anticipate more? Perhaps. Could I have said things differently, probed more possibilities, so that others could have used my informed musings to tip off the Prophet, so that History would now be different? Maybe.

Incessantly, I ask myself these questions. And I never have any clear answers. Except that there are some things you can never forget. Some things for which you never forgive yourself. And some things for which you know you ought never to be forgiven. Never. As someone once said, pass me the hemlock for I deserve it and from my own hands. If this were a simple Brer Anancy tale, the ending would have been obvious. Irony of ironies: the dreaded Brer Anancy curse inflicted on the self-same Brer Anancy. *And because Brer Anancy was so poor a judge of character and neglected his duties, from that day forth he is condemned to keep telling the same story over and over again until he gets it right. So when you hear the wind howling at night, and you're tucked away snugly in your bed and still can't sleep, you'll know why. It is Brer Anancy howling like the wind, still trying to tell you so sweet a nighttime story, you'll just curl up and fall fast asleep.*

And then in keeping with the ritual, to prove that everything had turned out just right, I, the narrator, like a judge sentencing himself, would give the benediction by saying, *Jump on wire; wire won't bend; so that's the way the story end.* Or as some of the other brethren might choose to say, *Jack Mandora, story over, me ain't tek none.* No matter what, there would be a natural ending and the listeners would just shake their heads and move on.

But, unfortunately, such clean endings only happen in folklore. Now you understand why the sense of impending failure is always second nature to me. And, believe me, defeat does leave scars. The same way that back then the chains had been broken from the people's ankles, but they were so used to dragging the balls, their muscles and spirits so atrophied, that the new

Negroes and Negresses, the very people the Prophet was to lead, acted as if they were still not free. The wounds where the balls and chains had cut into their flesh were too fresh, the pain still present in their minds, the scabs too visible. How can you forget? A people set free physically, a people given a dream and a vision, but a people whose minds were still enslaved. The scars do linger, still influence everything I do.

For these reasons, I'd be the first to say that I am too tentative this time around, perhaps too crabby and definitely too distrustful. But how can I be otherwise, unless I want to suffer the same fate as the last time? Unless I want to set up myself and everyone else for unimaginable disappointments once again. Unless I can cleanse my conscience and ignore my own scars. God, how I would personally like to pick up from where that great prophet left off. How I would like to atone.

So you must understand how often I relive that dreadful but pivotal time in our history. How every day I see flashes from those times: the picture of the Prophet festooned in his uniform, the smartly dressed courtiers of his realm: the Knight Commanders of the Distinguished Order of Ethiopia, Knight Commanders of the Sublime Order of the Nile, as well as the lesser nobles and the commoners.

Then there are also those haunting images of the long days sitting in the Atlanta prison cell with the Prophet. Just me and him and his thoughts. Deserted and denied. A great man reduced to watching ants crawl up a wall, to second guessing the truths he knew and preached. A visionary counting the rays coming through the cracks, but ultimately surrendering to bouts of despair as the sun withdraws and plans its attack for the next day. It is fun to record private thoughts, to see ideas take shape and develop. To see them go forth to excite and exhort others, to move people to act. To hope, to dream, to live for the future. But, after a while, it becomes tedious to just watch the ideas formulating but nothing becoming of them, just withering and dropping uselessly like scattered leaves before the wind.

While the Prophet is dreaming, others, even among his own, are railing against him. Ras the Impaler, one of our best writers calls this dear man. A conspiring murderer, others claim, for look at what happened to this brother Eason, his very right-hand man whose main sin was simply to challenge him by taking the title of leader of the American Negroes. An outsider, the intellectuals scream, no more than just a leader of West Indian Negroes at the most. Worse, shout others, a mere buffoon and con man fleecing the very people he claims to be saving, taking on the airs of another time and culture — a megalomaniac planning to become a despot and tyrant, an idiot consorting with people in white sheets spouting racial hatred and burning crosses on his own people's lawns. How could he join with those who preach racial purity and separation? they scream. Send him back to that damn little island he came from, they demand, as one by one, all of the so-called Talented Tenth, all these homeboys, all the young bloods, viciously deny him. This man, they cry, is the epitome of what happens when Africans of little formal education and class have a little power, just look at him dressed like a peacock, with all the trappings of grandeur that swell the head, the kind of thinking that causes Africans to destroy one another in their dictatorial lust for power and control. Can you imagine anyone, any African really, actually saying such scandalous things? Well, some of our so-called best minds did. Certainly by now, the cock should have crowed thrice, especially when these talented men petitioned the attorney-general to deport him. That's what I mean about a little knowledge being dangerous. Some of the people making the loudest noises were so-called diarists. Think on that. A weapon, I tell yuh.

From the cell, I can hear the denunciations. Bitter and vile, they are. The fact that he is, as they say, jet black in complexion obviously has a lot to do with these spiteful condemnations. I know I will offend some people by saying such things, but all I can say in my defense is that God loves the truth and the truth shall set us free. Yes, I can still recall how their faces all turned red when the Prophet retorted by calling all his detractors *paughy* mulattoes, *perjohnnies* all, white integrationists in half-black skins, an admixture of white and coloured blood, people vainly searching for, as he puts it, that elusive social equality between the races. They can't take it, can't swallow this kind of truthful criticism. Instead, they become vicious, they want to lynch the Prophet on the spot, especially when he says,

> *If all o' you so talented as you claim, how come you can't rally our people in unity and strength? Why do you still prefer to see a difference in West Indians and Americans? Why kill me because I am West Indian? Aren't we all Africans, torn from the bosom of our beloved Motherland?*

And then he made the prophecy that still rings in my ears, that really made them turn all sorts of colours when they heard it.

> *All of you talking foolishness about this being the century of the colour line, hear me nuh man. It ain't gonna* rass-clate *happen. All of you talking about casting down your bucket, better start thinking again, for every day you take the bucket to the well, one day the bucket bottom will fall out. By the end of this century, if our people don't stand up as mighty Africans, the black people of the Americas will still be beaten in the streets by police. They will still have to riot on the streets for simple human rights. There will still be one justice for blacks and another for whites. Even sports*

figures and actors will feel the pressure. The gap between those of us born in this land and those coming from elsewhere will be just as wide if not wider. Our men and women will be battling one another at every turn and our children will despair for the future. Nothing will have changed, although I hope to God I am wrong. But I don't think so.

Those were his exact words. I have double-checked the tapes several times. Even the words he said to his followers, those whose knees were weakening:

There is absolutely no turning back. There must be a going forward to the point of destiny. Destiny leads us to liberty, to freedom; that freedom that [Queen] Victoria of England never gave; that liberty that [Abraham] Lincoln never meant; that liberty, that will see us men among men, that will see us a nation among nations; that will make us a great and powerful people. Do you tell me you cannot make it? And I say, "Shame on you!" Have you not, you British Negro soldiers, made it for British colonization of the west coast of Africa, when, by your prowess, you conquered the innocent and unsuspecting native tribes? Did you not make it, you American Negro soldiers, for the white Americans in the Revolutionary War, in the Civil War, and when you climbed the heights of San Juan? Did you not make it at the battle of Chateau-Thierry and Argonne? You French Negro soldiers, did you not make it at the battles of the Marne and Verdun?

Nowadays, I listen in to the various reports from places like Los Angeles, Chicago, New York, San Francisco, Miami, from just about any American city, and all I can say is that, boy, that Prophet was really a prophet for true. He knew what he was talking about. Don't we now hear our women dumping and shiting all over our the brothers? Huh, don't we? Don't we hear our men slating our women, calling them beef and whores? Are our children not dying in the projects with no hope? Where is the vision? Aren't we still sending our young men to prisons or on Programs? For these reasons, because his words about the future were so right on, sometimes, I am glad that I ended up in Canada on a farm far from any major city. Maybe this way I can be a bit more objective. For we must remember that at times even the Prophet, even the founders of the Niagara Movement and the National Association for the Advancement of Colored People, had to seek refuge in Canada, of all places.

What a wonderful, long-suffering man. The Prophet heard the denials of him but never once became bitter or sour, never once sought retribution even when he became despondent. *Forgive them, Father, for they know not what they do or say.* I swear, I heard those words from my Black Moses. My people will come around some fine day, he would always claim, some day when the sun shall smile on them, when they have built a new home. Obviously, that day has not yet arrived, and I fear it never will. I still weep for a people that can be so ignorant. For a people that can eat its own with no recrimination or remorse. For this, I trust nobody.

And, yes, they did ship the Prophet back home. By then, I didn't know whose heart was broken more, his or mine. All I know is that I started to foul up on the job. I couldn't carry a straight line. My views seeped into the reports. Emotion choked my voice, giving it an indecipherable timbre. More storytellers triumphantly take over important events on my channel. They simply talk over me. Soon they are drowning me out for days on end. Envious, they are. It's like everyone has lost confidence in us. The Prophet has no people to lead. I have no listeners. Both of us in the same boat, our missions in life on hold. The envious cutting our throats while kissing us on the cheeks.

Picture this. The *S.S. Santa Marta* is reaching the mid-point of the journey to this place called home and I, as I later found out, am totally confused. I am reporting about all the happy people with me and the Prophet on the luxurious vessel *Yarmouth,* of the Black Star Line. We are going home in style. I had seen the hundreds of people gathered on the docks in New Orleans, the people walking in procession, some holding the umbrella over the diminutive figure walking up the wharf to the ship in the heavy rain. And the people standing in silence for his great speech.

"Good-bye America," he says, holding his silver-headed Malacca cane, wearing a snappy tailored brown checkered suit. "Farewell, my people." Vindication for the Prophet. The little man from the East has come and proven the Prophet correct. As far as I knew, we were on our way to Africa, the provisional president coming in out of the cold to build his empire on the west coast of the continent. For we had already established many, many outposts along the coast and elsewhere on the continent.

As the ship cruises into the harbour, I report that hundreds of thousands, perhaps millions even, of people are lining the coast to receive this important delegation. Oh, how crazy I have become. It must have been the tension and frustration. Or denial. That is what happens when a chronicler tries to influence the future. I wanted so badly for the Prophet to be right.

As we sail into the harbour, I go on deck with the Prophet to report what I think is the excitement of our arrival from this multitude of people. It is a welcome fit for a conquering hero, I rave. I watch as the Prophet wipes the tears from his eyes. Tears of joy, I rant with elation, tears of vindication and exhilaration. Back to the Mother Continent.

But, alas, it isn't a harbour in Africa. It is Jamaica. Only at the very last minute do I realize my error. Only then do I discern that they have stopped broadcasting my reports. Mother Nyame pulled the plug without warning. My accounts are unreliable, to put it mildly. Someone is dispatched to, as they put it, *assist* me. The storyteller doesn't even bother saying hi, to introduce himself, to tell me he is there to help me. Not a word, which is why I am now so suspicious of my new colleague. I can only think that the new storyteller must have come on board surreptitiously with one of the black guards that harassed the Prophet so badly. Perhaps it was when our ship arrived at Cristobal in the Central zone. When we transferred, as I later learned, from the U.S. fruit ship *S.S. Saramacca* that brought us out of New Orleans, a transfer that, somehow, I missed in my reporting.

Anyway, this guy shows up without warning and takes over. I now have no purpose in life. I am no longer the accredited storyteller, for I am cut off from my calling, the same way the Prophet has been denied his vocation. And then fate strikes. As soon as we come off the ship, it happens. I remember only briefly the shadows of the wings above me. In my confusion, I don't even try to escape. A death wish, perhaps. My brain is registering nothing, so I don't flee.

The hungry bird mercifully ends my misery with one gulp. So quickly does it happen that I do not even get the chance to put the age-old Brer Anancy curse on all those who had tricked us. You know how those stories end, something about how Brer Anancy getting so vexed that from that day on fowl cock never had teeth again, or zebras would always have stripes.

In any case, the end is quick. I don't have to watch the future unfold. The new storyteller picks up the narrative with, I later find out, only the slightest of blips. But without a curse, the story of the Prophet and his tormentors cannot be laid to rest, and that is why I know that he must return. That is why I believe I am back for a second stint.

When I do return almost thirty years later, the first thing I do is find out what happened after I was removed from the picture. What I discovered makes me feel relieved that it didn't fall to me to finish that story. It would have been the equivalent of serving a life sentence on death row, a slow torture. The jailing in his native Jamaica, the harassment of immigration officers when he entered Canada to teach or visit friends, the hurt of seeing the great edifice he was building around the world crumble, with no roof. No way would I have wanted to journey with the Prophet to London, to watch him become an outcast, when even the woman he loved so much, the same Amy denied him access to his two children and left him alone, with his acute bronchitis and asthma, to die like a dog in that cold damp city. To face the indignity of having to read his own obituary published in papers around the world, the result of an over-enthusiastic but equally uninformed diarist. Such indignity was enough to kill a horse, let alone a prophet, so that it must have been a great release for him when that cerebral hemorrhage claimed him.

In many ways, Johnny reminds me of the Prophet. Not in the sense of the Prophet's brilliance or his way with words. Not his penchant for hogging the spotlight and for being confrontational. Not his way of refusing to acknowledge his mistakes, for yes, the Prophet was human and in hindsight I would now say he made mistakes. Johnny is plainly none of these things. But what they do have in common are leadership qualities, that aura about them. Some people are just born with it.

But, yes, at times I still feel I am being punished. Obviously, I messed up on a very big story. In my way of thinking, the time had come for my reincarnation, but to be quite candid I sometimes feel there still isn't any confidence in my ability from Mother Nyame and the others. The obvious thing for them to do, I rationalized, is to take the easy way out — send me to a place where the story doesn't really matter in the overall scheme of things. Give me a chance to redeem myself with a minor assignment. And if I do prove myself, maybe they can elevate me. If I don't, it would be like writing one of those squibs that fill space in a newspaper but which nobody is expected to read. So where is the best place to send me? Some isolated farm behind God's back, among people virtually imprisoned.

Was I disappointed? I pleaded for a chance to prove myself. Is there no redemption around this place? I asked. Why must I continue to atone for the deeds of another time? But they keep telling me, we are not punishing you. We are not in the business of punishing, of vainly trying to correct or make amends for history. So stop overreacting. You should consider it an honour to come back as a storyteller. We are concerned with the present only — leave yesterday to history and tomorrow to the future. All assignments are of equal importance, Mother Nyame insists.

I am not totally convinced, obviously, because nothing makes any sense. I return to the Caribbean, an ideal place to work, an area that is my specialty, indeed expertise. Still, I am thinking that in the Caribbean nothing can go wrong, not with so much so fresh in my mind. I know the people, the culture and the lay of the land. I am returning at a time of liberation. Prophets no longer have to go abroad. They can lead their own people into a Promised Land right at home. There are so many stories to tell about young nations. So many inspirational leaders. Stories about people taking their future in their own hands. Of a downtrodden and dispossessed people rising up. All elements of a good, gripping story. Who could screw that up? Even in the area of sports, there is much to report. How, for example, these young nations could produce a single united team that has ruled unchallenged in the international arena for several decades, achieving on the cricket field what Prophet Marcus, himself a fine cricketer, hoped the black army of a United Africa would accomplish, as all those decades later Fidel sent his young tigers to fight and die in Motherland and by winning broke the back of apartheid in that now famous battle in Angola. How I wished I had been there to record that battle instead of just listening to those gripping reports. I wanted so dearly to tell good, meaty stories. Do you remember that line from another story where someone boasted that the Battle of Waterloo was won on the cricket fields of Eton's school, a victory beyond a boundary? I wanted to remain in familiar territory. Instead, they sent me to a farm, where I am the very first storyteller. A place with obviously no future. A prison for the body and soul if ever there was one.

Even my return is suspicious — why was I sent back immediately as storyteller, skipping the phase when we alternate as human and storyteller, as visible and invisible. After the incident with the Prophet, I should have returned as a human to demonstrate to others what I learned from watching and reporting. The same way that the Prophet is now off somewhere working as a storyteller and, hopefully, waiting and learning for his next chance as a human.

But instead of being asked to choose my parents, I just hung around, doing nothing. Just waiting and waiting while others who came back after me got their call and made their human choices.

Finally, I ask Mother Nyame what the heck is going on. That's when she breaks the news to me that I am going back as a storyteller one more time. "You won't be choosing any mother and father this time," she says, trying to pretend she is joking. "So you may as well stop watching all them men and women doing their business and having fun together. Sometimes I can hear your heart beating louder than the people you are watching, hoping we'll call your name at that critical moment."

Then, to make it worse, she gives me this lulu of an assignment. Why not see this as some kind of experiment? Mother Nyame says to me. We here at head office want you to watch closely and see if there is anything we can learn from these men. Treat them as isolated specimens. See if we can learn anything from having so many of our African men living in this prolonged isolation — you know, on a farm, in prison or even at jobs where they feel there's no future, no chance of integrating into the emerging international economy. We're anticipating big changes in the next millennium and we have to know what to expect from our men. Find out what you can about the social skills of these men and how adaptable they are, how successful we can expect them to be in a colour-blind world. For example, what would happen if in the new century we stopped sending so many African people to prison, if we emptied all the jails in those wretched societies of all our people? How would we integrate them? What would happen if we no longer put off avenging our people, if we were to come on chariots of fire, to burn down the old system of Babylon and build a temple with a roof of gold? If we were to overcome.

So you'll understand why I have second thoughts about this Program. Who could want a more boring assignment? They can say whatever they want, but I believe they are still punishing me, testing the limits of my endurance. For I'll live and die by the teachings of the Prophet, a brilliant man who would have looked Mother Nyame straight in the face and said nuts to this idea of integration. How I wish I had his strength and vision!

Now you know a little bit more about me. Yes, I'm a little complex. But I hope you'll now understand any slant I might bring to the rest of this story, a tale that I expect to really get going tomorrow, when everyone wakes up for the first morning of this new season.

chapter seven

But, hey, what's happening here? Watch that Winston character. You notice how he's acting? Look at him slowly pushing open the door and how timidly he's walking into the bedroom. I tell yuh, it's hard to sleep with something like this happening, with trouble settin' up like rain and looking for some place to fall.

For the longest while this youngster has been standing around outside in the dark, as if afraid to come into the light. While he's thinking, all this time I'm trying to get comfortable, ruminating about a past experience or two, with nothing too strenuous to report as the boys get comfortable in the old digs. Hardly anybody's paying attention to Winston, not even that foolish storyteller trailing his arse and now shivering she own self from the cold.

Now, as things start to quieten down even more, with people starting to think of breaking off some good sleep, this guy makes his move. He decides to come in out of the dark, if you get my drift. Now you watch him! Look at how his eyes circle the room. He's noticing how severely cramped it is, how musty smelling and poorly lit. To him, it is even worse than he expected. Oh God, I tell yuh, those vibes from him are so strong, so disapproving.

And what does Winston see? Along the edges of the room are large rusty nails on which the men hang their clothes. Winston stares at the men. They don't seem to mind the dreary surroundings or the fact that there's no privacy in this place, either, something Winston certainly can't come to terms with at all.

To his surprise, most of the men have already stripped to their underwear, some are naked. From the look on his face, to put it mildly, obviously Winston is taken aback by how the men are talking and carrying on, as if they are at ease with one another's nakedness. He hopes nobody expects him to behave this way. Now he is shuddering as that familiar queasiness runs through his body, the same feeling he always gets when another male looks at him too closely, tries to touch him or otherwise act too friendly. From what I can tell, from his body language, his expression and of course those strong vibes, he likes to keep other men at a distance — they should not touch him with their bodies or their eyes; for they are not women and he does not like anyone taking his sexuality for granted.

He does not mind being with men, for there are things a guy can only do and discuss with men, but they must keep their distance, must not invade his privacy. Well, I can tell you one thing: this boy is going to be in for some kind of a surprise. More of a shock than this. For in these cramped quarters, undoubtedly, keeping one's distance, not brushing against other naked men or having them stare, will be a tall challenge, if not well near impossible. And Winston must be realizing this, for even I can feel the rumbling in his stomach, the quickening of his heartbeat. He's so disappointed. This is not what he expected, not at all. I don't know if we should feel sorry for him, he and his ambivalence. This is only his first night on this Program, after all. But I can also understand why Tommy loses patience with this sapling. Well, let me tell you something straight up: this guy will have to mature really quick if he is to get used to this life. And you can tell anybody that if I, the reigning Brer Anancy, the king of storytellers, tell yuh so, it gotta be so.

Mark my word, I am not wrong too often, but I can almost guarantee you that this Winston isn't going to last too long on this contract. No way. He doesn't have the right mettle. Look at how soft his hands are, his long nails, and now the look on his face. It reminds me of the time another Brer 'Nancy turned up at the construction site and asked Brer Fox for a job mixing the cement. It was a disaster, if you remember that story, the reason why the house never turned out as planned, why Brer 'Nancy had to bail out early and find work elsewhere. But by then the damage had been done. You remember that story, don't you? Another house without a roof. Well, I think the same thing is happening here. A disaster in the making. It's only a matter of time before this one is back in Barbados. Clearly, this Winston person doesn't have the temperament for the job. And when he goes, I hope he takes all other intruders, all other misfits, visible and invisible, with him too.

I'll admit that with the men standing between the rows of beds, the room looks even more cramped, like a playroom for miniature dolls that has suddenly been invaded by giants. That's true. The naked bulb hanging from the roof doesn't cast sufficient light in the room, so the long shadows are merging into one another, forming strange, oblong beings on the walls and floors, naked shadows that must look to Winston as if grotesquely intertwined. Indeed, I can see that. Another bulb protrudes from the wall at the end of the room, but it isn't burning. Maybe Stewart forgot to check the wiring as he had promised.

Trying to make the most of a bad situation, at least for this night, Winston looks for an empty cot. There are seven rows with three cots each stacked in bunk-beds, with hardly any room between them. This arrangement reminds Winston of military barracks, the kind of dormitory he has seen in movies. Each row has a narrow wooden ladder either at the front of the cots or leaning uselessly against the wall. Most of the men, apparently oblivious to Winston's staring, are standing between the rows of cots talking or mechanically unpacking their clothes and hanging them on the sides of the room or on the edge of the beds.

Winston sees Johnny sitting on the bottom cot of the first row of beds. With his height, Johnny has to bend his neck so that his head won't brush the distended bottom of the cot on top of him. The space between the second and third beds looks even more limited. Winston wonders whether anyone could actually sit up on the second cot, and if they did, whether their feet would dangle in the face of the person in the lower bed. Could someone tickle your feet that way? He frowns at the answer that comes to mind.

All but one of the six remaining bottom cots in the formation are occupied, with Tommy claiming the first cot of the third row. The second one, between Tommy and Johnny, is unoccupied.

"Why don't you take that bunk over there?" Johnny says, obviously in response to Winston's indecision. Winston takes up his suitcase and throws it on the empty cot. He sits on the edge of the bed and purposely fumbles with his shoelaces to look busy.

"Hey, you! What you think you doin' there?" a voice shouts across the room. It is coming from the far corner where some men are trying to fix the light switch for the bulb in the wall. "Get the hell away from that bed, man. This is only the first time for you up here. Who the hell you think you is? You can't expect to get a bottom bed just like that. You gotta climb up when the nights come just like everybody else."

Winston looks up to see a big strapping man in his late thirties approaching him. See, I keep telling you that trouble's settin' up like rain. Looks to me like we're in for a good shower before we can get some sleep. Through the man's white t-shirt, Winston can see the bulging muscles. The man is angry and throwing out his hands threateningly as he approaches. I brace myself for the sound of something, perhaps Winston's head, being squished.

"That's okay, Delbert," Johnny says, rising from the bed to his full height and heading off the man. Beside him, Johnny looks much shorter, thinner and older, no match if the man should continue to act aggressively. "I tell the youngster he can have Grafton's old bed. For the next while."

"But, Johnny," Delbert says, his voice dropping in a plea for reasoning. He stops in his tracks and is now talking with Johnny as if he is a junior addressing a master, as if they have exchanged sizes and physical strengths. And, to tell the truth, it's at moments like this that I really hate Johnny.

"You know that ain't fair at all, man," Delbert pleads, while the youngster stands by paralysed with fear. "Not fair at all. He ain't paid his dues yet, Johnny. Everybody done agree it is me next in line to get a bottom bed. Like you and Tommy, there, Johnny, man. So it ain't right that he should get treat different from all o' we who's been waiting we turn."

"You're a' old campaigner, Delbert." Johnny is almost whispering. "You're strong. A little climbing won't hurt you when the nights come."

"I don't mind the climbing, Johnny. It's the principle, man. That's what binds all o' we here in this cabin together, man. The principle o' the thing. It just don't look good if anybody gets a cot on the floor the first time 'round. That's all I'm saying. The principle, man."

"I know," Johnny answers softly. He walks up to Delbert and, putting a hand around his shoulders, steers him away from the cot, from any confrontation with the frightened young man. "But don't forget what the Liaison Officer tell me, personally. To keep an eye on him." Johnny, his mouth close to the offended man's ear, is talking as if they are sharing a secret. "And you can never tell with these young people. You know, when the night come. No woman 'round here, as man, you know what I talking 'bout."

These words carry around the silent room, causing the men to laugh loudly in unison, breaking the heavy tension. Winston feels uneasy, he doesn't like being laughed at. Neither does he appreciate having everyone stare at him. Slowly, he starts to unpack, trying to figure out a way to undress without exposing himself. Maybe he should wait until all the men are sleeping. On second thought, he is already too tired from the long day and travelling all night. And from the way the men are talking, it doesn't look like they are planning on going to sleep too soon. He decides to sleep in the clothes he is wearing.

Delbert, his anger apparently appeased, throws a handful of clothes on the cot above Winston. Moving swiftly, he returns to the corner where the men are still struggling with the light switch. Obviously, Johnny's words were enough to mollify him, but you know how I personally feel about abusing seniority and status. I think Johnny is wrong, very wrong, if anyone cares to know what I think. Once you start breaking these little codes and understandings anything can happen. You open the door to degeneration, and the order that has been established, maintained over the years, just goes out the window. It's a big gamble. Call me a staunch conservative if you like, but I believe there are some tried and tested things with which you just shouldn't mess.

But it is truly heartwarming to see how these men respond to Johnny, how they are willing to accept his judgement. And why are they so accepting? Because of seniority and trust built over the years. Isn't that ironic? Still, I like this show of respect. It reminds me of the better times with Prophet, when people would come to his yard for the simplest of advice and take his word unquestioningly. It is always better that way, to keep things in their natural order.

Now the men appear to have forgotten Winston. This is to his liking. He can observe them this way. And, maybe, if the men aren't looking, he can quickly take off his clothes. Under the blanket. Except that Tommy is constantly drawing the attention of the men to that side of the room. Stretched out under the grey and blue blanket on his cot, Tommy is again having a fit of coughs. Johnny strips, gets into his cot and pulls the blanket up to his chin. No sooner has he settled into the bed than a voice calls out to him from the other end of the room.

"Hey, Johnny," the voice, already filled with laughter, is saying, "anybody ever tell you what happen'd to our good friend Delbert when he went home at the end of the last season?"

"No, Henry. What happen'd." Johnny's response is like that of a straight man in a comedy act, everyone playing his part. Tommy is breathing heavily, as if he is finally getting to sleep. Occasionally, he still coughs loudly, automatically putting a clenched hand to his mouth.

"Well, let me tell yuh, if he didn't tell yuh heself," Henry continues. He is shorter than Delbert but just as broad across the chest and shoulders. His voice booms through the quiet room. "This man here, my very best friend, playing he didn't want to write home and tell the woman he had, Joyce's she name, when he's coming home, saying how he planned to turn up at the house and surprise she. I mean, everybody here done remember how at the end of the season he went out and spend up all his money buying up all sorta things for this woman. I mean rings, clothes, powder, shampoo, you name it. Even talking 'bout marrying she as a surprise. Well, surprise she my *rass*. *He* was the one to get the surprise of his life when he walked in the house real quiet so and find a man sleeping strong, strong, strong in *'im* bed, in *his* pyjamas, in the house he pays the rent for. The said same pyjamas that my friend Delbert buy a couple years back, after he meet this woman for the first time and she start to put some culture in he, saying only proper men does sleep in pyjamas, 'cause everybody done know none o' we don't sleep in no pyjamas up here when the nights come."

Winston eyes open when he hears this. How could a bunch of men sleep together in the same room without clothes? They must be what Bajans back home would call a bunch of *bullers*, he thinks to himself. He better be careful how and when he is sleeping.

"But he did carry back these pyjamas and he never wear them, not once," Henry continues. "He keep saying how he's keeping them for when he's back home and he and Joyce got company, visitors, in the house."

"Well, Delbert, boy," another voice joins in. "It would be a different story if he did find the man naked, eh." The whole room is laughing. Even Delbert doesn't appear to mind the jibes aimed at him.

"Tell us what else happen', Henry," Timmy says. "Tell us the rest o' the story, man. All I can say is that whatever Delbert get, it serve he right. I always say don't trust no woman when you up here. You could never tell what she's doing while you're working your ass off trying to make some money for she. That's why I don't have no woman at home."

"You ain't got no woman, period," Delbert says, still laughing loudly, trying to shift the attention onto someone else. "'Cause none o' we never see you with no woman up here either. Only the old whores 'round Sarnia. And that was before you say you found Christ."

"That suits me fine. I would be able to save my money and get off this slave-labour program a lot sooner than all of you who're throwing away good money every year on them women. This goddamn program and the women are the same: no good for nobody."

"Let Delbert tell you guys his business, himself," Henry says, bringing the conversation back on track. "'Cause all I would say is that the next-door neighbour had was to phone for the police. And I'm in my little house when all o' sudden I hear one loud knockin' on the door 'bout midnight and I wondering who in the village know I'm home and coming already to try to borrow a piece o' change from me. 'Cause you know the people o'

Barbados. Think we bring back the world o' money or something. So I peep through the window flaps and who I see out there in the dark, but my own good friend Bertie looking for some place to rest his head for the night. The police put he outta he own house, his very first night back on the island. Out of the said same house that he did paying rent for even from up here."

"Don't surprise me none," Timmy says. "You just can't trust no woman."

"I get things fixed up before I left, though," Delbert explains. "I got she arse out of the house and I got my mother looking after it for me. All the same, I ain't the only one in this room that's getting horn while we're up here."

No sooner are these words spoken than Delbert realizes their implication. An unnatural silence overtakes the room.

"Who else getting the horns at home?" Winston asks, quick as a flash. Everyone in the room, obviously with the exception of this Winston, must realize what is happening. I, too, jump at the mention of this talk about this horning business, but I know it has to be a mistake by Delbert, for there is no way any of these men would be so cruel to Johnny. A heavy silence descends on the men. Even Delbert refrains from gloating and busies himself with fixing the light switch. Fortunately, the words seem to have had absolutely no effect on Johnny. I scan his face quickly, looking for any evidence of hurt. Not a sign. Not even a shift in his facial muscles. Sometimes I wonder about this man. So much like Prophet putting on a brave face, even as they shackled him and led him onto what I thought was the Black Star Line. Johnny has to know everybody is watching him, or listening for a response, that Delbert is referring to him. But he gives away nothing.

"Whoever he is," Winston continues, "he can't be no man if his woman got to have another man when he's away." Out of the mouths of babes, I dare say. These last words echo throughout the room. Not even Johnny can pretend he hasn't heard these damned words from this foolish boy. The remark brings only stone silence. Everyone tries to appear busy.

"Okay. Let's get some sleep now," Johnny says after what seems like an uncomfortable eternity. "Somebody turn off the light." The order breaks the spell cast by the misspoken words. The men, anxious for the opening, abandon trying to fix the switch and head for their cots. Several of them refuse to use the ladders, but grab the sides of the wobbly cots and pull themselves up, shaking the entire beds in the process. All I can say is this serves Johnny right; this is the thanks and gratitude he gets for saving the arse of this youngster this very night. I tell yuh, me know trouble when me see it.

Winston gets comfortable under his blanket, but still decides to sleep in his clothes, even after the men turn out the light. He doesn't even appear to have caught on to what is happening, how like some unwanted guest he has intruded so rudely into a very private conversation. This youngster has a lot to learn, most notably when to keep his damn mouth shut. And knowing Johnny as well as I do, it will damn well be a cold day in hell before Johnny will again extend a hand of friendship to this Winston. Not with he embarrassing Johnny so bad. I tell yuh, this guy is pure trouble self.

chapter eight

Suddenly, just as Winston feels himself surrendering to a deep sleep, several rough hands grab him. Startled, he tries to jump to his feet. Instead he finds himself straining against their collective strength, just like in his dream where a *soukouyan*, the woman with a cow heel for a foot, is chasing him to suck his blood. He can't move. The hands pin him like a helpless doll to the bed. Coming out of the sleep so abrubtly, he is confused. He doesn't know where he is and an unnatural cold bites his ears and nose.

Winston hears, and feels, his heart beating loudly. This is confirmation of his worse fears, of that queasy, uncomfortable feeling. Because of the darkness, he can see no one. But he hears around him what he thinks are people, maybe animals, perhaps even *duppies,* those dreaded zombies or walking dead that only attack at night. They are breathing loudly, very loudly, panting really. Perhaps they have been running all night and are so anxious to make the snatch and start the return journey before the first rays of sunlight they cannot pause to catch their breath, like in those ghost stories he heard when he was a little boy.

More than anything else, Winston is aware of the strong hands. He remembers the parables the older women always tell children before bedtime, when it is dark and the stories must be scary, when simple Anancy stories just won't do. Stories about how duppies always have strong hands. Once they grab hold of you, nothing can pry you from their grip. Nothing, not even a scream or a cross or garlic or sand spread across the doorway, can break the death grasp. Nothing can snap their hold until the captured soul is deposited on the other side.

From what Winston can tell, a different person or thing is holding each of his arms and legs. He doesn't like feeling so helpless. Momentarily, he thinks these developments must be a new twist in his dream. And to his amazement, he hears his own voice screaming, loud, clear and childlike, something that never happens in his nightmares. This is when Winston realizes he is in big shit, that he is awake.

Through the sleepy haze, Winston begins to see the reality of the situation. He is not in his bed in Barbados having a nightmare. He is not in his bed with a duppy riding him. He is not going to be able to get out of bed, find the guitar that he can hold on his chest and strum, feel the comforting vibration in his chest, until a peaceful sleep claims him. He will not hear his mother snoring sweetly in the nearby room.

When he screams, the naked bulb in the ceiling weakly springs to life, as if, tired and sleepy, it is responding reluctantly to a signal. The filament crackles loudly, the light flutters rapidly, attempting valiantly but seemingly half-heartedly to drive out the darkness. For the first time, Winston sees the pranksters and almost dies of fear. The eight or nine people around his bed are each wearing a khaki-coloured coat, obviously taken from the bundle Winston remembers seeing in a corner earlier that night. Underneath the coats, with the musty smell from being bundled together for several months, are bed sheets, wrapped around the men's bodies from shoulders to ankles. More frightening, the men are wearing pointy paper bags over their heads with holes for eyes. They are breathing heavily, like deranged people. My God, aren't our people funny: look how we like to mimic the very people that would kill us, that would segregate us, castrate us and even lynch us. The same people with whom Prophet had his misguided negotiations, or even Elijah Mohammed. All these bastards under the hoods need now are some burning crosses. It's too funny, I tell yuh.

Winston screams again, at the top of his lungs. Obviously, this isn't a laughing matter for him. The terror in Winston's voice, ricocheting off the walls and the ceiling, returns unaided to him, just like for those pioneers dragged from their beds and strung up. The hollowness of the scream touches me, if I may say that much. It reminds me of the piercing wails of the Prophet when they came in the night to beat him, on the night before he was to leave for what I thought was the inaugural trip of the newest Black Star Line ship. When the men came to his cell, the official-looking people, the so-called lawyers for Prophet, when they told him their intentions, he responded with just such a long shriek and growl. At that point, I should have realized he was no longer a man. The transformation, the initiation, the castration really, was now complete. Just like all those brothers penned up for life in prisons. The hopelessness of the growl was the signal of a job complete, a beaten man, the ending of the end. *Jump on wire; wire won't bend; so the story must end.*

Even now, remembering that plaintive howl curls the hair on my legs and back. I tell you, if I didn't know better, I'd swear there was something special about this Winston fellow. Something special even in the way he responds to adversity. A signature in his voice. Just like Prophet.

"Leave me 'lone," Winston splutters, twisting his body to escape the hands. "You all are homos, you know, a bunch o' damn *bullers* or something? Look, you better leave me 'lone, yuh hear?"

Realizing no one will aid him, Winston is trying to sound brave. I recognize the camouflage in his voice. It's not quite working. He is too young. With time, if he is truly like Prophet, he will learn to hide his true feelings. Indeed he must if he ever hopes to be a leader of any sort. Winston must learn to stand in the face of adversity and command his body not to tremble even though every nerve may be going crazy. Practice will help this youngster to master the art of deception. The great leaders always do. Just like the Prophet, who had it figured out so well — I could never tell for sure when he was not being genuine. And don't forget, according to the folklore, I am supposed to be the trickster, Brer Anancy incarnate, the one with the final say, who gets to put the curse that runs for generations and generations, who could be man or spider, sometimes neither just to trick yuh. But Prophet was a real chameleon, why so many black leaders, so many of them false prophets, come to nought. That was why I was so easily fooled on the ship, when I really thought Prophet's smiles were of joy, not realizing they were the only alternative to crying, to holding his head and just bawling for blue murder. Winston will have to work on that tremor in his voice, such huskiness that betrays his paralysing fears. Then, he'll have the disguise down pat.

"Ah. Is the youngster ready to be given up?" one of the men intones solemnly. He is standing directly under the naked bulb, hands folded across his chest. His shadow is underneath him, as if it too is seeking protection under the coat. Coming from deep in the speaker's chest, the voice is muffled, but brassy and authoritatively serious. He is an imposing figure, standing in his own shadow, in his darkness. "I ask again, is the youngster ready?"

The men holding Winston bow in unison, then fall on their knees paying homage, but still holding tightly to the legs and thighs of their victim.

Winston looks across at Johnny, who appears sound asleep. He hopes his scream might rouse Johnny to intervene and end this nonsense, but it doesn't. Realizing he is on his own hardens Winston. His countenance changes, an edge appears around the eyes, his jaw tenses. From the look on his face, I have no doubt what Winston is thinking. He is proud, he will not beg for help, not even from Johnny, who must be dead to be able to sleep so soundly with such a racket. Winston will not give the men that satisfaction, not twice in the same night. No, he is not going to call out to Johnny, to wake him and beg him to intercede. Never would anyone say that he needed the same help twice, that he repeats mistakes, that he is not a fast learner. Never, he tells himself, grimacing as he strains every muscle in his body to break free, to stand on his own.

Occasionally, a loud snore breaks the tension in the room. It is from Tommy, oblivious to what is happening around the room. This surprises me. Usually, Tommy is among the first to rag newcomers. At first, I thought the person under the hood was Tommy, until I realized the size of the man. Now, the only contribution Tommy makes to this initiation are long snores and the occasional cough. Totally unaware of the noise around him, Tommy instinctively pulls the blankets and sheets over him, as if so cold. Johnny too turns over on his side, pulls the blanket over his shoulders and returns to sleep.

"You better leave me alone, yuh hear me?" Winston shouts at the top of his lungs. It's clear he must fend for himself. This untrained youth will have to fight his own battles. He will have to lead himself. Even Johnny has turned his back on him. "Otherwise I'll tell the Liaison Officer."

"Oh Lord, not the Liaison Officer," one of the men stammers, feigning fright. "Don't tell he on we, yuh hear? 'Cause we're so scared of the big, bad wolf. Don't tell Brer Wolf."

"He done tell me already to let him know right away if anybody up here troubling me," Winston struggles on despite the laughter. "Remember that. I could get everyone o' you in big, big trouble by telling the Liaison Officer."

"I say again," the man under the light intones solemnly, "is this youngster ready to be inducted into the Holy Order of Migrant Workers — the Edgecliff chapter?"

"I think he is, oh Honourable Grand Wizard of the most Holy Order," says the man holding Winston's head. "But I'll tell yuh this: for a youngster his age, he's strong as shite, man.

Real strong, even if he don't look it. Hurry up, man, and let we get this thing over with real quick. We can't hold he down much longer."

Hearing this, Winston seems to find greater strength to struggle. His movements cause the men to stumble and to bang into the cots as they try to contain him. Despite the coolness of the night, a sweat breaks out on Winston's face as he strains and grinds his teeth.

"Okay, then," the Grand Wizard says, rocking back on his heels, his hands still folded across his chest. "Shall we offer him up as the virgin he is, having never been touched by a woman except his mother, grandmother, aunts and sisters? Not knowing true life." Loud snickers break out around the room, not only from the men holding him. His anger growing, Winston continues struggling, stiffening his body to resist, but with little success.

"Should we treat him like a virgin? Or should we think that he's a threat? So that we gotta cut out all two both of his balls before anybody gets any wrong ideas about he being the ram goat 'round here?" A pair of rusty scissors appears in the Grand Wizard's hands. He loudly snaps the blades open and shut above his head. "Before this young village-ram, this damn *gorgon,* think that selfishly, he can start taking away all the things that once belonged to all o' we?"

"Cut them to *rass* out," says someone holding Winston's head. "Cut out he balls right now. Show 'im who is boss 'round here."

"Yes, we cannot forget what already happened over who gets the bed," the Grand Wizard continues, sounding as serious as a judge laying out the case before ordering the execution. "Next, he will think he is some big *meguffy,* some big-time leader telling us what we should and shouldn't do, looking out only for heself. So, should we cut him down to size early?"

"Shite, man," someone holding one of Winston's legs says. "Not the scissors, man. No, no, no. Not the scissors."

"Cut them out now, I tell yuh," screams the voice at Winston's head.

"No. No. No," the other man pleads. "Oh lost, man. Give him a chance, man. We don't have to neuter he like some blasted boar-pig back home. Not the blood, man. No need to shed the blood of sacrifice."

"Give me the scissors and let me cut them out if you frighten or something," shouts the man at Winston's head. "Give me the damn scissors and let me make short work o' he right now."

"No, man," says the one pleading for Winston. "I got a good reason." Now, there is a long expectant pause. "'Cause there ain't anything to cut out." The punch-line delivered, everyone is laughing, even those still in their beds. "From the way I seeing things right now, if you know what I mean, from where I standing, I can't see no woman worrying she head with he." Winston again finds hidden strength in his bid to break loose. He hates people laughing at him. Just hates it. "So give he a break and put 'way the scissors. Let we just dump him. I don't think none o' we would ever have to play second fiddle to this one here. Not with that size, brother. So let we just dump him."

"You mean into the *co-oold*," the Grand Wizard emphasizes the last word, "into the icy water that cometh forth from the tap in yonder bathroom?" I like this part of the ritual best and to tell the truth I can't help laughing at the youngster. He's a natural; he's playing his role so well. I agree this rite is the test of a real man. Tommy was always such a master at this kind of thing.

"Be Christ, yuh right," the man responds. "Into the bloody water."

"So said and so shall it be."

With that the Honourable Grand Wizard also grabs hold of Winston, putting his big hands under the young man's struggling body and helping to hoist him into the air. The earlier struggle has virtually exhausted Winston. With ease, the men lift him and, marching him like a rag doll raised over their shoulders, they pass the kitchen and head toward the bathroom.

One of the men runs ahead and turns on the shower. "No," bellows Winston when he realizes what is happening. The only response is the trampling of the feet of the men carrying him. And a rattling sound in the pipes, followed by several loud bursts of water as the pressure equalizes. The icy and rusty-looking water settles into a steady flow, the sprayers bouncing off the concrete floor. The force of the water is causing the shower curtain to buffet as if by strong winds.

"No. No!" Winston screams. Now he is not even trying to hide the fear. "Don't do this to me, man. The water's too cold. I'd catch a cold, man. I was under a warm blanket all night. I might catch pneumonia or something. Don't do it to me, nuh man."

They hold him under the water, in all his clothes, including the tight jeans he had bought the day before to make him look special for his first international trip. They hold him so that he receives the full force of the water in the face, causing him to splutter and to feel the burning sensation in his nose. They hold him down on the cold cement as the water beats on him, freezing his entire body, turning the tips of his fingers white and causing his teeth to clatter. And the men laugh and jeer. They cheer every time the Grand Wizard makes some meaningless incantation. They continue to shout as the fight seeps out of Winston.

After what seems like an eternity, they lift him off the cement and take him not to the bedroom, but outside into the freezing cold. They run around the cabin, leaving their tracks, sometimes falling in the snow, until they arrive at an apple tree whose top is just above the snow. The Grand Wizard breaks off a cold twig and sticks it in Winston's mouth. By now Winston is so cold and shivering, he no longer has the strength to resist.

"Winston St. Clair Lashley, this is the first of the apple you are tasting on this farm, Winston, my son. Let's hope that this, the first taste, is sweet, the sap of a living tree, not bitter from a tree that's already dead. For that taste will be an indication of what your stay in this cabin, of what your stay on this very farm, will be like. Winston, my son, you are now one o' us, whether you like it or not. You will share in our joys and in our sorrows."

"True, true, true," the men chant.

"Now, Winston St. Clair Lashley," the Grand Wizard continues, "now, in entering this bond with all of us, do you swear to secrecy, to never tell anyone back home, no matter how tough it gets, never to tell what you'll experience over here? Do you swear to that?"

"I ain't swearing one blasted thing," Winston splutters. "All I know is that..." They drop him in the snow, on his face. Muffled sounds escape from him.

"He did swear, sir," one of the men says, the tone in his voice daring Winston to contradict him. Doesn't this sound like the same kind of narrative you hear about all those destructive gangs and posses that are so much rites of passage for our youths? But this is simple, fun stuff. At least he doesn't have to go out and waste anyone, just to prove he's a man, just to be accepted and initiated.

"Quick, man, let we get things over with real soon," the man pleads. "This cold out here's busting my arse, man."

"With that oath, Winston St. Clair Lashley, you have also promised to dutifully play your part when we need you, and to do so without any of us having to ask. We are now all brothers. On this farm. This exposure to the cold is the first test of your strength of character. And you have survived it well, my brother. But this could very well be the mildest of things you'll experience on this farm, on this Program. Perhaps the harshest test of all will be the fact that your brothers are depending on you not to let them down, to share that strong bond of secrecy, not to let our wives, our women, our children, mothers, aunts, fathers, friends, not to let them think for one moment that we are questioning our lot, that we are not willing to carry our cross in the hope of making a better life for them and for us. For generations, the men from the Caribbean have forged this bond. We will strengthen it. So welcome, my brother."

"I ain't nobody's blasted brother, let me tell you that," Winston says. He is recovering some of his strength; his teeth are knocking even louder from the cold. The twig from the apple tree sticks to his bottom lip. "As soon as you all put me down, as soon as I get my hand on a rock-stone or something, I'm going to lick down one o' you that's holding me out here in this damn cold."

"God, he's a tyrant," someone swears. "Like a blasted dynamo, man."

"I ain't taking this light. I'll stab somebody. I'll lick in the head o' one o' you with a big rock the first chance I get, mark my word. Just wait and see. As soon as you all let me go."

"He got a lot o' fire, eh," the Grand Wizard agrees. "Like he's a real fighter, boy. Don't give up too easy. That is what we need, another fighter. Take him back inside. The ordination is done."

In the far distance, the sky is gently accepting the weak first rays of a new day. If we were home, I would say the battle is about to resume, the enemy is advancing after a strategic retreat, that this could very well be the day of which the doves cooed.

Finally, Winston is back in the warm bedroom — but his clothes are freezing. As soon as his feet hit the warmer floor, Winston starts to strip hastily. He is down to his sopping underwear when he becomes aware of the laughter and whispers. He looks up and sees all the men, except Johnny and Tommy, who still appear to be sleeping, looking at him. The men are back in their regular clothes, or in no clothes at all. The Grand Wizard was Preacher Man. Winston feels like a man possessed by spirits.

The underwear feels so cold against his body, Winston simply has to get rid of it. Even if it means exposing his nakedness.

"You may as well go ahead and take it all off, unless you want to catch pneumonia and spend your first weeks up here in a hospital," Delbert says. "Up here, you'll find there's a damn lot o' things that you won't like doing, but that you gotta do anyway. You won't get to hide anything."

"What all o' you looking at anyway? And where is my clothes?" Suddenly, the panic hits Winston as he realizes someone has hidden his suitcase. It is no longer under his cot. "What you all did with my things, man? No more foolishness. Please."

"Ah, look he's crying. A little cry-baby," someone says. "Well you ain't see nothing yet. Many o' night you're going to look back on this very night and laugh when you think of how tough life on this farm is. Wait until the blasted farmer come over here tomorrow bright and early and start giving out orders one after another, left, right and centre. This life ain't easy, and that is what we're trying to warn you about, big boy. You'll see what we mean. It ain't anything like what the people at home think. Nothing."

"Who got my clothes?" Winston pleads. He sneezes loudly, then again and again. By wiping his nose, he can hide the tears running down his cheeks. "I'm cold man. Too cold. Who's hiding my *rass hole* things?"

"Okay, guys," Johnny says, without turning over on his side. "Enough o' this horsing 'round. Let's get some sleep."

Johnny has witnessed it all. He was not sleeping as Winston had thought. Winston feels betrayed. He could trust no one. He will trust nobody, regardless how much they talk about brother-this and brother-that. After all, Johnny was the same mentor the Liaison Officer asked to accept Winston as a student. And what does Johnny do the first time Winston expects him to speak for him: he stretches out on his bed and pretends to be sleeping.

Winston is so angry he feels like walking over to the bed and driving one big kick at Johnny. Right between those naked shoulders exposed above the blanket.

The men around him return to their beds. Someone turns off the light. In the darkness, Winston takes off his freezing underwear and gets into the bed, pulling the smelly blanket up to his nose. He feels comfortable, thinking nobody is watching him, not realizing that at least one storyteller is recording everything, not even the cover of darkness can hide anything from me.

In the refuge of this darkness, I am again reminded of Prophet as I hear Winston's thoughts. How this place is nothing like what he expects, nothing to keep him on this farm, everything so different from anything he had dreamt. Such disappointment! Winston tries to rub some heat into his fingers and toes. They are so numb and burning from the thawing. In the darkness, he does the only thing that can satisfy him. He cries silently and swears to get even for this humiliation. Softly calling his mother, he substitutes his thumb for the warm memories of her nipple. Poor boy, how he wishes for a piece of candy to take the bitterness from his mouth.

chapter nine

"How yuh feeling, man?" Johnny asks, sliding quietly onto his bed. Although Johnny tries to pretend all is well, I can still detect flickering notes of concern in his voice. Obviously, he is not asking this question in the hope of getting an honest answer.

The question is no more than a comforting noise, an assurance, really; something to let Tommy know someone still cares deeply about him. And this someone is a trusting buddy who at the same time can be blinded by unquestioning loyalty and unshakeable optimism into thinking that, while things might appear a bit brown at this moment, they are bound to improve.

But this loyalty works two ways. There is also the unspoken understanding that Tommy should know that if things were really getting worse, his friend would say something. Tommy would not have to suffer unbearable pain all alone, with nobody appearing to notice. But it would have to be excruciatingly unbearable pain. Not some *nay-nay, flimsy-flimsy* thing like a toothache or a sore throat. Otherwise, this friend simply would not ask the question; he'd just let things ride, so there would be no need for denials and lies, no need to put the other person on the spot. That's the way men are.

Until the friend confirms the agony is beyond what any man can bear, what any man should be expected to endure, Tommy will have the confidence of knowing that all is not lost. There has been no validation for the thoughts swimming through a weakened mind that, maybe, just maybe, enough is enough. Like in that old story of the man on the cross who cracked under the weight of carrying all mankind on his shoulders. He snapped under the pain of the moment and cried out in surrender, I give up the ghost, shouted, *Father, me can't tek it no more. Nuh more, man.* Or in all those stories we have on file about that one and decisive sting of the whip, that final lash on a bloodied and welted black back, that causes the warrior or leader to drop his head, to submit, to be neutered. Until Tommy reaches that thin point, until he can no longer balance on the edge of tolerance and capitulation, he would have to hold strain, just being patient while bearing and grinning. He must expect no commiserating, no hand holding in the dark, if he lets go too soon. For he is a man. Not a boy and certainly not a woman. But a Black man. So, a friend's just asking a question is a sign of hope, a verbal pat on the back. I tell yuh, these men are like that, that is how they stay — such rituals and contradictions!

Still, knowing all the games these men play, I find myself wondering if my imagination isn't acting up on me. Or maybe it's because I know Johnny so well. But of late, despite his casual approach, perhaps even a pretend indifference, I can't help noticing the dwindling hope in Johnny's voice when he somewhat mechanically enquires about Tommy's health. Something in me cringes, it gives me goose bumps all over, when I think I hear the cover dropping. I don't know. I can't quite explain it. But there is something wrong with the timbre of the voice. To me, it is virtually confirming that Johnny doesn't expect, doesn't want a truthful answer to the question; it confirms to me that despite the situation Johnny still finds it so difficult playing games. And you know Johnny is always a straight-shooter. That's how he rests. So it must be just me and all my paranoia. I know that Johnny believes so strongly in everyone in this camp being a member of the same team. I know he wouldn't consciously disrupt the order of things.

If Tommy notices the tone, and I can't see why he wouldn't, he doesn't show it. Not today. It doesn't appear on his face as he struggles to keep his eyes open. As of late, he is in the cot beside Johnny's, folded into a ball with the blankets tucked firmly around him. We are now in our third week back at Edgecliff and life is beginning to fall into a routine. The men are up early preparing the greenhouses and don't go to bed until late at night. There is a harsh business bustle about the cabin, so palpable and heavy you can almost feel it. The men are preparing for the long haul, for the best they can make of their lot. All the same, you should see and hear what this place is like in the middle of the day when the men have gone to the greenhouses or to the small repairs shop to fix and prepare the various machinery. Half of them work on the implements, while the others sort and even plant some of the seeds for the year's crop of tobacco, tomatoes, carrots and cabbages. The cabin is deathly quiet, with only the howling wind coming through the cracks and the sound of Tommy coughing. For the cabin's lone occupant a dreadful silence is the only companion until Smokie returns a few hours before the rest to start the evening meal.

For all but one or two days since we've been here, three at the very most if memory serves me right, Tommy has always been in bed. He constantly complains of never getting enough sleep, even after a full day's and night's rest. With every passing day, his eyes appear to be sinking further into his head. The skin on his cheeks is drawn. Even Johnny can see that the multivitamin tablets are not helping. Yet, I am sure, Johnny has no second thoughts about buying them for Tommy, or that he will purchase another bottle when this one runs out. Otherwise, why would Johnny spend so much time reading the labels on the bottles around the cabin and looking at those pictures in magazines about vitamins and herbs promising miraculous results? Truthfully, I don't believe him when he claims to be reading up on the powers of ginseng, that new crop that every farmer appears to be trying his hand at these days.

"How yuh feelin', guy?" Johnny asks again, this time trying to overcome the distance in his voice. "Wha' happen, you ain't feel like talking, or goat got yuh tongue?"

It is really heartwarming to watch these two men together. The close bond and understanding are really gratifying, like how at the end of the day neither man can wait to tell the other what has happened in his absence. Sometimes, I wish Maude could see them together. Don't ask me why at times like this, with so much uncertainty around, why I always think of Maude and Johnny and the coldness of their relationship. But I can't help it. I see these two running a talk just like brothers and the first thing that flashes in my mind, when I see the look of contentment, abandonment and relaxation on their faces, is Johnny and Maude. Especially when Johnny tenderly asks about the health of his good buddy and gently prods him out of his despair into conversation. When I see that, I can't help wondering why the same Johnny doesn't feel such closeness and caring for Maude, or for that matter, for anyone back at home. I guess, as with the Prophet, I will never understand the intricacies of exile.

"This damn cold holding on to me tight, tight, tight, man," Tommy says, the unusual honesty clear in his voice. He still coughs a lot. "Won't let go o' me for nothing."

There have been other changes I must tell you about, which I think prove one or two things about this life. For one, Johnny has asked Winston to exchange cots with Tommy, so that the older man is now in the bed next to Johnny. Of course, there should have been no need for Johnny to explain the switch. Everybody knows there are some things, as men, you don't have to express in words. Everybody, that is, except Winston, who obviously still has a lot to learn. Nothing can stop him from asking questions. Like a little child experiencing life for the first time. Fascinated by every turn in life and new experience, unable to inwardly digest the information without a stream of words rushing out of his mouth. Somebody ought to tell that boy to first put his brain in gear before opening his mouth. So, somewhat petulantly, he balked at giving up his cot, asking Johnny all sorts of foolish questions. Of course, he hasn't received one single answer from my man Johnny yet, and I hope he isn't holding his breath for a reply.

"How did the boys do in the greenhouses today?" Tommy asks, after loudly blowing his nose in the toilet paper he keeps under his pillow. Oh, another thing I forgot to mention. The other storyteller, the same young ill-mannered brat, is still around and growing more obnoxious by the day. Nothing lady-like about her, a real *leggo-beast* fuh true. She is as much a nag to me as Winston must be to Johnny. Morning, noon and night, she is running at the mouth. And saying what? Nothing of interest. She, too, should put her brain in gear first.

"They're okay." Listen, can you still hear how softly Johnny answers? A man of class, I tell you. A real team player and a true friend. In truth, he is. Really. "Except, perhaps, the young fellow."

"You mean that trouble tree, Winston?" Tommy asks. "What he's up to, now? 'Cause I don't know what the hell we'll do with him."

"He's still complaining about the cold," Johnny replies almost apologetically. "Still getting on the men's nerves, but not as much as before. He keeps asking why we don't send you to see a doctor."

"He should mind he own business," Tommy says, "should try and stop being so much trouble and hindrance."

Well, as I was saying about this storyteller, somebody was telling me that, perhaps, there is a reason for this one coming on the trip with me. That person says that I should accept her presence and reach out to the newcomer, you know, pool our efforts, me and this *nowherian,* since she just turn up from nowhere.

This same person says that, maybe, the time is right for me to become a colour commentator. You know, that I should sit back and relax, allow this new gal to carry the main narrative and reports, that I should use the wisdom of my age, seniority and status, to comment occasionally on specific matters. Easy work. Just analysing things. Like when you're watching sports on television and some guy is explaining a brilliant play on the field, or talking about some irrelevant piece of gossip that has absolutely nothing to do with the game. Or in politics when some highfalutin senior statesman makes an instant assessment of what somebody is saying and you know it is all lies but everybody is too respectful and accepting of this bullshit because it is coming from someone with experience, someone who should know, someone you respect and trust, someone politely offered a job just to keep shame off his face.

I don't know about this colour commentating thing. It doesn't sound right to me. What do you think? I mean, aren't these colour commentators old and decrepit, people long over the hill, one or two bastards just living off their reputation? What is that old saying now: them that can, do; them that can't, teach, or talk about what they used to do when they could. Doesn't sound too attractive to me. I'm not ready for retirement, partial or otherwise. I can still carry the show on my own, both reporting and commentaries. I don't need some little pup to make me, after all these years, into a second banana. Suppose I have to correct her in the middle of a report? Will we just quarrel and shout at each other and confuse everyone? 'Cause you know how difficult it is to reason with women. Furthermore, suppose I find out this young narrator has the traits of the trickster, how would I handle it?

No, I'm a loner. Always have been and always will be. I don't like this colour commentating thing. I want to do more that just analyse, more than just make some inane comment now and then, more than just sit back on my arse and put up my two feet. That ain't me at all. And, for sure, I certainly don't want some kid, especially this one still wet behind the ears and with no manners or sense of professional decorum, leading me around by the nose, not me, an experienced, old whore. No way. I'm too old for that kind of treatment. I still have a little bit of my pride left and I demand, at the very least, a little respect. So I think I will have to raise this issue directly with Mother Nyame, ask her why she's sending me help that I didn't ask for in the first place. I need to know if it is true what that same fella has been saying to me — that times are changing; that new technology is forcing us to look at the way we do things, reevaluating this and that, looking at how we can make our stories more entertaining by separating the reporting from the commentating. But why change a process that has worked so well for eons, and still works so well. Why change?

Johnny reaches under his cot and pulls out the bag with the diaries from Panama. I had been wondering how long he was going to ignore the damn things. I kept hoping Johnny would just avoid them. Those diaries, as I've said before, can be weapons in the wrong hands. Even in the hands of a Johnny, I dare say, they could wreak havoc.

Let me get one or two things out in the open about these bloody diaries, and things like them. I want to say right up front that I am very concerned whenever I see people trying to dig too far into their past. And it isn't me alone that has these concerns. I am sure that you know from your own experience of some poor fool who immersed himself into the study of history only to end up a bigger fool.

What I am telling you ain't no Anancy story. These same people with all this bookish nonsense in their heads don't know that leaders are born. Leaders have to be good and faithful storytellers, those who in their previous lives handled their narratives exceptionally well. They learn so much through observation that they are able to come back in the next life with a mission of pointing the way. Storytelling, the type I've been doing all my life, is the best training. This is one reason I want to complete this assignment on my own, to show my capabilities so that, hopefully, I can come back the next time as, perhaps, the next Prophet. It won't be asking too much 'cause I know my own abilities and strengths; I know I can do the job. I know I am better than many of the people returning with a special mission. That's why I just have to see this exercise through to the end. So that nobody can hold anything against me, won't deny me my rightful dues.

But let me get back to these diaries. My experience with history is that, for the common man, it doesn't show how to avoid repeating mistakes. History is simply a road map connecting these mistakes one after the other. The only link between the past, present and future is the legacy and the continuation of these missteps. I fear that badly written diaries can sidetrack a weak and insecure leader, especially when what is written doesn't square with what the leader knows innately. The leader could become confused. Which story is correct? The one recorded by Mother Nyame, and currently beyond the reach of so many people, or those half-arse and biased jottings in some obscure book that should never have seen the light of day? Really! Utter confusion. This can even happen when the human and the storyteller think they saw the same things! That is why a leader should follow his natural instincts, those gut feelings that are his soul reacting to all that he has learned and absorbed instinctively in another time. So take my word — there's no need for diaries. Nobody needs them. Not a true leader. Not anyone, really. Not when there are unbiased and properly trained storytellers like me recording the true history, workers like me doing their job the old-fashioned way.

Obviously, Johnny doesn't share this view. That disappoints me because I expect better of him. Truth be known, he is not even aware of what he could be unleashing by cracking open those musty books. I hope he is prepared to deal with whatever he is letting loose, for it could be worse than any virus now at large in these barracks. I mean, just look at him going about it so obliviously, like a child playing with dynamite. I wish I had the strength or the power to permanently seal those diaries. That I could force Johnny and all those diary-readers to turn away from a path that could lead to destruction.

But I am helpless. Johnny is in charge of his own destiny. He is the leader. In this life, I can only record. And besides, those editors vetting me back at head office are always drumming into my head that I should never try to influence the unfolding of history and time. Just tell it like it is, baby, Mother Nyame always says. KISS me, baby, she says, just keep it simple, stupid. And who am I to doubt the Great Mother, especially when I need her to recognize that I am doing a good job, so she'll promote me and send me back next time as a leader. So I always try to do as she tells me.

As a result, Johnny is now on his own as he, unwittingly, enters a strange land and time. And look at how he is approaching this crucial and defining moment so casually. I tell yuh, ignorance is indeed bliss. This is like the time long, long ago when Brer Fox invited Brer Rabbit to supper. Come into my lair, Brer Fox implores, sounding so innocent. All the nerve endings in Brer Rabbit tell him not to go. But does he listen? Not when he can only think of food. He goes, expecting servings of a sumptuous supper. Instead, as you guessed, *he* is served up for dinner. What is it the old people like to say as admonishment? *Hard ears, you won't hear; bum-bum will feel.* Yes, how many times have our arses paid the price because we would not listen to anyone, even our inner voice? Similarly, the instincts in Johnny's soul must be going wild. They must be rebelling. His bum-bum must be preparing itself for the inevitable sting of the whip. Yet he ignores all these senses at his own peril. Letting his legs fall over the sides of the bed, he spreads open the books and proceeds to tempt fate. How I wish I were a leader.

"I'm real sorry I had to miss the seed planting again," Tommy says. Perhaps, instinctively, he is trying to keep Johnny away from this danger. Sometimes fate makes these things happen. Tommy probably doesn't even know he has been elevated to saviour, leading Johnny back onto the path of the straight and narrow, away from the road of sweet enticement.

"It's okay, man," Johnny says. He starts to read the damn diaries, silently. Oh, well. At least Tommy tried.

"Things like that make me feel as if I ain't pulling my own weight," Tommy persists. He hawks and re-swallows the bile. "But I hope to be good enough to try and get out tomorrow." He coughs and blows his nose, all of which, I can swear, is an unconscious effort to distract Johnny. "A man ain't no use around here if he ain't helping out."

"You had anything to eat yet?" Johnny asks, turning a page of the diary.

"Still don't feel like it. I ain't got no appetite these days," Tommy says apologetically. "Somehow, these days, I just don't feel hungry at all. What Smokie cook today?"

"Rice and peas. With corn beef."

"Sounds good, eh," Tommy says.

"Your favourite food. Maybe he made it just for you. Want me to get some for yuh?"

Tommy shakes his head. The food obviously does not appeal to him. Or he doesn't have the strength to stir from the bed. Still, it would be so cool if he'd ask Johnny to get him a plate, so we can get Johnny to take his nose out of that diary. It would be so easy to get Smokie to cooperate by ladling a plate full of food.

Over the noises, we can hear Smokie's voice as he circulates among the men in the other room. "Come on, *nyam* the damn *bittle* I spend all the blasted day sweatin' over," he says as he dares the men to eat more, to fatten themselves as protection against the cold. What cook doesn't like people eating his food? "When yuh out all day in the field and the blasted cold hit yuh in the bones, you're goin' to be glad for a little fat on yuh ribs. That's when you done know which god yuh servin'. I tell yuh, that cold does suck the marrow right outta yuh bones, makin' yuh look thin, thin, thin like some *bone-rakie* dog." Before Johnny, Smokie too had tried to tempt Tommy, if only to eat a morsel. How I wish it were as easy for Tommy to fall for Smokie's temptation as it now appears to be for Johnny and those journals.

"I don't know why, but I can't stop myself from thinking about poor old Grafton," Tommy says. His voice sounds as if it is coming from a distance, maybe as far away as his thoughts at this very moment. "I remember how when he was sick and..."

"Don't you go thinking no foolishness, man!" Johnny interrupts. "It's just a bad cold you got."

"You really think so?" Tommy asks, evidently welcoming this assurance.

"Yes, man," Johnny continues the reproof. "Coming sudden so from the warm weather in Barbados to this cold."

"Really?" Tommy says, jumping to fill one of those interminable pauses so characteristic of Johnny's way of talking.

"It's a surprise that all o' we didn't catch pneumonia as soon as we step off the plane," Johnny finishes the thought and lapses into his usual silence.

"I know what you mean," Tommy whimpers. "What you say about the weather is true, true. It's just that I don't like feeling so helpless. I mean, having you and the boys do everything for me, even washing my blasted clothes. Even Barbara didn't wash my clothes at home. Makes me feel useless, man."

There is that silence again, this time resulting from Johnny concentrating on that damn diary. I don't like him so inattentive.

"You'll be better soon." He pauses again, turning a page. "Once we get a couple o' warm days," Johnny consoles, somewhat dismissively, if I may say so.

"I don't know," Tommy says, adding softly, "I hope you're right, man. I really hope so."

"Just watch," Johnny pauses as if concentrating on something in the diary. Their conversation is even more disjointed than usual. It got to be testing Tommy. "By the time spring rolls around, that cold will be long gone."

"Maybe I should go outside and see if I can organize the dominoes," Tommy says weakly. "'Cause if I can't help with the planting, I must be good for something else around here."

This does not bring a response so he continues, his voice a listless monotone, "And besides, with Grafton gone, I guess I gotta be the one to draw up the teams and enter the names in the tournament. That's what Grafton did most o' last year. You decide if you're playing in the tournament this year, Johnny?"

"Don't know yet." He doesn't look up from the diary. A scowl breaks out on his face as he reads. My heart misses a beat. I know that distant sound in Johnny's voice. He is focusing his thoughts on something else. To me, the red flags are waving. Danger!

"You gotta play, Johnny. You's one o' the best domino players 'round here. You gotta play. With Grafton gone, if we want to win this tournament and go to Toronto. I don't know what you have against playing in this tournament. In all your years up here, you ever went to Toronto yet, Johnny?"

"No." He noisily turns a page in the diary. "Unless you counting the airport."

"See what I mean?" Tommy gets to his feet gingerly. He holds on to the side of the cot and leans against it heavily.

His joints feel sore, and he staggers to gain his balance. "That's why we gotta win," he continues, trying to pretend nothing unusual is happening, that his legs are not wobbling under his weight, that the room is not spinning wildly and his head hurting so badly, throbbing like a drum. Tommy is thinking that if Johnny doesn't see his pained movements, or doesn't say anything even if he does notice, then there is no need to blame the symptoms of his cold for his awkwardness. Not that I believe that a simple cold has anything to do with what is happening to Tommy. But I am no doctor. I am just a storyteller. Still, I think I know better.

"I hear the Jazz Festival in Toronto is really nice," Tommy says. "And some of the men keep saying that if we get to Toronto, maybe we can organize a bus trip to New York. What you think? You ever been to New York, Johnny?"

"Uh huh."

"Uh huh, shite," Tommy says realizing that Johnny is not giving him his full attention. In his heart, he is happy to get the confirmation that Johnny doesn't notice when he stumbles. But just the same, he knows he should protest the apparent inattention. "What's that you got yuh head buried down in, saying that you reading, anyway?"

"One of the diaries I tell you 'bout. That my grandfather Percy did keep back in 1902. At the time of the building o' the Panama Canal. Listen to this here, Tommy. What you think? *February 15,* Johnny begins to read:

> *Our ship,* Hopeful Bless, *left the careenage this morning. It was loaded down with people. Couldn't hold a next person. The dockside was full of people wishing we God's speed. Everybody saying this was one of the biggest events on the island. Everybody says they glad they come to see we off. The schedule of the ship's sailing had been listed in the Advocate*

newspaper three weeks now. This morning from early, every cat and dog that is anybody on this island did find themselves at the wharf, including the Governor wearing all his fancy clothes, dressed in his coat and tails. Even the poor people come out in their Sunday best, women looking pretty, pretty in long white dresses and hats with feathers and silk veils on their heads, the men in three-piece suits and tails and bowler hats that really cut style. The priest, Father Ambrose of the Cathedral, said we are blessed as God is showering our departure with bright sunshine and calm weather, so that we would not be facing those choppy seas we've been having recently.

"Christ," says Tommy. "You sure that's a diary and not a book he's writing? Man, that grandfather o' yours sure did write down a lot in that so-called diary, if you ask me."

"The Governor," Johnny continues, ignoring Tommy's wisecrack, *"said all of us chosen for Panama should feel very lucky. We are ambassadors for Great Britain and the colonies. We are the cream of the crop, he said. Every man chosen for the program had to complete at least standard six education and had to be an apprentice for three full years. We should always remember we are to make the Empire proud."*

"Sounds to me like we own Liaison Officer, if you ask me," Tommy chuckles. The laughter sounds forced, as if he is also gasping for air.

Me, Egbert, Ezekiah, Terrence, Hopeton, Hezekiah and Adam, the seven o' we Lodge Road boys plan to stick together. The seven o' we real happy the government choose we from among all the thousands that apply to work in Panama. We calling weself the Marcus Garvey brigade. The seven o' we say to weselves, we will give it a good shot and that we will stick together. We don't know anybody on the ship. It looks to me like this is the first time any of we on this ship ever leave the island. So we had agreed, that since we didn't know anybody in Panama, we will stick together and look after we one another. We called this our bond. Just like in the Bible.

"Sounds like what we have up here, eh," Tommy says. "You sure you ain't pulling my leg, man? I mean, you sure them is diaries you reading and not some book you trying to write or something? 'Cause it don't sound no different between what you're reading and what I see happening 'round here right now."

Johnny flips a couple of pages and resumes reading. "Here's another bit. Listen to this part, Tommy."

February 17. This trip ain't going too good at all. We picking up more people at all these islands. Can you believe it. The ship is packed tight, tight with people. Everybody is tripping over everybody else and elbowing them one another. Now I understand what it was like when my own grandfather and the old people did tell me about the slave boats from Africa. The seven of we from Lodge Road manage to find weself a little section of the ship for we own, where we can hang out and talk. Yesterday, I came down with a bad bout of sea sickness. Vomiting and having cold sweats. This same thing happened to everyone. The doctors working really hard to keep up. We can't wait for this ship to get to Colon.

"Sounds like a hell of a time they're having there," Tommy says, breaking into the dry hacking cough. He starts walking toward the door, but the coughing stops him in his tracks. He leans against the cot and steadies himself. "You know, Johnny, what you just read there reminds me so much o' the first time I signed up for the contract. I don't think I ever tell you about this, but it is always on my mind. I was only eighteen years old, a strong young pup, when they up and send me to America, to Florida, to cut canes. Now, I never did cut canes in me life before, although the same canes used to grow all around the house at home." Tommy spreads his hands in an arc, using his body as the centre, to represent the house with the canes enveloping it.

"But the immigration officer in Bridgetown takes one look at me and decides I was strong enough to cut canes and he up and send me to Florida. I didn't question it because I'd been used to hearing the fellows coming back from America and boasting about how much money they make cutting canes. I used to see them bringing back all them pretty clothes, yuh know them banlon turtleneck sweater and those *stingy-brim* hats, so I decided to sign up. No skin off my nose, I said to myself back then. Remember I was only a little fellow thinking anything is better than staying home and doing nothing. I keep telling myself, it's a job, man, a chance to put some money in yuh pocket. Above all, I'd get to see some place overseas. 'Cause you know what it's like when yuh young and yuh don't want to stay at home on the island no more. And you figure you'd want to make a living abroad, off the little rock."

Tommy blows his nose in the soaked paper, folds it and puts it in his back pocket. "*Shite,* I need more paper for this nose o' mine."

Johnny closes the book and places it on the bed. With quick steps, as if in a race with Tommy or some invisible person in the room, he hurries over to the table at the far side of the room, where the light still isn't working, and unrolls a wad of toilet paper. He gives the paper to Tommy.

"Thanks," Tommy says. Johnny shrugs his shoulders and returns to his cot. "If anything ever happen to me, not saying that

I wish myself anything bad, but if anything happens to me, I know you'd take care of things. I know I can depend on you, Johnny." He wipes his nose, opens the paper to examine the soiled portion, and puts it in his back pocket with the rest.

"What foolishness you talking 'bout now, Tommy?" Johnny snaps angrily. "What you expect to happen to you? Why you gotta be talking such foolishness, even in joke?"

"But as I was telling yuh, Johnny," Tommy continues as if the questions don't matter. As if they are only a response to what most people would consider a mere throw-away line, but which he nonetheless knows Johnny fully understands. Even after all these years, I still marvel at the bond between these two men. "They up and send me to Miami to cut these friggin' canes. They had a whole bunch o' people from all over the West Indies. 'Bout sixty or so of we in all. And most o' we young and never see 'Merica before and the work real hard. Every darn morning, they would give yuh three big-arse rows o' canes to cut, and a row is 'bout a mile long with the canes growing as high as this cabin here."

With difficulty and slowness, Tommy raises his right hand to show the height of the cabin and the canes. Watching him labour at such a small task, I cannot help thinking, how in the past, this would have been such an easy manoeuvre for Tommy. Johnny must be thinking the same thing. I mean it is that obvious. Now, the stiffness causes Tommy to expend great effort and energy, his body moving as though prematurely aging ahead of the mind and the will. He grunts and gasps for air. If Johnny notices, in effect gets a visible answer to his questions earlier, he doesn't let on.

"And you'd only get two half-hour breaks to eat and shit when the day come. It was tough as shite, man. Especially for youngsters like me that weren't use to that kind o' hard work."

"Like Winston, eh," Johnny says.

"Be Christ," Tommy agrees.

"It ain't no different from when they sent me on my first job," Johnny says. "On a merchant ship."

Tommy coughs again, the momentum pushing him toward the open door. He is thankful for this. With the coughing, he can lean against the door frame without having to stagger and, perhaps, further raise Johnny's suspicions. In the camp, it is no good being sick. It is no good being a burden on anyone. He doesn't want anyone to say that, after all, he should have stayed at home this season. Or that if his sickness is going to be prolonged, he should stop being so selfish and give up his spot on the team to someone back home, someone who can make better use of it. As you can guess, this room is buzzing with tension, which prevents me from knowing what they are all really thinking. But it's electric, if you ask me — these two friends give off such heavy vibes, each playing his game, each trying not to display the hand fate has dealt him.

"Well, one day," Tommy perseveres, ignoring Johnny's interjection. He is determined to finish his story and to make an important point. "I see this Jamaican fellow working beside me. He was kind o' oldish, older than all o' we on the contract. And I notice he's actin' real strange, kinda funny. You know, you could always tell when somebody's up to something or the other from the way they acting. So I decide to keep a' eye on him while I'm cutting the damn canes. This same Jamaican fellow did tell me cutting the sugar cane was too hard and that, after all this time on the contract, he had finally come to realize that the money they were paying out would never be enough for even a dog to live on decently. So he decide to get off the Program and get some insurance money for the rest o' his life. Not that he did tell me anything about the insurance, but I later put two and two together. Now, this is a man with a wife and six children to take care of back home. So he couldn't run off the Program and live illegal in America, not like the rest o' people that run off when the nights come, disappearing into the dark and getting lost in the bush and swamps with all those alligators down there in Florida. I talking about the very same people that eventually got married and got their green card to stay in America. He had the wife and children to think 'bout. And how you think he'd do it?"

"How he'd do what?" Johnny snaps.

"Get the insurance money, nuh."

"I don't know."

"Man, when nobody did looking, I see this fellow put he right thumb like this," Tommy clenches four fingers and extends his thumb against the side of the wall, "on a cane root and then when he thinks nobody looking — *whack!* He cut off his thumb. I see him with my own two eyes. *Whack!* One lash. The fucking thumb jumping 'bout in the cane field, the blood gushing. They carry him to the hospital, bandage his hand and put him on the next plane home. That's how he got the insurance money."

"So what that means?" Johnny says. "Why you gotta tell me 'bout insurance money now?"

"I never tell anybody anything. As usual, we keep one another's secrets. These days when I think back to back then, I still can't fault the man, because when you're desperate you can do strange things, and nobody can tell what thoughts go through a man's mind when he feels kind o' left out in life. The insurance money looks real tempting. I heard he built a real nice home in Jamaica and gave his children a real good education. One o' them now studying to be a doctor or something, from what I hear. He got through better than a lot o' we on that Program. Even more better than the guys that run 'way illegally and now scattered all over the States. And about fifteen o' them did run off that year, too. What you think Johnny?"

"I don't think nothing. 'Cause I see men take worse things on the merchant ships I worked on and they never had to resort to anything so stupid or desperate. For you got to remember, where there's life, there's always hope," Johnny says sternly. "The same thing happened to these men here in Panama," he waves the diary, "to those who went to the United States in the Second World War as munition workers. Some of them went knowing they'd get killed making the bombs and gunpowder. But they didn't go running off no contract. Not even when they could not even go into the cinemas in the Deep South in America because o' the colour o' their skin. Not even when one or two of the munitions factories did blow up and killed everybody working inside. They had a job to do and they stick to it."

"And you think they were right to do that?" Tommy asks. "Slaving in a munition factory to save another man's country when they couldn't even watch a movie in the cinemas of that same country?"

"Where there's life, there's hope," Johnny repeats. I can't remember the last time I saw Johnny so animated, talking so long and passionately. But you know what they say about still waters, or rather about sleeping volcanoes. Well, that's Johnny when he blows.

"That's what these diaries is about!" he shouts. "I think we on this farm have things a lot easier. I know, because I've been on the ships. And I can tell you when men are at sea for six and seven weeks at a time, and you ain't got nobody to talk to, you can't have life no harder. All yuh ever get to do every day and night on them ships is scrub decks and stoke fires and work hard as shite. If you think cutting cane's bad, you ain't know 'bout working on a ship — a floating jail, that's what we called it. But where there's life, there's hope. One or two setbacks — no matter how low you sink — how sick you feel — shouldn't cause people to give up hope. To start thinking all sorts of evil things, just because they're down for a short while."

"How long you worked on a ship?"

"Eight months. Went from Barbados to Aruba for oil. Then to the States and then to Portugal and England. Then they started this program here in Canada and I transferred. I was among the first on the Canadian Program."

"I had two trips to Florida," Tommy says. "And they were hell self. Pure hell. Death couldn't be no worse." Tommy cocks his ears and listens to the sounds coming through the open door. "Like the boys done eating and starting up a domino game, eh."

For the first time since I have known these two men, this is the closest they have come to quarrelling. Yet, it is a different kind of argument, more passion and caring, nothing like the coldness and hurting I witnessed between Johnny and Maude a few months ago. It is also the first time in a long while that I have seen Johnny so angry, Johnny a man of so few words at the best of times now feeling compelled to argue and speak his mind with such force, and to his best friend. Obviously, something has struck a nerve, causing these two men to disagree philosophically. Perhaps, it is understandable that this should happen. With all the hours Tommy is alone in the cabin with only the sound of the wind. With the men out working and he alone with his thoughts. All that silence, the cold and the coughing. Tommy has all this time on his hands. He can think too much about what would happen if this and that were to take place and who would take care of Barbara back home. All those wild thoughts just running through his head. Once or twice I hear him mumbling whether Barbara would be like Pearl, finding things so hard. It is a good thing nobody is ever in the room to hear him talking to himself. But at those times, I find it easy to understand why Tommy can't keep the thoughts inside his head. He has to voice them, perhaps in the hopes that if they escape his mouth, he will be free.

I cannot swear, but I don't think Johnny would allow himself to fall into such a depression. He is always the steadying one, always believing, as he says, tomorrow will be better. Sometimes the men joke about this. They mimic Johnny. If on a bad day the men pick only ten bushels of apples, or ten carts of tobacco, they console one another by saying they can always double the harvest the next day. *We'll do better tomorrow, man.* Johnny is always telling them the farmers will find something to grow in place of the tobacco. He is always so confident this new fang-dangled crop will actually make money for the farmers and let them hire more foreign workers. Tommy knows this about Johnny and now, as he tries to change the conversation, also tries to forget the argument. Tommy knows he should keep listening to Johnny and be optimistic. Johnny would never set him wrong, Tommy tells himself.

"This brings me back to the question I ask yuh earlier: you playing or not playing in the tournament?" Tommy says.

"I *don't* know." The anger hasn't totally dissipated from his voice.

"And if we win, the jazz festival or the trip to New York…?"

"Who says there will be a choice?" Johnny snaps. "If the season ends early there might be no choice."

"You don't mean to say you expect the…" Tommy's voice trails off. "Did Stewart tell you anything about…"

"No," Johnny sighs. His voice is almost back to normal. His frustration is with himself. For losing his cool instead of understanding the stress Tommy is under. "I don't know nothing new." He is talking slowly, softer. "Stewart ain't tell me nothing new. I'm just… just… just thinking aloud too. Just like everybody else."

"I see," Tommy says. He watches Johnny while listening carefully to the sounds coming through the open door. He can hear the shuffling of the bone dominos and the loud slamming of the pieces on the wooden table.

"I better try and drag myself outside and see what they're

doing," Tommy says. "Maybe playing a domino or two will make me feel a little better."

"Try and get some food in your stomach, too," Johnny says. His voice is calm as usual, but I can still detect the tension, as the pressure intensifies. "You got to force yourself to eat, to build up your constitution."

"You coming?"

"No. I'll stay and read a bit."

Tommy drags himself slowly, painfully out of the room. Johnny can hear the men laughing and swearing on the outside and then the room going silent as the men realize Tommy is there. Johnny reopens the diary and begins to read the fine penmanship of a grandfather from almost one hundred years earlier. As he reads, he begins to realize that nothing has changed, in almost a century. Not for the people on the migrant workers programs in Latin America, the United States of America or Canada.

At the same time, Johnny realizes he isn't always keen to welcome change. Most of the time he is positively afraid of change, particularly if it is the kind he experiences off the farm. Like the change he still plays over repeatedly in his mind. One of the encounters is at least two months old, but still fresh in his mind. Every step and punch as new and vicious as that night. In his mind, he is back home and totally lost in a land that should still be familiar to him. Instead, it turns out to be an island as foreign as anything on this earth.

As he reads, Johnny gently rubs the tips of his fingers over his eye. This is the reminder, the result of not understanding change. He knows that even if the reminder came from a strong fist it is the social and physical evolution in Lodge Road that accounts for the scar over his left eye. Change, he just can't handle too much change. Not at this stage in his life. He can't keep up or adapt as quickly as before. And now he has the scar as a reminder, or the occasional throbbing in the eye to spawn another wave of doubts. And he has the punch from Maude that didn't leave a physical mark.

The scar and the tenderness underneath his eye remind him of what can happen when he doesn't know the lay of his so-called native land any more. Remind him of straying into an alley after a drinking binge with practical strangers at the local rum shop, only for youngsters to mug him, people he doesn't know and couldn't even identify. Kids born and raised in Lodge Road since he joined the Program. In the harsh, modern reality, he realizes these youths don't respect him the way they do the older men that actually live in the village, the way, as a youngster, he respected his elders. And he doesn't know these kids because he can't meet them on a daily basis, doesn't know their names, doesn't see them playing with his own children or waiting at the side of the road for the school bus. In his mind and theirs, the person they continually beat up is a stranger to them, a foreigner in their midst — worse, an outsider pretending to be one of them. They aren't beating up on a member of their extended family.

Yes, there is comfort in keeping things the old way, Johnny reasons, and in the isolation on Edgecliff Farm. When Johnny thinks like this I can empathize with him. I remember what happened to the Prophet and his ideas for revolution. What happened to people like Shaka, Martin Luther King Jr. and all those African heroes whose actions storytellers like me have always chronicled. And I get the idea that this thoughtful man will never do anything rash just for the sake of change. In these troubling days, the latter is the only assurance I dare to hold. *A colour commentator, my god.* Perish the thought. The last time I looked, no leader has ever been a colour commentator. And I don't think that will change in a hurry.

chapter ten

In the darkness covering Edgecliff like a heavy cloak, the men walk slowly eastward, away from the almost empty cabin. They are heading in the direction of the bleak fields. Only the crunching sounds of their heavy boots against the ice, gravel and stones break the morning stillness. This noise travels long distances in the tranquillity of the young day, over intervals of time, space and even memory.

The sun, struggling over the horizon, is not the enemy of old; its visit is not a harbinger of struggle, desolation and genocide. It is like the coming of a friend. For in this strange world, as someone once said in some story stuck in my memory for its irony and practicality, yesterday's enemy is today's ally. With this in mind, I want you to watch how these men move hypnotically toward that from which they have always run; notice how quick they are to embrace to their bosom the very thing they spurn elsewhere; admire if you can how they have become the men they can never be at home. For something in their training, an unemotional discipline buried deep within tells them this is their lot. This is their fate for coming back, not as storytellers, but as men — black men at that.

So, just close your eyes and listen to the sounds. Watch the figures moving into the darkness. Don't they remind you of soldiers? The very kind of people — strong, mature and disciplined disciples — the Prophet wanted for his army, don't you think? Just imagine if that man's dream had come through, what a wonderful world we would be in now. Doesn't the sun, so far in the distance, and on a morning so cold and humbling, look to you like the fury of an approaching war, of a battlefield over the horizon lighting up with great big explosions? Maybe we'll see a mushroom cloud. Isn't that what these elongated rays tell you? These rays, so unfamiliarly soft, so weak and *papecie* at the beginning of such a truncated day. We are so used to seeing such weakness, such capitulation, at the end of the day, at the battle's end, not at the beginning. If there is such certainty of defeat at the start of the day, what is left to take anyone through the remainder of the battle, what will motivate people to go on fighting? What is to stop them from just hanging out on stoops, or under street lamps, or just bouncing a ball all day, as we see in just about any black community in this part of the world today?

Only soldiers can answer that question, only people who enter into a theatre knowing certain defeat awaits them, but nevertheless march right on, accepting death as natural. Soldiers, I tell yuh. Programmed. The Prophet Marcus could have used these men in his liberation army. Soldiers, mere soldiers, with my man Johnny as the general.

Before us is a scene I was waiting for you to witness. There is something here that is both foreboding and nostalgic. Watch how these men walk in silence, moving seemingly by memory. Note how carefully they avoid the potholes that have now become small lakes of ice and water. Their feet intuitively know their way around. Stripped of any emotion are these men. Walking as if in a trance. So that cold and the mist, the ice and the burning in their toes and fingertips shouldn't matter. They take solace in each other's presence, as if warmed and comforted by the unspoken knowledge and confidence that each of them has someone less than an arm's length away. Someone with whom to share the experiences of this bitter cold. Fellow travellers with whom to silently suffer such searing loneliness. In the darkness, they are not alone.

On mornings like this, I can tell you from experience, you

believe spring is years away, and not just a few weeks as the calendar promises. On days like this you can't help wondering which of these men wouldn't jump at the chance to trade places with Cuthbert, which of them wouldn't like to be a singer, a dancer, a politician, a doctor or even a restaurateur, just like anyone else. Anything but an agricultural worker trying to nurse life out of an unforgiving and uncooperative earth. Anything but the feeling of their balls swizzling and recoiling into their protective sacs.

Yet it is days like these when I can't but notice the strengthening bond between these men. When I can't help to remember former times. When I wish the women back home, women like good old Maude, could at this very moment see them, could admire their tenacity and sacrifice. Soldiers they are, if not by profession, by temperament and dedication. Soldiers, not ambassadors, not emissaries. Just damn well cannon-fodder. And it riles me no end that some of their women, black women at that, at home in comfort and sunshine, have the guts to say that these hardworking men are no damn good, that they can't be trusted, that they can't love, can't be tender and nurturing. Some things I just don't understand. Sometimes I wonder what more anyone can want from this lethal combination of melanin and testosterone.

But back to the scene. Notice that although the men huddle in threes and fours, the groups are in such proximity that, from a distance, all of them appear to merge into one large bunch of faceless people advancing in some programmed uniformity against the ravages of the elements. They walk in unison, like those inmates we see picking up paper and litter from the side of the streets, lumbering resignedly toward the sun that half-heartedly signals another day of hard labour. Tell me the truth: of what else do they remind you? Dredge up images from your own memory; recall stories from a grandmother or teacher, tap into the eternal story that runs in all our psyches and tell me what this scene reminds you of.

Don't they look like the slaves that four or five generations earlier were the forebears of these men slipping into the dark? I think they do. But then again, I am different, weird in my thinking. I can recall scenes from past lives. I remember seeing slaves walk in gangs like this. But that was supposed to end, according to that story in our archives, that episode with the special effects capturing the chilling voice of bellowing town criers and griots, for Mother Nyame spared no production costs recording those exceptional chapters, the ones that contain these famous and immortal words:

> *All and every person who on the said first day of August one thousand eight hundred and thirty-four shall be holden in slavery within any such British colony as aforesaid, shall upon and from after the said first day of August one thousand eight hundred and thirty-four become and be to all intents and purposes free and discharged of and from all manner of slavery, and shall be absolutely and forever manumitted; and...slavery shall be and is hereby utterly and forever abolished and declared unlawful throughout the British colonies, plantations, and possessions abroad.*

If you doubt me, check the records for yourself. And for these men to come to this, now? So many years and generations later! Oh, for a Marcus Mosiah Garvey. When will you come again? Other times, in my memory they are not slaves, but what we call apprentices, people supposedly free or, shall we say that lovely word, *manumitted* for a royal sum of 150 million pounds sterling by dear old Queen Bess, or was it for a mule and forty acres south of the border? Of course, even after manumission most were still tied by law to the plantations at "slave" wages until the year of our Lord the said old one thousand eight hundred and thirty-eight. So strong a case have we for reparations, I tell yuh. Later, we called them indentured servants, maybe because we like to alter a name or a title here and there without really changing the narrative of the stories we are recording on the wind. I can't remember from which country, or even island, these scenes in my memory spring.

All I know is that the old faded pictures are so similar to this portrait of these men out in the dark this morning. Scenes and pictures covering over five hundred years, all combining to form a single story about experiences on both sides of the Atlantic Ocean.

Still, despite all my memories and images from times past, there is something different about this group. Those slaves in my memory complained bitterly about lack of freedom and longed to go back home. It is the master's whip that keeps them in line. Even still, they rebel constantly and burn down the plantations the first chance they get. They run away when they can and do so often. They are always looking for a sure-fire path back home. Such is the case also with the apprentices — the magistrates, the original Liaison Officers, move from plantation to plantation as arbitrators, tying them to the land of former slave owners. The indentured labourer has no choice for he can't pay his passage back home, or he would have deserted this strange land without a glance backwards. The slave, apprentice and indentured labourer have no choice. And those from whom this bunch sprung didn't have to endure such bitter cold, or try to survive in a land so alien and different from what they knew. At least the sun is always as hot at home or in the strange land where they wail in my memory.

But look a' life, though, nuh. These people on Edgecliff Farm actually choose to be here, for theirs is not the case of the wicked taking them away to captivity and requiring of them a song. That is the major difference. Every year they literally outbid others, such as the taxi driver Cuthbert, for the opportunity to be on this Program. Why? I have no rational answers. Is there something so ingrained in the black man's psyche that he must do this to himself, that he will never be free? That he must still be looking for what even to this day we still call *Panama money* — selling our bodies and dreams in a foreign land for token remittances to send back home?

These men of Edgecliff Farm share the same purpose, urgency and, apparently, even the same taste for clothes. They are all wearing similar heavy khaki-coloured coats with remnants of imitation fur around the necks, with a thick lining on the inside and a big heavy-duty zipper to the front. Every one of the coats unashamedly shows the twenty-five years of wear. That's how long ago they were purchased for the first group of workers. Remember, after all, this started out as a temporary Program, a stop-gap measure to ease a labour shortage that was expected to be only fleeting, so nobody in his right mind did any long-term thinking or planning. Since then, the coats have been handed down from year to year, as this farm has been passed on over the generations. Young boys on the islands back home learn from their absent fathers that their future can come only from producing food for foreigners to eat. Even as youths they understood how they must resign themselves to living like disposable domestic servants in the homes of foreigners or, as in this case, in the remote side-houses and barracks on Canadian farms. These coats contain that history, in the mixed odours of sweat and dried bloodstains from the bruised bodies — the traces of the men present and gone, so-called envoys who share like a protective bond these musty and ever-thinning coats.

When new, the coats had hoods to protect the head and the ears, just as the men, when young, had so many dreams. Most of the coats no longer have the capes, and the older men have lost their hair, as their bodies sag with age and their legs slow a couple steps. The zippers, too rusted or missing large tracks of teeth, do not work. Some buttons on the outside, providing another fold over the zippers, are also missing. The men simply tie pieces of string around their waists to keep the front closed against the biting wind.

Even then, the coats fail them. Reaching only halfway down the thighs, they expose the flanks and legs, so that the men's pants are soon soaked from the water kicked up with every step. For most men of average height and build, these coats would be adequate. But for the strapping men that now share them, the coats are too short and too narrow. And, like everything else on Edgecliff, they are too thin and soft with age. On cold mornings like this, the ironic curse of these men is obvious: the same strapping build and height that qualify them for the Program become their vulnerability in such weather. And even if the coats don't work, the men must.

As they walk toward the day's rendezvous, the men stuff their gloved hands in the coat pockets in search of any warmth and protection they can find. The frosty mist forms small droplets of water around their mouths, in the beards of those who could not find the time to shave or who recognize that a face of hair is at least some insulation. Their noses run and their ears, fingers and toes burn from the cold. They continue to walk silently and purposefully into the field. The formation is broken by two stragglers lingering behind the main group. They look like an unwanted tail on some grotesque animal.

Johnny and Winston are the two stragglers. The emerging bond between the two men of different generations is already beginning to set them apart from the rest of the group, although they too remain an integral part of the gang. Let us go down now to where the men are and listen in on this conversation. There's one really good thing about the decrepit coats — all the cobwebs from over the years. What more could a spider like me want for protection from the cold?

"Cold, eh?" Johnny says, increasing his pace to fall in step with the long-legged youngster. This morning, Johnny was the last out of the cabin, so he could have a final word with Tommy, who is spending yet another day in bed. I have now lost count of these sick days. While the others move ahead, Winston waits back, perhaps for no other reason than that he likes being in the older man's company, even if they always argue. I tell yuh, the old women back home are right: two rats with big balls can't live in the same hole. They must fight, and it doesn't always have to be physical blows. Brer Rat done know this fact of life. That is why to this day he ain't got no family, 'cause it's Brer Anancy that make them things happen. Remember, it was Sly Rat who crept up from behind on Brer Rat, intending to dethrone him by snapping off the oldster's private parts hanging so big behind him; how, thank God, it took a shout from Brer Anancy alerting Brer Rat just in time. When the youngster snapped his big teeth shut, it was only on Brer Rat's tail. Whew, what a near miss. And that's why to this day we always can come across the odd bob-tail rat, and you know for yourself how funny and out-of-place they look. It appears inevitable that Johnny might have to put a licking on this guy, duke it out with him, just to prove who is the real man around here.

I think Winston is also hoping that Johnny will share with him some of the personal information on Tommy. The youngster is like that, damn nosey. Of course, Johnny never does. And Winston never asks, perhaps hoping that by fixing Johnny in his gaze the old pro will break down and spill his guts. Obviously, he still doesn't know my man Johnny. I guess he is also still waiting for an explanation as to why Johnny shifted his *rass* out of the cot next to his.

But never mind all these mind-games, I want you to take a

good look at these two so-called rats. Tell me are they not, in perhaps a few ways, not too many though, because we don't want to overdo the comparison, but aren't they like two peas in a pod? Answer me! Notice how they are now matching each other step for step, left foot to left foot, right to right, as if joined by invisible strings in some puppeteer's hand. Such things, little though they are, make you wonder. Such potential. If only this Winston wasn't such a pain in the arse.

"Spring is really late this year, man. All like now we should be getting better weather." Take note of the tone of Johnny's voice. He could almost be apologizing for putting Winston through such a trial. I don't usually hear him talking like this to any of the other guys.

The remarks appear to catch Winston off guard. Not that he doesn't think it is cold — he keeps thinking that no one should be working outdoors, and that it is so dark that everyone should still be sleeping. If he were to volunteer what is on his mind, somebody, Johnny even, might start snapping at him. But it is almost as if he and Johnny are thinking the same thing. The real surprise, if I may say so, is that Johnny, a man of so few words, is actually initiating this conversation. Several times in the three weeks since we moved from the greenhouses to the open fields, I have noticed Winston walking beside the older man. I can always feel how much he wants to talk with him. Every time, he forces himself to refrain from saying anything for fear of appearing to intrude on Johnny's personal thoughts. To me, he is always picking his moment, learning how to wait for the right opportunity before moving in for the kill. To some degree, I think this guy Winston is starting to learn one or two things. At least he can hold his tongue. Which reminds me of the lessons Brer Anancy had to teach the baby that cried, cried, cried all the time. In that story all the baby ever did was eat and cry, cry and eat, eat and cry. That baby became the tongue of the world and from then on we've had trouble trying to control it. Winston's tongue is still his biggest baby, except when he is around Johnny.

I can understand this reluctance to intrude on Johnny's space. To do so would be a fighting gesture and this young rat better be ready to finish anything he starts. I, too, notice how Johnny always seems so preoccupied of late, especially when he's reading those diaries. He and Tommy are the only ones that read, even to the point of missing the domino games in the camp after Smokie has served the evening's meal. Already you know how I feel about those diaries. Now, I'm thinking more than ever that Johnny is overdoing things, setting himself up for a big fall. Every evening the two of them are reading in silence — Johnny from his diaries, Tommy from the stack of yellowing letters from his wife over the years. Tommy has three red rubber bands wrapped around the collection. Sometimes, Johnny and Tommy argue with Timmy, who shares the same views I do about the two of them being blatantly antisocial. But most times, they just sit and read, alone in their private thoughts and worlds. Tommy, between the sniffles, enjoying every word from his wife, reliving the nostalgia as if courting her all over again.

"Christ," Winston answers, clapping his hands and then rubbing them together for warmth, "I didn't expect to be working outside in this kinda cold. Man, I mean, I can't even stop my poor teeth from knocking. Look at me; see how I'm shaking like some old man, nuh."

Johnny doesn't look but instead fumbles with the flap of the breast pocket of his coat. He fishes out a crumpled pack of Wrigley's spearmint gum, the top of which is already torn off. He takes out a stick and extends the pack to Winston. "Here. Take a couple o' pieces."

Johnny unwraps a stick, folds it in half and places the dingy-looking piece of gum into his mouth. He chews slowly and firmly, swallowing the sweetened saliva, his big Adam's apple bobbing up and down as the juice goes down his throat.

"It should keep the jaws from feeling seized up," he explains. Johnny is chewing slowly, unconsciously teaching the young man how to get the most out of the gum. "Like it's freezing off or something. The cold can make your jaw feel that way. As if everything turn numb or dead. You had coffee this morning?"

Winston doesn't answer. He fumbles clumsily but unsuccessfully to unwrap a stick of gum. His fingers feel fat and numb. It reminds him of the impossible task of using the lamp light in his mother's house to thread a very small needle to make a patch. A reminder of the many times he had ripped his pants while playing with the boys in his village and his mother had to patch or darn them. Clumsy. Like the time at school when his teacher took the class into the science lab and allowed them to use microscopes. He never managed to pick up the strands of hair with the bumbling tweezers. It is the same now with the gum. He has absolutely no control over his fingers. Except that in school, in the Tropics, students don't have to worry about the cold. Of course, other things — just ask Brer Donkey why he tries to find the back door — intervene to stop them from becoming the scientists of their dreams.

"I don't drink coffee." He is not looking at the older man as he speaks, but instead still fumbles with the wrapper. "Always makes me nervous. Even when I was a little boy. My mother could never give me no coffee. Make my stomach upset and turn sour, sour all day."

"You gotta try and put something warm in yuh stomach in the morning," Johnny says. "Coming outside in the cold like this," Johnny can hear the authority in his own voice so he tries to moderate the tone, "with no heat in the body, ain't no good for a young fellow like you."

"But I can't take the coffee," says Winston. "And that's the only thing we got to drink on mornings."

"Buy a little oatmeal porridge. The next time we go into town."

"I don't like porridge, neither," Winston says. "Too heavy so early in the morning."

"Try and get something to warm up the inside. Otherwise, you could catch pneumonia easy so. Getting hit with sickness 'round here ain't no good at all."

"Like Tommy, eh."

Johnny is watching from the corner of his eyes how Winston fumbles with the gum. He acts as if he does not hear the last statement. By now, almost all the flavour is gone from the piece in Johnny's mouth but his jaw is warm and loose. Without appearing to notice, he sees the gum, still wrapped in the second silver layer, falls from Winston's hands to the frozen ground. Winston stoops to pick it up, but the gum shifts every time he places his numbed fingers around it. The frustration is getting the better of him. The youngster is sucking his teeth loudly. Without prompting, Johnny reaches past him and deftly grabs the gum, using the tip of his gloved hand to flip it into the palm. With both of them still in the crouch position, they look at each other and smile.

Rising together, they stand facing each other and then, almost as if of the same mind or perhaps because they are unable to look each other in the eye, they notice the other men lengthening the distance between them. Their first instinct is to run, to at least appear to be trying to regain lost ground. Johnny gestures as if to return the gum to Winston. But then, with his hand still extended, as if frozen by the cold wind, he stops. Smiling, he unwraps the last of the paper from the gum. Winston stretches out his hand to receive it.

"Uh, uh," Johnny says, shaking his head from side to side. He opens his mouth and points to the gum in it, as if daring a child to mimic him. Winston takes the hint and opens his mouth. The older man pops the gum in, taking care not to brush the youngster's lips with his dirty glove. They resume walking, chewing quietly. It is some time before either speaks and disrupts this beautiful silence.

"I know I got a lot to learn up here." It is Winston talking. He sounds resigned, as if he is really musing aloud to himself but also wanting to bounce some thoughts off the older man. Maybe some consolation for being so lost in this hostile environment, for being so useless and feeling that he can't even take care of himself, can't even unwrap a friggin' piece of gum without someone's help. He is thinking that it's no wonder the farmer wants to send him back home. Wants to send him back, even though he is strong and healthy, even though nobody is doing anything about Tommy and his condition. Not even Johnny would talk to him about Tommy.

Flick. Flick. Flick. That annoying sound is from Winston's laces, undone once again, the plastic tips lashing noisily against his steel-tipped boots. He stoops and tries to tie the wet laces. A few paces on, *flick, flick, flick,* the laces are undone again. "Damn things keep coming loose all the time." Petulantly, he stomps his foot in frustration. Boy, is he ever losing the war.

"Give them a good knot or two, man," Johnny encourages him. "Like if you're tying out the sheep in the pasture at home. You know, when the rain done fall back home and the rope's wet and slippery and you got to make more than one knot to make it hold."

"Johnny," Winston begins, coming to his full height, the laces now bulging with several strong bows. "Talking about back home, I was to ask you this long time now: how come we ain't get no letters yet? Not a word from home all this time?" Do I notice the rekindling of defiance in his voice, the old Winston returning from defeat?

"I don't know." Johnny drops his voice as if once again trying to internalize everything. But the pained expression on Winston's face makes him want to explain further, for the youngster's sake. "Like Stewart, the farmer, don't like goin' intuh town no more."

He pauses again, choosing his words carefully, trying not to look straight at Winston. "He never used to take so long to go into town. I don't know what's happening."

"Can't we go and get them we own selves, Johnny? I mean if..."

"Normally, he don't take this long. 'Cause he knows how much the men look forward to the letters. Particularly the first letters of the season. Them is the ones you want real bad. But I don't know. He like he's frightened to go into town these days."

"Why you say that, Johnny? I mean, look at how poor Tommy got to read the old letters to get by. Sometimes, I kinda feel sorry for Tommy, man."

"Well, I mean once upon a time Mr. Stewart used to be the one to take us into the town on Friday nights. You know, spend the whole night out with the boys. Me and he used to talk a lot on them nights. About everything — the farm, the men, the rain, the crop, things back home. 'Cause neither o' we did like to drink too much. And besides, somebody had to be sober enough to keep an eye on the men, so they wouldn't get into a fight or anything so. Now he's saying that if we want to go into the town he think he's send us in the school bus and he'll stay at home."

"But think of poor Tommy. What you think we can do, man?"

They have been gradually increasing their speed to catch up to the other men, nearing the beginning of the apple orchard. Again, Johnny refuses to take the bait. Perhaps this psychological war is back on.

"Another thing, Johnny," Winston says, the gum now

wedged between his teeth and the side of his mouth. "How come we can't wear any gloves when we pruning these damn trees? I mean it's so cold and everything, man."

"You can, but you'd bruise the young bulbs." He is still deep in thought, but the answer comes automatically, as if he anticipates such questions. "Would kill them that way."

"Gosh, I didn't think of that." Such ignorance makes Winston feel useless all over again. "I guess I really got a lot to learn, eh Johnny?" This statement sounds like both a plea for patience and a sign that he too is unsatisfied with himself and his progress. Perhaps a sign there will be no clear-cut winners or losers here.

"You'll do all right."

"I really don't know." Winston is again the voice of resignation, of hopelessness. He is chomping heavily on the gum, causing it to crackle in his mouth. "Right now I have five minds to pack up my things and go back home. But I can't. I got to stay. Because of my mother and sisters. I got to help them out. I can't turn out just like my father." Now his speech appears as slow, his thoughts as measured, as his companion's.

"You'll do all right. Just take your time. All of us went through the same feelings one time or another."

"But it's so hard, Johnny. Nothing like what I expected back home," Winston says. "And the men always getting angry with me."

"It's a good thing all of us had a reason for putting up with the hardships until we got used to them. Otherwise, we'd all just turn 'round and go back home the first time."

"I don't know, Johnny. I don't know if I'm cut out for this kinda work. I can't seem to get used to it, no matter how hard I try, man."

"You will," Johnny assures him. "You will find that every year there's a different reason, and always a very good one, for not giving up and going back. Once you start, it's like you can't stop. Even if you wanted to. It'll take you a few years, good, good."

"*Years,*" Winston snaps, "You say years. Huh, I really don't know about spending no *years* on this program. Just let me see if I can get through this one first."

They are catching up to the men at the head of the field. The foreman, in a long dirty coat, and off-white tam on his head, is already sitting on the high seat on the Massey Ferguson tractor, waiting. Every man knows that, except for Smokie, it will be many, many hours before any of them will return to the relative warmth of the cabin.

chapter eleven

Still steaming, George Stewart pulls the battered Chevrolet pickup truck off the main road into the parking lot across from the doughnut shop. He jams the brakes hard, bringing the truck to a final stop a whisker from the brown brick building. What a crazy man he is this morning, looking like the Devil himself?

Here I am tailing this man just because I want to find out for myself why he isn't going into town these days. Because of that question Winston keeps putting to Johnny about getting letters for Tommy, but also for me to see if there is any truth in what Mother Nyame is now saying. If she is right, if I have to become more than just some dumb storyteller, as she puts it, I guess I have to get around, roam far and wide, add to my store of knowledge, if you know what I am getting at, have a complete changeover since there is such dissatisfaction with me on high. Maybe an old dog can learn new tricks.

So when George storms out of his house and jumps into the van, I up and follow him, my frustration with everything as deep as his, 'cause nobody can blame me for assuming that, with the guys in the field in such warm weather, there isn't much that I can miss in one day. Not that I think it matters one fig if I miss a day in the great heart-stopping annals of these people, chronicles that I am now told must come fully dressed-up with commentary, something that even the great Prophet had to get by without.

And besides, from the way I feel today, I don't think anyone back at the head office would really care to hear my voice. Not today. They might be glad, happy in fact, that I am not competing with the insightful, dulcet tones of any of their favourite scribes. So I decide to hang out with George, if only for a change of scenery. 'Cause everybody is entitled to at least one day off the job every now and then. This is my sick leave, or what a teacher friend of mine likes to call professional development time.

But seriously now. To be truthful, the reason for this trip is that I want to get away from the farm to be alone with my thoughts. I want to think through some things. You see, I got around to having a chat with Mother Nyame. Finally, I screwed up enough courage to confront her. I just couldn't go on any longer with this young whippersnapper walking all over my turf, second-guessing me, literally spoiling for a fight. No, I couldn't take such indignity and open disrespect any more. Can you imagine what the other storytellers, some with bigger and more important projects, must be saying about me? And an old whore like me. Lord, how much lower can I fall — from the Prophet to this farm behind God's back, coming back a second time as a storyteller, skipping the leadership. Now the open suggestion that I can't tell a story straight any more, that someone must help me out. And a female storyteller too, not even someone who knows about real battles by real men. A damn first-timer, *tuh rass*. God, I have some pride too. I mean, it would be like Johnny having to answer to the dictates of Winston every day, no respect for age and experience. Johnny can refuse to answer questions from that boy. But I can't ignore that someone is trying to show me up in my job, that someone, in keeping with those well-known feminine wiles, is *dissing* me real bad.

So I up and ask the Great Mother what the hell is going on. Is there something about my reporting that you don't like? I ask her straight up. As you can imagine, the reason I take so long to talk to Mother Nyame is that I deal with this woman only when I have to. Women, as you know, are strange birds. Real strange and unpredictable. Check out for yourself all that trouble Amy Jacques caused for the followers of Prophet. Just look at how unreliable Maude is. Mother Nyame is no different, unreliable as hell. I still think that she could have turned a blind eye in the first place, that she didn't have to send me back for a second stint as a reporter. So now I try to deal with her as little as I can. I just hope my work speaks for itself this time, but then, I ask myself how can it when she is showing absolutely no confidence in me? Can you imagine the indignity of doing this bullshit a third time around, especially when they are suggesting that I can't even do the job now? Would I be able to do it any better, would I have the confidence and the assurance of their backing the next time? If I can't handle a stinking farm now, where will she send me next, a damn prison, exchanging the prison and black population of Edgecliff for say the prison of Sing Sing or wherever on this continent they warehouse black people? So I put my cards plainly on the table and asked her to come clean with me. Give me the respect I am due, tell me if you no longer have any confidence in me. Let's get it out in the open, I say.

And guess what she answers. Well, in fact, she says, I've been meaning to send you a note. We are thinking about making a few changes and, in fact, she says, we are thinking of asking you to become a colour commentator, our very first colour commentator in history. Neat, eh, she says.

Well, my head just drops when she tells me this foolishness. My mouth hangs open but no words come. Here I am, the one storyteller with the most experience and status in the entire stable, for, after all, there isn't another fella around who has had two back-to-back assignments. That gives me seniority and status at the least. It should also bring me better treatment, if I may say so. For that point, I won't even deal with the matter of why I am always the last to hear anything, why I had to first hear about this colour commentary crap from a friend, and why I wouldn't know anything official if I didn't up and ask a question. No *rass hole* respect. And that's not even taking into consideration that I have been on the job here at Edgecliff for twenty-five years now. But no, Mother Nyame tries to butter me up by saying it was she who specifically chose me for this prestigious ground-breaking project, that if I was successful, I would start a specialty service for others to follow, that I could possibly expand the role of the storyteller into that of a soothsayer, so that in future the people would know who is and who isn't a false prophet leading them astray, that I could revolutionize the business. Me, who supposedly needs all the help in the world with a half-arse story? Give me a break, don't insult my intelligence, woman. This could be my calling, she says. That I could use my extensive experience and knowledge to start *extrapolating* into the future. It is she that pick me for the job and how she hopes I won't let her down, that I won't make her look foolish for having this faith in me. As if she is doing me a favour. As if the fact that she picks me should mean anything to an old whore like me. What foolishness! Are we storytellers or not? I couldn't believe the insults coming from her mouth. Damn women! From a man, they would be fighting words. Somebody would end up with his balls bitten out clean, clean, clean — not just a tail bobbed off.

So what's wrong with what I am doing? I demand to know from Mother Nyame. By now I am not even trying to hide my anger and displeasure. I ain't laughing at all, not, as they say at home, one skin *teet'* laugh to make pretend. For I too vex, now. And what more can she do to me, deny me a promotion again? Could anything be worse than what she is doing to me now — making me a damn guinea pig? Giving me a task that I am sure to fail, 'cause none of us is trained for this business. Is my memory deceiving me or do I recall that, until now, it was this woman, the Great Nyame, she sheself always drilling in our heads: *the facts, the facts, and then more facts.* Now, she's setting me up for everyone to laugh at, to make me a damn fool. I can't believe it. Maybe I have some sign saying idiot all over my face so that anybody can make me a laughing stock. But not me. Wrong number this time, boy. Call again.

Well, she says oh so sweetly, it's not that we don't have confidence in you, you know, man. Not at all. But — and you know there is always trouble when a but comes up — but, she says, we want to move with the times. We want to make the reports more technologically advanced. We want our representatives in the field to adopt different styles. You know, to breathe a bit more life into their reports. Tell us much more than just the bare bones. Try different methods and perspectives, maybe even see if we should deal only with African people. Or if we should spend more time with other peoples. I don't know, I don't have the answers, but we figure you're the one to take on this challenge. You know, roam around, see things, tell us what they mean. After all, black people don't live in the world by themselves, so why not show us how they get on with other people? Is it a fact, for example, that other people have total control over their lives and future? You can do a whole series on that one issue. Explain to us what is going on; make sense of it for us. You can do it. Some people claim, quite rightly too, that we from Africa haven't changed our methods in the last five hundred years. We do things the same way we did before that great big exodus from the Mother Continent, before our holocaust. Now we are at the turn of a century and a millennium; now, after five hundred years, we've had a review here at head office and decided that it's time to try something different. For the old tried-and-true no longer seems to be working, at least not for the young people, especially our men. Why not do a major overhaul? So we would like you to start the ball rolling with some commentaries. If they work, we can go from there. Those were Mother Nyame's words to me.

Then she drops another bombshell. Apparently, she has been listening in on my reports of late, especially since I started talking specifically to you at the beginning of this season. And you know what? Mother Nyame says that the way I have been talking to you — you know, ad libbing a bit here and there, making the odd commentary, not sticking to just relating what is happening — all of these things help put the idea in her head. At least, thank God, she doesn't mention anything about the early shakes in my voice. Otherwise, God help me. You are a natural colour commentator, she says. You know so much. You can help us to break that narrow and confining mould of what we as chroniclers, as historians and writers, are free to do and still remain professional and even artistic. So why don't you spend your time concentrating on doing what you are really good at? Take your talents from under the brush. Why not leave the hard work to the young ones that have the strength and tenacity? In any case, she says, dropping another vote of nonconfidence in the lap of yours truly, these young ones are just out of training school. So they know the latest state-of-the-arts reports; they know what we at head office really want; they know how to handle change. Of course, I had to ask her what the last statement meant, if she was implying that I am old and decrepit, out of touch and simply no longer effective, just *dotage* from age like some human storytellers I know.

Ah, you always make so much of the slightest criticism, she says, laughing. I am still not convinced that her laughter doesn't ring hollow. Why don't you think about what I've just told you? she says. You don't have to make a decision right now. But I definitely think you'd make a good colour commentator. Think on it.

And what about this other dame, the one you sent over even though I didn't ask for help, what happens to her while I am *thinking* over my options? I ask. Is she still going to be meddling in my affairs or are you going to recall her, at least silence this unruly tongue, as in the Brer Anancy story, until I make up my mind?

No, she says, rather firmly. She stays. But think on what we've just discussed. *Right!* I think to myself. The writing is on the wall, fella, I tell myself, for why doesn't she make this one simple concession to me and ask this intruder to shut up for a while? It's not like I'm asking her to recall this girl-wonder right away or to reassign her. Just send the young thing on a vacation! But I guess that is asking too much. And it's only me. Then she expects me to believe all this claptrap about having confidence in me. If she does, why doesn't she show it?

So here I am trying to think, hoping that the ride with George will help to clear my head, will help to get me away from the action and my charges, just in case I am getting too close to them and losing my objectivity. Just in case I have to start commentating on other people as that Great Lady suggests. If I must, why not start with George and the Stewarts, working them more solidly into my narrative than before? What happens to them will have an impact on the lives and future, as she says, of twenty-one black men back on the farm. And in any case, I tell myself, nobody will be missing anything if I don't make a report today. They can make do with the, how shall I put it, the *fulminations* of that other one. They obviously don't need me. Not when Mother Nyame has her precious favourite on hand to second-guess me.

But I didn't expect this scary ride in the pickup truck, with this madman at the wheel swerving down the road, making wide and reckless turns. The vibes are pouring out of him so strong, like nothing I ever experienced before from him. Several times I had to ask myself if this is what it would be like following these strangers. What can I reasonably say in my comments? That they drive like maniacs? That they are crazy? All the time,

George is arguing with himself, his face red as a beet, the radio blaring with tasteless country and western music. Utter confusion in this strange world. I am not used to such displays of temper. And when we arrive at the bank's parking lot, I tell yuh, it is only the last-minute intervention by some unseen force that prevents George from ramming the truck through the damn building, valuable mortgage papers and loan agreements flying wherever they might in final liberation.

If this is what Mother Nyame wants for me, I'm sorry, but she'll have to find someone else to do it. My poor heart can't take it. Maybe get that other storyteller, since she is so good that she can't be shut up for one day, me say get *her* to do this running about. Leave me at the farm, where I want to be, where everything is as I like it. Come to think of it, that's a good idea. I am glad I am thinking that way — maybe I should make that suggestion, that Mother Nyame make someone else, even the youngster, the colour commentator and leave me alone. 'Cause my poor heart can't take this sort o' *botherations*. Lord knows, not at all.

But the saints of storytellers, and perhaps even Mother Nyame sheself, must be watching over me. They stop the truck just in time. George sits at the wheel after turning off the engine, sighing repeatedly and slapping the steering wheel with the palms of his hands. He rummages through the documents in the seat beside him. It's clear he is still so angry with Mary. *'Im bex, bex, bex no rass,* as they say back home. He sits telling himself that even after all their years together, she still doesn't understand him.

Oh, the poor man. He must feel like a boxer in the changeroom, psyching himself up for battle, making himself ready to kill or to be killed. When, on a morning like this, the very first day of sunshine bright enough to melt the snow, he would rather spend bonding with the men in the fields than entering a battle.

But Mary forces him to come into this damn town only to be embarrassed and belittled. Because of Mary, he will be sitting in an office, staring across the desk at this new banker and begging. Begging while thinking how long it would take for him to wrap his crusty agricultural hand around the joker's smooth, close-shaven neck and strangle the bastard to death. And if you believe George, he wouldn't even crumple the man's neatly ironed shirt collar in the process. And it would be all because of that woman, Mary, the instigator.

Goodness gracious, just hearing him complain, it sounds so familiar. Perhaps I do have material for my first commentary! Women are all alike whether black or white; whether human, Mother Nyame or a dim-witted, intrusive storyteller. Gosh, I would like to see the face of this mother when I offer up these comments officially. Brer Fooly-bird, I tell yuh. Even now, I can't stop laughing at the idea. Sometimes, I can be so funny and witty but, when I want to be, I can also be like a stepping razor, sharp, sharp, sharp and dangerous. As Brer Hyena says to Brer Crocodile when they meet at the watering hole to share the catch, you are a damn fool to be crying all the time when you can be laughing like me. Heh, Heh, Heh.

George opens the door, although he makes no move to get out just yet. He is not through cussing Mary. No, he grumbles, Mary could never understand why he wanted to skip this meeting, why he tries to miss all meetings like these, why he feels compelled to pretend that he doesn't even receive the letters. But the most recent letter was different, Mary was so quick to point out (and dwell on). This letter came special-delivery the previous day. The bank used a courier service that guaranteed same-day delivery and a signature as evidence of receipt.

George looks across at the doughnut shop and decides against buying the doughnuts now. He'll do it on the way out, after the meeting. In any case, time is getting away and the stupid banker would see him across the parking lot hanging out in the shop and keeping him waiting. He'll get them later.

He pushes the creaking door open wider. In the rear-view mirror, he checks how he looks. Noticing the stubble on his face, he feels proud of it, a rebellious sign that he isn't one of those smooth-face, soft-hands bankers. On an occasion like this, he wonders what it would be like if Johnny were in this very truck, getting ready for this meeting. What would this banker think? Would his eyes light up, if Johnny walked in and simply said he's representing the Stewart family? If Johnny were his sparring partner, or even manager for this fight?

After all, George reasons, Johnny knows as much about the farm as any of them, certainly more than the damn banker. If ever there were a crisis on the farm, George can think of nobody but Johnny he'd want standing shoulder to shoulder with him, fighting the common enemy. But, of course, Johnny won't do for this situation. And he won't do because the banker doesn't really want to discuss farming, as he claims in the letter, but money. And Johnny has no say in money matters. George adjusts the hat on the back of his head and swings his legs from under the steering wheel into the snow bank. Johnny would be a good ally against this banker, he muses, perhaps an even better partner than Mary. I smile at the suggestion.

His eyes catch the sign warning that parking is limited to fifteen minutes and that the spots are for clients of the bank. He frowns. George looks up at the clock above the bank's name. It is showing exactly a quarter to noon. The men in the field are probably taking a quick break. Maybe to rush to the outhouses. If he had his way, he would not even be here, far less robbing some poor slob of a parking spot. Now that he is here, though, he knows that he will need more than fifteen minutes. He needs hours, perhaps months, to explain the facts of farming to this brand-new banker from the fancy glass-and-steel towers of

Toronto. George slams the door closed. Fifteen minutes. This damn bank is as stingy with its time as it is with money.

With the hood of the old khaki-coloured coat flapping behind his back and the front zipper undone, George Stewart marches through the slushy ice and water. He makes a wide step over a pool of black oily water onto the first round of the steps leading into the building. He pushes open the glass door with the name of the bank painted on it and walks over to the counter. His noisy entry interrupts Mrs. Francis, who is typing somewhat bewilderedly at the word processor. She looks timid, unhappy and uncertain behind the new piece of equipment. For all the years George has been coming to this branch, Mrs. Francis has always been the bubbly secretary for the bank manager. She knows all the farmers and occasionally helps them fill out a form properly without the manager being any the wiser. Now, someone with the title of administrative assistant has replaced her. Someone who screens all the manager's calls and who keeps him up to date on all delinquent payments, instead of making a quick call first to the farmer to find out if the onerous duties of actually running a business are preventing him from managing the books. Mrs. Francis has been reduced to using the word processor for typing in the names of the farmers on the form letters demanding meetings between the banker and client. George remembers hearing talk that now that Mr. Francis is dead, this gentle woman will be leaving Sarnia for Toronto, or some ot her city, where she has no friends but where she would not have to explain anything in her life. She'll be gone as soon as she reaches her fifty-fifth birthday, the rapidly falling threshold for early retirement.

To tell the truth, I find all of this fascinating. But I am still at a loss as to how I could ever use any of this stuff in a commentary on the lives of those poor slobs on the farm. What is the relevance? Obviously, Mother Nyame knows something that I don't. But then again, maybe, if I remember her statement correctly, she doesn't know either. This is a shot in the dark. Maybe all I have to do is say it ain't working out, stop the experiment. Or I can be so bad in my commentaries that she would stop them right away in the hopes of maintaining an untarnished professional name. That's another good idea — maybe I should just screw up on the job.

"You must be George Stewart," the woman replacing Mrs. Francis says when he approaches the counter. She is about thirty years old, full-breasted and with a big smile on her face. Her teeth are white and look smoothly polished. Obviously, no smoker here. "I'm Celia Ashford, the new administrative assistant, and I've been reviewing your file. Mr. King will see you right away, Mr. Stewart."

She removes a latch behind the door and swings it inwards, gesturing with the palm of her extended hand for George to enter. The bank manager, in a grey pin-striped suit, comes out of the inner office. On cue, he mechanically stretches out a hand toward George. He, too, looks programmed, a clone of his predecessor now sitting at headquarters in Toronto, George thinks. "It's so good to meet you, Mr. Stewart. Come on in."

They shake hands firmly, like two fighters, not only of raw masculine strength but also of willpower and intellect. At the mention of George's name, Mrs. Francis looks up and nods. They smile briefly, communicating in silence. Mr. Walter King, the bank manager, steps out of the way and allows George to precede him into the office, into the squared circle. "Remember your luncheon appointment for noon, Mr. King," Celia says and walks away. The bank manager glances quickly at his watch, closes the door behind them, walks around the desk and sits. George remains standing. He doesn't even attempt to take off his coat. I must admit I agree with George. Why bother sitting for only thirteen stinking minutes?

"How's this weather treating you, eh, George?" the banker says with pretend familiarity, shuffling some papers on his desk. "People around here tell me they can't remember the last time we had such cold weather so late in the year. Think we'll have any summer, George?"

"I hope so. Otherwise, we may as well pack it all in."

The response, even for George, is unexpected, cold and brusque. Walter King looks up from his papers and finds George still standing. I know I am going to enjoy this fight. As you know, I like nothing better than a good rumble. It adds so much to a story — the drama of not knowing the outcome, the tension and conflict and, of course, the strong-willed characters. All elements for a good yarn. I love it. Maybe there is something in what Mother Nyame has been saying.

"You may sit, George. But tell me what you mean by that. By what you just said." Watch out, here comes the sucker-punch.

"Ah. Nothing really. Just that you'd asked if we'd have any summer. A guy like me, a farmer, gets kinda tired hearing them sort of questions." There would be no attempt to hide his anger. George isn't like Johnny, who, if memory serves me right, would sit there in the chair as soon as the bank manager offered it and accept all the terms dictated. That is exactly what he did on the house mortgage in Barbados. That's why he has to send virtually every cent back home. Why if this insurance thing that the Liaison Officer talks about doesn't pan out, and soon, Johnny could be up the damn creek. This Johnny who so stupidly sat down and signed his name to papers drawn up between Maude and a banker he had never met before the time for signing. That is why I laugh when George says Johnny would be such an ally in this office. I have my doubts. But back to the main bout here.

"I see," the banker says. He still looks confused by the response but obviously decides to let the matter rest. "Anyway, George, the reason we called you in today, take a seat, *please*, the reason is the line of credit. Please, take a seat!" His voice is now several octaves lower. "It's used up again and we haven't had any payments in the past, uh," he flips some pages, "in the past five months, to be exact. Not even the monthly interest payments, which you know you must pay, if not the principal too. And as you know you have to reduce the line of credit to zero at regularly specified periods; it's not a loan. I mentioned this in my letter of introduction around Christmas and again in the New Year when we sent out the calendars. It's not me, but head office, the auditors, who are asking questions again. And have a seat, George, I can't stand you standing there like that."

George smiles at the small victory. He has made his point. He settles into the chair.

"Well, that's because of the early expenses in the season. Happens every year," George says, talking slowly, his eyes wandering around the room. They settle on a picture on the wall. I follow George's eyes. Everyone in the picture is smiling and looks well tanned. In the centre of the picture is a man with a straw hat on his head, a broad grin on his face, obviously on vacation with a woman and two children on some tropical beach. To me it smacks of the typical tourist-trap picture. Obviously, not everyone tries to flee the tropical sun; some even burn themselves in it and take cheap pictures to decorate their walls at work.

"From our last March break," the manager says, noticing George's eyes on the pictures. "In *The* Barbados. I try to go down south whenever I can get away with the family." George nods. To him, the man in the picture looks a lot different than the one sitting in front of him. "Ever been to *The* Barbados, George?"

"Uh, no." Obviously these two pugilists are just exchanging jabs, keeping in reserve the Big Berthas, the real heavy punches. So they flick a jab here and there and keep moving. Like Brer Lion circling his prey.

"Aren't your men from *The* Barbados?" the banker checks the files again.

"Yes."

"Ah well, as you were saying, George."

"Head office," George says the words with disdain, "knows it is always like this at the beginning of the season. We always have cash-flow problems at this time of the year. It ain't nothing new."

"Why?"

"'Cause that's when we have all the expenses of getting the farm ready for the year and no money coming in. The flow will even out throughout the rest of the year. Always does."

"Not really. It hasn't for the last few years. And this year looks no different," King says. This round-house punch staggers George. "I have the accounts right here." King noisily shifts papers in the file, pausing occasionally to hold up a computer printout for closer examination. "In fact, your expenses are way up this year, George, way up compared with this time last year and the year before that, too."

"That's because I have to pay for the plane tickets up front." I think George is holding on here, tying up his opponent while trying to get some life back into his rubbery feet. "We used to pay for them in instalments. We've already cut back as much as we can on the farm, but there're still certain obligations that a farm must meet at this time of the year. And for me, one of them is paying for these tickets from," he pauses purposely, "Barbados."

"And what about the extra medical expenses this year?" the banker asks. "You also have to budget for them. I don't see any provision for them and your expenses are already too high."

"What medical expenses?" Well, count this as a knockdown. No slip here. No off balancing — just a clean knockdown, so start the counting.

"For the men. With all this sickness around. The way that

fellow died back there over the holidays. When we were in The... when we were in Barbados, we made sure we took no chances when dealing with the natives. You got to make contingencies, George. Haven't the government health people contacted you about changes to the medical coverage?"

"No," George says, shaking his head. "What expenses?"

"Oh," the banker says, sounding as if he has spoken too soon. Still, on my scorecard, clearly this is knock-down number two. "Nor the Liaison Officer, he hasn't contacted you either?"

"He called the other day and said he wants to come over and have a meeting with me this afternoon."

"Didn't say about what?"

"I guess it has something to do with plans for this year," George says. "Looks to me like I'm spending more time in *meetings,* just wasting time these days, than on real farm work."

"I see. And you do *plan* to plant tobacco this year, am I right?" King asks, shifting the conversation. But there is defiance in his voice, as if he is throwing George a challenge, daring him to say yes. George is letting his guard down, acting as if the fight is finished. I sense it has only moved to another plane, onto a level where he has no weapons, no defence.

"We gotta plant *some* tobacco. I mean, we just can't stop growing the stuff overnight. We need time to find something new to switch to."

"Of course. And, of course, you also know there is no market for tobacco," King says with condescension. I can feel the big knock-out punch coming. "Times have changed. It's not like when everybody was smoking, when it was cool to light up a cigar. Just the other day, I was reading in one of the Toronto newspapers that the government's planning a total ban on all smoking outside the home. Same thing in the U.S."

Obviously, in this battle, the banker knows he has broken through George's defence, to the point where he can now lecture and George has no choice but to sit and listen. Like a Muhammad Ali taunting a lesser opponent before putting him out of his misery. "Already, you can't smoke in airplanes, in theatres, in restaurants, at work. I myself don't smoke, but I was talking to this fellow in Toronto last week, and he told me he can't even light up a cigar after dinner in his own house without his wife and daughter screaming at him. Something they're teaching the children in school and once it's in the schools... well, you know what I mean. Anyway I got Mrs. Francis to photocopy this article I was reading in the papers from Toronto and I'll give you a copy when you're leaving. But planting tobacco, George, it doesn't look too good."

"We're all trying our best to change," George says softly. The fight is gone. He is about to surrender, perhaps even beg for his life. "There ain't a farmer out there that ain't trying other crops. Personally, we're trying to put some of the land under ginseng, but it takes three years to grow and harvest. The money from the Asian market is good, but three years is a long time."

"I wasn't thinking of ginseng," King says. "Everybody can't get into the same thing."

"What would you replace the tobacco with?"

"Cabbages," the banker says, as if anticipating the question. I watch as George's head drops to his chest, deflated by this wicked straight jab, his neck now sapped of its strength and will. I must have looked like that when Mother Nyame told me about that colour commentating shit. "Don't cabbages come from the same plant family as tobacco? If tobacco grows well out there, then cabbages would too. And have you ever thought of roses, George?"

Now the bank manager is pontificating in victory. It's nauseating, I tell yuh, just watching him *pompasset*, standing over this fallen warrior and daring him to get up. I wonder what Johnny would say if he were witnessing this. Would he, like some sympathetic manager, throw in the towel and end this mismatch, this humiliation?

"At this seminar in Toronto," says this king of the ring and all he surveys, "we were examining the same question you just asked. Government people were there along with our agricultural experts in the bank." Now, he is talking in measured tones, like a boxer carefully building up points, administering a beating at will. What remains is a chore, not a challenge, really. "It appears there is a really big market right here in Canada for cut flowers. I mean, think of yourself as a typical man — when you get the old lady angry, what's the first thing you think about? A bouquet of flowers, right. That's a trick as old as the hills. You'd be surprised at the amount of flowers we import in this country. Billions of dollars every year. Hundreds of billions if you consider the United States and the free-trade agreement. I guess North American men either know how to keep their women happy or they're always making them mad as hell." Indeed, how appropriate: flowers for the victor, nothing for the vanquished. "What do you say, George?"

"I'm willing to try anything," George says. "But with time."

"Another thing, George. I don't see why you need all these men from the islands." Now we dictate the terms of surrender, don't we? "You don't have all that much work for them and we in this branch have been trying to get you guys that import labour to shorten the season."

"But I need the men." How awful, what we are watching and seeing — a last-ditch effort to surrender with at least some pride. "Some of them have been coming to Edgecliff since my grandfather's time, God bless his soul. They've worked for my father and now for me. I just can't let them go. It's a commitment we…"

King doesn't reply. There is no need, and George knows it is pointless explaining further. The banker is staring at him, unimpressed, as if he has tuned out on the conversation. I hope George realizes that the victor always set the terms. "You haven't been reading anything in the newspapers about this sickness, eh?"

"I ain't got time to read. All I know is that I need an extension of the line of credit," George says, using the opening to plead his case. He knows the momentum is against him.

"How much do you have in mind this time, George?" The question comes slowly and coldly.

"Fifty thousand."

"Same terms and conditions?"

"I guess so."

King closes the file and places his elbows on the desk. He looks straight at George, as the door opens and Celia pokes her head in and points to the watch on her wrist. "Although I think you are already too deeply in debt, I am still going to give you an extension." He leans back in his chair, generous of spirit in victory. George relaxes his shoulders, unconsciously signalling final capitulation. "But only twenty-five thousand dollars. That's max. I can let you have that much only."

"That's half what I need!" George shouts. His voice sounds hollow. "What good would that do? I really need seventy-five thousand dollars, until the season gets going and some money starts coming in. But I thought I could squeeze through on fifty. I need the money for new equipment."

"Ever thought of going around to some of those farm auctions and buying used equipment, George? Can be pretty cheap that way."

George flashes a look of anger and bewilderment at him. This man would never understand, he thinks to himself, that only the scumbuckets of the world, only the sleazebags would buy farm equipment to help a bank raise a few thousand dollars, in the process of driving some poor family off its farm. Could he really expect George to buy another farmer's equipment at a bank auction? What nerve! he thinks. Boy, are the vibes from George pounding or what? His grandfather and father would roll over in their graves, George is thinking, as would all the now-dead farmers from around Edgecliff. The boys at the marketing board would never speak to him again. The men in the doughnut shop would spit on him, curse his name. But although these defiant words are on his tongue, the thoughts fighting in his head, he swallows them, succumbing totally to the inevitable.

"Three things you should be thinking of, George: one, buying used equipment — I have included in that package I told you about a list of all the auctions around this part of the world; two, stop growing tobacco and try something new — like the cabbages or roses; and three, use fewer men. It's that simple, George. I've been to *The* Barbados and some of the other islands down there and if I were those men, wild horses couldn't drag me away from that paradise for a place like this. In fact, George, we are making it a condition of the loan that you plant no tobacco this year. Understand?"

With this final uppercut, King gets up and walks out from behind the desk. The extended hand for the obligatory shake indicates the meeting is over, the referee raising the hand of the victor. "Miss Ashford will draw up the papers and get in touch with you, George, before we deposit the money in your account as usual. It's been good talking to you, *finally*." This is in the post-fight interview, when the television cameras hover, when the winner gives the obligatory hug and pretends to be genuinely interested in the welfare of the man he has just thrashed. "And by the way, George, ask your doctor or the regional medical officer for some information on how to protect the men from this sickness. I hear it's becoming a really big concern for the government people. For us too, who must live in this country. Can't have people with incurable diseases running wild on weekends, can we?"

George rises slowly from the chair. Truthfully, he reminds me of the battered boxer who doesn't quite understand how the battle could be over, how the finish is so different from what he expected. So he reluctantly gets off his stool. In his mind there is still so much to talk about. He has to try convincing this bank manager that nobody can change that quickly. But how can he? He is only interested in talking about some stupid disease and roses and cabbages. King stands by the open door politely indicating that George should leave.

In final defeat, George glances at the smiling picture of the man, woman and two children. He realizes what is different about King — he's wearing sunglasses in the picture. Maybe so nobody can see the flash of fire in his eyes, the flashes that George has just seen. Other farmers have talked about the humiliation of begging him not to take away their farm and of seeing only that firm, fiery gaze that made it clear there was no use begging, that the sheriff and the auctioneer had already drawn up the repossession papers. The referee has already counted to ten and is mercifully signalling the end of the battle. So much for the *mano a mano* stuff.

"Celia, give Mr. Stewart one of those packages we're giving to the farmers. The one with the clippings and the brochure on alternate crops. And if you can put your hand on one, give him a copy of the medical handout we've been giving our employees."

"Yes, Mr. King." She hands George the white folder with the name of the bank across the top. There are stacks on the floor beside her desk. "I'll be getting in touch with you about the line of credit, Mr. Stewart," she says. King returns to his office, purposely hitches his belt, as would any boxer hearing the announcer scream those covetous words *and still the undisputed champion*, and closes the door. "This time I hope it won't take so long to get you in."

Still dazed, George walks out of the bank, passing Mrs.

Francis' work station. She doesn't look up at him. He is glad she doesn't, so neither of them have to confront their fears about the changing times.

Outside, George lethargically opens the door to the pickup, moving like a man whose muscles are so sore he doesn't even want to feel the pain of breathing. He looks up at the clock. Three minutes to noon. Christ, he thinks, they didn't even give him his full fifteen minutes. Maybe their lunches are getting cold. A bout that was to last fifteen rounds ends before the fans are even in their seats. Just like the Brown Bomber and Max Schmelling. Remember? Except, in my books, the wrong guy won this time.

George checks his watch to confirm the time. Three minutes is not enough time to get over to the post office and collect the mail before the clerk closes the shutters for lunch. He may as well spend the hour in the doughnut shop across the street. He could buy a cup of coffee and get up to date on the town gossip. It wouldn't make any sense making another trip into town just for the mail, so he'll wait. George considers leaving the truck on the bank's premises and walking over to the doughnut shop. Then he changes his mind. With the way his day is going, he'd be towed away for sure.

Before he gets into the truck, he allows the folder to slip from his hand to the ground. He closes the door and puts the truck in reverse, letting the front wheel run over the white folder now in the black slush. That's what he thinks of the bank and its stupid advice, he tells himself. As he drives away, he sees Celia Ashford coming down the steps for her lunch break. "Damn," George says, as he watches in disbelief as the woman stoops and picks up the bank documents. This is enough to make George give up on plans for the coffee and doughnut, to get away as fast as possible.

He guns the engine and then just as quickly eases his foot off the accelerator. No need to speed, to rush home, he tells himself. There is plenty of time before his next meeting...er, bout. What is the urgency, anyway? Just so he can have another meeting, more bad news. But this one will be different, he tells himself, so he has to be calm and relaxed, if he is to be ready for another fight. This time it will be on his turf, in his house on the farm. And in this meeting with the Liaison Officer, *he*, George Stewart, would be the one laying down the rules. This time, *he* will be the one to beat the shit out of somebody, the one to be firm about sending back home any worker that isn't pulling his weight, no matter how new the worker is to the damn farm. George became so engrossed in his strategy that he forgets all about the doughnuts, and the letters too.

chapter twelve

Johnny pulls the hood of the sweat-stained coat over his head. He glances to his left, at Winston leaning cross-legged against one of the taller trees Timmy and his crew had just finished pruning. Winston, as if aware of the stares, defiantly pulls down his toque over his ears, shutting out all but the music in his ears. Plugged in as usual to his cassette player and radio, this guy is oblivious of the world and the resentment around him. Proof enough, I guess, that, indeed if you are listening my dearest Mother Nyame, that you *can't* teach an old dog new tricks.

Who would believe that this guy Winston could revert so quickly to his old ways? Especially when Johnny appeared to be making good progress guiding him onto the straight and narrow path. I guess some things never change, especially when they have seeped into your bones. One of these vices is laziness; youthfulness and laziness always seem to go together, hand in hand. I don't know of anyone who has found a cure for laziness yet. For what the hell do young people really know, even when they have the latest technology, when they are still green, still wet behind the ears, their heads full with only useless theories, with no experience to balance them?

In my books, the school of hard knocks still counts for something, for a lot, really. As the women back home keep saying, book sense ain't common sense because you really can't tell a man's intelligence from the size of his head. Definitely, a head is for more than just wearing a hat, or, a dingy-looking toque. Some things you just have to learn by experience. Then you store them away in your noggin. Of course, that is providing you are willing to learn and to listen to older heads. And to show respect and have manners. Because there is no short cut. To be young and full of theory is no cure for laziness. Hard work is, though.

See how Johnny is frowning? Those grimaces must tell you something. Instinctively, even if he can't hear me, Johnny knows what I am saying is true. A leader is like that. Any leader worth his salt would recognize the truth in what I am saying. The truth will burn his belly like fire, like swallowing a scalding piece of yam too fast.

And why is this? Well, once again, Johnny doesn't like the way Winston is behaving, and I don't blame him. I would be pissed too. Everybody, with the obvious exception of Winston, has to be aware of what Johnny is thinking. Even Johnny, with the goodness of his heart, can't ignore this guy's antics anymore.

If the boy isn't used to the cold and the constant bending, Johnny is thinking, even if he isn't familiar with the repetitive stooping and standing upright that makes everyone's muscles so sore, he should not make it so obvious. Even Tommy, his hands shaking so badly as he raises the knife to cut the dead branches, his graveyard cough heavy enough to keep him in bed, is putting out the effort on this his first good day in the field.

Johnny looks at Tommy and Winston and I know he is wondering at the difference between these two men. Obviously, one of them has a mortgage back home to pay, a mortgage that is cutting his arse even though he's up here in this cold. But that threat of foreclosure hanging over one man's head and not over the other's shouldn't be that much of a difference. Not unless you are buying my argument that age matters, that young men are useless until they acquire the wisdom of time and a few good debts to straighten them out as men, until they swallow the bile from the disappointment of paying a bill when you're broke, of having one or two young *pickneys* going to bed when you're not sure if the damn children's belly full o' *hungriness* or *bittle*.

Some men, if you can call them that, run away fast, fast from facing these situations. They just take up the two good feet God give them and just run, disappearing into the darkness, heading for places they don't know, running from the responsibilities and commitments they know. That's why I admire all these men here in the field. The ones that stay behind as real men. Despite all the hardships, they work diligently, from sunrise to sunset, so they can have a dollar in their pockets. Every last one of them works.

Everyone but Winston. This is because quite simply everyone but this boy has a purpose in life. I can't offer any other excuse; I won't try to defend the indefensible. Like Tommy, I like to speak the truth, even if it is as hard and sharp as nails. The truth will set you free; you must shout it from the mighty mountain top, the prodigious hilltops, the curvaceous peaks, the stone mountains, the lookout mountains and from every hill and molehill. And if I may add this line to that old refrain, from even the snow-capped Rockies to the cold-arse apple fields of Ontario. Let truth, like freedom, ring. And common sense too.

For the one truth every last one of the men realizes is that the faster they finish this chore the sooner they can return to the warmth of the cabin. That makes sense to me. That kind of thinking is as clear as a whistle, a sign of the wisdom coming through experience. Which only goes to say that, indeed, in my heart, I cannot blame anyone for feeling resentment. Not at all, I can't set up my face, can't really get annoyed, at anyone getting angry with this Winston, this keep-back.

And there are other truths too. On top of everything else, the wind is biting and getting colder by the minute. The men are hungry. It is early in the season, so their bones are sore. All around it's just uncomfortable, plain and simple. But the men have a job to finish. A task to complete by day's end if the farm is to start getting back on schedule for the expected planting and the delayed season. In a case like this, teamwork matters. Nobody can afford to carry a keep-back; everybody should pull his own weight, behave like a man. Teamwork is the key. On a day like today, especially when it turns so cold unexpectedly, this is what decides how soon we can all be slamming a few dominoes and drinking a cup of warm coffee back in the little shelter we call home. Brother, these are the cold-arse facts of life on this farm.

Waiting for us inside that cabin is not only the warmth and comfort of a familiar place, but the doughnuts and beer Mr. Stewart picked up from town. There is also the fight on television, on the American station we get when the reception is good. Yes, the first big fight of the season. The men have already made their bets, although I don't think anyone dares to bet on the white boxer. To tell the truth, nobody even knows the names of the fighters, has never heard of them before, actually. But when there is a boxing match between a white fellow and a Black, the decision is automatic. Everybody expects one decision, and in boxing, the result is even more certain than the coming of spring. Blacks and boxing, just like that melanin and testosterone I keep talking about, that the Prophet always talked about.

So we have this fight to look forward to, if everybody contributes and we can all get out of this cold that is busting we arses, making our balls feel all swibbled up and small; we can watch this whatever's-his-name beating the shit out of this white guy. The boxing, just seeing the Black man all sweaty, throwing them lefts and rights, would warm up every part of any Black man's anatomy, if you ask me. And after the fight, a few of the boys might stay up to take in a basketball game. Of course, here again seeing the basketball depends on the reception from the American station in Detroit. If everything fails, if there is no boxing or basketball on the tube, then there is bound to be at least a hockey play-off game on the Canadian station. Of course, only a few of the men would watch, and then only to kill the boredom, an excuse for the opportunity to eat doughnuts and drink Mr.

Stewart's beer, while others just play dominoes and quarrel with one another. But, as you know, all of this depends on the damn television working. I really think Delbert is on to something when he says that maybe the men should throw a few dollars into a hat and buy a new television. Or maybe they can ask the Liaison Officer to find a good second-hand set, as long as it ain't from no farm auction. The men wouldn't like that.

Johnny knows how anxious the men are to get out of the cold. Besides boxing and basketball, they're also interested in what is happening in the Grapefruit League at the start of the baseball season. Once that season gets going, everyone would be rooting for his own team. I expect even more fights between the men and Winston over the boom-box radio will break out. Winston, poor guy, still can't get it through his head that the men want to listen to sports and maybe the news, not music. And that is all he listens to, music. Always searching for some new station, when all the men want him to do is keep his arse quiet and leave the damn radio on the all-sports station. That's why he always has the cassette player plugged into his ears. When the batteries run out, all hell breaks loose with him and the boom box, until he somehow manages to get a new set of batteries.

Now you can put yourself in Johnny's shoes. He sees all of this in front of him — the anxiety and the celebrations. And he knows the frustration and resentment, the isolation from receiving the men's anger, even if unspoken, is enveloping Winston. Johnny shakes his head. The sooner the men get the day's chores over with, the sooner they can relax and start doing all these things that make them happy, that make them bond as a team.

So I hope you now have a better understanding why Johnny is so upset at Winston. I am taking this time to explain it all because I feel in my bones that something is about to happen. Everyone in this field understands the situation. Everyone but this little fool, the dreamer, the spoiled child. How many times do the men have to tell him that everyone must pull together? I mean, they told him that much the very first night on the farm. Otherwise, why do you think big men would dress up in hoods and all that foolishness, tramping through the snow and ice on their very first night back up here, if it wasn't to bring home to this guy the truth that they can only get by, can only succeed, as a team? At this stage of the game, the men don't think they should be telling this guy the same thing over and over a million times. I don't blame them for thinking this way.

So lately, the men hardly say anything to Winston. When they do, whatever they say is usually accompanied by a curse or two. Sometimes it is an entire phrase, or even a sentence, enough to turn the whitest hair blue, as the people like to say back home. When the men done talk, nobody can doubt how they feel toward Winston. There can be no doubts about anything. These men can have an acid tongue when they're ready. Yet even the cussing is not affecting Winston. Otherwise, why would he goof off now? I tell you, it must be really bad when even Johnny, a man of such tolerance, gets offended. Must be really bad, in truth, when Johnny realizes he cannot hold back the men for too much longer, cannot prevent them from strangling this guy. Who can blame them for these thoughts? Certainly not me. And I don't think you will either.

Still, let me give you one more little bit of insight. Of late, even Johnny cannot hide his own growing impatience with Winston. This is very important. You see, sometimes I hear when Johnny hints to this youngster, telling him that he should shape up a bit, pull his weight, show a bit more initiative. But you know Johnny. He would rather hint at these things. That is where, be Christ, I fault him. The man's too soft with this Winston fellow; I mean he acts like he is a ripe pawpaw, so softy-softy, as if this guy has something on him. So Winston has to read between the lines to get the message from Johnny. Me, I would let it hang out. And as everybody done know, my mouth ain't have no cover. I can't pretend 'cause nobody ain't going to rub shit in my mouth and tell me it's black cake. I ain't that foolish or bewitched. And besides, nobody never work no obeah on me or rub oil to-turn-muh-head on the I and I.

When I'm really angry, I raise my voice: instantly everybody knows how I feel. They don't have to rely on no hints. I'm just like most of the men on this farm, like the ones with balls enough to complain bluntly to Johnny about this fellow. I don't blame them. I would do the same. 'Cause I don't agree with Johnny that a kind word turns away no wrath, or whatever apology he makes for not confronting Winston. How long can he assuage the men, when Winston does not help his own cause, when he continues to mope around, and in full view at that, not doing one damn thing to help out? And on one of the coldest days, *rastah*.

To tell the truth, I really admire the men for their patience; and I thank God they have so much forbearance. For at any moment, I swear, I expect one of these men to stop all this grumbling, rake up his hand and give Winston a good cuff right up against the head. That would teach him. Mark my word. It won't be too long before the men settle this matter one way or another.

But, at last, Johnny appears to be coming to his senses. He can't pretend any longer not to notice; he cannot cover for this boy forever. Johnny knows the youngster's *don't-carish* attitude can only cause greater hard feelings among the men. I mean, who, in the middle of the day, in the middle of a field, has the time to listen to music on a Walkman, or to search for some radio station playing music he likes? Only the Brer Dreamer.

I just hope he ain't somehow managed to find a way to listen to that other storyteller talking about him. There is something about that boy and his music, something that could destroy what we have here on this farm. Especially if he starts believing in his dreams, starts listening to the quiet voice over his shoulder. I hope his storyteller is truthful enough to point out how self-centred and selfish this Winston is being. I hope the voice over Winston's shoulder tells him the truth. Otherwise, what use is it? I know I would demand the truth, but maybe my word on its own isn't good enough any longer.

Still, I cannot see how any objective person could say anything different about this youngster, or about events on this farm for that matter. A real storyteller would only have to compare Winston's behaviour to that of the other men, all of whom are facing the same difficulties as Winston. None of the men likes working in the open fields so early in the year. And if they find out that Winston is drawing the same pay for doing less work, they are bound to rebel and maybe even, as I predict, strike the boy. Johnny would have to step in. But even such intervention carries a risk of further strife and divisions. For my part, I would think the men justified in claiming Johnny is condoning slackness. After all, nobody else gets to listen to a damn radio when they should be working.

As I was saying, Johnny is aware of the growing resentment. He also knows he cannot have this thinking spreading like some uncultured disease, like a nasty virus, across the farm. The price would be too high. Take my word, I know what I am talking about. I've seen the results of this kind of thing, have them indelibly inscribed on my brain, recall them whenever I think of the Prophet. No wonder he has been so long in coming back.

Johnny has to take care to inoculate and isolate this virus. 'Cause any rebellion or bad feelings so early in the season would destroy the camaraderie. That would be a disaster, almost as bad as something happening to the crops themselves in those early weeks and months after the planting, something to stunt the growth or even kill the damn plants. Then even the dumbest idiot won't have to ask what will become of the men on this

Program. This resentment, if it remains unchecked, is bound to hurt the friendship the men need to keep them working as a team. Remember when the foolish Brer Horse and his wife started snapping at each other instead of pulling in the same direction? You should never be unevenly yoked. And there must be a leader, with a strong, firm hand on the reins.

It is clear as sunlight: teamwork will be extremely vital during the harvesting, when everyone works minimum shifts of eighteen hours, seven days a week, when everyone is so tired his nerves are on edge. Take it from me, it is then that you need a friend. This is when you can't afford the luxury of second-guessing anyone's intention. If you destroy that confidence so early in the season, or if it doesn't develop at all after a bad start, then what will be left for those long dark days of the harvest?

Yes, it is at the harvesting that the men need one another most. When they rely on one another even for the small things of life. When every apple, plum, tomato or tobacco leaf the man next to you picks means you won't have to do it, means that someone else doesn't have to expend the energy, doesn't have to spend another minute in the field.

Johnny knows he cannot risk destroying this bond. In fact, I wonder why, knowing all this, he does not act quicker to stamp out this stupidity of Winston's. I think too much is at stake for him to gamble that this boy will come around on his own. Quite frankly, this is where Johnny must show his leadership. Otherwise, Winston will continue just doing what he's doing. And what is he doing? Well, even a blind man can see that this pretend rebellion, this insipid laziness, this selfishness and thoughtlessness by this young punk, is really at heart an incipient challenge to Johnny's leadership. Nothing more, nothing less — a challenge to Johnny. Winston is simply saying, let's see who has the biggest balls 'round here, fella. Show me yours and I'll show you mine. So let's get it on, man.

And so much comes with this challenge. So much negativity. If it spread, such open rebelliousness, the men could start thinking of themselves as individuals. They might forget that because they are so isolated on this farm, that when the going gets really tough, they will need one another. None of them could really stand alone and hope to survive. Johnny knows the results of an upsurge in selfishness, of every man trying to cook for himself. He could imagine the fury every evening from every man, tired and hungry, fighting over the rights to the single stove. He knows too what happens when the men refuse to share a slice of bread or soap powder for washing, when everyone miserly holds on to even the occasional mouthful of cough medicine or ganja cigarettes. That is the worst thing that could happen to this team.

But obviously, Winston doesn't know what he is starting. I hope you don't mind my dwelling on this matter, but this is clearly another example, I tell yuh, of the need for wisdom from the school of hard knocks, from relying on the experienced and trusted. Do you remember the story of the idiot who opened the Pandora's box, not knowing what would jump out? The same thing is happening here with Winston throwing down this challenge to Johnny. I mean just look at this Winston fellow, so full of vim and youth, acting just like some new ram on the scene, deliberately invading the territory the older ram marked off with his piss, clearly challenging, clearly and openly *dissing* the older fellow. Beating his chest, flexing his muscles. But in offering this challenge, he runs the risk of disrupting all the well-established patterns on this farm. With this challenge, the old order will be questioned and perhaps thrown out, with nobody knowing what, if anything at all, will replace it. Change for change's sake, I guess.

History tells me what the outcome will be. On this farm, and I am as sure of this as I am of the stars in the heavens, the result would simply reduce the men to a collection of individuals. I don't even have to stray into the area of predicting or extrapolating, although as you know I can do that as a so-called colour commentator. But history is replete with these examples, so I am not adventurous here in saying the following: That because of the breakdown in order, by disrupting the life that everyone knows, it would be easy for any of these men to forget, or even not to care, that a companion is running low on soap, deodorant, cigarettes even, on money for the mortgage back home. They will not care that someone, still in the field, needs help to wash the underwear soaking in the basin with the dingy soapy water for so many days. If selfishness steps in, what next? Resorting to stealing, questioning the deservedness of pay cheques, carrying grudges? And then the fights, with knives, forks, farm implements and, the most cutting of all, words. Harsh words.

Johnny knows he cannot let this happen. They left Barbados as a team. They would have to survive as one. He will have to reinforce his authority one way or the other. He will have to maintain predictability at all costs.

Without saying a word, Johnny resumes cutting the dried twigs. From the corner of his eye, he watches Winston walking aimlessly out of the orchard onto the lane between the two apple groves. Now, Winston is leaning on the tractor on which the foreman had perched for most of the day before walking off into the distance. The foreman climbed down because of a sharp drop in the temperature. Obviously, he couldn't take it any longer and headed for the warmth of the farm house and the much-heralded meeting with the Liaison Officer. Minutes before he left, the Liaison Officer's car swung into the driveway but is now hidden from view by the house. The tractor is in full sight of the farm house. Johnny knows it is common for people to spy on them from the back windows of the house. Several times, the Liaison Officer has told him things that he could only know from watching the men or from having someone spy on them, possibly from the kitchen. Winston doesn't know this, doesn't know so many things.

Johnny shakes his head and continues to prune the tree. He has to keep his tongue under control. He feels it wouldn't make sense bawling him out in front of the others. Maybe he'll have a quiet word with him later. In the meantime, he hopes nobody notices, or that Winston picks up his knife again soon and at least looks busy. Boy, I tell yuh, I have this problem with people who are just too scared of confrontation. You know, people who only want appeasement. If Johnny had been around then, with his appeasement shit and not wanting to fight publicly, Hitler would still control the world; Mandela would still be breaking rocks on Robben Island. If Johnny were a leader during slavery, none of these men would be free today, not with his unwillingness to fight. I tell yuh, there comes a time when a man has no choice but to fight. And you know I love a good fight. Brute force — sometimes that's all it takes to settle an issue, especially when the alternative is to talk until you are blue in the face. Look at this youngster sauntering off wherever his mind takes him, Walkman blaring in his ears, contemptuously drowning out everyone and everything within a hundred miles of him.

Somewhere in the distance, Johnny hears an engine roar to life. It is rough and in need of oiling. Momentarily, it takes his mind off Winston. The noise is coming from west of where they are standing, in the direction the foreman went. Almost immediately, Johnny closes his mind to the sound, letting it become no more worthy of attention than the whistling of the wind through the trees or the birds chirping in the distance.

"Johnny, what that youngster doing over there?" Tommy whispers under his breath. "Look at him with them earphones in his ears. He's listening to that Walkman as if he's back home. It looks to me like he wants to make things bad for all o' we or something, eh. He does be always like this all the time?"

Johnny doesn't answer. He doesn't want Tommy to join the group already thinking the youngster should be sent back home. "Look, Johnny, you better go and talk with that boy before the other fellows see what the *rass* he's doing and get mad as hell. He didn't do one arse this whole day, if you ask me."

"Okay," Johnny whispers. "I'll be back." See what I tell yuh? If Tommy notices, Johnny has to know the others are aware also. Obviously, he cannot wait until later to talk to Winston. "Keep cutting 'til I get back."

Johnny sticks the tip of the pruning knife into the frozen earth under the tree. Slowly, he shuffles off toward Winston, trying not to attract attention as he passes the men.

"Look here, boy," he scolds when he is close to Winston. He is still trying to keep his voice low. "Why don't you try and make yourself look busy, nuh, man? You don't know the people in the house over there," he jerks his head in the direction of the farm house, "could be watching you all like now."

"What you want me to do if I'm tired, man?" Winston shoots, a wave of anger washing over his face. One of the speakers from the earphones drops to his waist. The volume from the other causes him to shout. "I hate this bloody place. I hate this work. I hate this cold. I hate it. I hate it. I hate it." None of the men would talk to him like that, Johnny thinks.

"So don't come saying anything to me, man," Winston continues. "'Cause I ain't used to all this hard work in this blasted cold. I got to rest now and then to get my strength back. I ain't used to all this hard work, not like all of you hard-back people. So leave me 'lone to listen to my music and catch myself."

Winston wipes his nose with the back of his hand and flounces off. Almost as an afterthought he adds, "Think I care who watching or not watching me. The Liaison Officer doesn't have to hide and pimp after me; he can come out in the clear and see what I'm doing."

"Nobody stopping you from takin' a rest now and then," Johnny calls after him. He is now forced to raise his voice as Winston walks away. Johnny sound so sympathetic it is enough to make anyone puke. Yet it is clear that the unexpected rebuke still stings, as painful as if the young man had slapped Johnny in the face. It forces Johnny on the defensive despite his moral authority to confront Winston. The men stop pruning and look in the direction from which the voices are coming.

"You can take a rest, but don't make it look so plain," Johnny shouts, obviously getting mad and rising to the challenge. "We can't keep covering for you, not when you're marching off and leaning up against some tree every five minutes. And in full view, too."

Now Johnny is angry with himself. With the men watching, he is in a bind. The old ram, if I may say so, can no longer make believe that the young pretender has not invaded his territory. All pretence is now stripped away. We are facing that *mano a mano* situation. I predict it can only get worse with he and Winston leaving each other no chance to extricate themselves from this public dispute. And, Johnny is painfully aware, this upstart is openly challenging his authority. There can be no doubt. The only solution, as I see it, is for Johnny to slap down this punk. He has to show there is only one authority, one leader on this farm. Then I, too, will have the legitimacy to say to that usurper narrating the other story about this farm not to be so presumptuous. My man is still in control; no little boy is going to upstage him; the same way that I am in control.

"I don't want nobody covering for me," Winston shouts. I can hear deep anger, frustration in his words. He throws out the words like missiles from a cannon aimed at anyone in its way. "Let me tell all of you something right now: as long as I'm on this Program, when I'm tired, I'm going to pick a rest regardless of who like it or who's watching. I ain't no bloody slave for nobody, man."

Winston turns around to face Johnny. He defiantly straps on the earphones and cranks up the volume. Now, he is walking backwards, away from Johnny and the men, but into a mammoth piece of farm machinery coasting clumsily between the groves. As it moves, it belches black smoke. Winston cannot hear it. The driver is facing the other way, unaware of Winston walking into the path of the machine with its exposed and rusted blades.

With swiftness that belies his casual approach, Johnny lurches and takes Winston tumbling into the trees with a body tackle. Instinctively, Winston, thinking he is under attack, screams at the top of his voice and begins defending himself. They roll under the trees, the younger man coming out underneath the pile, the earphones and the Walkman long separated. As they struggle on the wet grass, the machine rumbles by, its blades picking up pieces of stick and clumps of grass and spitting them out to the sides in millions of little pieces.

Johnny gets to his feet slowly. The machine lumbers on, destroying all in its path. Instantly, Winston's anger turns to horror when he realizes the close call. He remains seated on the wet grass, a frozen look on his face, with Johnny towering over him. The enraged foreman, now aware of what is happening, swears loudly at Johnny and Winston and raises an index finger at them.

Winston slowly stands to his full height. He replaces the toque on his head, pulling it over his ears, and searches for the Walkman. "Christ, what happen' there?" he asks with a mixture of bewilderment and astonishment. I guess he can still feel the strength of the older man's hand. Now he knows not to mess with Johnny. There isn't going to be any of this shit about the king is dead, long live the king. There can only be one leader on this farm, and it is Johnny. The same way there can be only one Prophet and he must return to complete his work, to lead his people into a new land. The same way there can only be one storyteller on this farm, and it must be me. For I am storyteller, grandmother.

"Look, all I'm going to tell you," Johnny says through closed teeth. He is furious, out of breath and systematically clenching and unclenching his massive fists as if he wants to pound some good sense into Winston's head. "All I'll tell you is that you gotta start looking after yourself, you hear me? You ain't no damn baby. And watch your bloody mouth, too. Watch how you talk to people 'round here."

Tommy runs over and places himself between the two men. He puts his trembling hands on Johnny's shoulders, allowing Winston to back away. "Don't bother to bring yourself in no trouble with this half-ripe young fellow, Johnny. We done know he only got a lot o' piss in he balls and don't know no better. And, from the way he's behaving, you can bet your last dollar he ain't going to be around here too long. He can't last with all that piss in him."

"He won't be any fucking good dead." Now Johnny is screaming, and boy what a temper! Even I have rarely seen this side of the old guy. "Let me tell him that. Piss or no piss." Johnny is still trying to get around Tommy to Winston. "Remember Cleveland? Twelve years ago this April? Many o' you here on this farm won't even know who Cleveland is, far less what happen' to him. He was fooling around too. Just like just now. In front o' one o' them said same machines. The first machine like that we ever had on this farm."

As Johnny talks he begins to calming down. Tommy still remains between the two men. Others are gathering around.

"Christ," Johnny continues. "I never hear a man scream so long; so loud when the damn thing hit he. Like when the butcher comes to the house to slaughter a pig back home, how it squeals and squeals from the first stick o' the knife. Must have bre'k every bone in his body. Every one o' them. Like pieces o' dry stick or dried sugar cane that you can bre'k across your own knees. You could hear them cracking. The doctor say he was long dead before the fucking thing done pass over he."

"You mean these things so dangerous," Winston asks with wide-eyed bafflement, still adjusting his toque. All the while he is continuing to put distance between himself and Johnny. But the encircling men hem them in, creating a ring from which neither can escape still holding his shame. No escape, the battle to the death. Just like in the school yard, when the boys form a ring and the two combatants inside have to fight until one wins, until one surrenders totally and abjectly. There can be no retreat. The foreman parks the machine and marches back furiously. It all comes down to this pivotal moment. I tell yuh, may the better man win!

"All I'll tell you is that they shipped Cleveland back home in a pine box. So mashed up his own family couldn't even see his face at the funeral. They just dump him in a goddamn hole right there in Westbury Cemetery back home as if he was some pauper."

"But the family must get something from the government," Tommy says. "Some kind o' insurance, eh?"

"Goddamn, you people make me so sick!" Johnny's still shouting. "Here I am trying to show this guy how dangerous a farm is and you can only start talking some foolishness 'bout insurance money again. Why you so interested in insurance? I don't know why you gotta be talking 'bout insurance money morning, noon and night."

"Don't get angry with me," Tommy pleads. He, too, takes a few steps backwards, as if he expects Johnny to lash out at him with his fists. "Just that we gotta realize that on a farm like this anything can happen. We gotta be prepared for the worse and make sure we got everything in order."

"I don't want to hear no more 'bout insurance money, right!" Johnny snaps. "Nobody up here ain't planning on deading off, you hear me. We come up here together, as a team, and all o' we're going back home together, as a team. Nobody deading off."

The foreman arrives and the men start dispersing. How anticlimactic, and it's all because of Tommy and his insurance foolishness. I'm surprised at Tommy. Why doesn't this idiot go further? I mean, why doesn't this fool use that very moment to ask Johnny about the insurance on the houses back in Barbados, if the Liaison Officer told him anything about the insurance? What bad timing! 'Cause at this moment, when something so pressing as who has the authority on this farm is about to be settled, everyone is really interested in insurance. Right? My god, what could Tommy be thinking? I mean, you must have heard of King Ja Ja and of King James the Fifth, so let's get out the crown and proclaim this one here the fool he is, a real King Foolie the Fifth. How could he let Winston get away? Like opening a hole in that school yard ring and letting one of them get away to run to the school-ma'm for help. And before Johnny could put his hand on Winston and teach him a lesson or two. Now, in front the foreman, obviously Johnny can't belt this guy a few good ones. All because of Tommy, the moment passes resolving nothing. "Lashley," the foreman says, just like any monitor acting for the school principal, "come with me. Let's go and talk to Mr. Stewart."

"I think Mr. Stewart went into town, Bob," Johnny says quickly. Surprisingly, he appears calmer. "Let the boy continue working. If he leave now he'd only get docked the full day and lose the pay."

"Well, I don't see why not," the foreman says. "I don't see why not."

"Of course," Johnny says. "That is unless you want to pay

him a day's wages for not working and then have to face all these men here." He raises his hand in gesture toward the other workers. "For treating one man different from the rest."

The foreman thinks for a moment. He seems torn between his feelings and the financial reality of what Johnny is telling him. "Look," he starts gingerly, as if feeling compelled to explain, "the short time I've been here helping out George, I've been watching this guy here. I don't think he's worked one full day yet. And it ain't me alone that notice it. Mr. Stewart too. This farm can't afford any loafers."

"That's okay, Bob," Johnny says forcefully. "If it's a problem, then it's a problem for we the workers. Remember, we agree as a team to do this job. As a team. If we, as a team, ain't happy with how a fellow is working out, then as a team, we'd raise that with the Liaison Officer ourselves and get that straightened out *weself*."

Turning to Winston, Johnny says, "Why don't you go back to the cabin over there and start helping Smokie to prepare the food for today? He might need some help."

Winston walks away, with his tail between his legs. The foreman raises his hands, either in frustration or as an indication he is washing them of the issue, and likewise begins walking toward the machine. Johnny picks up his knife from under the tree and continues pruning. Tommy, to his left, breaks into another prolonged fit of coughing. He sounds like one of those drakes honking.

"Careful, Johnny," Tommy says between the coughs. Only Tommy appears to realize how much Johnny is still seething. "See that you don't cut off a finger, now," he says. "Not unless you want some...*insurance*."

"And you're a next one," Johnny grunts. "Insurance money!"

But the honking, from deep in Tommy's chest, drowns him out.

The Liaison Officer, in an immaculate black winter coat that, so help me God, really looks like a boxer's robe, comes into the cabin minutes after the last of the men returns from the field. He is carrying a brown cardboard box which he places on the table, using it to push aside the scattered dominoes. The foreman, George Stewart, Mary and their daughter Jessica quickly follow him into the room, walking single file, as if in some order of precedence. Without being called, the men gather around the table, not rushing off as usual to wash the day's sweat and dirt off themselves, to harass Smokie about his cooking or to finish the laundry soaking from the morning, or even the previous day.

The appearance of all these important people at once points to something meaningful, especially the presence of the Liaison Officer, in the cabin for the first time this season. The men wait expectantly, watching the officer adjust his coat around himself. They try to read the expression on the faces of the visitors, but I don't think the men are coming up with anything. I hate it when the tension is this heavy. It makes me so nervous.

"How all you guys feeling?" the officer finally asks in a soft voice. He sounds nothing like the man giving the harangue the last time he spoke with us at the airport in Barbados. This makes everybody even more nervous. This man likes to blow his own horn, very loudly too, at every opportunity. When he doesn't, well look out. Something is definitely wrong. Now, he is looking at the men around him, staring like a doctor into their faces, as if trying to identify those that might be sick. Outside, the darkness is settling over the farm, the dusk not as heavy and thick as the day before. So I guess there is some hope that the longer days will lead to spring. But who can know for sure, this is Canada and the weather is always freakish.

"I know it's still a bit cold out there," the Officer begins, putting his coat on the back of a chair near the table and flexing his muscles. "But you guys can take it. In fact, I was listening to my car radio on the way in and I heard the weather man say we can expect better, warmer weather, from this point on."

The Stewart family drifts around the room, still in their coats, looking anxious to flee the house as soon as this errand is over. Or, maybe, they are keeping their coats on for some kind of protection. I don't know, but it looks kinda suspicious to me.

The Officer continues to examine the faces of the men, stopping briefly to stare at Winston, who has an awkward expression on his face, as if, at first blush, he is sceptical of the words of the government official. The officer is about to publicly rebuke Winston, openly drawing to his attention the unfavourable reports from the foreman, when it occurs to him that Winston might not have heard a single word. He is too busy making eyes at Jessica, obviously flirting with him too, and under her parents' noses. The officer smiles.

What can you do with young people? This Winston is just like his uncle, the one working in the Prime Minister's office back home. The Liaison Officer can already hear the uncle squealing with delightful laughter when he reports to him, maybe as early as his next phone call home, the audacity of this young Lashley. Flirting with the boss' daughter right out in the open. As if he doesn't really think that he is a Black man.

The Officer smiles to himself. He could imagine what the Stewarts would say if they discovered this flirting. And all this time I am thinking of that saying by the Prophet: *We must prevent both consequences. No real race-loving white man wants to destroy the purity of his race, and no real Negro conscious of himself wants to die, hence there is room for an understanding, and an adjustment. And that is what we must seek.* Yes, this is the Prophet at his best on this miscegenation nonsense, saying so boldly, even if some now say so foolishly: *The White American*

Society, Anglo-Saxon Clubs, and Ku Klux Klan have my full sympathy in fighting for a pure white race, even as we are fighting for a pure Negro race.

Ah, young people, this one has probably never ever heard of the Prophet. Winston is truly Barbadian, full of balls, and daring enough to be making eyes with the farmer's daughter. Just like all the men the Officer knows, including himself. What they wouldn't do for a skirt. And that was why he had to talk to the men seriously.

"The reason that I'm here, and that Mr. and Mrs. Stewart are here too, is to discuss something serious with all you men," the Officer says. "Now, let's be frank. I know men will be men. I'm a man too, so I know what I'm talking about. And I know it ain't no fun living up here on a farm. You guys look forward to going into town on Friday and Saturday nights, when you can get a piece o' tail, don't you."

He stops for the buzz to go around the room. Between you and me, it's really funny, and noticeable, how the vibes actually diminish when a person is speaking; they are so much stronger when they are just thoughts.

"Heck, I don't blame them neither," George Stewart says. "I provide the transportation, so I guess I'm as much an accomplice. I remember when the men first started coming to Edgecliff, how I used to drive the truck into town and wait for the men while they had their fun. Sometimes we used to be gone for an entire weekend, right Johnny? Cross the border into Michigan. They used to come back on the farm just in time to start work Monday morning, most of them flat broke too and having to borrow against the next week's wages to be able to send home even a small remittance. That's when you people in the government decided to impose the forced savings at source. But these days, the Officer is right, everybody got to be careful."

"That's what I'm talking about," the Officer says. "Guys, you got to be safe. You got to protect yourselves. I'll be the last person to say don't have any fun. After all men'll be men. But I gotta tell yuh: be safe. Use some of these things here in this box."

He reaches over to the table and turns the box over. Hundreds of condoms in all colours and shapes pour out, some spilling onto the floor. The men laugh nervously. Tommy breaks into an even louder coughing fit and leaves the room.

"I know some of you find it funny," the government representative says. "I know some of you, as men, swear never to use these things. But you got to. You got to be careful. With all these strange sickness knocking around, you never know what you'd butt up on, if you're not protected. And I ain't talking about a clap or anything so, like when one of you can't pee you ask Mr. Stewart for a phone call and I come and take you to the doctor for a couple of injections to set you straight. I ain't talking about that. So walk with these in your pocket. That is all I have to say. 'Cause if Grafton did use one or two o' these he might still be around today."

The formal part of the meeting is ended. Johnny watches as the men hover around the Liaison Officer and George Stewart with their questions about everything except what they just heard.

"And how you're finding the farm work?" Mary Stewart is asking someone to Johnny's right.

"Fine, ma'am. Just fine." Johnny turns to see Winston, a broad smile on his face.

"I'm glad you're liking it," Mary Stewart says. "When I first saw you I said to George he's just a boy. They seem to be getting younger and younger as the years go by. Or maybe I'm getting older. But you're settling in, eh?"

"Yes, ma'am." Winston might be answering Mrs. Stewart with his voice, but his eyes are communicating something else entirely with Jessica. And she is sending back the same messages, laughing with her eyes. Johnny notices as Winston passes by and Jessica gives him what could only be the batteries for that stupid Walkman that almost cost him his life a few hours earlier.

Idiots, Johnny thinks. The two of them will only create more problems if they start anything, if they take this flirting any further. He storms away to look for Tommy. Johnny also knows it is time for him to have a chat with the Liaison Officer about Tommy seeing a doctor.

chapter thirteen

From the outer room, the voices of the men seep through the half-open bedroom door. Irritatingly, they arrive in competition with the whistling sounds of cold air burrowing through the cracks in the sides of the cabin. Nothing is tolerable any longer: not the lingering cold, not the isolation and uncertainty; everything, it now seems, is simply vexing to the spirit and harmful to the body.

Together, the voices and the taunts of the wind are bringing the same frightening messages of continuity and hopelessness to Johnny sitting silently on his cot reading his grandfather's diaries. Like a hawk, I watch him flipping through the pages, feeling as if I am observing a stranger. You got to be so careful these days, trust nobody and nothing. And as I watch him, I can't help wondering about the changes overtaking this man of late. It is true, I guess: you can spend a lifetime with a man and still not know with whom you're really dealing. So many changes in his mind, so many head trips of late, that he does not seem a bit concerned that this bloody cold weather continues to hold the farm, the entire country really, in a grip much longer and firmer than ever experienced.

Once upon a time, not so long ago, these things would matter to Johnny. They wouldn't let him sleep, would make him wonder day and night what would happen to the men in his charge. Now, nothing seems to intrude into Johnny's private world. Not even the voices or the wind. Not even his gut instincts as a leader. Changes. Like him gone foolish or something.

And it's all because of those damn diaries. Frightening tools,

I tell yuh, that's what half-baked diaries can become in the wrong hands. Those diaries and the ranting and raving by someone called The Minister, somebody claiming the mantle left vacant since the Prophet, this person, I dare say, who follows the teachings of one Fard Wallace, who if you remember turned up across the border there in Michigan with another road map to the Black man's redemption but is supposedly just another itinerant Bajan immigrant, just like these men here. But once again on such a matter as the one about this Fard and his roots, I got to say *Jack Mandora, me ain't tek none* 'cause there are some things I am not willing to swear about.

Still, we hear this pretender on those radio stations coming across the border, the same stations that this idiot Winston listens to when he is not moping over that tasteless, insipid music. The same preaching and lectures that Timmy and his Black power shit are turning these simple men onto. I have no doubts whatsoever that this man, The Minister, isn't the Prophet, he just can't be, even though they appear to have so much in common.

So many changes, and all of them telling me just one thing: how in the absence of strong and firm leadership it is so easy to totally befuddle some people, even those from whom you expect better. Even Johnny. For as the saying goes, where there is no vision the people perish. And, sad to say, these days I see no vision, not for these men on Edgecliff, and not for Black men — as long as Mother Nyame remains in charge of all our stories.

Sometimes, here at Edgecliff, the voices and the wind are no more than an indecipherable din, humming and steady. And like the wind, when fortified by a mean gust, the voices are at times boisterous, bubbling, loud and antagonistic, as noticeable as the frenzied draft whipping up the ice and snow outside. Other times, it is no more than when in their dying wane, these northern winds angrily bash the remnants of the slowly receding winter against the cabin. Voices of promise that are as effective as the warm southern breezes rising to confront the cold but which manage to succeed only in cloaking the farm in dense fog.

From the sounds alone, Johnny knows the men are beginning their nightly game of dominoes. This is their main recreation. Their ritual. Johnny hears them laughing, shouting and teasing one another. This noise should be reassuring. A sign that, finally, life is falling into a pattern. An understanding that, ultimately, the warm weather must arrive to break the unrelenting grasp of this cold. The signs are everywhere, as ubiquitous in the barracks as the buds struggling on the outside against greater odds this year. If there must be change, this is one I like and support. Controllable and expected change, not haphazard and scatter-brained, not opening a bottle and just letting a genie jump out. That is madness.

But change that is predictable. So Preacher Man no longer talks at every chance about religion and the need for the men to save their souls. The annoying vigour and constant proselytizing born of his first Sundays back at church is waning. No longer does he preach at the faintest opportunity, his mind concerned more about temporal man now than with the spiritual or celestial. A good change, if I may say so. Only Timmy is still so harshly branding all the men, including himself, mere slaves for maintaining a system that works against them, that keeps poor people the world over subjugated. But even here, the expected changes are beginning to appear. The militant magazines from Detroit, the same ones that reinforce these hostile views, are once again piling up, waiting for Timmy to find the time to read them and then to harangue his colleagues with his newly found knowledge. That will end soon. If everything goes as expected, Timmy won't have time for the magazines until he unties a bundle of them in Barbados, and that's providing the government people at the airport don't deem them seditious and confiscate the whole lot. Otherwise, that's when he'll catch up on his reading, just in time to replenish his anger for the next trip up. Until then, he will have to make do with the Minister's rantings, and that too might become limited when the major league baseball season gets in full swing.

Over the voices, Johnny hears the rough knocking of the bones one against the other, the sound of the men shuffling the dominoes on the wooden table. And then it is mere minutes until the unmistakable sound of victory, as someone smashes several dominoes onto the table in a seeming fit of delirium.

This cabin definitely has its own rhythm, the beginning of a real cycle, just like life itself. And it is so comforting when that ritual is fully established, when everything is in its place. As the captain tells Brer Anancy in that loveable yarn about becoming a sailor, on a boat there is a place for everything; but everything must be in its place always. That way there are no problems on the high seas, in the storms of life. Everything and everyone in its right place. No unexpected changes. No surprises. Just predictability.

Johnny knows he cannot begrudge the men this excitement. For even the dominoes embody a dream for them: the aspiration that, after several years of trying, this could be the season they win the domino tournament, the chance to escape the unforgiving farm life for a weekend of fun and frolic in Toronto, to maybe even charter a bus and head for New York or Boston, where they can link up with other farm workers like themselves. A brief respite from the hard labour while they look at the beautiful costumes and dance to the pulsating rhythms of brass and steel drums and ogle almost-naked women prancing in the streets. To listen to the music of well-known jazz players from around the world. They have heard so much about the jazz festivals, the blues and calypso music, the rich slice of Caribbean, African and African-American life that brings so many hundreds of thousands of people the world over to the streets of

Toronto and New York. The same festivals that beckon so strongly over the years. The call always appears to reach them over the wind, even though these festivals and all their beauty remain beyond their reach. Even though the dream of answering this summons dies every year, just as the winds start to turn cold. When the umbilical cord linking Edgecliff and the Black experience abroad is severed once again.

But Johnny recognizes something else in the enthusiasm over the domino games. It is a signal or perhaps, even more crucial to the psychology of the men, an indication of how they will survive the isolation of the farm when the winds have become warm and less threatening. The mere fact that the men are now practising so seriously tells Johnny that, mentally, they are bonding into cliques. They are preparing for the long haul, devising ways to overcome the tedium of farm life. They are hard at work in search of the elusive victory in the tournament that will point the way to Toronto and the festivals. Yes, the men are beginning to sound like a team. For Johnny, the refreshing hum of the voices is testimony enough.

Johnny closes the diaries and puts his hands over his eyes. Anyone not knowing him would think Johnny was simply resting his eyes from too much reading and in such poor light. But I know better. I can hear the thoughts swimming through his head, colliding like icebergs. In his mouth is the overpowering taste of the meal of just a short while earlier. The only person still not eating is Tommy. But by now the men are used to Tommy only picking and nibbling at his food.

The meal on Johnny's tastebuds is the green peas and rice Smokie whipped up for the men. This time Smokie outdid himself. Once again, he demonstrated he is a master at improvising and turning out something that is not merely palatable, but tasty and nostalgic.

Although he devoured the food some time ago, Johnny can

still envision the heaping piles of rice and peas on the plates and in the soup bowls. On his plate, a thick and delicious-smelling butter sauce covers the mountain of rice. The sauce is fortified with some greasy concoction from several cans of herring and tomato sauce. This is a ritualistic meal. It is the last of the green pigeon peas from back home. By the time the peas run out, the men are usually well ensconced on the farm.

As Smokie makes the rounds, he loudly reminds the men that they better eat slowly, relish every mouthful of these peas, for they will be the last to cross their lips for almost a year. "Make sure yuh don't swallow too quick, yuh hear me, 'cause this is the last little bit. So let the taste linger," he says. "Let it go down real easy."

In his mind, Johnny can see the looks on the men faces, a look caught between bemusement and dismissal, of thinking Smokie will always be Smokie. No change here. But they also know the full meaning of what Smokie is saying. They know why Smokie does not treat this as a usual dish, as something that he slapped together hurriedly, that he simply allows the men to shovel into their mouths while waiting for the next man to play a domino. No, everything must stop, must pause for a while so everyone takes notice of this turning point. To give respect and reverence where it is due.

I hope you see what I mean when I keeping harping on the importance of tradition, of ritual, of things not changing from day to day at somebody's whim. Of seasons running their courses, as they are expected to, as everyone prepares and adjusts. I wish Mother Nyame would take the time out to observe what I am seeing here. Then maybe she wouldn't be so hasty for change, any change. She would know better and my job would be a lot easier.

Johnny shifts his long legs on the bed. Yes, he knows the story, the symbols of this last meal. It is as true a signal as any that the men should have settled in on the farm. By now, they should have filed away the memories of the last Christmas and the visit back home, even thoughts about Grafton. For life must go on. Even Johnny acknowledges to himself that, until this meal, it is really asking too much to expect a complete and full transition from the men. How could they? Not when almost every time they sit at the table, Smokie comes up with a pot of green peas and rice.

This meal, more than anything else, is the traditional Christmas dish in Barbados, the one piece of cooking that really reminds the men of fond childhoods, of love and of genuinely belonging to a society. Of the importance of having around them mothers, sisters, wives. That special touch, a refinement for their rough edges. For while Smokie might cook as good as any woman, he does not possess that elusive quality, that nurturing of the female. He is just a man who happens to be a good cook.

Johnny knows that the same way some people must have roasted turkey or goose on the festive table, these men must have green peas and rice, ideally, with slabs of baked pork on the side. At Edgecliff there is no pork, except the pickled pig trotters on the occasional Saturday. Still, in the Smokester's hands, the herring and tomato sauce is an adequate substitution, even if some of the men complain that the food needs lime juice to cut the fish's rawness, even if in their criticisms they are unconsciously calling for that special touch and refinement they now miss. As long as there is one green pea still in this cabin, these expatriates will cling to the memories, never fully accepting the reality of life in limbo. Perhaps the same way the Prophet hit such a chord when he urged every Black man to return to Africa, if only to the continent longingly stored away in every heart.

But every time Smokie produces a pot of rice and peas, the men cannot help remembering poor Grafton, now dead but whose spirit is as present in the cabin and around the domino table as if still there in the flesh. Johnny knows that he should be the last to talk about letting go of memories. Everywhere he turns, he sees a reminder of the last time with Grafton. The memories are always so fresh. Grafton, jovial and refreshingly optimistic as usual, is joining them for the Christmas dinner. It is at Tommy's house in the beautiful Barbadian countryside, in that part of the island to which the birds always head at nesting time. The occasion was even more memorable because it was on a warm day, with bright, bright sunshine after several days of heavy rain, a combination of nature's best that turns the island into a paradise of lush tropical vegetation, the strong rays of the sun that sting his skin and make him feel alive.

Tommy's wife, Barbara, is outdoing herself, leaving the men to gather in the backyard to admire the greenery of the breadfruit tree leaves, the *dunks* trees, golden apple, mango, ackee and clammy cherry trees. They are in the lap of such idyllic splendour, beauty painted by the rains and framed by the blue sky, the moderating breezes blowing across the island from the Atlantic coast to the Caribbean shore, bringing the feeling of standing in the midst of green canes as they bow respectfully before some conquering hero.

In the house, Barbara is fussing as she lays on the traditional Barbadian spread for her boys. Johnny remembers that Barbara would call them nothing but that — *her boys* — all twenty-one of them. Her boys are to want for nothing on this day. Her boys are to do nothing, except help themselves to a glass of ice and rum or to the slabs of great cake piled high on the plate under the plastic cover shielding it from the flies. Or to the coconut water, soursop punch, rum and corn oil ... the works. A smile breaks on Johnny's face as he recalls how Barbara refused to let Smokie so much as enter her kitchen.

"You's one of the honoured guests, Sir," she tells Smokie when he pushes his head into the kitchen. The smile broadens on

Johnny's face as he remembers the exchange. Barbara can tangle with the best and Tommy is so lucky to have a woman like that, someone who cares and looks after him so well. If Tommy has to go back home, if he has to retire prematurely, Johnny knows Tommy will be in good hands. Barbara would take good care of him, the same way she did all the men that day.

"But I only want to help you dish out the food," Smokie protests. It's to no avail. Barbara can be as tough as nails. A good woman is like that. Johnny glances at Tommy wrapped in the off-white bed sheet, looking like a mummy.

"Not today. You keep your arse over there like everybody else," Barbara rebukes Smokie. "Take your arse over there and sit it down quiet at the table. Get a drink like everybody else and wait 'til you hear me call all o' yuh to come and eat. Wait like a gentleman, so that I can serve you like a gentleman. Now get outta here quick, quick."

Barbara has put a lot of thought into the planning of the meal. As if some sixth sense or foreboding that women seem to possess is urging her on. Or perhaps it is simply out of some misplaced pity. Johnny would never know. Yet he recognizes how hard she worked to make the occasion a lasting and impressive gift to the men — one day of over-indulgence and absolute rest, a thank-you to the men from Barbara and all the women.

She keeps saying she wants everyone to be happy, to celebrate, as if simply repeating these statements is enough to make them happen. To smile and to gather in the backyard, under a large green tarpaulin and to sing old Christmas carols like *O Come All Ye Faithful*, and the less-known but loveable West Indian Christmas calypsos like *Drink A Puncha-creamer On A Christmas Morning* and *Mamma Sita, Donde Santa Claus?* Don't forget *On the first day of Christmas my true love gave to me: one doctor bird in an ackee tree* — just like when she and all the women and all the men on the Program were young and brimming with love, hope and ambitions. She wants her boys there at home in her backyard singing, she says, until the voices of well over sixty people ring out in the village, bouncing sweetly off the rough walls of her home, their home for the day, the biggest and newest bungalow in the area, the voices travelling across the parish, if not the entire island, wanting to lift the roof of her house as a stellar salute to these heroes.

And between the singing and celebrating are the several helpings of food and drink, more than their stomachs could ever hold. Apart from the traditional rice and peas, there is the *jug-jug* made from the crushed green peas with bits of meat mixed in, there is also the doved green peas and, of course, sorrel, falernum and rum and so much coconut water, sweet bread and pudding. But always green peas and rice rule the table.

Little do they know that this meal is to be their last with Grafton. Nor, Johnny thinks now, do any of them suspect that Tommy will not be able to shake the stubborn cold that plagues him throughout the meal; that he will not lick it, as he promised, in time for the return to Canada and that even now, six weeks into the season, he still has that hacking cough. Even after drinking the last of the strong bush tea Barbara brews for him, after collecting fifty-two different bushes, roots and herbs and boiling them into a brownish and bad-tasting concoction, and which he smuggles into the country. Tommy still can't shake it.

Instead, it's getting worse, so much so that Johnny now finds himself suggesting to Tommy that he stay in bed all day or that he leave the field two hours ahead of everyone and to go straight to bed. For once Tommy doesn't object; he no longer tries to argue that he will be fine given time. He doesn't attempt to explain that it is the unseasonable cold weather that has robbed him of his appetite, making him so weak and his resistance so low. Only the Liaison Officer is not convinced that the time is right for Tommy to see a doctor. No longer does Tommy protest, not even when the Officer advises him to hold on a bit longer. Instead, at Johnny's urging that there is no loss of face from at least checking out a doctor, Tommy is quick to meekly bow his head, accepting defeat, and slowly drags himself off to the cabin in the distance, much the same way Johnny remembers Grafton leaving the tobacco field one summer afternoon, never to return.

The meal has its memories. Johnny closes his eyes to shut them out. To close out the hurtful thoughts of what happens when he is at home. Unconsciously, he rubs the tips of his fingers under his left eye. Maude and the three children flash through his mind and, mercifully, he is glad they do not linger to haunt him, to make him feel even more guilty for what happens back home. The spot under his eye is still tender, although the scar is all but gone. But the healing is not complete and his eye is still sore and occasionally throbs. Although he likes to tell himself he isn't generally superstitious, he remembers his grandmother saying that a throbbing left eye is a sign of pending pain or misfortune. The same way that a thread in the hair signals the arrival of a letter from overseas, or an itching palm promises gifts of money, usually from the same source. From Panama, in his grandmother's case.

There are other things that Johnny doesn't want to recall. Certain coincidences that I think, as a faithful storyteller, I must draw to your attention. One of them is the fact that Johnny got the blow to his eye the same night he received the news of Grafton's passover, the term people at home still use for a stroke. *A passover.* That is how we all remember Pearl describing the seizures that left her husband speechless and his face twisted, before he died in the back of a taxi en route to the hospital. Although he was sick, as thin as a rake, the change happened so suddenly that none of the men had a chance to say farewell to Grafton, although individually and spontaneously on hearing the news they did gather in the crowded casualty department of the hospital to comfort Pearl and to offer any assistance and money to give Grafton a decent funeral. Later, Pearl would tell them how the doctors said they shouldn't have been so surprised. Grafton's immunity was washed out, that while he looked so-so on the outside, inside he was dying every day.

Johnny must be remembering these things too. Look at how he is gingerly feeling the scar under his eye again. Impatiently, he is wishing it would fade, disappear from his face and memory, the same way he wants some images from back home to release him from their grip. Johnny doesn't like the way the men look at his eye. Silently, he wonders how many of them know the full story, for as Grafton's death demonstrates, back home news travels quickly. Still, because nobody says anything, he wonders if the men understand how he came by the *licking* back home; how he almost had his eyes punched out in a back alley in the streets of Lodge Road.

Lodge Road, he thinks ruefully, repeating the words in his mind. *Lodge Road.* This is the village where he was born and grew up and which he knows so well that he could sit on his cot and, walking down the roads in his mind, point out the houses and the names of the people living there, recall every stand of trees. People who, he now knows, must all be dead. But on this night he finds out the hard way that the village he carries around in his head no longer exists after an absence of almost twenty-five years, that in this very village with houses and new families where the trees once stood it is now possible for him to get lost on a dark night, especially when he has a few bad rums in his head.

If the men knew the full story behind the scar, they would appreciate, pretence to the contrary, that even Johnny harbours in his heart frightening thoughts about what would happen to him if he was forced to return home. If there was no more work on the farm. If he had to return to that strange island to pick up the pieces and to try to make a living for himself. After so much time in Canada, Johnny has doubts whether he can fit back in to the old setting. If he would have any friends, if he could, in reality, simply go back home and be the head of a family he does not know and which does not know him. Whether, in a real sense, as far as the people in Lodge Road are concerned, it is not *he,* Johnny, born and bred in the same village, who is now the stranger; not the people living in those houses where in Johnny's memory there can only be mahogany, tamarind and dunks trees.

And that leads to another thing. Anyone who knows the story behind the scar is also aware of his problems with Maude and the children. They should now understand why he went drinking that night after the quarrel and why, once the rum shop closed and Johnny was so reluctant to return home straight away, he took what he thought was the longest route back to the house, if only to delay the inevitable.

Instead, he made a wrong turn. It was soon after this misfortune that Johnny, to use his actual word, *discovered* the so-called diaries. It was almost as if that beating, more so than Grafton's death, was a defining moment for him. Now he sits here on the bed reading diaries while the men play dominoes.

Johnny looks over at Winston's empty bed and sighs. I know he is thinking how nice it would be to be that young and unspoiled again. To have an uncharted future. Free to not make any unrealistic ties to back home. Free to not have a mortgage. Seventeen is two generations ago for him, Johnny thinks. It is like opposite ends of a rope — the beginning and the frayed end. But the frayed end can be frazzled for a million and one reasons, one being why Winston slips out of the cabin for a rendezvous in the darkness.

Johnny sighs. Little does Winston know that he isn't fooling anyone; it is only a matter of time before George Stewart discovers these late-night trysts, the ones that send Winston home, the big bulge in his pants, so late that he arrives in the field all bleary-eyed, but still listening to a borrowed cassette and relishing his memories from the previous night.

"I think I got to call the Liaison Officer, Johnny," Tommy says hoarsely from under the covers on the cot. His voice is unusually weak. He is talking slowly as if searching for words, as if forcing the frightening thoughts and words out of mind. "Man, I don't like the way I feeling. It's like I getting worse. *Me can't tek it no more, nuh longer, man.*"

"What you mean?" Johnny can feel the accelerated fluttering inside his chest. He decides not to try to humour Tommy, not to play the old game of pretence.

"These cold sweats coming too regular, man. I like I got to take a chance and try and call the Officer. See if he can take me to see a doctor or something soon. Maybe the doctor'll give me some tablets or something and make me feel better."

"Want me to talk to Stewart?" Johnny pauses, not wanting to appear over-anxious or agree too hastily with Tommy. "'Bout calling the Officer in Toronto, I mean."

"What you think, Johnny?" Tommy says. "I mean, I don't really know." Suddenly, Tommy is having second thoughts, shocked by the reality of what could happen if his worse fears were confirmed. He is throwing himself at the mercy of his best friend, exposing himself — fears and all — looking not only for advice but assurances. "I mean, just suppose he does carry me to the doctor and they find out something wrong with me and... and... that they got to send me back home? Already you helping me out with the few cents every month for the mortgage back home, even ignoring your own situation back there."

"Don't worry 'bout that. You got to put your health first, man."

"I know, Johnny. But just suppose, that's all I'm saying, man. Just suppose they say I can't work no more. You know I would be going back home to Barbara and the children without one blind cent. And you know what that means, Johnny. I still got the house loan from the credit union back home to pay off every month. Tell me, Johnny. You think I should call the Officer?"

"You got to put your health first. Only you know how you feel and if you say *yuh can't tek it no longer*, then you must know." The awkward silence seems so inefficient, so hollow. This is not the way a man should think. They know they have to do much better, must accept, grit their teeth and bear what is coming their way. Refuse to give in, the soldier wounded but still fighting.

"Even so, what so wrong with going back home, Tommy? You ain't like some o' we. You got something to go back home to. You got Barbara."

"Living with Barbara," Tommy begins tentatively, "ain't as easy as it..."

Winston walks through the door, flops heavily onto the cot and stretches out. Or maybe the sound I hear isn't the flop on the bed, but Johnny's heart falling, or my own heart dropping so unexpectedly. I wish Winston would disappear, just go *poof*, like a magician. But he is going nowhere. His presence, like a curtain of lead dropping between the two men, brings the conversation to an abrupt end. With their eyes and with shakes of their heads, Johnny and Tommy communicate that they will suspend the conversation until a more appropriate time. Some things are simply not to be shared with everyone. Some pain is always to remain behind the mask.

Winston senses the tension but tries to ignore it. He likes being with the older men. After the near-beating in the field, he has been keeping to himself, becoming less of a pain in the arse. Now, if I may say so, this joker only has to work on his timing. Also, hanging out with Jessica seems to be doing something for him. At least his attitude is a bit more acceptable and bearable, one change I do declare welcome. Johnny swings his legs on the bed and opens the black diary on his cot.

"Listen to this, Tommy," Johnny says. He is reading another passage from one of the diaries. My heart flutters faster. Those diaries make me so nervous. I don't know what it is about them that leaves me so frightened. I hate dabbling in the past like this. "Listen to this and tell me what you think."

> *April the thirtieth. Panama is nothing like what me and the boys expected. Everybody's saying that if they did know what we were getting into, they would never have signed up in the first place. Some of the men want to go back home on the next ship. They say we're doing all the hard work and then the Americans still claiming it's them that building the canal. But none of us can leave, at least not yet. We would have to pay the passage up front and nobody got that kind of money. Big mosquitoes buzzing around your head all night long, making it so you can't sleep, night or day. Real big mosquitos not like the small puny things we got at home. No good water to drink either, making the men complain more, complain that they should not be working sixteen hours a day, in the dark and even on Sundays when they should be at church.*

"That's the same thing we're doing up here right now," Winston says. "Just that we ain't got the same mosquitoes."

"Don't talk so soon," Tommy says. "Wait 'til summer come. Then you'll see real mosquitoes and black flies that can bite holes in yuh, man."

"Shit, man," Winston says, sucking his teeth in disgust.

Johnny looks over at the youngster, as if surprised by his *cheupsing* sounds. He resumes reading aloud.

Yesterday, we went to the new living quarters. All the men disappointed. We'd hoped to find some women there. Not even one woman to cook the food. None of us can cook. We never had to cook at home. The men vex too because they have to do their own washing. The men wondering when we will have time to do all these things when we have to work so long on the canal seven days a week.

"Ha, ha, ha." Winston laughs. "They should be real glad they ain't got Smokie cooking for them. Ha. Ha. Ha. Otherwise, they'd be wondering if the soup they get to drink's make out o' the same water they does be washing the clothes in. Ha, ha, ha."

I was made a water boy today. The American foreman say that I look too small and young to be handling dynamite. I now got to walk up and down the canal with a bucket of water on my head and a cup in my hand. Water boys make only eight cents a day. Not the twenty-two cents the other men get. I had to tell the foreman, I don't like what he's doing. That I might look small, but as the Jamaican friends we meet 'round here say, me talawa, *and I still got big responsibilities back home. In the end I had to give in. I need the money.*

Smokie enters the room and sits on the edge of his cot. He has retired the chef's hat and apron for the evening, one of the first times since our return from home that Smokie is not wearing his cook's outfit almost up until bedtime. The usual smile is gone from his still sweating face. From under the bed, he pulls his suitcase into the aisle between the cots. The powerful springs snapping the latches against the hard leather produce loud bangs as Smokie opens the valise and takes out a pair of blue running shoes. Carefully, Smokie wipes some undetectable dust off the tips of the shoes and places them on the floor. All eyes are focused on Smokie and his shoes. For Johnny, this is the most telling sign that life is settling into its routine.

"What's them you got there, Smokes?" Winston says.

"What the hell they look like to you?" Smokie answers abruptly.

"Shoes?"

"Not just shoes but shoes for runnin', young fella. Let me tell yuh somethin' right now: if you ever wake up and find these shoes missin' from under this bed o' mine, don't ask what happen' to Smokie. Don't ask for me. Don't go in the kitchen lookin' for no food, neither. And, I beg yuh for god's sake, don't call Stewart or the Officer to start lookin' for me. Just give me time, plenty o' time to get away, to make tracks. 'Cause everybody would done know that with these shoes gone, I'm burnin' up the road, smoking it down, slammin' tar. Runnin' like hell. I'll be sailin' into the darkness on my way to Toronto."

"Don't start now with that foolishness," Johnny says sternly. "You and this runnin' business. Only start putting foolish ideas in people's head. You forgetting what the Officer say." You don't know how relieved I am to hear Johnny say this. I was beginning to have my doubts.

"The Officer can kiss my black arse, that's what he can do for me." Smokie turns over the shoes to examine the soles. "He got to look after himself and I got to look after my-own-self."

"Not by running. Ain't no future in that," Johnny says. Gosh, I feel like shouting *attaboy, Johnny*. Talk yuh talk and tell them the truth, brother.

"Why you don't try them on and see how they fit?" he throws the shoes and Johnny catches them. "You and me does wear the same size shoe. You can use them to run too. I'd get another pair. Runnin' would be good for you, *Johnny*."

"Yeah, but you'd never hear me talking 'bout running,"

Johnny rebuffs him quickly. "After twenty-five years up here, I don't know of one fellow that got away with it, even if they did get to Toronto. Especially, if they say they're running alone. They only end up running 'round in circles in the night. First thing in the morning, the police and the immigration people find them and ship them back home. Everybody left behind on the farm then put under a curfew. People watching you everywhere you go, like prisoners. Ever think about the rest of us? So you can go and run if it suits you." He throws the shoes back at Smokie.

"And besides," Winston chimes in. "What about Angie? What about the poor girl you keep saying you're going to marry and start a restaurant with? What 'bout she? She still crying all this time, Smokes?"

"You's a rass-hole idiot or somethin', man?" Smokie says with derision. "I mean. I up here doin' my thing; she down there doin' she thing. How the hell I's to know what she's doin'. I got to look after myself, man. I got to be realistic. Not like you and that Jessica, stealin' out at night and playin' with blasted fire. You better watch out before you find yuhself in big trouble."

"In what trouble you talking 'bout?" Winston asks sheepishly at being confronted with what was supposed to be his secret. "Trouble from just *talking* to a woman?"

"You better take one good look at the back o' yuh wrist, yuh hear me?" Smokie says. "That's all I'll tell yuh before you start seein' stars and thinkin' yuh fallin' in love and all that foolishness. Just take one look at yuh wrist and see what you see. See if you don't see blackness, the colour of your skin. Still the same colour since yuh left Barbados. Not white, you hear me. Now, I done tell yuh that, you can cut your suit to fit the cloth. A word to the wise is *enuff*."

"Don't mind that smart-ass, Smokie," Delbert says from the doorway. "That Winston will always find a way to make things bad for all o' we. It's like he got some *duppy* on he shoulder for bad luck. Now, he's going after the farmer's daughter. I tell yuh that guy got balls. What next?"

"More than that," says Timmy walking in on the conversation. "You know, he's just a weak Black man, just like so many of the Brothers nowadays. You know, just like the Mighty Sparrow says in his calypso, *I never eat a white meat yet.* That's this youngster here. I'm sure he has some little girl from his village or school waiting for he back home. But, no, he has to run after a white woman. Weak, man. That's what he is. Weak." Timmy turns on the radio and starts searching for his favourite station. "I think all the Brothers that saying they want this white meat thing should listen to this here Minister. He will set them right. He will lead them into the light."

"Why don't all o' you just mind your own business, nuh? Tell me, what does what I doing have to do with any o' you?" Winston shouts. "What you want, anyway?"

"Funny you should ask," Delbert says. "But we've been looking for you long time this evening for a game o' dominoes. Remember the bet? Time to put your money where your mouth is. But it's like you hiding out in here. Like you can talk a lot better than you can play. Johnny, you should hear the chat this fellow here does put down, hear how he's always bragging 'bout how hard he can play dominoes. That's all he's talking 'bout since you send him over to my gang. We keep telling him to put his money where his mouth is, you know, put the pay cheque on the line like everybody else. But he's only a mouther-man, all talk, no action."

"Man, I can beat all o' you. Even with my two eyes shut," Winston boasts. "You should hear what everybody does call me at home. Nobody can mess with me and a domino. I am a real hard seed. The number one seed."

"Well, why don't you come and play then?" Delbert challenges.

"Just tell me when you want me," Winston says dismissively. "I'll be there. Just name the time and place."

"How about now?" Delbert challenges.

"Now?" Winston looks at Johnny, pleadingly.

"You could think of a better time?" Certainly, you can't miss the taunt in Delbert's voice or the snickering around him.

"I didn't mean *right now*. I was talking about, you know… another time, right. I don't want to clean out you guys so early. I mean, I'm giving you guys a chance to…"

"Time waits for no man," Delbert says. "It's now or forever hold your peace. Step up or cut the talk forever, man. Come and let your arse pay for your big mouth."

Winston walks slowly from the bedroom to the outside room where everyone is waiting for him. If you listen carefully, you will notice there is no shuffling or banging of the dominoes. They are waiting for the lamb. Smokie puts the shoes under the cot and hastens after them, pulling the billfold from his back pocket, offering to take Winston as his partner. Johnny closes the diary and puts it in his valise under the cot. He glances at the backs of the men and at Tommy, eyes closed, under the covers, seemingly oblivious of everything in the room.

chapter fourteen

Winston takes his seat at the table. The confidence of a few minutes ago is now gone from his face, vanishing like a brief shower on a sunny day. You will forgive me for not feeling sorry for this boy. Indeed, I don't think that, knowing me, you're too surprised I have these sentiments. I am always consistent, to say the very least.

In a situation like this, I can't help wondering what this new storyteller hiding out somewhere on this farm is saying about this lamb before us. Really, what can she say? Indeed, what can she say? Before calling it a day, I'll check in to hear for myself what her take on this night is, what story she is spinning. I am expecting a big laugh, and I don't think I'll get any surprises there either, just good belly-rolling laughs. Already this storyteller, if she's any use, must be cracking up anyone listening to her reports. And listen, maybe there's even a *colour commentator* listening, you know what I mean, if you can forgive me for laughing so much.

Lord, how my side hurts, like it wants to split open! Which only goes to show there really is a God and she doesn't like ugly. There is justice in this world. Truth and tradition will always reign. Perseverance will too. All pretenders are bound to fall. In the end, only the righteous will be saved. Only the faithful will escape the wrath and the sword.

Just watch and see for yourself — but try not to laugh too loud. Notice how Winston glances sheepishly at his partner, Timmy, busily shuffling the white dominoes. This is pure comedy, the pairing of these two against such pros. Pure comedy, man.

Timmy places the palms of his hands flat on the twenty-seven dominoes and mixes them with quick, firm twists of the wrists. It is magic the way an expert like Timmy handles these dominoes. And there is such style and finesse. When Timmy has shuffled the dominoes sufficiently, he raises his hands from the table, pulling them back as if the dominoes are suddenly too hot. Pure style, I tell yuh. Flamboyantly, he hits his two outstretched index fingers against the edge of the table, the signal for the men to start drawing their pieces. Winston seems mesmerized by this act. A mere babe in the woods, I tell yuh. Finally, with delayed action, he lurches for his share of the dominoes.

This, however, is not true of the sure-handed. Just look at them. See how they go about collecting their dominoes. It is art itself, an elaborate ritual that cannot be learned overnight or mastered by anyone watching with bulging eyes, hoping to learn on the fly. This is so funny! Notice the consummate ease with which Delbert and his partner Henry reach into the pack and pull the dominoes toward them. Without looking up, they sort the dominoes in their hands, adeptly holding their seven pieces in the palm of one hand with their fingers folding over them, a foil from prying eyes.

Let's keep an eye on Winston. He is the one, in case you don't know, nervously fumbling with his dominoes, trying to gain control of them. Unlike those of his rivals, Winston's hands seem too small to hold all the dominoes. Poor boy! And they are shaking too, a sign of how much the pressure is getting to him. And someone had the gall to suggest to me that this Winston could be a leader! Bah, I say, tell this leadership shit to the marines; let them sail away with that mother-lode. Nobody in his right mind would buy such crap. A leader, in truth! I mean, how *can* he, when he cannot even handle a little pressure? When he sweats and trembles at the first sign of discomfort, when he becomes a nervous wreck because people are watching him perform. Leader, my foot! If he's a leader, then I can be one too, and I'm only a spider, a storyteller awaiting my true calling the next time around.

Just look at the pain on Winston's face as he realises the men now ringing the table are staring at and analysing his every move; know the fear in his heart. These men can taste the fear. They can smell it the same way wild animals in a pack can always detect the wounded and lame, the lamb for the slaughter. Winston knows these men are anxious to expose him as the usurper and windbag he really is. And, I say, it's about time, too.

I tell yuh, the look on this guy's face is something I will freeze in my mind forever, so I can call it up whenever I want a good laugh and I will keep it there just in case someone back home is foolish enough to carry through on the rumours flying about. You know that somebody plans to recall me; that the other storyteller is doing such a good job, finding new and interesting things to say by focusing on one Winston St. Clair Lashley; that they plan to end the story I am telling about Johnny and switch the emphasis of the story about this farm to some fool-fool thing about this little guy with the so-called leadership traits; and that they know I won't even bat my eyes at this Winston fellow so they might have to move me. I guess I should keep a sharp eye out for any birds circling overhead. You can never tell when someone might get you to do their dirty work, eh Brer Bird?

Whoops! What's that? Oh, just the sound of one of the dominoes falling to the floor. No big thing, I guess. What's that you're saying in Winston's defence? That we shouldn't be so hard on this guy, that he is magic? Well, if you say so. But tell me, though, how do you personally account for what we are seeing? As Winston reaches uncertainly for the domino on the floor, another slips his grasp and ends up exposed on the table. Do I hear someone say clumsy, clumsy? Ah, you are too harsh, too critical of an up-and-coming young Black man. Isn't that what we always hear when we criticize certain people, when we don't toe the line?

Winston makes a quick grab for the upturned domino, his lips trembling in what I believe could only be a desperate prayer. But guess what? In the process, he loses several more pieces. They slip right through his fingers to the floor. As if his fingers are coated with butter. Mercy, when is this comedy of errors going to end, I ask you? And they haven't even played one domino yet.

Finally, Winston, poor thing, retrieves the elusive dominoes and haplessly lays his entire hand out on the table in front of him. He isn't even trying any longer to hold the seven dominoes in his hands, not like his opponents. His face burns and his lips are dry. He licks them. Sweat appears on his nose. He's aware of the giggling around him and of the scorching heat in the room. He is ready to play, or so he thinks; the opponents are ready to start the slaughter, but Timmy isn't. Puzzlingly, Winston's partner refuses to draw the remaining dominoes from the pool. Instead, he stares at Winston, a smile of benign amusement on his face.

"What you waiting for, Timmy?" Delbert asks. "Draw your cards. I think I'm going to collect a lot of somebody's money tonight." To no one in particular, he adds, "Double six pose."

Timmy still doesn't move. Henry and Delbert look at him again. Everyone looks at the pool of money. Timmy continues to alternate stares between his untouched dominoes on the table and his partner.

"Looks to me like somebody can't even play with seven and they want eight, eh," he says, finally. Delbert and Henry make a quick count of their pieces by holding six in the palm of one hand and professionally knocking the seventh against each individually. All eyes focus on Winston, who, seemingly unaware of what is happening, is still trying to control his pieces.

"Spread yours out, young fellow," Timmy says. Winston

complies with the command, putting the dominoes in a line in front of him. Notice this time that he is placing them face down. Well I'll be damned, I guess our hero *is* indeed a fast learner like everybody claims. Timmy reaches across the table. "One, two," he is picking up each of Winston's dominoes with the tips of his fingers and slamming them down on the table rather forcefully — *smack, smack* — as he counts. "Three, four, five, six, seven" — *smack, smack, smack, smack, smack* — "and," he pauses, holding the last one in the air, "eight. SMACCKKKK. You can hear the slam right across the farm. God, is this guy ever mad, or is he just bemused at being so badly taken-in by this Winston fellow? "People does play dominoes with only seven cards, you hear me young fellow, *not* eight. Lesson number one, I guess."

He is now talking like a school teacher, not a confident partner, and certainly not like a follower. The onlookers are laughing loudly. "Now shuffle them!" Timmy commands, pushing the six remaining dominoes closer to Winston, mixing them with his eight. Awkwardly, Winston shuffles the fourteen dominoes. The onlookers roar even louder. Timmy raises his eyes to the ceiling.

"Timmy, boy, I hope you ain't planning to go into town next weekend?" Rat Face Simpson says, playing the role of the set-up man.

"Why?"

"Because I can't see you having a cent left when Henry and Delbert through with you." The men laugh louder, Delbert and Henry reach across the table and shake hands. "As they say back home, Timmy boy, somebody's arse will pay for their mouth. Looks like your arse's in a sling too."

"Lord, have mercy," Timmy says. "The boy like he fool me bad, eh. Good Lord, I mean it now look like I shudda ask George Stewart to lend me he daughter. She like she'd be a more better partner than this one I got here."

"Don't feel too bad," Rat Face continues. "If things get really bad, when Henry and Delbert done clean you out, me and the boys are willing to lend yuh a couple of dollars to see you through the week. We're in the charity business. 'Cause yuh gonna need some help real soon, man."

"You think so, eh?" Timmy says. "Charity. You mean I'd be so broke."

"As sure as there is a tomorrow, my man," someone else chimes in. "If you want proof, just look 'cross the table and see who's your partner, who's sitting there just shitting *heself* right now."

The men are whooping it up. I haven't seen them so happy in a long time. It makes me feel happy too, helps me to forget my call back home. And why not? Here is proof of what I've been saying all along — experience beats youth every time. I just wish someone would tell that to Mother Nyame and to that youngster she has on this farm with only the task of showing me up. But, as sure as my name is Brer Anancy, I know I will have the last laugh. As the old story goes, he who laughs last, laughs best. How true! And don't expect me to show any charity. I like going for the jugular, every time. I plan to laugh 'til my belly's full. This is my revenge.

It is at this point that the cabin door opens. I tell yuh, there is a God who answers prayers, especially those of this Winston. As they say, he probably has horseshoes up his arse, because he can be so lucky. I guess that's what Mother Nyame means when she says that this Winston is magic. What about him is magic? I asked. She could not give me a good answer. You will see, she says. Time will tell. That's the best she could offer for an explanation. I should give this guy a chance to blossom, she says, leaders aren't always born. Some are developed and trained, she says, but they must get a chance to prove themselves. What foolishness, a total denial of all we have learned over the centuries. And she tells me this nonsense with a straight face. How stupid does she think I am? Now you understand why I am so flipping angry, why I delight in observing this night's happenings, why I keep kicking myself for calling home in the first place.

George Stewart, Mary and Jessica walk in. The men jump to attention like soldiers receiving a surprise inspection from a commanding officer. The sound of shuffling feet followed by abrupt silence brings Johnny to the door of the bedroom. Only Winston is still sitting, still trying to figure out the dominoes.

"Did any o' you 'round here hear somebody crying out for help?" Delbert asks, as the three angels of mercy stroll in. All eyes are on Jessica.

"Got some letters here," George Stewart says, obviously unaware of the intended joke. He seems in a better mood as he drops the bundle on the table. This is kind of surprising because Mr. Stewart normally brings the letters in during the day, just after the men come in from the fields. Suddenly, the men are no longer interested in the dominoes. Winston sighs with relief, like a mismatched boxer saved by the bell, glances at Jessica and hangs his head.

"I was going through the letters before I brought them over, sorting them really," George Stewart says, as if trying to make it clear that he does not mean he was prying, "when I came across this one here." He raises it beside his face. "From the Immigration Department. Albert. Albert," he repeats, "Jonesie." He is looking around the room for the addressee.

"Here." Albert comes running out of the group to accept the long brown envelope. It is flat and official-looking with the words Immigration Department written in bold across the front. A broad smile appears on Albert's face. His hands tremble. Ignoring George Stewart, he waves the envelope above his head for all to see. "This is it," he shouts gleefully. "At last. This is it, boy. I keep telling all o' you that the reply was coming any time. I think I got my papers."

He goes into the bedroom, several men following him, and gently pries the envelope open. This will be a keepsake, so he has to handle the envelope and these important documents with special care. Several official-looking forms fall into his hands. Stapled to them is a high-quality printed letter on a piece of white paper, French on one side and English on the other. He flips it over to read the English.

"Everythin's okay, man?" Smokie asks. He is standing besides his cot, with the blue running shoes underneath it. Smokie kicks the shoes further under the bed as if ashamed of them.

"Yes, man. They say in a couple o' weeks they'd start processing the papers. Send some more forms for me to fill out. Want more information, I guess. Just an update of my finances. That's all they want. It's looking real good, man, I know it just have to work out for me. All them years got to count for something no matter what the other bad-minded people say. Now I can get my entire family up here with me. Make a new life for all o' we," Albert Jones says. He begins reading silently, smiling all the while.

"I sure hope they don't disappoint you," Timmy says, leaving the room. "You can never trust these damn people, you know. The system ain't set up to help people like me or you."

"What you saying?" someone challenges Timmy. "Don't start pouring cold water on a good thing."

"I just saying to be careful how you walk. Until you get that visa in yuh hands, don't count the chickens." Timmy says. Believe me, Albert probably doesn't even hear him. His head and thoughts are elsewhere. He is entirely absorbed in his reading. Or, if he does hear Timmy, he chooses not to respond.

"Don't mind Timmy," Rat Face Simpson says. "I glad for yuh, Albert. Because you're clearing the way for all o' we."

"I hope so," Albert says softly. "I really hope so."

"'Cause if you get through, more o' we can follow and get we papers too," Simpson says. "That's much better than we all saying we running off the contract like some bunch o' runaway slaves or clowns. And with things not looking too good on the farm these days, you never know."

Smokie slinks out of the room. But not before he pulls down the edges of the sheets over the bed, to make sure nobody sees his running shoes. That's so funny, I tell yuh. In the outer room, Smokie sees the men sorting through the mail on the table. "Here's a couple for Tommy," someone shouts.

"Give me, here," Johnny says. He is standing to the side of the room talking with George Stewart. Someone brings over the letters. Johnny takes them and continues talking to the farmer in hushed tones. Jessica and Mary are standing beside Johnny and George, watching the men sort through the mail. As the men find their letters, they disappear from the table. Some remain in the room, others literally run into the bedroom to read from the comfort and privacy of their cots.

Eventually, only Winston is standing in front of the table. Only the dominoes, fourteen in one group and seven each for Delbert and Henry, stare forlornly from the table at him. The big pile of letters has disappeared. So has the pool of money. It is hard for Winston to believe, but there is no letter for him. Winston slumps with disappointment on the bench. He and Johnny are the only ones not to receive a letter. Johnny does not seem to mind. Winston is devastated.

"Before I go, I want to tell you fellows that we start planting the tobacco next week, if the weather holds fair." George Stewart says. Mary gasps, quickly stifling her urge to speak. Her husband pushes ahead of her. "Better late than never, but the weatherman says spring should finally arrive this weekend." George is also happy because the money from the bank finally came through today. That's when he collected the letters.

But nobody is listening. Nobody appears to notice Mary's response, except Winston. Even Johnny has gone into the bedroom to hand Tommy his letters. George Stewart steps outside into the cold. Jessica lingers momentarily in the doorway, watching the distraught young man. She seems uncertain what to do. But despite the initial hesitancy, Jessica also steps outside, leaving Winston alone at the table watching the useless dominoes.

"Will you walk up!" George shouts in the dark. "For a young woman, you're acting mighty strange these day. I don't know what your mother is telling you, but we have to have a chat."

The sound trails them into the darkness, leaving me to wonder if George Stewart has finally caught on to what is happening. And if he has, Lord how would I like to be there when he blows his stack. I mean, you don't really think George is falling back on that age-old ploy of getting angry, or appearing to be angry, before anyone — say a disappointed wife for example — can get angry with him? Attack always being the best form of defence, as every man, every general, knows. I think not.

In any case, I can't take the claustrophobia in this room any more, not with everyone running off and reading letters, acting as if time has stood still. Obviously, nothing is going to happen in this cabin for a while. For after reading the letters will come the sighing and the looking off into the distance, with every man feeling sorry for himself and wanting to be alone. It happens every time, without fail. How I hate it when the men get so mellow and misty-eyed.

I might as well cruise around the farm, clear my head, take in a fight or two to get my adrenaline up, to feel like a good old male child. Maybe I can use this opportunity to take Mother Nyame's advice and listen to what other reporters in this big universe are saying, to how they are saying it. This way, I might even get Mother Nyame out of my system.

"I thought you promised the bank not to plant tobacco this year," Mary says when they enter the kitchen. Well, it appears I may have been wrong. How unusual. She takes off her heavy coat and places it in the closet by the door. It's much windier than I thought, so instead of going for a walk I decided to latch onto the Stewarts. I want to find out for sure if Mary and George are catching on to what is brewing between their daughter and Winston. I didn't like the way Mary was looking at George in the cabin, especially when George was addressing the men. I could feel the chill coming back between these two, and the way they looked at Jessica told me something else was up too. So here I find myself in the middle of this discussion, with Mary reaching into the closet. Mary finds two hangers and holds out one each to George and her daughter. The coldness in her voice is almost enough to make Jessica, and certainly George, refuse her offer of a hanger and keep their coats on.

"I thought the bank said we're not to plant tobacco this year," Mary repeats. "I had to sign the papers too, remember."

Jessica hangs her coat up in the closet and pushes past her parents into the living room. I guess it's only a matter of time before Jessica's parents confront her over Winston. Something in my guts still tells me this isn't going to be a good night for the boy. Indeed, I notice that his storyteller has been relatively silent this night, very carefully selecting what to report, I suppose, most noticeably not mentioning a word about the domino fiasco. Which only makes you wonder if this is the type of selective reporting Mother Nyame expects and wants. Are we to become censors, reporting only what makes our charges look and sound good? Is that what this honourable profession has come to? Can we speak no ill of the living, too?

Well, let me be truthful and say this right up. Another

reason for my coming here is to officially put on record — in my own words, if you please — what a disaster of a night this has been for Winston. It will be my crowning pleasure, no censorship here if you please, to report every word and thought as Mr. and Mrs. Stewart confront Jessica on her misguided escapades with one magical Winston Lashley. Then nobody can say someone has not told the truth; someone has not done his duty and in the most professional manner. Our job, despite what others now claim, is not to make our charges look better than they are. After all, they are *human*.

"Don't you have anything to say, George?" Mary says, obviously annoyed by the silence and by George ignoring her.

"Think I'll let some guy from the bank tell me how to run my farm?" George answers, finally.

"But George, that was a clear stipulation. I read it on the papers," Mary says. "If you knew you weren't going to abide by it, you shouldn't have signed."

"I had no choice," George says.

"But you promised. *We* promised."

"I need the money and I would have signed anything. You want to waste your time planting roses? Or would you prefer cabbages?

He sits at the kitchen table. Mary puts a mug in front of him and fills it with black coffee. George automatically feels into his pocket and pulls out his pipe. He looks at Mary, frowns and, apparently changing his mind, places the unlit pipe on the table.

"Talking about promises," he says, "don't forget that we promised Johnny that we'd call the Liaison Officer to come and have a look at that Tommy fellow. Christ, that's the last thing I need right now. Sickness on the damn farm."

"What's wrong with him?" Mary asks. They can hear Jessica on the piano in the other room.

"How would I know? Maybe too old. When the Liaison

Officer comes over, I think I'll also have a talk with him. About that Winston Lashley. I don't like that youngster, not one bit. We should send him back, too." Ah ha, now they are getting to the real issue. I am all ears now.

"You know that the Officer could pull the men off the farm," Mary says soberly. "He could stop them from working if he finds that, contrary to what you promised the bank, you're planting more tobacco and putting everything in jeopardy."

"What the hell would he do if he pulled them off my farm? Send them back home and lose the next election?" He picks up the pipe and holds it in his hand, hefting the weight. Instantly, Mary starts to sneeze and rub her eyes. "Farm them out to other farms around here? You see any farms hiring people? To do what — grow roses? Or are you into coleslaw too? Christ."

He sips the coffee. "And another thing," he says angrily. "We have to talk about that daughter of ours." The piano music is getting louder, drowning out the radio. "What's she's up to now?" George listens carefully. He hears something on the wind. Loud singing from the cabin and the accompanying music is wafting over the silent night air. The men appear to be celebrating something.

"Listen," he says, gesturing with the coffee mug toward the cabin. George sips more of the coffee. With the wind blowing strongly in their direction, they can hear the clean strumming of the box guitar, the metallic tinkling sound of the steel pan, the rhythmic beating of spoons and forks on glass bottles and the voices of Smokie and Mighty singing in sweet harmony.

"Guess they're having a party," George says. My heart leaps to my mouth. I didn't expect them to have a party. What is different this time? Whenever they get letters, the men just go off, find a corner or some quiet spot and sulk. And that can last for hours. I guess I better hurry back and see what's going on behind my back. Christ, this kind of thing is enough to make me think

I'm really getting out of touch. I can't take these unexpected changes, man.

"Maybe they got good news in the letter. Could be in the letter for Albert Jones." Mary says. "If he succeeds, it will be a good sign for all of them. I guess they can't wait to give up working on a farm."

"Well, we should be the last to talk," George says gruffly. "Look at our very own daughter." Wait, not so fast. Maybe I can wait a few more moments and hear what they have to say about Jessica and Winston. "Our dear sweet daughter, eh." Here it comes, I think. "The one in there on the piano. Just dying to go to some blinking college in Toronto and study music. Everybody wants to run to the big city. Nobody interested in farming no more."

"I'd really hoped you'd change your mind about the tobacco," Mary says. Is that it? Nothing about these two love birds? I can't believe it. I got to go and see what's happening in the cabin. I can't take any more shit about growing damn roses, or cabbages or even tobacco.

"And do what?" George bellows. "Let the farm go to ruin?" He gets up and takes another sip of the coffee. "I'm going to bed." He marches out of the room. Suddenly the house is almost quiet, except for the music from the radio and the cabin. Jessica is no longer playing the piano.

Before slipping into the darkness, I look at Mary, a striking picture all alone with her fears. She knows George is making a big mistake but she does not know how to stop him. I really feel sorry for her, because I know what it is to see someone making a great big mistake, when you are so helpless to do anything. She has George. I have Mother Nyame. She can only stand at the window and look out into the darkness and hear the men making merry. And me, I must hurry over to the cabin and find out what, indeed, is the cause for this unexpected outpouring. What the hell does anyone have to be happy about?

chapter fifteen

My friends, I ain't happy at all. And when I am unhappy I have to share it. I can't keep things bottled up in me to give me a some kind o' ulcer. 'Cause I'm sure you done know so many people that long gone and dead off with grief lumps because they won't let out how they feel. They keep the grieving to themselves. Not me. That won't happen to me. *Atall*. So bear with me if you find me spending a tad of time letting you know how much they're unfairing me.

To start with, look for some changes in me from now on. More commentaries. Yes, you heard me right. More commentaries to spice up my reports. That, my dear, is what Mother Nyame keeps bitchin' about. And what Mother Nyame wants, Mother Nyame damn well gets. So, with life in these parts settling into a predictable routine of late, I've been thinking that maybe I should use any spare time I have to try my hand at something new. Time to attempt a commentary or two. What do I have to lose? At the very least, I might get the Great Mother to shut up for a while and to stop her whining. That alone would be worth the risk.

Now, I don't know about you, but I think that if there is one thing deserving a commentary it is the damn effects of letters, the coming of news, on people. More precisely, I would want to comment on the impact of letters on these men around me. That's what started my troubles. Remember how excited they were the other day, when George Stewart delivered that pile of letters?

I don't have to remind you how the letters set off one big

round of celebration, the drinking of a few grogs and Mighty beating on the steel pan. So much noise, you would think somebody won the lottery. When I get back in the cabin, all out of breath from dashing across the farm and almost killing myself by running my blood to water, I am simply amazed to find out nothing of note happening, nothing really changed. Except for the fact there's no sulking. Just that the men received their letters and are in a damn good mood.

Now let me say something else before I go any further. And I hope you still have the patience to bear with me. It's only a little bit longer, so hold on. Obviously, everybody knows I am not used to this commentary thing. We are not fooling anybody on this one. As I had to say to Mother Nyame: Look here, nuh, but remember you never give me no formal training in this area, not like the schooling I get on how to scrupulously gather facts, how to be precise with details, tone and the weight we place on every report. She says nothing on this point.

But, these slights aside, I am willing to give this commentary business a try. I have an open mind. With this new attitude, this willingness to accommodate, I hope everyone will see this change of mind for what it clearly is: a firm demonstration of my commitment to being a team player, my willingness to experiment within reason, my wanting to be as helpful as possible. Yes, the continuing fuss at head office is a factor. I can't deny that. But it definitely is not true that I am making this attempt because Mother Nyame is threatening to let someone else, maybe even that unlettered storyteller already positioned here on Edgecliff, start a trial run of commentaries if I don't feel up to the task. There is absolutely no truth to that rumour. So let's kill that one, once and for all. And, in any case, as everyone knows by now, I never give in to no threats. I didn't with the Prophet, not even when it would have made sense to compromise myself and desert that great one, so I don't see why I should now.

However, I grant you this, and let me choose my words real carefully so as not to offend anyone, it is true that I wish there were others besides me experimenting with this art form. Then I could listen in and see how they're doing, how to do the job. As just about everybody done know, it's very lonely being a pioneer. How can you breathe or sleep with all that weight, all those expectations, on your shoulders? Just reflect on all those stories from that school in Little Rock just a generation ago or even of that young man's masterful performance on the fairways at Augusta, Georgia. Pioneers for a race — never an easy task.

With this in mind, it doesn't surprise me that there is a rumour abroad that Mother Nyame is cracking down on me and asking me to move over if I don't think I can do the job. All I had suggested to the Great Mother was that I didn't like the idea of pinning the success or failure of a new agenda squarely on my poor shoulders alone. Especially when it was something for which there were no clear, definite instructions or desirable outcomes, only some nebulous notion of trying something new and seeing if it would work. What kind of mandate is that? And why get mad because I ask a few very relevant and pertinent questions? I like to be as specific as possible.

But Mother Nyame can be a real uncompromising bitch when she wants to. And I should have known something was up when she up and call me, when right off, without even a good hello and how are you doing, she straight 'way starts asking me a whole set of questions like am I going to do these commentaries we've been talking about or will she have to find somebody to do the job. Brer Anancy, she says, in that serious voice that she can throw on yuh when she's ready, it's time to shit or get off the bloody pot. Time is getting away. We need to start doing some new things to spice up our overall reporting. The new millennium will be here and you still won't have made up your mind, she says. What will it be? What is your decision?

So I am the guinea pig. The whip speaks. Now my friends and trusted colleagues around the globe are calling me and asking why the Great Mother is so mad at me. Is it true, they ask, that she is going to promote this storyteller on the farm and give me a junior role, if any role at all? My friends are so concerned; they do not want anything to happen to me; they do not want my assignment interrupted again; they worry about what will become of me if I do not come back as a leader but as a storyteller for a third straight stint. Try your best, Bro, they all tell me. Give it a chance. Pour some water in your wine. What have you got to lose?

And, with these messages ringing in my head, all I can think is that this crisis wouldn't have happened if those letters hadn't arrived, if the men weren't so happy that some alarms must have gone off at head office, maybe some other storyteller sticking her nose in my business and running at the mouth. When they checked in I was not on the job. It had to be the letters. Otherwise, why would Mother Nyame read me the riot act and remind me that a good storyteller should never be caught unawares, should never be found sleeping at the switch, that if I tried commentaries it would encourage me to anticipate more so that I wouldn't be caught with my pants down again. And, of course, she had to trot out the old canard of how I screwed up with the Prophet and that I should be careful, very careful. God, talking with her, I couldn't help thinking that there must be quite a big file on me at head office, a dossier well-thumbed through and dog-eared.

Luckily, I know how to improvise and I know my history. I can be flexible because I am well-schooled. The one thing I do know is how African people over the years have always made commentaries by preaching. Yes, preaching. This is something Black folks accept and understand, but which other tribes often castigate them for, for being too preachy, too pedantic, too didactic. But preaching is the closest form I can think of for a commentary. Here I am thinking of the social and political reflections by people like Malcolm, Martin, the Prophet and even his evil nemesis Mr. DuBois, who, if I should give Jack his jacket, still had one or two good things to say once he got over being so jealous of Prophet, or of artists like Robeson, Baldwin, Wright or Hughes. All great preachers, all solid commentators.

I hope Mother Nyame, of all reviewers, understands what I am doing and that she doesn't become too critical too soon. In any case, if anyone accuses me of being too pedantic, not that I really expect them to, then I can argue that I am in good company. It's an African and Caribbean thing. What use is a smoothly told story without a strong moral, without a well-argued point of view, without the conversion of some poor sinner?

And let me tell you another thing before I launch into this commentary business. This might surprise you, but I've decided to pay closer attention to, I know you're not going to believe it, but, yes, to Winston. I can understand your shock at hearing such a statement coming from me. And to tell the truth, I am as puzzled as you why my bosses find it necessary to have a running narrative on this Winston. At least, Mother Nyame insists relentlessly, mention more of him in your reports. Then she gets my friends to call and ask why I am being so stubborn in refusing to give this boy a narrative or two. Well, it's like I just can't win. I can't please anyone, no sir. Everybody ganging up on poor Brer Anancy. So, from now on, I won't go so far as to provide a running narrative, but I also won't totally ignore him either. Now nobody can say I don't compromise. Now I can have an easy living like everyone else, a living without anyone calling my arse and threatening me. I'll compromise on this one.

There's another reason for my compromising. Although I know it is highly unlikely that I am wrong in concentrating on Johnny, I cannot sleep well with the thoughts playing in my head that, once again, I may be missing something momentous. Mother Nyame was pretty blunt in making that point and it's nagging at my conscience. And she really hit me where it hurts, gave me a good kick in the balls, by throwing my record at me. I have to admit she is right, though, unless I want to take her on point by point and only succeed in muddying my own waters. After all, she gets to call the final shots. She is the Great Mother Nyame, possessor of all stories. Plus, when she's in such a bad mood, it's no use talking, let alone arguing, with her. And, as I said, this time it was she that called, not me. This time she would not even allow me to talk, to even explain. I guess it's true to say that she set down the rules, read the riot act really, on a couple of things. Well, Mother Nyame warned me not to be so narrow-minded, as she put it, as I was when I continued to follow and report on the Prophet all the while ignoring one W.E.B. DuBois, all the while arguing that the phony disputes between Blacks from the mainland and those from the Caribbean weren't worthy of being recorded. I mean, what can I really say to this criticism? I was obviously wrong; I suffered, and still do, because of the petty divisiveness I so stupidly overlooked.

The truth be known, and I am not repentant in the very least, I still think to this day that the argument that divides the followers of the Prophet and Mr. DuBois, in the wider scheme of things, is still spurious, so very bogus as to still not deserve any consideration. This is another legacy, if I may make a commentary here, if I may become preachy, that is still paralysing African people so many decades later, almost a century later. And for what? Because of the ego of one man? Because of this endless and dry debate that I am better than you because, purely by accident, I was born one place and you the other.

I mean, I can still hear the Prophet destroying that argument. I can hear him shouting from the hilltop that what we are really discussing is a moot point. That because the slave boat dropped us off in Bridgetown, Kingston, Demerara, the Carolinas, Havana, wherever, we must remember we had no choice. We must remember we were all in the same slave boat, he says. We must remember that we now have a choice of walking up the gangway of the Black Star Line and going back home to where we are all equal. The Prophet can lead us back into the Promised Land. What a mind that man had! How I agree with him! That's why we must await the coming of a true Prophet, someone like me who knows the real history of all these things.

But I digress. As Mother Nyame so brutally points out, my mistake was in not seeing Mr. DuBois as the rising star, the leader about to do in and overthrow the Prophet. In my books he was the Anti-Christ, arguing that we need not go anywhere to redeem ourselves, even though in the end, years after Prophet's demise, it was the very same DuBois who saw the light, recanted, ran away and even died on the continent. Life can be brutal, Mother Nyame tells me. She says she doesn't understand why I expect things to be so predictable, why I keep searching for this one messianic leader. We are at the end of a millennium and it is vital that we look to the future, she persists, that we do not remain stuck in the past, fighting all these old battles. Let's move on and show this new spirit of openness, of looking forward with eagerness to what's ahead, to a brand-new future. Sometimes I wonder, with the Great Lady's thinking so close to this DuBois fella's, if she didn't side with the enemies of Prophet back then. But, for obvious reasons, 'cause you know who has my future in her hands, I can't express that thought too loudly. Still, it nags at my mind whether she had a hand in this tragedy.

When she gets going like that, who can argue? Women can be so persuasive if you are not careful. But I am an old-fashioned male, and I like, in most cases, for things to remain they way they are. I am for known systems and order. For as the Greatest One says in another story, I am your God, who never changes. I am the same yesterday, today and tomorrow. Now that is consistency; that is reliability, predictability. And who am I to tell the great Creator of all things under the sun and on the earth and in the waters that it is necessary to change? Of course, Mother Nyame would not accept this argument. She simply said I was acting more confused by the day and ended the discussion.

So, most humbly, I am keeping a closer watch on Winston these days. Why fight with Mother Nyame over this idiot any more? Why not use him to make my points for me, to rub salt in Mother Nyame's wounds when the time inevitably comes for me to say I told you so? And I want you to be my witness. I want you to see him for yourself, to realize what I am talking about when it comes to this Winston idiot. I want you to make up your own mind whether my doubts are misplaced. Tell me truthfully if I am wrong. You don't have to worry about pandering to me. I am an adult. Just judge with an open mind for yourself — does this Winston have leadership potential? Listen to him well, watch his moves. Tune in to his thoughts. Would you, in good conscience, waste your precious breath on him, if you were in my shoes? That is the question.

And what better way to link my commentaries and Winston than through letters. I mean, just look at how the disappointment of not receiving any letters still weighs so heavily on Winston. This, I think, is a great test of his mettle. The letdown causes his boyish face and shoulders to droop, as if carrying around a thousand pounds of lead. What does this tell you about the fibre of someone who can be so emotionally distraught over such a small thing as not getting a letter?

I know that all of us go through periods of being homesick, of just dying for the comfort of the familiar, but a leader has to be immune to such feelings. Or he must somehow override them, suppress these periods of prolonged disappointment. A leader must move on in life like a moth attracted to a bulb. The danger, imminent or otherwise, does not matter. People like Martin always live in the crosshairs of the inevitable, so does a Malcolm walking onto the stage at an Audubon ballroom. But maybe I don't know any more. I am from the old school.

So let me bring you up to date on Winston. This youth is smart enough to realize the men have noticed that he gets no mail. It has now reached the point where Winston dreads seeing Mr. Stewart making the walk across the green fields to the cabin, especially when the farmer has under his arm the canvas sack. Every time he sees the farmer, his heart drops. This is the power of a letter, I guess.

Winston is now afraid to even look into the pile for fear of the resulting disappointment. And believe me I'm not being sarcastic or mean-spirited when I make these observations. My heart is pure, you can take me at face value. Winston feels alone in the world; however, this feeling should not be so strange to a leader. Here again, I think of the Prophet or a Nelson breaking rocks on Robben Island. I think of any leader burning the midnight oil, worrying while the world sleeps, blissfully unaware of the personal turmoil and the loneliness of having to make monumental decisions.

Winston feels adrift from everyone that he loves and cherishes. He is thinking nobody cares about him, nobody wants to inform him of all the developments back home. It's as if nobody thinks that he worries about his mother and three brothers and sisters. As if the members of his family don't feel anxious about him. A day doesn't pass that, secretly, he doesn't hope for some message from home, that he doesn't envy Tommy, rolled up his bed, reading his latest letter.

And talking about Tommy, I am pleased to report that something is having quite a startling effect on him. It must be the words in the letters in combination with the medicine. Even in the midst of his troubles, Winston, or anyone for that matter, cannot help noticing the change in Tommy since his visit to the doctor, since the letters began arriving with some frequency. Tommy isn't shaking and coughing as much. No longer is he spending all his time in bed with the bad feelings and coughs. Tommy can now work a full day in the field. Planting the tobacco seedlings is the toughest part of the job. With his recovery, Tommy seems imbued with extra energy as if he is a new man, his tongue twice as sharp and swift.

The rejuvenated Tommy is once again captain of the dominoes team. As a leader, he flexes his muscles and is not as accommodating as Johnny. As captain, Tommy makes it clear that Winston shouldn't even think of sitting at the same table where the men are playing. That is what I like about Tommy, why I am so happy he's coming around and looking like his old self. Tommy, as I've said, does not bite his tongue or condone foolishness. I hope Mother Nyame hears his quotes in my reports. He isn't as soft-hearted as Johnny. The Tommy I know would never risk denying the men a chance of winning the domino tournament simply to appease an upstart like Winston.

If it were up to Johnny, I have no doubt he would let Winston onto the team, so that the youngster could feel he was contributing something. Not Tommy. Only the truly deserving is worthy of praise. We are not on some kindergarten soccer team where we have to carefully placate fragile egos by making sure even the clumsiest kid gets time to play, where we have to appear fair. Life, as we all know, ain't fair.

I agree with Tommy that if Winston wants to contribute anything to the team, he can give moral support. He can lead, if I may use that word, from the sidelines. But let the real generals carry the war. This is what Tommy means when he tells Winston in plain language that even though he is a member of the farm community he can only expect to travel with the team to the games on the farms. That is the full extent of Winston's help for the team. No playing time. Winston, as to be expected with his pride and all, has declined the offer on the few trips so far. I guess his leadership pretensions get in the way of his common sense.

As we talk, why don't we go over to the cots where Winston and Johnny are sitting and observe them more closely. I can sense the bitter thoughts going through Winston's mind as he sits brooding. Everything is boiling over in his head — that there is again no letter; he doesn't feel part of the team or have any real affinity with the men on the farm; and he is not sure if he should even remain at Edgecliff. I don't know what you think, but the look of impatience on his face tells me Winston wants to say something to Johnny, but the older man is reading one of those diaries and Winston seems reluctant to interrupt.

In the other room, the men are playing dominoes. The noises torment Winston, feeding his feelings of uselessness. Mighty is playing his steel drum and singing bawdy songs. Smokie strums on his guitar and improvises calypsos on the spot. I do not have to tell you that such merriment comes from one source: George Stewart and another bag of letters. Let's listen in on the two in this room.

"Johnny," Winston is saying softly, his voice a mere whisper.

"Um," Johnny answers, if that's what his grunt is. He continues to stretch out on the cot, his upper body resting on his arms and the pillow.

"Johnny, you realize that me and you is the only people that don't get no letters?" he asks.

"Uh hum," Johnny answers.

"How you feel 'bout it?"

"Don't feel no way," Johnny says. He still isn't looking up from the diary. There is a scowl on his face as he tries to decipher the scribblings in the books, sometimes difficult because of the faded ink. Winston has noticed that Johnny's mood always changes when he reads the diaries.

"I can't get used to it, man," Winston confesses. "Maybe I ain't been up here long enough."

"That ain't got nothing to do with it," Johnny says. He closes the book and swings his feet onto the floor. He is now sitting, his back bent, facing Winston. "A lot o' men can't take it when they don't get no letters neither. Just look at how Tommy keeps reading and re-reading all those letters even with the new ones he gettin'. I think he has every letter, from the first one he ever get up here. But me, I'm used to it."

"But you got a woman back home," Winston says. "And three children."

"Yeah. The oldest boy's almost your age."

"You must think 'bout them a lot. How they getting 'long without a father? Even now, I still think a lot about my father and how he run off and left we back at home."

"I ain't much of a father, if you ask me."

"What you mean?" Winston probes. His eyes search the older man's face, look beyond the lines of his hardened and stretched skin and into his watery eyes. Winston can smell Johnny's perspiration from the day's work and see the sweat and salt marks at his hairline and on his forehead.

"My biggest boy's sixteen going on seventeen. In all this time, I have spent what...thirty-two months with him. Less than three full years with him by my countin'."

"That don't make no sense, Johnny," Winston says.

"Two months a year at home. Sixteen years. Thirty-two months," Johnny explains.

"Oh," Winston says. "I see but..."

"Not enough to be a father to anybody," Johnny interrupts with a hollow deprecatory laugh. "The second boy is fifteen and I spend even less time with him. And Melissa, my little girl..."

He smiles at her name. He returns to the diary, leaving the thought and smile lingering. Winston notices that Johnny doesn't say anything about Maude.

They sit in silence pondering what Johnny is trying to explain. Occasionally, they look at each other and exchange a sheepish smile. But after each smile, Johnny appears more serious, his face tenser and the muscles in his upper jaws systematically clenching and relaxing.

"I was reading that diary there," Johnny finally breaks the silence. He points to the book on his cot, as if Winston is seeing it for the first time. "It got me thinking a long time. Lots of things in it remind me of when I first came up here. Got me thinking like never before. Some o' the same things my grandfather went through in Panama and then my father in Cuba, I went through too. In fact, we still going through. Like nothin' ever change."

They lapse into silence again. I hope they will shift the conversation away from those bloody diaries. They give me the willies. I feel like shouting out, they are no good for you! Don't read them any more! Over the noise from outside, they can hear each other breathing. Johnny gets up, then takes a couple of steps in the direction of the bedroom door. He stops as if an invisible rope is pulling him back to the young man.

"You know, I read them diaries there, and I think about my grandfather. He was twenty-two when he went to Panama. My father, twenty when he went to Cuba. I left when I was eighteen and you... you're seventeen, right?"

"Eighteen this year," Winston corrects him.

"We seem to be getting younger every generation." Winston rises too and start walking toward the door. Johnny feels like putting an arm around Winston's shoulder to console him, but refrains. It is obviously a real struggle for him not to hug the youth.

"If I was seventeen, eighteen, starting my life over again, I would really seriously ask myself if I wanted to spend the rest o' my life up here."

Well, hold it, I can't believe what I am hearing. Is this Johnny speaking, the Johnny I know? It would never occur to me he would think, far less express such a thought. The farm labour program is all he knows, the only life for him. Johnny always defends it. So what is he saying? Now he sounds almost treasonous. What can we expect next? That he would join Timmy and call for an end to the program, even though he is always the first at the airport for the return trip? Or linking up with Smokie in the foolish talk of running off?

Somehow this youngster always seems to find a way to unsettle Johnny, to make him say the most inane thing in an apparent attempt to impress this Winston. I tell yuh, if I didn't hear this conversation for myself, I would not believe it. Indeed, what's next?

"Look at me. Look at Tommy, Smokie," Johnny continues. "Look at all o' we after all this time. Sometimes, when I done reading them diaries, I does wonder to myself."

Winston walks out of the cabin to be alone. It is still bright out, but the light is fading. A pleasant breeze is spicing the air with the sweetness of the early spring plants and flowers. At least it isn't as cold as before, Winston consoles himself. Even if it is just as lonely as when he first arrived. He looks at the house in the distance and wonders what is keeping Jessica. He decides to sit on the steps of the cabin and wait for her. His eyes fall on the sapling, the same one now budding and coming alive, that had been part of the ritual supposedly making him a member of the Edgecliff group.

Winston walks over to the tree. He breaks off a twig and places it in his mouth. As he returns to the steps, he realizes the twig he is chewing is still as bitter as when he first arrived.

Winston strips down to his underwear and is crawling into bed when he hears the surprisingly loud scurrying about in the outside room. Only minutes earlier, Jessica had left from sitting with him on the steps. The wind had changed direction suddenly and it was becoming a bit nippy. They had chatted for more than an hour and Jessica did cheer him up a little, even getting him to laugh at how he plays dominoes.

"Anyone can learn to play dominoes," he remembers her saying. "Even me. I learned from Johnny, when I used to trail him around the farm like a puppy. And, besides, you can borrow books from the library on anything these days."

As he reflects on the evening, Winston realizes that their talk probably didn't do much good for Jessica. When she was leaving, it was obvious that something was still bothering her, something she doesn't feel like telling him about just yet and which he didn't press to hear. Something bigger than her wish to leave the farm and study in Toronto. Whatever it was, Jessica obviously still had to think it through, still wanted her private moments, forcing her to decline his offer to walk her back to the house. Perhaps the next time he will be considerate and give her plenty of time and opportunity to talk out her problem instead of mourning so much about himself. He will provide a willing ear and even a shoulder.

But he could not help feeling a bit morose as he watched her departing into the darkness. Even then, Winston realized the winds were really getting much colder and that the rain was starting to sting so violently — the drops bouncing off the ground — that he decided it was best to go inside and get an early night's sleep.

"Quick. Quick," he hears a shout in the next room. "Next, we'll have a darn funnel."

"What's the matter?" Winston hears Johnny's question.

"Hail. As big as golf balls," says the first voice, which Winston now identifies as George Stewart's. "The tobacco plants. God, I can't remember the last time we had this kind of weather so late in the year. And not a damn word on the radio."

A crashing sound penetrates the room, as the table falls to the floor and the dominoes scatter. Winston jumps to his feet. He tries to picture what is happening in the other room. He can tell that the men are running to the corner of the room where the winter coats and rubber boots are stacked in a pile.

"Tommy!" Johnny is shouting. "Take Delbert and some of the men over to the fields. The rest come with me. Over to the barn. For the heaters. Kerosene in them, George?"

"We might have to get some from the drum in the back of the house," George answers. "Mary will show you. God! Who would expect hail like this so late? Just when we planted the damn tobacco. I just happened to look out the kitchen window and see these things bouncing off the ground. When I got outside, the ground was covered with the damn hail. Christ, how I wish someone had noticed this was happening and alerted me. Didn't any of you guys hear nothing? On the roof?"

"I don't think so," Johnny says, rushing to catch up to the men running ahead.

Winston pulls his coat around him and steps through the door. Immediately, he understands why George Stewart is so concerned. The steps to the cabin are covered with the little balls of ice, some of them coalescing like misshapen glass marbles. He remembers playing marbles at home and his opponents shouting: *Down taw, no brush. Up taw, back to the line.* Still more hail is falling heavily on Winston's head, stinging his face and hands, the same way it had a few minutes earlier when he still thought it was rain.

Winston curses himself. He should know better, should be

more alert. Nobody should have to tell him the difference between ordinary rain and hail. He should have known what was happening and given the early warning. This is just another sign that he has no right to be on a farm, Winston tells himself. Another sign he should *up taw* and head back to the line to start all over again.

In anger, he kicks some of the hailstones from the steps. For the record, allow me the pleasure of simply saying I rest my case about Winston and this leadership madness.

chapter sixteen

Like mischievous children playing peek-a-boo with aged men, the first weak rays of the morning slowly appear from behind the trees in the distance. A strong breeze is beginning to warm the land, driving away the last of the overnight fog, partially compensating for the dissipating lukewarm heat from the yellowing flames.

Wearily, the men drag themselves from the fields. In the half darkness, some of them mill around the tractor carrying the heaters and the oil drums. This hideous vehicle stands forlornly in the pathway between the fields, an unwanted reminder of how these people have no control over their fate, not even with the use of machinery and contrived heat.

The men say nothing. Maybe this silence reflects their tiredness. Or it could be caused by the darkness, or from realizing they have soldiered all night in vain. The men in this ragtag army do not try exchanging feigned hopes for the prostrate plants. They know that even the strongest rays of the sun will never cause these plants to rise again. The evidence is plain and convincing for all to see. All across the fields, it looks like *baccoos*, those wicked little spirits that can only do harm, had spent a busy night in illicit play, carelessly stomping on the fragile plants in some twisted humour.

With the sun finally rising, the men can at last go back to the cabin. The crisis of the night is over, dead, kaput. But a new one awaits them. This is the wake, a moment for personal reflection, a time for the sun to try to heal and preserve where the men failed. For the sun comes as a friend, the cavalry charging out of the distance. A conqueror not of the men and their hopes but of the fears and hurt welling up inside them.

When they get inside, they can warm their hands so as to lose that stiff and clumsy feeling. In their hurry to save the plants, most of them forgot to grab gloves from the cardboard box beside the pile of coats. Eight hours later, their hands are still paying the price. In the warmth of the cabin, they can catch a couple hours of sleep and think about their uncertain future.

No one has to tell them that the night's devastation might be the final blow to their contract. No one has to tell them that the damage done might be beyond the repair of the sun, no matter how triumphantly it spreads and struts itself over the land over the coming summer. Nobody has to tell them of the danger for each and every one of them from having nothing to do, when the men may prey on themselves as relentlessly as the sun does back home.

For when there is no work, when there are only the heat and discomfort of the warm air and hot rays, when there is no hope individually or collectively, what then is there to do? Maybe they will not call it black-on-black violence as some would. And perhaps they won't call it such because this is a farm in Canada and not a project or some slum ghetto elsewhere. They will lash out at even the best of friends if they stand between them and redemption by the rescuing sun. With the dousing of hope, a man is capable of killing his own mother. Remember what even his closest friends did to the Prophet.

So the men drag themselves from the fields, wearily, silently and deep in thought. Everyone is beaten. All of them discouraged. No need to talk about how hard they had worked to beat the odds. Even Winston toiled like never before. And, can you imagine, without a single complaint, too. But they still feel like failures. All around them is evidence of the ruin.

"Mrs. Stewart is making coffee over by the house," George

Stewart says from the tractor seat. His eyes are red and his face drawn. His hands and clothes are dirty. He, alone, is not wearing a coat. He had come to the field in heavy cotton shirt and jeans and had worked all night, dressed as if it were summer.

Still without a word, the men begin retrieving the heaters, many of them already cold. The bad weather has come so late and so unexpectedly that there wasn't enough kerosene on the farm to keep the flames going all night. Not that it matters. From early on, it was obvious that the losses would be heavy. Instead of trying to spread the heat thinly over the farm, George Stewart and Johnny decided right away to concentrate on the fields shielded from the wind by the apple and pear trees. And what cruel irony. No sooner had the men positioned the heaters than the spiteful wind immediately changed direction.

"We did our best," Johnny says as the men file pass him. He is standing by the tractor to the left of George Stewart. Shoulder to shoulder, they look like two beaten generals. As the workers trudge past him, Johnny sees the hurt on their face and the weariness in their uncertain steps. And, as usual, Johnny rises to the occasion. He taps the men on their shoulders and backs, a reassurance to keep their hopes alive. Nobody on this farm — including George and Mary Stewart — can afford to lose faith at this point, Johnny thinks. And he knows it is up to him to make sure that this loss is not followed by prolonged despondency, something undoubtedly more crippling to the farm and the men's future than anything encountered so far.

"Have some coffee. Get some sleep," he says to no one in particular. Nobody replies. Johnny, a true leader, a prophet in his own right, is now a lonely voice in the arid wilderness of hope. The men just move in single file toward the house, their heads bowed, their eyes fixed to the wet ground.

Winston is sitting on the empty oil drum in the yard when Jessica motions to him with her disposable cup of coffee. He is the last to get something to drink. Every time the tray passes his way, he declined, taking one or two cookies from the glass plate but refusing the coffee.

"Black or regular?" Jessica asks.

"Black," Winston answers.

"And as weak as I can make it and still call it coffee, right?"

"Uh huh."

"I thought you'd want it black. All the men like theirs regular, except Johnny," Jessica says, handing him the steaming cup. "Johnny has always taken his black. For as long as I can remember." Underneath her brown coat are the jeans and running shoes she was wearing when she and Winston sat in front of the cabin hours earlier. "Just like Johnny."

"Why you say that?"

"You remind me of Johnny when he was younger," Jessica says. She surveys the yard with the pools of water underfoot, the dirty and muddy boots on the men's feet. She could not help noticing how obvious it is that her father is avoiding her mother. All morning, her father has remained in conversation with someone, mostly Johnny. As her mother comes closer, he always moves away. They have been making circles around the yard and each other.

This issue will come to a head inside the house, Jessica figures, when the men are gone. In her head, judging from those strong vibes I am picking up from her, she can hear her mother insisting that George should have listened, that he shouldn't have defied the bank. And she can hear the same old argument from her father that he had no choice but to gamble just one more time on tobacco.

Jessica sighs loudly at the thought of her parents' incessant arguing. I feel sorry for her, and I wonder if Winston even realizes what this young woman is going through. Jessica takes a big mouthful of hot coffee. She plans on telling her parents soon about her decision, the same one she partially discussed with Winston the previous night, a discussion that still leaves her feeling hollow and empty but just as determined. Jessica knows that her parents will also argue with her. Still, as she had reasoned with Winston, she has no choice. This night of ruin makes her decision even more imperative; it's almost impossible for her to remain on the farm.

"Why you say that?" Winston persists. She looks at him, hearing his voice in the distance. "How you could know 'bout Johnny when he was young?"

"When I was a little girl. He always used to come over to the house. I used to trail him around. I liked being with him and hearing the way he talked. It sounded so different and funny to me."

"Oh," Winston says. He recognizes that her heart isn't really in the conversation. He sips the coffee and watches Jessica watching her mother and father battle each other across the yard, in the full view of the seemingly unsuspecting men. Finally, her mother had caught up to George and Johnny. They are near by the steps to the house. Johnny looks uncomfortable standing between them.

"Shit," Jessica says, just loud enough for Winston to hear. Even from across the yard, it is obvious Mary is crying openly. This is what Jessica doesn't want, what she fears. Her father is looking to the sky.

"You know, I should've warn somebody that this was happening," Winston says. He sips more of the coffee and makes a face. "It was starting to hail when we were talking. I should have said something."

"Me too," Jessica responds. "But my head was so fucked up, somewhere else."

They notice that Johnny has escaped and is talking with Tommy. Once again, the coughs are taking hold of Tommy, trying to strangle him. Unsuccessfully, he is attempting to suppress the coughs with sips of coffee.

"I think I'll go and see if the men want any more coffee," Jessica says. "What about you, Winston?"

His cup is still almost full. He makes a face and before he can answer, Jessica walks off. Her mind is on comforting her mother, on helping her parents cushion the hurt from realizing that the farm is probably truly lost. For the past two years, she has dreaded something like this happening. She has lost friends who had to leave school prematurely to help on the farm, only to see their education, dreams and then the family farm slip away. Others simply gave up and moved to Toronto. She too is bound for Toronto, for the Royal Conservatory of Music, as soon as the government approves her student loan. As soon as she tells her parents.

Johnny looks anxiously about the cabin. With the men hanging around in the building all day long, the already small space appears to have shrunk even further. It does not help that the men are walking about listlessly, half dressed and with long drawn faces, just getting into one another's way, or that the black and white television no longer works.

Johnny shifts his weight on the cot and brings out one of the diaries from underneath the bed. Across from him, Winston stretches out on his back, a matchstick in the corner of his mouth, and stares hypnotically at the mattress above his head. Since the storm, Johnny has detected a change in Winston, a sign of maturity that displays itself in less complaining, but in more solitary thinking. That is good, Johnny tells himself, and I agree. Under these conditions, so strained as they are, the last thing the men need is to have to put up with anyone's whining.

Johnny glances around the room. As usual, Tommy is under the covers, reading his stack of old letters, seemingly oblivious to his surroundings. Tommy's recent visits to the doctor have not done much for his coughing or to ease his pains that flared up after the night in the field. Tommy says the doctor wants him to take a whole series of various tests, as soon as the Liaison Officer can take him to the clinic. Some of the other men are resting in their cots, but the majority of them are aimlessly walking between the bedroom and the outer room as if in search of direction. They don't know what to do with the unexpected free time.

These four weeks following the hailstorm have been like nothing Johnny has experienced. Dispiriting uneasiness and edginess have overtaken the farm. The men fear that the worst is still to come. And they believe that Johnny, from his conversations with George Stewart, knows full well what is going on, but refuses to level with them. In all his years on the farm, Johnny has never had to deal with such coldness and suspicion. Little do they know that he too is frightened by this endless uncertainty. That he, too, in the early hours of the morning finds himself waking from bad dreams, despairing about the future, bathed in warm sweat. But he has to hide these concerns. He has to look cheerful in the hopes his pretend happiness will help the men to relax and, possibly, to forget.

But it is not working. No matter how much he tries to tell them that nobody knows what is happening, not even the Liaison Officer or George Stewart himself, the men always walk away with their heads bowed, looks of disbelief and betrayal on their faces that tear deeply into every fibre of Johnny's body. Johnny knows he is telling them the truth whether in private conversations, when they unashamedly admit their fears, or in long open discussions in the bedroom before they go to sleep. "There is simply no way of knowing what to expect," he tells them, "not until George meets with the banker. Everything is in the bank's hands."

"In the hands of the Lord," Preacher Man says.

Johnny has explained whenever he could that the storm was so devastating in the region, and because there is now such a heavy demand on the banker's time, that the meeting to decide the fate of Edgecliff wouldn't happen until four weeks from the day of the storm. Other farms that are closer to the edge financially have to be dealt with immediately. While George Stewart is spared the immediate pain of having to throw himself at the mercy of his creditors, the uncertainty lingers heavily over the cabin. Time creeps by so slowly, making the wait so heavy and drawn out, giving the men too much time to think. This wasting away is no good, Johnny thinks, and I agree. Such despondency will only sap their energy and willpower, robbing the men of the strength to accept any additional bad news. But, after much agonizing waiting, the day of reckoning is here. Johnny tries to distract the men and keep their spirits up.

"Listen to this," he says, flipping a page in the diary. "Here is another passage that my grandfather did write in Panama."

He looks from the opened book to see who, if anyone, is listening. None of the men appear to be paying attention, but he begins to read. He knows they are listening, if only with one ear. Like Johnny, the men are hooked on the stories in the diaries. And what are they but running commentaries from that dark period decades ago, the echoes coming alive through Johnny's reading to the assembled men. Now they are ready for another instalment.

"Last night," Johnny reads, haltingly.

> *Seven more men died from the malaria. We found them stiff as logs in their beds. This brings to twenty-three the number of people dead so far. Some people*

saying that the malaria caused by the dirty water we got to drink; others say it's from the mosquitoes. Today, the foreman put up a sign on the door saying that from tomorrow all of us have to line up every morning in front the cabin for a dose of quinine.

"A dose o' what?" Henry asks.

"Quinine," Johnny answers.

"I never hear nothing named so," Henry says. "What is quinine?"

"People used to take it for malaria," Johnny explains. "Real bitter."

"Can't be as bitter as workin' on no contract," Preacher Man says.

"I ain't surprise that you ain't never hear about it," Timmy says. He is sitting on his cot with his legs dangling over the sides. "A lot o' we own people don't know their history. That's what's wrong with all o' we Black people, even the ones like we up here on these farms and not knowing if they'll send all o' we back home or not."

Suddenly, you can feel the tension.

"I keep telling all o' you that we's only the latest of an exploited people, a people with no control over we own future," Timmy says. His voice falters, sounding as if his reflexes to flee are beating the shit out of his desire and wisdom to stand up and fight. But either way, Timmy has to appear confident: he must run as a sissy or stay and fight as a man. "We's a people that can be bought and sold easy so. It goes back to when our foreparents were dragged outta Africa and brought to the West Indies as slaves. We is a pilgrim people from then on and we won't stop roaming until we become we own masters."

"But what that got to do with…what you call it again, Johnny? Quin-what?" Henry interjects.

"Quinine," Johnny says.

"People like you, Timmy," Henry says, seemingly ignoring Johnny's answer, "only make me real vex with all this slave nonsense talk all the time."

"You see, that is why I don't like talking to ignorant people," Timmy responds angrily.

Maybe the reflexes to fight are staging a comeback, or maybe there is only so much any man can take. Johnny realizes that like Henry's, Timmy's nerves are also on edge; he's ready to explode, to lash out at anything and anyone. Actually, everyone's nerves are frayed.

"These ignorant people who don't know any better," Timmy parries. "Here I am tryin' to explain the ins and outs of this system that we working under. The same kind o' system that our foreparents laboured under in Barbados, in Panama like Johnny's reading in them diaries, in Cuba and America and which all o' we still got to live under up here in Canada in this day and age. Ignorant people!"

"Who you calling ignorant?" Henry shoots back. He advances threateningly toward Timmy. "Who could be more ig'rant than a big man like you talking the same foolishness all the time? If things so bad why you still on the Program after all these years? Why you is always the first to come back up here? Why you don't just put your tail between your legs and run off?"

Johnny quickly positions himself between the two men. Timmy sucks his teeth loudly and stretches out on the bed.

"See what I mean?" he says. "Try to explain something to somebody and the first thing they do is look for a fight. Well if anybody wants to fight with me, I'm ready to fight them, too, so help me Christ."

"Why you don't come down here and say that," Henry challenges him. "I'll bre'k in yuh arse right here on this spot."

"See what I mean?" Timmy repeats. "Preacher Man, isn't it

the same Bible you read that says 'where there is no dream the people perish?'"

"Not me. Don't put me in that," Preacher Man says curtly. "The Bible also says: blessed are the peacemakers, *bo*."

Johnny leads the enraged Henry through the bedroom door to the outer room. He comes back and picks up the diary. Perhaps it isn't such a good idea after all to read such touching material to the men. On this crucial day, the men aren't in the right frame of mind. Not with so many thoughts running through their heads; not with every one of them on edge until Tommy returns from the clinic; not with everyone just dreading the arrival of the Liaison Officer and any bad news he might have about the Program.

And it is definitely not a good idea when the men have time to think and amplify, to extrapolate and commiserate, to feel elation one moment and despair the next. No, the time isn't right, the men's psyches too fragile, for such discussions. With the men's heads running so hot, tempers so short and hope all but gone, anything can happen. Johnny knows this.

Finally, you are seeing a perfect example of what I've been warning against for so long. Diaries can be such weapons, bombs really. I don't trust them. I've seen what damage they can do. Now you, too, are seeing with your own eyes what I could only tell you, even if it is just a brief taste, like a squall on the outer edge of a hurricane. One sampling and you don't need to feel the full impact of the hurricane. That's why I am glad Johnny is finally putting away those diaries, hopefully for good.

"Anybody for dominoes?" Johnny queries. He closes the diary and places it under the bed. "Don't forget the tournament next Wednesday. We gotta keep practisin' 'cause them boys from Lowerthon Farms real good. Come Timmy. Don't lay down there mopin'. Come and play a domino."

Johnny looks at his watch. A quarter past one. In another

fifteen minutes or so the uncertainty should be over. George will be meeting with the bank manager. In a few hours, we can expect him to report to the men the outcome of the meeting and their fate. If the Liaison Officer shows up with George, it will be obvious. But at least, Johnny thinks, he wouldn't have to try to amuse the men any more.

The Liaison Officer does show up, but without George Stewart. As soon as he steps through the door, the deep frown on his face indicates something is wrong. Without saying anything to the men around the dominoes table, he walks into the bedroom and closes the door behind him. A few seconds later, Winston comes out of the room, obviously asked to leave by the Officer so he can be alone with Johnny and Tommy. Nobody can hear what they are saying, although they keep hearing the muffled sounds of Tommy's repeated coughing. The domino games drag on with nobody saying anything, with nobody really winning or losing.

Eventually, Johnny and the officer come out. The officer stands in the middle of the room, his hands in his pants pockets. The games stop. Still not smiling, he looks around him, as if searching for the right words to say, as if looking for the right face.

"Any word from Mr. Stewart?" Johnny asks, obviously to get things going. You can see from the looks on the men's faces that this question surprises them. They are wondering, heck, if the three of them didn't talk about George Stewart and the farm, then what the France did they have to keep them so long behind closed doors? And instantly you can hear that uncomfortable rumbling in the chest and bowels of every man; you can hear the loud flutterings of their hearts. And you can see the beads of perspiration breaking out on the face of even those who tend not to sweat too much. I hate the feel and smell of fear and trepidation.

"No," the officer says. He is not talking as loudly and pompously as we know he can. "That meeting was postponed for another week or so. But I'm more concerned about something else." He looks around the room, as if afraid to make eyes with anyone. Not only is there now the rancid smell of fear, you can also taste the insipid odour of the wounded, a stench that only a beast of prey can like as it seeks to savage the weak and wounded.

"I can't really go into details about it because it's a private health matter," he scratches his head and runs his hand through his hair, pushing it back, "but I might have to make arrangements for all of you to get a blood test like the one Tommy just had."

The men stare at one another, not knowing what to make of this news, but realizing this talk of a blood test is a serious matter because of the look on the officer's face, because of the way the officer has lost control of his hands. If there is one thing every man is trained to decipher, from the shift in the eyes of a potential attacker, the feign of a boxer, to the awful smells of weakness in the vanquished and of power in a conqueror, men know how to read body language, even the slightest movement of the hands, and how to react accordingly for their own protection

"I'll come and get Tommy in a day or so," he says. "We got to do some more tests. Depending on his results, the rest of you might not have to have no test. But I don't know," his voice drops unconvincingly.

"But all of us had blood tests at home just before we come up here," Winston says. "At least, I did. So why we need more people sticking up we arms for?"

"I know. But you might have to do it again." He turns to leave and is almost through the door when he spins around and says, "Oh, I almost forgot. You guys won't be going into town any more. The health authorities are asking that we keep you on the farm until they know the outcome of the blood tests. If you have to get anything off the farm, give me or Mr. Stewart a list. We'll try to get it for you."

Without another word, he is gone, leaving Johnny to explain what he doesn't know and for the men to listen to the sound of Tommy's coughs.

chapter seventeen

Jessica stands awestruck in the doorway, as straight as a pin, her auburn hair blowing in the wind. She is both surprised and enthralled by the beautiful music coming from the silverish steel pan and by the muscular young man playing it. The haunting music stirs feelings deep inside, gnawing at those very emotions that she wanted to leave behind in fleeing her parents' house only a few minutes earlier.

A mixture of loneliness and subtle desperation emanates from the pan. And, at the same time, it is so unforgettably exhilarating, a soulful sound that has us simply enraptured.

I can imagine what Jessica is thinking, if the music would ever allow her thoughts to gel. Really I can, for as I also stare at this man standing so ghostlike under the naked light, the strange mixture of shadows and light amplifying yet contrasting the very essence of his sheer blackness, it is as if I am seeing him for the very first time.

And what a beautiful blend of melanin and testosterone! What a specimen, the type the Prophet and honourable Elijah always said we should strive to be, that we will become, if we live right and eat correctly. The Minister would have recruited him instantly. So struck am I that I really have to look at my feet so I don't step on the scales that must have just fallen from my eyes.

Alone with his thoughts and emotions, he is rhythmically, yet effortlessly, tickling the notes on the open-faced pan, tapping his feet almost absentmindedly to the music, but freely sharing his thoughts with anyone willing to listen.

It is obvious that Jessica still can't quite believe that this young man, the muscles in his back and upper arms beginning to firm up like those of the other men from the heavy manual labour, this young buck standing with his bare back to her, could express such deep feelings. And on such an unconventional musical instrument, a contraption that she is sure she will never study at the Royal Conservatory.

And, to tell the truth, Jessica is not alone with these feelings. I feel that way, too, and very much so. As if a part of my heart is missing. My soul needs salvation. That's why this music, so haunting and personal, touches me so deeply, because I am hurting too and real bad.

I do not know what else I can do to please everyone. And the Lord knows how I try. But sometimes nothing is enough; sometimes it is so difficult to resist giving up. Sometimes, nothing matters any more. Walking around the farm, just being alone with my thoughts, isn't really helping the situation. I can only ask why do I find myself in such a predicament? Why am I so sad and depressed? So despondent? And is this a fitting reward for all my hard work, caring and dedication? I just don't know.

Take this morning when I woke up to find changes of mammoth proportions all around me. For some unexplained reason, something told me as soon as I rolled out of bed that I should check out the reports Mother Nyame has been receiving. It was just that gut feeling that makes the hair on my back stand on end, the premonition that something is amiss and, as is now undoubtedly the case, I will be the last to know.

When I check, my poor heart almost gives out; I'm thinking I must have stumbled into the Tower of Babel; I am thinking this can't be for real, someone is messing with my head. I keep changing from channel to channel, but the result is always the same. The stories are in all these different languages — nation languages, I think people call them. Only the odd one here and there is in English, French or any of the more common

European tongues. It sounds so strange hearing these languages. Nothing musical to them. Or is it the fact that mentally I'm not prepared for this surprise?

Anyhow, I stand there dumbfounded, my brain refusing to register anything. I must have remained like that for a full hour. How can this be? I keep asking myself. Am I sleeping? Didn't they always drum into our heads that our reports must be in a language that is useful to the largest number of people? Isn't it still true that we have to use one of these European languages? Well, then, I am thinking, why am I hearing all these funny languages? Why are they wasting time and effort with a language that at the most maybe a few hundred thousand people speak here and there?

And the worse was still to come — in no time I discover that the other storyteller on this farm has been spilling her guts in two or three languages, usually at the same time. And to think this is the same Miss Twerp that I condescended to by going out of my way to bloody-well call her, taking the initiative to befriend. It's me that had to be the one to swallow my pride and say, what the heck, this business of not speaking and not being courteous can't go on forever; it is too juvenile and short-sighted. Why not call up the youth and say hello? I said. After all, she is not responsible for her presence on the farm. If I should be mad at anyone, it should be with those that sent her, not this Miss Plain Jane who is just doing her job.

So I say to myself, why not be the one to show you have manners and class, that you're mature, old enough, comfortable enough with yourself to just call up and see how this gal is getting on? And when I do, she sounds so surprised, as if she expects a bolt of lightning to knock her dead. So that she comes across as really frightened, as if she wants to keep her distance, as if she thinks I'm thinking of hitting on her or something, but all the same she's giving the airs that she only talking to me because it is me that call her, that want to make friends. I mean, she couldn't wait to end the conversation, which I am thinking is really strange — in my books you don't act this way when someone extends a hand of friendship. Not unless you are devious-minded, unless someone like this scrawny-ass rebel really believes that males act generously to the other sex only because they have one thing on their mind. Which, as everybody can swear, certainly isn't the case with me. At least not with her!

What's up? I say, unintentionally putting her on the spot. And right away, before the words could drop from my mouth, she answers quick, quick — *nuthin'*.

"How you mean nothing?" I ask, like a fool not picking up anything.

Just that I kinda busy, can't stop to talk now, she said.

"What makes you so busy? Girl, you gotta make sure you don't run your blood to water working too hard, yuh hear me? Anyway, chile, did you check with any o' my commentaries?" I continued, trying to sound as friendly as possible. All the time I'm thinking this Miss Prim-and-Proper is nervous as shite because she knows to whom she is talking. Obviously, I think, she still has some respect for her seniors.

Nah, man. I ain't been listenin' to nuthin', she says. *Too busy husslin', getting ready fuh tomorrow, I guess.*

"So, what's happening tomorrow?" I ask. Then, you won't believe it, but there is this long silence, so long that I have to ask Miss Big-and-Powerful if she's still there. But as the old people like to say, the damage already done: 'cause mouth open, story jump out. The only thing that makes me certain she is on the other end of the line is this loud gulping that I keep hearing. Now I know she trying to recover, the poor innocent. The gulping and the gears in her brain just changing and grinding against one another.

"What's up with this tomorrow thing?" I repeat.

Oh, nuthin', she says, speaking slowly and carefully enunciating her words. *Nuthin', I guess.*

You're sure you lie? I ask.

Nah, man. Trust me, brother.

Well, you know me by now. Anybody tells me to trust them, automatically I do the opposite. A hard and fast rule with me. Especially if it is a person I don't know or one acting so timid and uncertain, behaving as if he or she spoke too fast and just wishing he or she could reach out into the air and grab back the words. So we say goodbye, promise to talk to each other again and just end the conversation.

But I am no fool. I know Miss Pretend doesn't really want to talk to me again. You can understand how all these signs and signals add up to this ominous feeling in my heart, how I can't sleep, and how I wake up this morning with all this foreboding. Then, as I was saying, I check out these reports first thing this morning and all these strange tongues and languages coming at me like wildfire. I didn't know there were so many languages in this world, so many derivatives of what we call English or French or Spanish. Everybody speaking some fancy language, wrapping his tongue around fancy words and phrases, sounding so happy and hip. And all the storytellers sound so young, like they're just out of the classroom.

Only me, the fool, not knowing what is going on. Which only confirms in my mind that there is a hidden agenda somewhere, that this Jezebel on this farm is part of some scheme or plot against me. She had to know what was coming down the pipe and she could have told me. She could have tipped me off, as one professional to another, so I wouldn't now look so stupid and out of touch. But she didn't and for that, all I can say is, this bitch is going to dead bad. Yes, that's the worst curse the old people back home can put on anyone, especially on a wayward youth. Mark my word, this Miss Virago is going to die bad, stretched out on her back, her eyes open wide and staring blankly into the nothingness of the sky, her legs waving in the air. Yes, she will die bad because the God I serve doesn't like ugly and doesn't reward the deceitful. So now you understand why what some of the gangsta storytellers and rappers would call the conniving females I am describing as nothing but bitches and whores. Or why the young boys make such fun at them while singing — *There's a brown girl in the ring, tra la la la la la. 'Cause she likes sugar and I like plum*. Now you understand.

Of course, for the rest of the day I just cuss this *rass-clate* deceiver blue, nonstop. I was nasty, man. And I didn't limit my thoughts and words to her alone. No, I also turned on her grandmothers, her grandfathers, her mother and her father. Then I turned to any brothers, sisters, uncles, aunts, cousins and nieces she has. I cussed them all, just letting loose my tongue in their arses. I even touched up her unborn children and their children's children, too. For how could she do this to me? To me, the champion storyteller? *A riddle, a riddle, a ree, godblindmuh, in she back-side.* When I was through cussing, her ears must have been ringing like a bell. I cussed her stink, stink, stink. She deserves it.

I don't mind admitting that it is really taking me some time to get over this shock. Yes, I can admit it because, as Brer Jackal said to Brer Fox, confession is good for the soul, so show me your motion, *yuh think I mekking fun*. But, my God, I mean, that shock this morning almost killed me. To think all these thing happening behind my back and nobody bothering telling me nuthin', the same way all those people had schemed and planned in the absence of the Prophet, the same way I am always the last to know anything. Every minute that passes, I am getting more and more angry. I can't control myself. As the man says, I feel like bombing a church now I find that the preacher is lying. I feel utterly betrayed.

With my blood running hot, I do another foolish thing.

Without thinking, I just up and call Mother Nyame and ask her straight what the hell is going on. Well, she starts bawling me out right off the bat — about how she doesn't like my commentaries; that she doesn't think what I am trying is working; that she had something else in mind; that she thinks my going on about letters and diaries is pathetic and so on. It's like nothing I say or do is worthy of any praise.

Finally, I get a word in and I say, is this why we have to have this Tower of Babel nonsense? Didn't we come a long way in standardizing how we do business, how we report and act? To which she just says, look man, don't bother me with your foolishness. You is the one always talking so much about history, she says. So let me ask you, wasn't there a time when African people had their own voices and spoke a multitude of languages, when they told their stories in their own tongues? Wasn't that a glorious era, one we should try to recapture? Then came all these European tongues. Look here, she says, this is the ending of a millennium. We got to get back our history so we can move forward. And anyway, she says, I'm busy right now, too busy for all this talking. I have work to do. I have to listen in and find out how these new guys are working out. When I got time to just sit around on my fat arse and lick my mouth, I'll contact you.

As you might expect, I am a basket case. I don't even know how my reports sound, if they make any sense in the least. Something keeps saying to me, Brer Anancy why do you keep kicking against the pricks? I am hearing this voice and it is ripping up my heart, because the pricks are indeed hard and sharp. Yeah, why kick against the pricks, I ask myself, why don't you just give up and know your place? Why not become another Brer Jackass for everybody to ride yuh? Why do you keep on fighting and fighting, expecting so much from a people that are just vipers, snakes in the grass? Oh, you vipers and hardhearted people, I hear another prophet proclaiming in another story, and

I wonder if this kind of chastising and cursing will always be the only role for the true prophet and his storyteller.

Needless to say, I am in a fog all day. At one time, I find myself wandering around the bedroom and climbing onto the bed of Jeremiah, a real booze-head of a man. As luck would have it, I arrive just as he is hiding the last of his bottle of rum, just as he removes the bottle from his mouth and one drop, just one little drop, falls next to me. Well, shit man, for the rest of the day I am practically tipsy. My head is spinning. But for once I feel mellow, *irie, man; real irie*.

I can forget the heartaches and the pain, the rebuff and the lies from this Delilah on the farm and from Mother Nyame. I feel free and uninhibited. I am really sweet. I just feel like passing the chalice, man, to lively up myself. Except that everything is in that fog, everything moves so slowly, so exaggeratedly slowly. So that when the men climb onto the school bus to head for the domino tournament, I don't care. I don't want to go. I just want to roam around the farm, feeling the wind in my face, singing and reciting my poetry, man, and hoping to God that one of the birds now appearing in this part of the country will spot me. I wouldn't even resist. Then how would Mother Nyame, if she still got a conscience, feel when she knew she was the cause of my demise? I guess she would just jump at the opportunity to get one of her favourite connivers to take my place, maybe somebody speaking Swahili or something so. But I would be gone, out of my misery.

Just when I feel like throwing everything in, I start to hear this sweet music in the distance. The haunting melody calls earnestly to me. It is freedom and redemption. Somebody understands, the music says. Get up and go into Nineveh and tell the truth. In the melody I hear Brer Anancy saying to Brer Donkey, why you'll be a real jackass *fuh true* if you don't get up and start living; if you don't start braying for your own self, braying loud and long. And that was after Brer Donkey keep complaining about how it is he who always has to pull the big-able cart uphill, the load so heavy that when he gets home he ain't got the strength to bray loud enough to let the master know it's time to bring him food and water. This music is so real and invigorating. It puts a joyful sound in my heart; it makes me feel as if I want to live again. I want to just jump up and shout hallelujah, thank you Jesus.

So I begin to walk slowly in the direction of what beckons me, enjoying the music and feeling that I am floating on air. I am really taking my time because, as you know, taking your time ain't laziness — hasty ox drinks dirty water. And for some stupid reason, I start thinking of Frankie back home and how he likes to stop and smell the flowers. In my mind, I see him cuddling the petals in his hand while listening to a steel band playing in the foyer of the airport, welcome the arriving tourists to the land of sea and sun. Don't ask why I am thinking these things, because I don't know.

The music pulls me to the cabin and I understand what people mean when they say they hear the song and feel the pull of the mermaid and they can't resist. The same way Brer Donkey felt when he kept swimming and swimming even when Brer Fish cautioned him, hey man, the sea ain't got no back door, yuh. Brer Donkey just couldn't resist. The same way I can't. The same way that, obviously, Jessica can't either.

Now I see Jessica standing frozen inside the door, her eyes fixed on Winston's long slender fingers, her own hands folding tightly around the plastic shopping bag behind her back — the bag with the book in it.

When she left the house, Jessica expected Winston would have already left the farm with the others. And she has a reason for thinking this way. Everyone knows how anxious Winston has been to get off the farm, especially since none of the men is now permitted to go into town unsupervised. She had hoped to drop off the plastic bag to whoever was playing the instrument and to leave clear instructions that nobody but Winston should open the bag.

But there before her eyes stands Winston under the naked bulb, absorbed in his thoughts and his music. Jessica feels the palms of her hands sweating from the heat of her own body and from being afraid of interrupting this artist. She doesn't want to break the peace, she doesn't want to intrude on the serenity, interrupt the privacy, the sweet but agonizing music providing a refuge. A sanctuary that even she can enter.

It is the music that pulled her from the house in the first place, the notes like those of some pied piper beckoning her away from the uncomfortable presence in the farm house. When she first hears them, her father was sitting at the kitchen table, smoking his pipe, a sure sign that something new was bothering him, an indication he was building courage to raise some troublesome matter with his wife. Smoking the pipe in the house, knowing Mary will ultimately protest as her sneezing increases, is his way of going on the offensive. As far as Jessica can guess, this probably wasn't the case when he met with the bank manager earlier in the day.

"Mrs. Francis moved to Toronto," she remembers George Stewart saying. "Looks like she couldn't take it any longer, seeing so many old friends in such trouble. Now, tell me — what can a woman her age hope to do in Toronto? But it's like everybody just gotta run to Toronto."

Jessica gets up from the table, empties the excess fat from the beef into the garbage and quickly washes the plate, knife, fork and coffee mug under the running tap water. Placing the utensils in the plastic drainer, she wipes her hands on a striped towel that hangs from a nail on the wall beside the old electric stove.

"But who am I to talk?" George continues. "Even our own daughter wants to go and live in Toronto. Doesn't she?"

Jessica walks over to the side table between the kitchen and living room, picking up the book she had placed there when she returned from school. With her back to her parents, she reaches into a cupboard underneath the sink and takes out one of the neatly folded plastic shopping bags with the words Dominion printed across it.

"Where are you going, honey?" her mother asks.

"Out for a walk," Jessica answers solemnly.

"All the way to Toronto?" George adds sarcastically.

"Be careful," his wife calls to Jessica. "It's getting dark."

"I'll walk over by the cabin," she says.

"Didn't the men go to Lowerthon's tonight?" her father asks, puffing a big white cloud of smoke into the air. Her mother waves the whitish bluish blob away from her face as the smoke circles over the table and dissipates into the air.

"Well, if all of them went to Lowerthon's, then who's playing that music?" Jessica asks, grabbing the opening to get back at her father. She steps out the back door before he can answer.

Indeed, Winston is the last person Jessica expects to find playing the steel pan. Until she sees him standing over the instrument, Jessica has seen nothing in him that would betray such musical talents. Nothing in their conversations, not even when she talks of playing the piano and going off to Toronto. Nothing to tell her that the two of them share such a deep love for playing music. Yes, they had exchanged cassette tapes and he talked once or twice about his guitar at home. But nothing like this. She had expected to find Mighty playing the pan, for apart from Smokie, there is no one else in the cabin that has ever played a musical instrument in front of her.

Winston finishes the tune and takes a deep breath. He still isn't aware of Jessica's presence. He shifts the short stubby drum stick from one hand to the other. Each stick is about six inches long and has red rubber wrapped at the top. He knocks the two sticks together and mutters softly, "One, two, three" and starts to beat to the up-tempo rhythm dictated by the tapping of his feet. Suddenly, apparently finally feeling the stare of the eyes in his back, he stops and swings around to face Jessica.

"How long you been standing there?" he asks softly.

"A fair bit now. Don't let me stop you." She walks into the cabin. "You played very well."

"I learned to play at home. The boys formed a band to enter the competitions at Crop-Over."

"At what?"

"Crop-Over. That is what we call carnival at home. Just like Caribana in Toronto or Labour Day parade in New York."

Jessica looks around the empty room. On one of the tables are several dirty dishes. Some shirts are on the back of chairs. But the cabin seems lonely, hollow and eerie without the men in it. The music seems to have more of an echo than at other times.

"Where're the others?" she asks, knowing full well in advance the answer.

"Playin' dominoes?" He begins drumming again and to hum the words to the song.

Beautiful. Beautiful Bar-ba-dos.
Gem of the Car-rib-bee-an Sea.
Come back to my i'-land, Barr-ba-dos;
Come back to my i'-land and me.

"Why you didn't go with them?" Jessica asks, waiting for him to pause in the singing. For me, instantly, hearing the song's lyrics, it is obvious why I am thinking of Frankie and back home. Pure nostalgia got me, man.

"You know I can't play dominoes."

Please come back where the night winds are blowing, he continues to sing, raising his voice slightly.

Please come back to the surf and the sea.
You'll find rest, you'll find peace in Barr-ba-dos;
Please come back to my i'-land and me.

"You should learn," Jessica says. "It isn't *that* difficult."

"Don't want to," he answers, continuing to play the melody. "None o' the men ain't got no time to teach me, anyway."

"Then you can use this." She produces the plastic bag from behind her back. He stops playing momentarily to glance with bewilderment at the package.

"I borrowed it from the library. Here's the deal: I'll help you to learn to play dominoes and you can teach me to play the steel pan."

"You crazy or something?" Winston says. "You know Mighty would kill me if he catches me." But as he is talking he is thinking through what she has said and even before he finishes protesting a smile breaks on his face. "You want to make a quick try, now?" he says, handing her the sticks.

She places the bag with the book on the bench nearby, takes the sticks and steps in front of the pan. "Maybe we can practise when the others are away on nights like this."

"Then when you get real good and you're in Toronto, you can play for Caribana," Winston says. He points to the indented and raised parts on the face of the drum for her to hit for the different notes. They run through the musical scale.

Winston steps behind Jessica, takes her wrists and resumes playing the haunting melody. "This song always reminds me of home," he says softly. She feels his chin on her shoulder. The warmth of his breath against the side of her face and ear gives her goose-pimples. There is strength to his grip, a natural rhythm in his movements and a soothing huskiness in his singing that makes her temporarily forget the problems in her parents' home, on the farm and even her plans to run away to Toronto. For a brief moment, she is willing to escape to the Caribbean with Winston.

Beau-ti-ful, Beau-ti-ful, Bar-ba-dos,
Gem of the Car-rib-bee-an Sea.

They are so cute. But as I watch them, I can't help also thinking, who would want to kill them first if he caught them in such a compromising position? Would it be Mighty for fooling around with his steel pan or would it be the black nationalist Timmy, who would undoubtedly frown on such a coupling? Perhaps it is the lingering effects of the alcohol or the hurt from Mother Nyame, but I don't care to know the answer. I really don't. For Winston and his music have me back in Barbados and I am happy. For me and for these two. Or so I think.

chapter eighteen

It's funny, when you think you have fallen as far as anyone can possibly go, you can always look around and see someone lower than you. Somebody is always worse off. Some poor slob, and, brother, isn't that a real fact of life? Thinking of this helps me to put my situation in some kind of perspective. This world might not be as bleak for me as it is for others. For I'm still blessed. Do I hear somebody saying Amen, brother? Indeed. Amen to that.

And when I find myself thinking about the vagaries of life, of the kind of hand that we get dealt when we creep out of the egg, a veritable collection of dispositions and traits, of so many things written into our stars, of, for example, deciding who can be a leader and who quite simply cannot, I have to come back to the discussions I've been having with Mother Nyame of late.

Yes, dear ones, the Great Mother does call, when she isn't too busy, just as she promised. And believe you me, my brothers, I am still most surprised to hear her voice. And before anyone can say *jack-boot-slipper*, I just fall under the spell of that familiar but enchanting sound of laughter and happiness in her voice. It is such an unbelievable pleasure to hear her cackle like the hen that just laid the egg. Such a pleasure to feel that warm, comfortable glow massaging every part of my body with that sweet serenading tone.

Oh, the voice and tone that bring back all those sweet memories hiding somewhere in our soul, our psyches. Some of them we don't even know we have. When the voice makes us remember our mothers singing us to sleep. Remember — it is dark and raining, fork lightning cutting the sky and there is no man around. She is promising that we will grow up to be a big, strong man, to be mummy's big man, to protect even mummy.

Mother Nyame possesses that disarmingly friendly tone that says without having to actually mouth one word that I must be a real jerk to think someone as nice and gentle as her would be angry with me, or would allow me to keep a bad mind or, as some men like to say, have a real hard-on for her for any length of time. Ah, I tell yuh, these females and the ease with which they get us to do anything they want. We are such putty, just wet clay, actually, in their hands. They always know how to get us to sleep the restful slumber of babies.

Needless to say, today I am as happy as any man who not only falls helplessly underneath the charm of a very special woman, but gets the ultimate reward, the soft treatment that leaves him completely drained, with a sleepy but contented smile on his face. Yes, I am like that man, so bring on the world, my brothers, I'm aready for battle.

How can I keep feeling sorry for myself and any mess I might be in when all I have to do is simply look at these sorry souls for men before me? When I only have to think of their utter privation and how, no matter how hard they try, because they are human and men, they cannot cross the gulf that separates them from women.

They will never get to hear the sweet voice of their mothers lulling them to sleep again. The voice and kisses stitching the wounds, balming the pains. They will never hear the promise that every imaginable thing will be okay. No calm voice to tell them they don't have to keep fighting every minute of the day, that it is all right to take some time out to rest and regenerate. That after a night so dark and frightening, everything will be fine. In the light of day, they won't have to spend time vainly reaching for conjectures. They won't have to search relentlessly for things that, as men, they are not good at finding; apparitions they are not programmed to handle well even if they try to confront them manfully; assurances they can just get on with what they are good at: working, fighting and, once in a while, playing.

If they are lucky they will have a master general leading them into battle against power they might never know or comprehend, but which with such strong leadership they should never fear. For at the end of the day, the reward for every man should be to come back home and to lie beside a woman, any woman, and hear his mother's voice.

When I think of these things, that's when I feel that I am especially blessed. For as Brer Anancy, a simple spider, I can understand, while still experiencing all their fears and expectations because I am male. But because I am not human, I do not have the same hang-ups as a typical man. I do not have to always be appearing to be trying to bust out of my natural limitations. I don't have to break out of the cage into which every animal finds itself. And to add a bit more poison to the witch's brew, let's be honest, to be Black or African is an added handicap for these men.

Before I go any further, let me tell you about the new arrangement I have with Mother Nyame. I think we now have a better understanding of what we both want. And while we are at it, I should also draw your attention to something that is happening to the men in the field even as we speak, something a tad bit disconcerting because of an unexpected development last night, but which might impact on my new arrangement. As I say, the anxieties are small potatoes, really, something to note, while not getting too worried. But, of course, these things, or how people react to them, are important. At least I believe little trials like these go to show character.

So, before I explain any more my dealings with Mother Nyame, I want you to cast your eyes over to the men. Notice how Johnny is behaving. A bit unusual, I should say, the way he is eating himself out with anxiety. Still, as I keep telling Mother

Nyame, my confidence in him remains unshakeable. Johnny is one man who knows his onions, I tell her. At the same time, he also knows his limitations, one man who's immune to having to strive for that special reward at the end of the day. As you know by now, going back to the cabin and finding a letter from home is not a high point for him.

There he goes again, just in time for us to see: anxiously glancing down the road every few minutes. This man is going to make himself into a total wreck if he doesn't calm down and relax. I think it is so funny; I don't know why Johnny keeps beating up himself so much. I didn't expect last night's incident to scare him so much, to leave him so jumpy, as pathetic as any of the men in his charge. But funny things do happen.

Yup, last night's unexpected development is definitely bothering him. And, uh huh, you are right again, that is another furtive glance, and still another and another. Now, by the minute, they are becoming more open. I am seeing those looks too and can't believe my eyes. Indeed, you might be quite right to ask, what the heck is Johnny looking for and why is he so nervous? Good questions, I say. Very good questions. But bear with me.

Well, believe it or not, and you must trust me on this one, Johnny is actually looking for any sign of the red and white minivan he expects to approach from the north. That's right, the little old van that would bring Tommy and the Liaison Officer back to the farm.

Which takes me back to what I was telling Mother Nyame. I got to share this last bit with you before telling you about last night. So wait. Now, Mother Nyame keeps asking what I think about Johnny and whether he might now be past his prime and ought to be replaced as the acknowledged leader for our purposes. Not that anyone, she adds, is saying he is over the hill or can't get it up. Just that she and a few others are wondering these things, and since I'm the one on the scene and with the most seniority, she said she wants to find out what I am thinking of Johnny in comparison to, let's say, someone like a Winston.

Well, as I tell Mother Nyame, I have unqualified confidence in a man like Johnny. He is caring but fair; he lives by the rules and he's always upfront with the men. Most of all, he's unemotional. This is not a man who goes off and acts rashly, doing erratic things. He is very predictable and loyal. In other words, I tell her, he is closer to my image of a father, not a mother.

Because Johnny knows his limitations and lives well within his boundaries, everybody can sleep well at night knowing he is in charge. He is a father watching over the crib, making sure everything is in its right place, imposing some sense of discipline and order while the heavy raindrops fall on the roof, while we gather strength to fight the next day. He's the one who'd jump for a hammer and some nails if the wind in the storm started ripping shingles or the galvanized zinc panelling from the roof over your head. A protector and defender, definitely not a nurturer.

Yes, he may not be big on the vision thing, but we can't expect everything, and certainly on that controversial topic of vision nobody is saying Johnny is the Prophet incarnate. He's just a good conservative general efficiently executing a task someone has the luxury to dream up. Definitely no prophet here. And having gone through one experience with a prophet already, that's what I like about Johnny.

Indeed, so much confidence do I have that he will always do the right thing, and a solid job too, that I am willing to put everything to the test, I tell the Great Mother. Johnny is a good man, I tell Mother Nyame, as solid a man as any. Throw anything at him and he will never come up short, I assure her.

You know what happens to me when I end up in a sweet piece o' talking: man I get a little carried away and start one loud boasting. Hear me say: you know what is true, Mother Nyame — Johnny reminds me of an old story, one of your favourites actually. And I begin quoting chapter and verse like rass, improvising as I am going along: *Hast thou considered my servant Johnny, that there is none like him in this world, a perfect and an upright man, one that feareth God, and escheweth evil?*

Hearing me quote that famous passage breaks up Mother Nyame. She just can't stop laughing. She is in fits, I tell yuh. She says Brer 'Nancy you's still a character fuh true; you's still your old self, man, a true true trickster who can make even the most sourpuss laugh their belly full. If I didn't know her so well, I would think she is laughing at me, thinking, holy shit Brer Anancy done gone over the top, he's certifiably nuts.

But I know her different laughs. I know when she is just *shit-talking*, having a good time and all that. Because in keeping with the spirit of that moment, she comes right back at me, playing along and quoting from the same story. Just like the answer and call in those classic African stories, the wonderful improvisations of duelling rappers or calypsonians, the verve of the storytelling contests. She says, just like a damn Signifying Monkey to my Brer Anancy: *Put forth thine hand now and touch his bone and his flesh and he will curse thee to thy face.*

By now, the two of us are laughing so much that we lose control. It is so great. All the while we are laughing, I am telling myself, boy this sure feels good, this is lifting my spirits, this is the apex. From here I can only go down. And I am thinking this is the happiest moment for me since returning to this farm. Ah, we just end the conversation on that high note, with the two of us laughing so much we can hardly talk.

At that moment, I am feeling the meeting of our minds is complete, we are conceiving something here, just like in the quiet moments after the heated outpouring of passion between a man and a woman. At this moment, I realize that Mother Nyame knows the point I am making. She also knows that I expect her to hold me to a fiery test.

And she has been testing me in the weeks and days since then. Indeed, up until last night she was still at it. Knock on wood, I can honestly say that despite all that has been thrown at us my man Johnny stands his ground and makes me proud. He has done nothing to make me ashamed of him. A weaker man would have wilted by now. Not Johnny. Not my rock of Sharon. That is until this very moment, when he started all this silliness. How I wish he hadn't chosen this moment to lose his equanimity. Get a grip on yourself, Johnny! I can't have you losing your good disposition at this moment. Not now, *godblindmuh*.

Every minute that passes and there is no sign of the minivan, Johnny becomes more worried, helplessly jittery and jumpy. Obviously, from the ugly looks on his face, Johnny is worried in a big way. I mean, it isn't usual for him to act this way, not for a class act like Johnny, always as cool as a cucumber.

I think I can understand why, though. It only goes to show once again how committed this man is to his people, something that everyone has to admit is admirable. But I also have to say that his nervousness is getting to be a bit much. Actually, it's beginning to bother me, as you can probably tell. It is making me wonder if I am missing something, if I talk too fast to Mother Nyame without reflecting on what she's saying, even in a joke. For as the women back home like to tell one another, especially when they take offence at something somebody says, wise people say many a true thing in a joke; fools just skin their teeth.

So let me give you Johnny's view of what happened last night. Every time he plays it over in his mind, the evening starts on such a high note, with such celebration. This is the night they defeat the men from Silverton Farms, to enter the finals of the domino tournament, the night Tommy gives them such a scare.

Until then, Tommy has been coming along well, appearing to finally have shaken that stubborn cold. Even his sense of humour has returned, and as usual nobody could good-naturedly rag another man, friend or foe, as well as Tommy. This night, he is in high spirits, taunting and mocking the men from Silverton as they lose game after game.

"They got some young women back there in Barbados that can play dominoes more better than any o' you here," he taunts the men. "They would give me more better competition tonight, a better run fuh my money than any o' you. Look, play a domino. Yuh taking too long to study which one you'll play and then you' always play the wrong one. So, stop all the studying, play one and let me win off your hand, yuh soft shite, you."

Tommy is the general leading the charge in this battle. His performance is as much to demean the opponents as it is to keep his players fired up. At times, Johnny can only shake his head across the table at his partner's taunts, dares and even outrageousness. Maybe it is the excitement from winning, the exhaustion of expending so much energy, but whatever it is, Tommy is to have an anxious and painful night. A night that leaves the men so concerned and frightened that none of them would get any sleep either.

On the way home, Tommy starts coughing uncontrollably. At first he claims it is the fresh night air, or that perhaps while berating his opponents, he slipped and swallowed some peanuts or something the wrong way. An unexpected coolness in the air makes his throat feel raw, he contends. It will stop when he is in bed, he says between the coughs. But the coughing doesn't stop, except for the hour or so when he finally falls asleep.

It is about two o'clock in the morning when Johnny is awakened by the muffled groaning. "Oh, God. Me can't tek it." In the darkness, he can tell immediately the noises are coming from Tommy. Johnny jumps out of the bed and switches on the light in the middle of the room. The sudden glow causes some light sleepers to shift, to pull the sheets over their heads, but none of them gets out of bed.

"Oh God. Oh God," Tommy is whimpering quietly to himself, his face buried in the pillow. "Oh, God." He is kicking his feet, letting them rise and fall loudly on the stiff mattress.

"Tommy, you all right?" Johnny asks. He stoops at the side of the bed and rolls his friend onto his back. "What happen'd?"

"I don't feel too good," Tommy says. He is talking loudly, as if having decided that, with his secret discovered, he may as well be fully open with everyone. For the first time, Johnny sees the tears running out of Tommy's eyes.

In the twenty-one years he has known Tommy, Johnny has never seen him cry, never had to confront such fears in another man. Grafton had held up much more bravely, never once letting his mask slip, never once forgetting the promise of his initiation, the commitment to bear all hardships without so much as a whimper.

But Tommy, as he is wont, is different at this weak moment. Johnny pretends not to notice the tears. Possibly, the weakness is only a passing phase, which Tommy will correct at the first opportunity. Everyone will just try to forget, as if it never happened, as if he never slipped. "I don't feel too good, at all. I don't feel too good."

"Where hurting you?" Johnny asks.

"All over. In my chest. My back. My head. All over, Johnny." The tears are flowing freely, silently. When I look in closer, I am just shocked by the frightened look in Tommy's eyes, a look of desperation, like that of a mortally wounded animal.

"Try sitting up."

"I don't think I can," Tommy says. "I feel cold and weak, weak, weak."

Their talking is waking the men. Several of them are now

hovering around Tommy's bed, asking what is happening and how they can help.

"Smokie!" Johnny calls out. He has succeeded in getting Tommy to sit upright on the cot. "Smokie, go and make a cup of ginger tea there or something."

Smokie, still rubbing his eyes, walks into the kitchen.

Just then, for some unexplainable reason, Winston catches my attention. He is sitting on his bed, looking as confused as everyone else. He doesn't know what to say. His eyes flit from face to face, searching for answers and assurances. He has seen nothing like this before. While he has been warned, in what he still thinks is an exaggeration, not to get sick on the farm, he does not expect anything as horrific as this.

"Somebody should call a doctor," he suggests. Nobody pays any attention to him, and I am just as keen to ignore him too. But there is something unusual about Winston this night, a kind of aura, a force circling him that makes me want to keep him in my view.

"Oh God, no," Tommy shouts a delayed response, almost raising himself off the bed. "No doctor. Don't wake up the Stewarts to call no doctor." Winston slumps his shoulders and remains sitting, physically, and obviously mentally, apart from the men around Tommy.

Smokie returns with the cup of tea. The steam is escaping from the water and there is the sweet smell of the ginger.

"Here," he says, handing the cup to Johnny. "See how this taste."

"Take a few sips," Johnny encourages, holding the cup to Tommy's lips. With his other hand on Tommy's shoulder, Johnny tries to get him to lean forward, toward the cup. "This will help to settle the stomach. Make you feel better. Maybe get you to belch."

Tommy carefully takes a couple of sips. At first, he holds the hot liquid in his mouth, as if his stomach is rebelling, refusing to accept it. Finally, after a struggle, the tea goes down with a loud gulp.

"That's good. Take another," Johnny says, holding the cup to his lips. Tommy's hands are on Johnny's holding the cup. Johnny notices how his friend's hands tremble and how the palms feel so cold and clammy.

The second sip goes down easier, but the third and fourth are more difficult. Then it all comes rushing up. Everything that is in his stomach. It splatters on the floor and on the beds, in the cup of ginger tea and on Johnny's hands. Everything comes back up: the split green peas and rice from the evening supper, the peanuts, coffee and chips from the tournament and, of course, the sips of the medicinal ginger tea — everything from deep inside Tommy's stomach.

"Help me, Johnny," Tommy pleads. "I feel real bad. I wish Barbara did be here. She'd know what to do to help me, eh, Johnny."

That is when we realize Tommy is really sick. That is when the men understand they have to call the Liaison Officer first thing in the morning, no matter how much Tommy protests, how much it inconveniences their representative. No one says a word, but they are agreed. In the silence, they look at one another. Johnny and Smokie help Tommy to his feet. They lead him away to the bathroom. The vomiting stops. Other men are stripping the beds, using the sheets and coverings to mop the floor. Immediately, the room smells sour and of sickness. Winston sits transfixed on his bed.

"Want me to run over to the farm house and wake the Stewarts, to call the doctor?" Winston asks in his confusion.

"What we should all do is say a prayer," Preacher Man says softly from the back of the bedroom. "Things like these is a sign. When everything else fails, in the end we can turn to Christ."

Timmy sucks his teeth loudly. "We shoulda give he a good dose of ganja tea, if you ask me, not ginger tea." He sucks his teeth again, but this time sounding less assured than before. "And maybe a little weed to smoke on the back of it, too. A little weed always help me."

No one answers about the doctor. Without anyone noticing, Winston slips out of the cabin and trots over to the Stewarts'. When he returns, with hardly anyone noticing his absence, the men are still fussing over Tommy, trying to make him feel comfortable in his cot, piling blankets, towels and sheets around him to make him warm. Winston says nothing, although he keeps an eye out for the first sign of the light from the ambulance.

———

No matter how much Tommy tries to minimize his sickness, he cannot hide it from the doctor at the emergency ward. He gives Tommy some big white tablets and orders him to rest and to report to his own doctor the next morning. First thing the next morning, Johnny phones the Liasion Officer from the Stewarts' and tells him to come and get Tommy. From that moment, everybody is on tenterhooks.

Any diagnosis like Grafton's would mean trouble for Tommy, Johnny tells himself. This is at the root of what is troubling him: he has some serious doubts about Tommy, and his mind, I must admit, is really going a bit wonky on him. It must be the lack of sleep. That is the danger of anticipating too much, another way of proving, as I do tell Mother Nyame, that nobody should concern himself too unduly about living in the future. So why does she want me to start predicting instead of just simply reporting things as I see them?

This here is a good example to back up my point. For we can see how someone as strong as Johnny is tying himself in knots thinking that if the diagnosis was anything like Grafton's it would mean for his best friend pain and soreness from the poking and running of tests. Tommy would return to the cabin in a worse mood, Johnny thinks, as his mind runs ahead of him. Having Tommy in such a mood wouldn't be any good for the sick among them or for any of the men. Everyone would start wondering, who is next?

Johnny is telling himself that at a time like this, with so many things going off the beam, the men need one another — a chain is as strong as its weakest link. They cannot start being suspicious of one another, thinking one morning they might just wake up and find the chain rusted from the inside and broken, one of the men dead in his bed.

If the worst happens to Tommy with some unexpected diagnosis, the men would have to lean on one another for support and moral sustenance. They would have to support Tommy; stop worrying about themselves and whether they, too, should get checked out, and early. If just thinking of the future can frazzle the brains of someone as cool as my brother Johnny, can you imagine a weaker mortal in this situation? Mother Nyame, I hope you are taking note.

Still, there is no way I can possibly convey how much Johnny wishes the minivan would show up. I too am beginning to wish this damn vehicle would just appear and end this maddening waiting. It would put Johnny and the men out of the misery of thinking. It would let them know immediately if there was a possible monster lurking in all of them, the time bomb on which they can only wait. With some news about Tommy, at least they would know what to expect. They would know if they should even worry at all.

Until the minivan shows up, my dear, Johnny remains almost beside himself with worry. And right now, I'd be the first to say he doesn't look too much like any leadership material I know. I just wish he would bloody well snap out of whatever funk he is in.

I hope you don't think I am going on too much, sounding, as I hear one of my colleagues saying, like the father who takes his little toddler to the friendly soccer or baseball game and keeps shouting and berating the kid from the sidelines, demanding that the poor darling play not simply for fun, but seriously, like the young man he is, the man he must become from early on.

In my heart, I just have to believe Johnny is trying not to transmit these concerns and fears to the men with him. He has to know that they already have enough on their minds, including all the missed wages since the storm. All of them have commitments back home and not getting a regular pay cheque is troubling them more than they want to admit.

Neither George Stewart nor the Liaison Officer is holding out much hope the situation will get better quickly. However, the officer is always at pains to remind the men that they still have jobs. Indeed, I would shake his hand for making this point. Really, nobody should have to remind these men they are still the envy of people like Cuthbert in Barbados and the Caribbean or even Mexico.

But, of course, I have to acknowledge that such commitments don't sooth the men, especially when the Officer reports that so far the government has not passed the legislation insuring the men's earnings. When he does this even Johnny starts thinking about the mortgage for the house he is building back home. I mean, he is acting as if Maude doesn't have two strong hands and a brain, as if unlike all those strong African women before her, she doesn't know how to cut and contrive, doesn't know that if you don't have a horse, ride a cow.

Another unexpected development weighs heavily on Johnny's mind. For the first time, the men are not too anxious to receive letters from home. Neither are they writing. How can they? Johnny keeps asking himself as if interceding for the men when, in fact, he should be challenging them, like a general demanding that they behave like real soldiers. But not Johnny. He argues the men's case in his head, sympathizing how nobody wants to send home a moneyless or — as they would say in Barbados — dry, empty letter. And then again he starts wondering how Maude, like the rest of the wives and girlfriends, is reacting to the infrequent remittances and whether work on the house under construction is suffering.

In his heart, he knows that the construction has to be suffering, for what little money he makes is hardly enough to meet his own needs, let alone Tommy's. The thought flashes across Johnny's mind that Maude might carry through on her threat to write Mary Stewart about the mortgage payments. She might feel more comfortable dealing with another woman.

But Johnny is not too sure. He realizes that he can no longer swear about Maude, if he ever could; he does not know with any certainty how she reacts in given situations. The thought frightens him, and rightly it should, because Johnny is beginning to act like some weakling, no longer is he impervious. And I keep wondering if he has started taking a nip or two from the bottle of rum when I am not looking. This is the woman with whom he is building a house, the place in which they will spend the rest of their lives together, with each other. They will be getting to know each other at a stage in their lives when their friendship should be unquestioned, when they should be totally committed and predictable. I can't understand why this man always seems to be expecting miracles.

Johnny wipes his brow and forces himself to stop such musing. He does not have time for such thoughts, for worrying about the future, about mortgages, about people who are now strangers to him, about Tommy and Barbara. What a surprise it is still for us to realize the true situation between those two. Johnny remembers what Tommy has said about what life with Barbara is really like. When all along we've been thinking Tommy and Barbara are like two love doves, you know, as the saying goes, when one says I do the other adds me too. Two love birds always in agreement.

Johnny tries to clear his mind of all these thoughts. Right now, standing in this field on this farm in Canada, there is precious little he can do about these problems, he tells himself. So why give in to such negative thoughts, why not just be positive? For no matter what happens, in Barbados or at the clinic in town, his main concern is, and must remain, the welfare of the men. He must keep their spirits up. Tommy and the men are relying on him for guidance.

Johnny glances around the field. He sees the treeline in the distance. The birds, perhaps gulls, flying in the distance, are following the tractor and the plough. He sees the birds, hears the wind rustling the tops of the trees, but no sign of the damn car. If you watch closely, you will also see how the other men appear to be moving in slow motion, none of the usual banter and putdowns so usual when times are different. The tension is heavy, too tight, sucking up all the mental energy, making the men distrustful and ill-humoured.

Johnny looks across the field. Where the hell is that car? he mumbles under his breath. Instinctively, he places an open hand over his eyes to protect them from the blazing sun in the cloudless sky. Just as quickly, he drops his eyes down again. He has to be careful how people see him reacting. So far, all the men have been going about their duties as if it were a normal day. Even Winston asks few questions. And that's another thing about this Winston fellow: in the last few weeks he appears to be striving for his independence, just doing what he likes or thinks necessary. Somehow he always seems happiest around Wednesday, the day everyone but he piles into the school bus and heads off the farm for the dominoes tournament.

Winston is with the half of the team picking the scrawny leaves on the tobacco plants. The others are taking turns sorting the leaves in the back of the cart or resting from the arduous task. To be fair to him, and just in case you hear another report bragging about this, Winston is the only one not to have taken a break since lunch. Johnny stands with the men sorting the leaves. This gives him the opportunity to keep an eye on the road without raising the suspicion of the men. A chance not to make evident he is as deeply concerned as they.

Johnny smacks his lips loudly, partly to moisten them, but also to vent his frustration. Anything to help him to relax, to concentrate on picking the tobacco. No matter how much he tries to tell himself that he is too pessimistic, that he always anticipates the worst in the hopes of getting a pleasant surprise when the outcome isn't as bad as he expects, he cannot shake this dreadful feeling.

The mere thought of their finding something dreadfully wrong, maybe life-threatening, dark and mysterious inside his best friend, causes goose pimples to appear too frequently. After all, Tommy is not only his best friend, but is also his age. And that is the unspoken fear of every man facing the effects of time. He and Tommy, and all the men, are no different, even if they never talk about these things.

Maybe this is what Mother Nyame is hinting at when she asks what I think of Johnny. Their bodies, their resistance and resilience, are not as strong as they used to be. They are now more susceptible, maybe the body's way of getting even with them for all those wild days, for working too hard, not taking tonics and vitamins, not exercising enough to keep fit and trim, drinking too much and not eating correctly.

These, Johnny knows, are the fear of every man, fear that

escalates as the first grey hairs appear on the head, but particularly in their beard and moustache or even in places of the body long considered the fountain of eternal youth and life-creating.

A chill runs down his spine, despite the heat of the day. Nothing can stop Johnny from remembering the horror of the previous night, when even the sounds of the wind and the rhythmic breathing of the men in the darkness weren't enough to lull him back to sleep.

"I think I'm headin' back to the cabin now," Smokie is saying. He stands beside Johnny, cleaning the dirt from underneath his fingernails with a twig. "Gotta put the pot on the fire."

When Johnny doesn't answer, Smokie stops cleaning his nails and puts a hand on Johnny's shoulder.

"What yuh thinkin', man?" Smokie says. "I'm here talkin' to you and you actin' like you ain't hearin' me. Like you somewhere else."

"Nothing, man," Johnny says, quickly catching himself. He shakes his head as if to clear the cobwebs. "I just thinking a bit."

"I was saying that I goin' now," Smokie says. "So that I can start the pot for when the men come in later. It's gettin' a bit late now."

"How late it is?" Johnny asks, forgetting that he checked the time only a few minutes earlier. He looks at the watch again, and then in the direction from which he expects the car. "Three twenty-eight. Christ, it's getting late, man. You must go, in truth."

Smokie picks up the dungaree jacket from the back of the cart containing the men's utensils, their hats and clothes and the big water cooler. He too glances down the road longingly, then at Johnny, before walking off. In the distance, all they can see are the birds hovering. To me, they look like vultures, maybe even those ominous Caribbean birds of death, those damn gaulins or carrion crows, or what the Bajans call them damn long-neck turkeys that fly so high.

chapter nineteen

The steady drizzle meticulously forms pools of water in the backyard, each drop spitefully celebrating its ascendancy, each proving, as the old Brer Anancy story foretells, the inevitable triumph of water over fire.

It's been raining all day, the initial thundershower starting just after midnight, triumphantly ushering in the first heavy downpour of the summer, with the heavy, dark clouds wilfully blunting all day long the kamikaze-like rays of the sun. This is truly a god-awful looking day, by any standards, a miserable time to be outside in the dark and the cold.

Mary looks through the window above the sink. In the darkness, she sees George Stewart pacing impatiently, expectantly, behind the house. Johnny is standing to one side just watching him, looking as out of place in these surroundings as anything I can remember. Nobody needs this type of weather, Mary tells herself, and I can't agree with her more. But what can she expect?

Indeed, what can *we* expect, I am thinking. This dismal weather comes with the land. After all, this is Canada, home of strange weather, a country that *is* winter, as someone so wisely claims in another story. A place that, paradoxically, some people like Albert Jones and many others in that cabin over there in the distance would like to call home. After all, aren't they deemed residents? Johnny, fortunately, sees Canada for what it really is: a nice place to visit but that could never really be home, an alien soil in so many ways, with this beastly weather topping the list. Just like what Prophet thought — no matter how many times he came to Canada, no matter the reception he got this side of the border, even when he set up his correspondence school of philosophy here to teach them Americans when he couldn't go back to the United States, Prophet could never fully take to this place — always had to be leaving.

In this country, like other things so strange and unusual, the sun can be banished for days on end. When it resurfaces, often for a few short hours only and with virtually no sting or strength, it always tries to present itself as an accommodating friend, not as a rested and revitalized warrior ready to do battle. So often it comes back like the bully who disappears for weeks on end, eventually showing up looking frail and weak, only to explain that his absence is due to a stint in hospital, a sojourn that leaves the patient still alive but drained of spirit, strength and fire. In such a weakened state, how can a bully even feign to be anything but a friend? How could the sun pretend otherwise? Nobody would believe the sun we encounter in this country is the same one people fight with every day at home.

Like Mary, I am depressed about the weather and the mood it throws over everything. And I blame the sun for giving up the fight so easily. And, indeed, it is true that it takes a dark and dreadful day like this one to make people think about their experiences back home. To wish they could feel the presence of a strong glancing ray on their skin. It is like when you have a cut on your toe or finger, and it has partially healed, but still throbs so annoyingly. Remember how sometimes you felt you couldn't stand the throbbing one second more? How you wished the damn thing would just hurt really bad, instead of frustrate with this deadening throbbing? You wonder if you are going crazy, when you covet searing pain over a throb.

Well, all this rain makes me feel that way about the sun. It makes the men wish they had a real enemy to fight with, not some phantom hiding behind a bank of clouds. I guess it is true what the first Brer Anancy told Brer Fox: you never miss the water 'til the well run dry. Well, if I may correct that old-timer a little bit, right now we are having too much damn water flowing into a well that is already overflowing, if you know what I mean.

Because one thing about the sun, no matter how hot it gets, no matter how much you sweat or get tired, the first ray that burns your skin makes you feel alive. It quickens you. The sting is like a good hard slap to the face, causing the blood and the adrenaline to start flowing. Makes you jump to your feet and want to do damage in your own defence, to protect yourself from further indignity. That's what the sun does when it burns your skin. It challenges you to fight back, to live, to try to take control, to even run. To do *something,* even if it means trying to escape. But with rain and dark clouds, what can you do but be passive and accepting? You just have to sit back and waste time, no heat, no boiling blood, no challenge. Just water cooling down everything and removing what little sting there might be to life. Just all those thoughts eating you out and all that time to do nothing, except be frustrated as hell.

I must agree with Mary that at this time of the year, we can all do without this kind of weather. Today's variation only saddens everybody. It adds to the deep gloom hanging so heavily over the cabin and, as I am now finding out, even this house. I cannot tell you how glad I was that George came along so unexpectedly and asked, well ordered really, Johnny to come with him. Like Johnny, suffering all this cabin fever and so depressed by the poor light all around and by the men getting on one another's nerves, on top of the incessant rain, I quickly grab the opportunity to get outside and breathe some fresh air myself. I couldn't wait to escape all the petty bickering in those cramped quarters, with the tempers rising, all that pent-up energy that can't be worked off because the men can't go outside.

Such god-awful weather, I hear Mary thinking, weather that

makes everything look so dreary and discouraging. Let's listen a bit closer to Mary as she muses about what's bothering her this evening, about life on the farm and, what else, the never-ending battle that comes from such isolation. As she peers through the window, Mary is wondering why George Stewart still remains so sure that she will never be a good farm wife.

She knows that, even now, she cannot fully accept the vagaries of this life, of farming and the weather — all of which combine to be so depressing on a day like this. Indeed, in her head she can hear George dropping his ugly remarks, the same ones that ring so loudly in her ears hours after their quarrel is supposedly over, when they accept a stalemated truce. Today he tells her she is the only person living on a farm perhaps anywhere in this big country, in all North America, if not the world, that actually hates the rain. The only farm wife, he says, that is constantly complaining about the mud people bring into the house on their boots; the only one whining endlessly about people smoking in her presence.

Women just don't understand men, George tells her, storming out into the rain and claiming, as his pathetic excuse for retreating from this particular exchange, that he thinks he hears the men coming with the equipment. He prefers to be alone, or with the men in the cabin, he says, even as he realizes that it must have been the wind he heard, that nobody is waiting for him outside, nobody is coming to his rescue, that he is just jumpy, impatient and obviously in retreat. Why he prefers to stand out in the rain talking to another man, why he marches off in the distance and returns some minutes later with Johnny, so the two of them can just stand around in the rain, anticipating the arrival of a cavalry of testosteroned reinforcements.

George acting like this reminds Mary of another story. The one about how domesticated turkeys are so stupid they do not seek shelter when it rains. They simply look to the skies with their heads upturned, running the risk of actually drowning in a brisk downpour. I too have heard this story. It's somewhere in our annals, the story of how Brer Fox tricked Brer Turkey Lurkey. Let me point out one important thing about that story: it is about *domesticated* turkeys only. Wild turkeys have a mind of their own; they know how to survive.

Mary doesn't like the idea of comparing her husband to a stupid turkey who isn't even smart enough to come in out of the rain, but at the moment this is exactly how she feels. She knows that George will always find refuge for his thoughts away from her company, even in the rain on an evening like this, even if, he admits, the workers whose company he seeks are not his intellectual equals. At least they are men.

And, according to George, that is what is important. A refuge in a pack of men. A man needs to be with other men, to draw strength, to reason and to bond, he explains. And a man needs a son, not a daughter, especially not a musically minded daughter who, at the first sign of problems, runs away from a father's life-business to study, of all things, music.

As she turns away from the window, Mary recalls that the voice so loud in her head is very different from another one a bit more remote in her memory, the voice of George as a young man. Even then he complained a lot. She can hear the young George arguing that although he is at university, he has no choice but to answer the call of his father. He has to return and take charge because Old Man Stewart is sick. A farmer expects certain things of a son, George says to her as explanation for his heading off to the farm, promising that she can come and join him later. Nobody even thinks of calling on his sister to save the farm. Nobody bothers asking her to take charge, at least until George graduates from university, even though everybody knows Johnny is doing a good job keeping things together. Old Man Stewart wants a man, the same way George these decades on still says that he now needs a son to at least help him think things through. Not a daughter whose only concern is to study some damn music, as if the frills of music can fill anyone's guts. As if this daughter has inherited all her genes, and a hatred for farming, from her mother.

Mary shifts at the window, swatting at a fly buzzing over her head. Maybe George is right, she says to herself. Maybe she can never be a good farm wife. Perhaps she has passed on this undesirable characteristic to Jessica, compounding the indignity for George by not giving him that son he wanted, that young male he needs so badly as confirmation that this land and the Stewart name will live on long after George joins his father and grandfather in the grave.

Obviously, men think about these things, she says, and they can become so aloof when they feel denied, when they feel a right is being withheld from them. For Mary knows that if she hasn't achieved the status of a good farm wife after all these years — and she tries — from the way things are going, it doesn't appear as if she will get much more of a chance to change. Although, that might not be a bad thing, she is thinking, because she is tired of pretending and faking. Here she reminds me so much of Maude, the first person I ever heard ask the question, what woman doesn't really get tired of faking?

Sometimes, like Maude, Mary just doesn't have any more patience with George or any of his friends, especially the ones who talked George into allowing them to spirit away their machinery and bring it to Edgecliff for safe-keeping. Something tells Mary that some day George will say to her that he should have listened to her and not accept the machinery, the same way that he has almost come to the point of actually acknowledging to her that yes, maybe, perhaps, she had a case when she suggested he shouldn't have gambled on tobacco this year.

But something also tells her that she shouldn't hold her

breath waiting for George to go the extra distance of ever conceding fully to her. For despite all the years they have been together, she can literally count on the fingers of one hand the number of times George has told her she was right about anything. She has come to accept that it just isn't a man thing to say those words. Not even when they try to convey sorrow or regret with their actions, with a gift or two if they are also feeling a bit generous, with the usual hangdog expression on their face. A man can find a million ways to show he is sorry, she says to herself, but ask him to say it with words and he becomes dumb. No wonder the bank manager wants them to think of the roses business.

Looking at Mary and reflecting on what she is thinking, I cannot help marvelling at how much she reminds me of Maude and her frustration of having to deal with too much time. Neither can I stop reflecting on the products of this weather that is the fountain and perhaps excuse for all these thoughts, the same way that useless time bedevils Johnny and Maude in the off-season, driving them crazy and widening the gulf with every second.

First, the hail kills the tobacco plants. Who would think fate could be so harsh, Mary wonders, or would conspire to make her look so good, so correct in her thinking, unwittingly at her husband's expense? Nobody expects such weather so late in the season. When she was warning George Stewart that he really shouldn't take such a big gamble, she wasn't even thinking about the weather. All she was thinking is that he should abide by the terms and spirit of the new contract with the bank. She knew that she was being a wimp, just accepting the dictates of the bank, just willing to give ground until it was time to launch a counterattack with a swift, decisive strike.

So she pleads with him to pass up on growing tobacco this year. For just one year, she begs him. One year as a sign of good faith, until the situation improves. Then they can return to planting whatever they want. Maybe they can raise some money this year with a quick cash crop. After paying down a bit of the fully exhausted line of credit, George could return to tobacco if he still felt that strongly. But hold off on the tobacco, she beseeched him, hold off for just one year.

But as she replays those critical conversations in her mind, Mary recognizes when George is beyond listening. It is the same trait she sees in him even now as he stands foolishly in the rain looking into the distance. He can be so pig-headed. Every little thing becomes such a fight for him, so much so that he is more emotional than rational in his reasoning.

Even as they argued back then, he was making plans for another crop of tobacco. His prolonged bouts of silence and isolation tell her that much. He will prove himself to everyone by overcoming all the odds against him. He will remain in charge of his farm, protect this heirloom and preserve it as any man would. Nothing, nobody, will challenge, far less defeat, him. For here is the soldier marching into battle thinking he is invincible simply because he is a soldier. It is almost as if his manhood is on the line. He is at the point where he could surrender, perhaps even retreat, just as Mary suggests. But if he does, it must be with the full knowledge that he could no longer call himself a man.

Or he could rear up on his hind legs and fight for his territory. He is the one to piss on his own farm, not some banker. Everything becomes a challenge to his integrity, a confrontation that seems to grow more intense as he gets older. Mary believes that this kind of half-assed thinking is what's behind George and Johnny standing around outside in the rain. Otherwise, what good can they expect from the darkness swallowing them a bit more every second?

So, this pride and bravado combine to dare George to do one foolish thing after another. To gamble once more that tobacco will pay off. And in this case, that the sheriff won't come knocking with a search warrant for the machinery. The cries and pleas always seem to be the same: just this one last throw of the dice; it will bring freedom. It will allow him to, eventually, barge into the office of the banker and reclaim title to his kingdom and his manhood. Then comes the hail. Just as they had planted the seedlings. Bad luck, George swears, or bad timing? It would have been so different if they had kept the plants in the greenhouses for another week — for another four days really. Then they would have been spared all this agony.

More bad luck follows with the parched dry earth, a sun momentarily strong enough to go on the attack. Mary is never sure about this bad-luck claim. She only knows George shouldn't have planted tobacco in the first place. And she knows that he better have a damn good excuse if he gets a visit from the police.

Still, Mary can sympathize: what can a farmer do when even the weather is against him? She shakes her head and continues to rinse the dishes. Who would believe the same weather that produces hailstones as big as golf balls — according to George some of the men say they were as big as grapefruits — would then turn around and produce the extreme opposite, scorching sun that withers the plants to their roots and stunts the growth of even the hardened apple and pear trees? No real rain for a good two months. Not until this unwelcome downpour with the loud thunder and forked lightning in the distance. Such weather at such an inopportune time — in the middle of the harvest, the worst time for the rains to come.

When these misfortunes hit, George always withdraws into his shell and treats Mary as if she had bad-mindedly prayed and fasted for pestilence to blight them. Mary shakes her head in disgust. At this point in their relationship, there is no point in hoping George will ever change, will ever stop feeling that she is in competition with him, when all she wants to do is to help George think his options through and to provide a second opinion.

Maybe Jessica is making the right move, Mary thinks, the anger rising in her chest so much that she has the urge to open the window and scream at him, George you bloody fool, maybe your daughter is right! Maybe the younger generation of women is right not to stand for any foolishness. And maybe I should follow her too. I should just pick myself up and go to Toronto or wherever, so that you won't keep feeling that I am trying to stop you from being the man on this damn stupid farm. From doing whatever the hell you want and making sure you lose everything so much faster. So you won't keep feeling I am trying to castrate you by telling you how to run this bloody bankrupt farm. Then you can be man enough to come in out of the dark, into your own house and home when it rains.

Mary turns off the tap and wipes her hands on a small towel. It is already damp. Instantly, she feels guilty for having had these thoughts and for not appearing to offer more support and unquestioning loyalty to her husband. Maybe that is why she will never be a good farm wife. For the same reason George is so brutishly rebellious in his own way. She could never grow to accept being so vulnerable. So open to everyone and everything: from the bankers to the politicians now outlawing smoking; to the hail and the sun that kill the tobacco plants; to the fate that would allow all of this to happen at the same time, in the same year. To making Jessica feel that she has to pick this very moment to branch out on her own, leaving Mary alone to deal with her father and the farm. To deal with these uncertainties, the weight of which at this moment feels like too much for her. And the rain outside isn't making anything any better, only making George more distant and brooding, challenging even his own good sense and the law. It's all so confusing; she doesn't know what she really thinks.

As if he has heard the screams building in Mary's head, George Stewart pulls open the door and tramps into the kitchen.

Momentarily, he holds the door open for Johnny before pushing past him into the kitchen. He leaves a trail of dirt, water and the serrated imprints of the soles of his rubber boots. Mary casts an angry glance at the mess. Just as she is about to say something disapprovingly, to release the screams, she realizes that how clean she keeps the kitchen and house probably doesn't matter one fig in the greater scheme of things. The house is probably a complete loss. Especially if the men and the machinery turn up, if George goes ahead and gambles once more. That would be like signing a death warrant. So she picks up an empty glass and fills it with water from the tap.

"Anybody called yet?" George asks. He takes off his dripping raincoat and throws it over the back of a chair at the kitchen table. Johnny sits beside him at the table, still in his raincoat, as if he desperately wants to be out of this kitchen, to escape from all this tension. Pools of water begin to form under the table on the faded but clean linoleum. Mary shakes her head, while keeping the glass of water to her lips.

She swallows what is in her mouth and then empties the glass by throwing the remaining contents into the sink. She turns on the tap, subconsciously runs her hand under the water to test the temperature, in the hope of conserving the hot water, then rinses the glass and returns it to the draining board. All the while, she keeps her back to George and pretends to be staring into the darkening evening.

"Those guys should have been here by now," George continues. "I wonder what's keeping them."

"You think that's a good idea, George?" Mary asks. Her back is still to him, as she rearranges the dishes on the draining board.

"What you mean, *Is it a good idea?*"

"I mean what would happen if the police found out, George? Could we get into trouble?"

"We'll cross that bridge when we get to it," George retorts, the deep male grumble of defiance in his voice. Mary tries to tell herself that she is not really the target of his anger. Her dear husband is like a cornered animal blindly lashing out with a vicious paw, striking at anyone that comes near, even those who mean it no harm. "We farmers got to start fighting back. We can't let these damn banks keep walking all over us. Picking us off one by one. And using the law to put us out of business. We got to fight back, stand up for ourselves."

"I know," Mary says, still looking into the backyard. She is purposely not raising her voice. "But there is a lot of difference between fighting back and what you plan to do, George. It could involve the law and the courts. I don't feel too good about it."

"I ain't killing nobody, if that's what you're worried about. I'm only helping another farmer like myself to hide a few pieces of equipment until he can catch his hand and pay off his debts. If the auction goes ahead and they sell the equipment — practically give it away at the prices those things fetch these days — how will anybody ever get back into business again? And besides, I can't just sit here and do nothing, say no when another farmer, another man like me, comes to me and asks for help. For all I know, it could be my turn to go begging next."

"I really hope this doesn't bring any more trouble," Mary says. She finally turns around and faces George. Feeling somewhat uncomfortable under his wife's gaze, he walks out of the kitchen into the living room, leaving additional footprints in his wake. Johnny watches him leave, his eyes flitting from Mary back to George, wondering about the *shite* he now finds himself in.

Mary takes the mop from beside the refrigerator and begins cleaning the floor. She simply doesn't like the plan, but she is powerless to do anything. For this reason, if nothing else, she hates the farm, the helplessness she feels with George, all this rain and all this thinking and loneliness. George is always talking about missing another male like himself on the farm. He never understands that she too misses a lot, including the life she had to give up to pretend to be a good farm wife. She cannot be angry with Jessica for going to Toronto, for following her dreams. If she were Jessica's age, if she had her life to live all over, she would definitely head for the Big City, not sit out her life on a farm with a man with a bruised ego, a big baby always in need of some kind of mothering. Maybe Jessica has become too much of what Mary would have loved to be, and maybe that is another sign of just how much she fails to measure up as a farm wife. Still she knows she will miss her daughter and confidante.

Mary takes up the stack of letters from the table. She looks at the ones with Barbados stamps on them. Another thing she hates about being a farm wife, she says to herself. All these correspondences, including the most personal matters that she has to deal with, especially some of these letters from the wives and girlfriends in Barbados.

She walks into the bedroom and throws the letters on the table beside the bed. Sometime, perhaps later tonight, she will get to them. Then, someday, maybe after Jessica is gone and she has nobody to talk to, she will make the time to reply to the letters that ask why the men are not writing, why the remittances have stopped. And someday she might even tell the plain truth in her letters instead of guessing what she thinks the men would have her say if they knew she was corresponding with their women.

———

The last of the sun is disappearing when the door to the kitchen opens and three men in heavy black raincoats trailing water and dirt, their heads covered, march into the house.

"George!" the leader shouts into the house. They are standing in the middle of kitchen, next to the table with George's raincoat still hanging over the back of the chair. "We're here."

George comes into the kitchen and holds out a hand to the man that is speaking. "Got time for a coffee, Thomson?" he asks.

"Don't think so, but thanks anyway," the man answers. "We got the equipment back here on the truck. Where do you want us to put it?"

Mary appears in the hallway between the kitchen and the rest of the house. She is standing with her hands folded across her chest, her long-sleeved woollen cardigan unbuttoned at the front.

"Evening, Mrs. Stewart," Thomson says, immediately becoming uneasy in her presence, as if he expects a disapproving remark from Mary. It is obvious: the man is much happier dealing with George. The other men grumble something and nod in her direction. "Shitty weather, eh?" one of them says lamely. "I hope you are keeping dry and warm, Mrs. Stewart." The other men are also uncomfortable with Mary, like little boys caught in some compromising act by an authority, an action for which they are not proud, for which they expect motherly censure.

"The weatherman says it should continue like this for another day or so," she answers. It is an unenthusiastic response. She knows instinctively the correct tone to use, especially when the listener is looking at her and smiling but has long tuned out anything she is saying. Hers is a response with no connection. All that registers on the listener's brain is the movement of her lips and the expected smile, a sign that she is not attacking, at least not openly. Otherwise, she could just as well be singing the words to the national anthem for all the men know and care. Just as long as she smiles and does nothing to make the men spring into a defensive or attacking posture.

There will always be that insurmountable distance between

her and the men, between her and George. It is a distance that seems even greater when George is with the men. George seems to blend in with them, to be happier, leaving her alone and isolated. When she passes, the conversation ends, the men giggle, or just stare at her with those stupid bemused looks. They cannot wait until she moves on. No matter how civil they try to be, something is always missing, she feels so unwelcome. So often it happens.

Mary hopes her response masks the deep feelings of misgivings in her heart over what they are doing. The last thing she wants is for the men to think that they got into trouble because she did not give them her blessing, that she was the one providing the negative vibes that bring on the failures. But at the same time, she does not plan to hide from them that she disapproves of their doings. She will simply not get into their way physically. On the battleground of sheer brute strength, she would never win.

"I hope to leave these few pieces of equipment here for only a short while," Thomson explains, as if reading her mind. "Shouldn't be no trouble. We had to wait until the darkness, so that the spies watching wouldn't notice when we slipped them off *my* farm. These days a man doesn't know who's watching; who is your friend and who is an informer. That's why..."

"Let's get moving," George interjects. He buttons on the raincoat and pulls on his boots. "Come with me. Johnny, give us a hand here."

"Give my regards to Mrs. Thomson," Mary calls out as they are going through the door. That simple remark obviously wounds Thomson. Mary notices his wince and quick recovery. "Must be tough on Liz and the children at this time. Tell her to give me a call if there is anything I can do. Or just for a chat."

"Elizabeth and the children're in Toronto. I didn't want them around to witness what's happening in the next couple of days," the man says. "So I told Elizabeth since she's always wanted to spend time in Toronto, here was her chance. I will stand on my own. I ain't running anywhere. Not me. I will do what I have to do to hold on for as long as I can. So, she's in Toronto."

He is the last to step through the door, to become a ghost-like figure in the darkness. Mary finds herself standing at the half-opened door, hands still folded, watching and listening to the men walking and talking as they march single file across the yard. Would she too have to slip away from the farm without telling anyone, to avoid the shame, the same way Elizabeth Thomson did? Perhaps Elizabeth is away because she does not approve of what her husband is doing. Will it reach the point where she will have to choose between leaving and continuing to put up with George's antics?

"We can put the machinery down by the house for the workers," George is saying in the darkness. "If the sheriff and the auctioneers start searching farms in the area they would hardly look down by the workers' place."

"Remember to tell the men not to fool around with this equipment," Thomson says. "It could be dangerous. Somebody could get hurt."

"Christ, Thomson," George says, his voice growing faint with the distance. "You're talking about men who are accustomed to being on a farm. How many times must I tell you to stop worrying? They're not bloody well women, you know. These boys know how to goddamn well protect themselves."

The wind carries the voices away from the house. As I hasten out in the rain to join the men and see for myself what they are doing, I glance back and see Mary standing in the doorway, looking into the darkness, listening to the rain falling on a soaked earth. Once again, she reminds me of Maude, standing by the back door as Johnny left for the rum shop that night the youngsters of the village beat him and caused his left eye to throb, even now. I feel a little sorry for Mary, at her disconnectedness, and her private weeping and loneliness. I know she feels that urgent uncomfortable sense of foreboding which she cannot share with anyone. Not even with Jessica, who is playing the piano in the living room, practising some of the West Indian songs she hears the men singing from time to time.

Mary's mind returns to the letters awaiting her in the bedroom. Sometimes she wishes she could talk face to face, heart to heart to the women who write those letters. Especially the women her age. Indeed, sometimes she wishes the women were on the farm with their men. She and these women would probably form valuable friendships, and she wouldn't feel so alone. For, Mary tells herself, as the women in Barbados know, writing letters just isn't the same as talking, of just looking a friend in the face and peering deeply into the frightened eyes.

As I snuggle up and get comfy in Johnny's coat, I can think of only one thing: maybe it is good that it rains today, that there is no sun. For the sun would have only raised Mary's spirits and made her ready for a fight with George. At least with the passivity of the rain, she can be a typical woman, holding her tongue and her counsel, just hoping that the drenching will cause everything to turn green, bright and fruitful in a few days.

I, however, am not that optimistic. And I don't mind telling you, I hope it is a long time before I find myself in the company of this woman again, any woman like this one. It reminds me too much of that damn Mother Nyame. I can't wait to turn my attention to more positive things, which I hope will come as early as tomorrow when the sun rises and rules in a cloudless sky. Amen, my brother.

chapter twenty

"The damn drumsticks," Mighty says aloud, but to nobody in particular. "I can't find them damn sticks that I left there on my steel pan last time. I don't know who could be moving my things without even asking me. Like somebody playing my damn pan when I ain't looking, without even asking me first. But if I ever catch them, be Christ, I'll..."

He doesn't complete the threat, as if he doesn't have the heart. As if to promise to inflict further pain on another member of the group would be sacrilegious. How could he exact revenge when all the men around him are silently praying for divine intervention, not for themselves but for a friend, a brother man standing in the need of pray? Without the usual bragging, they are quietly making personal pacts with their God. They are promising to be upright, forgiving and much more. To be their brother's keeper. To personally start anew in return for the granting of just one last favour.

So Mighty catches himself and restrains his tongue from instinctively issuing the threat, the very thing that might fly into the face of the Redeemer, that might make a mockery of all their supplications. Mighty knows he would not want to walk around for the rest of his life thinking that he was the one to bring down everything just because he does not appear to have a pure heart. How can any of them in this room atone for themselves, far less anyone else, if their hearts are not pure? Can they really expect anyone to listen to their intercessions? Especially if they continue to think about harming one another, if they are selfish, acting as if they lived alone and all is fine in their world?

Mighty throws a suspicious sweeping glance in the direction of Winston, who is plugged into his Walkman as usual. Winston doesn't return the look directly. Instead, he continues to bop his head to the music and tap his feet. When Mighty isn't looking, he gingerly pats the back pockets of his dungarees. His hand freezes as he feels the narrow sticks in his pockets, but he recovers quickly, says nothing and pretends, like everyone else, to be ignoring Mighty. I dare say at least, he is learning how to appear cool under pressure.

The pall in the room remains heavy. As are the expectations. The feeling of foreboding saps the natural energy in the room, so that the men bathe, shave and dress without saying much. Nobody seems to have the heart for the usual banter. Nobody is anxious for a domino game, even though the farm is on its longest winning streak ever. Winning the tournament, and the elusive trip to Toronto and the Jazz Festival, is just one more night away.

Even Mighty is in a foul mood. Searching the cabin, looking under the cots, upturning the silverish steel pan in the corner, banging his feet on the walls. Occasionally, he mutters to himself something about breaking the arse of anyone messing with his steel pan. But everybody knows that whatever they are doing, individually or collectively, it is only to occupy their minds, to help them to wait. If Mighty wasn't looking for his sticks he would have to find something else to keep him busy and that might be more challenging.

"It's coming!" somebody screams. It reminds me of the sweet sound when the lookout on a slaver shouting Land Ahead! a sound that the cargo chained below in the hole of the ship doesn't understand, doesn't know if it signals the beginning of good times or the inevitable arrival of death itself. Suddenly there is a rush for the window. All eyes see the red minivan turn off the road and begin its slow approach to the cabin. As it moves, it bounces on its springs and kicks up clouds of dust. Immediately, a feeling of excitement overtakes us. Even from this distance, we can see two heads in the van. Two heads mean good news. It means Tommy is coming back home. Maybe what we think is some great sickness has been a false alarm. We were wrong to think there would be a need for additional tests, for Tommy to stay in the hospital overnight like the last time, that all the men might finally have to troop off to some clinic to be tested for God-only-knows-what.

The men become much more relaxed, almost instantly. They no longer seem to be carrying the sins of the world on their shoulders. The relief is palpable. It is the comfort from having triumphed over impatience and wild thoughts. It is the satisfaction from knowing that, individually, they have overcome those deep, unspeakable doubts that afflict every one of us. This sense of victory, of pending good news, produces mixed emotions. Yes, there is the feeling of relief. But the men still have nagging doubts, the suspicion that perhaps they should remain cautious to protect their hearts from the danger of disappointment.

Reality and doubt strike the men with full force. They could be reading too much into the appearance of two heads in a van. How can they tell from this distance that the second head belongs to Tommy? Suppose it is some doctor or nurse coming to explain the ins and outs of some incomprehensible things to them, some incurable disease, or maybe they're even coming to take their blood for immediate testing? How can they tell the second head is really Tommy's?

If these men are honest with themselves, they will admit that they are expecting the worst. They have already run through in their minds how they would react to any amount of bad news, to the presence of any of a million and one possible diseases in their midst. But until the van pulls up to the cabin, how can they be sure of anything, that Tommy is even in the van? And if he isn't, what do they do next?

The minivan pulls up in front of the door of the cabin. Even before it stops, we are all rushing the van. We are crowding the door, like little boys eagerly awaiting the arrival of a parent or a visiting relative loaded down with the sweetest candy. I know that I am supposed to remain aloof from these things, but for a moment I find myself just as caught up as the men. I will try not to let it happen again. But this is the result of tension getting too tight, just like, if I can say, when I was in that cell with the Prophet. However, from this point on I promise to watch for any slips on my part and to pull back if necessary. I must keep my perspective straight and not let anything colour my thinking or actions.

Tommy, wearing a black windbreaker and a pair of jeans and looking a bit drawn, slowly gets out of the car. He closes the door softly behind him, almost as if afraid to slam it. He waits for the Liaison Officer to join him. Together they walk ever so slowly and laboriously the short distance to the cabin and then up the board steps. The Liaison Officer, smiling and rattling his car keys, allows Tommy to lead the way. Tommy doesn't smile. He walks slowly into the cabin, very slowly, too damned slowly for the likings of any of us.

He heads straight for the bedroom. The men watch him walk past zombie-like, his mind elsewhere. They exchange baffled looks and try to read what they can from his sombre appearance, from the fact that he doesn't even say a word to them, from how slowly he moves. And, as if with one mind, they all cringe and prepare for the news, obviously bad news. Tommy's behaviour is very different from the last time. That time he almost bounded out of the minivan, telling the men that he was sorry for depriving them of a good wake, but that just for the fun of it they can still polish off the last of his rum in celebration.

"How'd it go?" Henry says, pushing past the Liaison Officer

and following Tommy across the room. Obviously, Henry cannot take the suspense any more. He is asking the questions on the tip of all the men's tongues. "What did the doctor tell yuh? How yuh feeling, man?"

Tommy does not answer. He seems to quicken his pace, if ever so slightly, as if seeking to escape from the men, particularly Henry. The Liaison Officer motions to Johnny and they move to the corner of the room, where they can talk without being overheard. The men notice this and Henry, sensing the worse, continues to question Tommy, beseeching Tommy to tell him, and all the men listening, that all is well with him. That the hours of tests by the numerous specialists at the clinic in town proved that nothing was wrong with him, or that whatever it was could be cured with rest, or powerful drugs.

"Gotta send him back home," the Officer whispers to Johnny, nodding his head in Tommy's direction. "The same sickness they're talking about in the news all the time." The broad smile is still on his face. The implication of what he is saying doesn't appear to bother him. "Tommy doesn't know yet. But I had a quick meeting with the doctors when he was dressing. They say his days of working on a farm like this are definitely over. So, it looks like home is the best place for Tommy. His wife can look after him."

"That bad, eh?" Johnny is at a loss for words.

The Officer nods his head. "We might have to keep a close look on some of the other men. Got to remind them to use them bloody condoms now they've started going back into town on Friday nights."

He places the keys in his pocket and begins jingling them with some coins. Johnny bites his lower lip and tries to conceal the hurt from his face. He casts a quick glance at the bedroom door as Henry's back disappears inside. They can still hear a frustrated Henry angrily questioning Tommy.

"Man, why you ain't talking?" he is pleading. "How you think all o' we out there feel, man? Answer me that. How you think all o' we feel after all o' we waiting here fuh you to come back and then you ain't saying one word? Like the damn goat eat yuh tongue, so you can't talk. What yuh expect we to think, nuh man?"

Johnny moves away from the Liaison Officer. With four quick steps, he crosses the room and enters the bedroom. Moments later, he reappears with an arm around a quietly protesting Henry, who is almost incoherently now trying to explain to Johnny why he is so anxious for the news on Tommy, how Tommy isn't being fair to the men.

"It's okay, Henry," Johnny says. "Give him some time to catch heself. It's been a long day. He's tired, man."

"If you say so, Johnny," Henry says. He drops his hands to his side in resignation. Tears build in his eyes and he quickly wipes them away with the back of his hand. "You, yourself, know how we feel, Johnny; he's one o' we, a brother, man, and we want to know everything, man. That he's okay, Johnny. You know what I mean, Johnny, man?"

Henry sits pitifully on the bench at the main table. He props his head in the palms of his hands, the elbows grounded on the table. The men look at him in silence. Some of them bow their heads so as to not make eye contact with one another and betray their inner doubts that are now stronger than before, causing their stomachs to churn. This way they can also hide their tears.

Johnny pats Henry on the back and whispers something soothing to him. Nobody hears what he says, but Henry appears calmer, if not more at ease. Johnny returns to join the Liaison Officer. Even as he talks, his eyes never stop flitting from one table to another. The other men could expose their feelings. But Johnny knows he has to keep his emotions under control, he has to keep his head even though everyone around him may lose theirs. He has to keep the cabin functioning, help the men through this anguishing period. Later, when alone, he can reflect on life. This, my dear friend, is the evidence to prove what I have been saying all along, of how in a crisis a born leader just takes over instinctively and worries about his own feelings later.

"Another thing, Johnny. How's Jonesie taking his news?" the Officer asks, speaking softly as if seeking illegal information. "I'm wondering if we should also send him back home with Tommy. I can have the two tickets issued at the same time."

"What you mean?" Johnny asks. He cannot understand why the Officer would want an escort for Tommy.

"The immigration people in Ottawa called me the other day," the officer explains. "They want to know how Jones is taking the news; if I think he would try to leave the farm. You know, run off the contract."

"Why?" Johnny asks, unintentionally raising his voice, but quickly recovering. "Something happening to Albert, too?" Now, he is even more puzzled by the question and turns to face the officer directly. This way he can see across the field in the direction of the farm house. He can see George Stewart, with clouds of smoke curling above his head, with the canvas bag under his arm. He is walking slowly toward the cabin in the evening darkness.

"You know why, Johnny. You know how much Jones was looking forward to the news that..."

"You mean they turn him down?" Johnny blurts out.

The reaction surprises the officer. He looks at Johnny in amazement. Suddenly, he realizes what he has done. "You mean, nobody ain't know anything, yet? The letter from immigration people in Ottawa ain't come yet?"

"Know what?" Johnny says impatiently. "Don't tell me they turn he down." George Stewart comes through the door and the

Liaison Officer, taking the opportunity to escape Johnny, goes over to join the farmer by the large table.

"Letters here," George says, dumping the bundle on the table. "I went into town today and decided to stop by the post office. You left a message for me on the phone, Mr. Government-man," he says turning to the Officer. "I saw your car and decided to come over. How is Tommy?"

"Not good. But let's talk outside." Turning to the men, the officer says, "I will get back to you guys" and steps outside with George Stewart. They talk for a while. George Stewart glances into the cabin several times. He continually takes the pipe from his mouth, sending gobs of spit into the dusty earth, as if he also needs his mouth to take in the information. The men watch suspiciously. The pile of mail remains untouched.

Minutes later, the engine of the minivan roars and the men hear the sound of the wheels rolling over the gravel and the sticks and twigs. Now the men are trying to appear as though they don't really care. The bundle of letters is disappearing. For a moment the men will have other things to occupy their minds as they devour the news from back home.

Johnny remains standing in the corner, arms folded across his chest, wondering why all the bad news had to come simultaneously. He watches as Albert Jones takes up his official-looking letter, smiles, and disappears into the bedroom, just as he always does when dealing with the Immigration Department. Johnny knows the worst isn't over. The suspicious side of him, the part he hates to acknowledge, reminds him of the saying that bad things always happen in threes. There is no telling when and where the next round of bad luck will strike, he thinks. Maybe at the domino tournament, if Tommy is no longer around to inspire the men, to be his partner. Whatever form it takes, in his heart Johnny knows more bad news is inevitable.

So engrossed is Johnny in his thoughts, or probably it is so unexpected, that he doesn't notice Mighty shaking in his direction a white envelope with white and red stripes on the edges.

"Like somebody write you from home, Johnny," Mighty says.

Johnny takes the letter and pockets it. His thoughts are on Tommy and Jonesie, not on some letter, even if it is his first of the year. Like no other time since my return, since my debacle with the Prophet, I have this indescribable feeling of dread. For the first time I am willing to concede that maybe, just maybe, I should never have accepted this assignment, should never have become a reporter in the first place, should never have listened to Mother Nyame, never have come back to a country from which even the Prophet ran away.

chapter twenty-one

From inside the bedroom, Johnny and Tommy can still hear the men talking in the next room. They all sound like they are in agreement, although it is Jonesie who is expressing their thoughts and disappointments most eloquently and forcefully. As usual, Timmy is making the most noise, pointing out that nothing surprises him any more, claiming that he knew all along that there was no way those immigration people would allow any of them to stay in Canada permanently. After all, he says, who wants kiss-me-arse apple pickers in their country? And that is all they are — kiss-me-arse agricultural workers, people who pick tobacco and apples and pears and tomatoes, people good for paying taxes too. Who wants more of these people in this country, when they can get them for ten months a year and then send them packing when the season done over?

"It's the said same thing Mrs. Price back home tell Boysie the night she butt up on Boysie grabbling up she daughter Rosie in the backyard. Boysie, she says, lemme know yuh intentions right now, and they better be honourable. If they ain't, don't bother setting yuh two foot on these premises o' mine again 'cause, Mrs. Price did say to him, why buy the cow if you can get the milk free?" Timmy says. "And that's what all o' we is, cows that people can milk."

Albert Jones, he testifies, and anyone who holds contrary views and dreams, is simply foolish and naive. After all these years in this country, stupid people like the ones he is now talking to still don't understand how the Canadian system works, how Canadians only want them for their labour.

"It reminds me of the lime skins," Timmy says. "Just like the limes that we use back home for making lemonade. You know, you start with a nice, young lime. A firm and juicy one, just off the tree, so that when you squeeze it the acid spray outta the skin into yuh eye, burning yuh eye and blinding yuh. Then these people up here take you and squeeze you dry, squeeze out all the juice and the pith from inside out o' yuh. Then they dash you away, like lime skins with no more juice."

There is silence, as if Timmy is waiting for someone to challenge him.

"'Cause, be Christ," he continues, "we's just dirt to these people. Damn dirt, if you ask me. All we good for is to come up here when the year come and work we arse off and then when they finish with we, or we ain't no more goddamn use to them, they pack we up and send we back home. They done with we. Just like that. Just like Frankie back home."

"But even if you know them things, you still can't be certain," Albert says defensively. "You can't be so sure 'til you prove everything for yourself, until you give everybody a chance to prove themselves. After all, you might think something, might have a real strong hunch, but you can't be sure until you got proof. I mean, who can blame me? I talk'd to the Liaison Officer. I talk'd to the people at the Canadian High Commission in Barbados. I talk'd to everybody that should know what's going on. And they keep telling me the same thing: that yes I should apply. Give it a try, they all tell me."

"They didn't tell yuh that they would turn yuh down, though," Timmy says defiantly. "You know what I feel when I think o' how these bloody people only using we? I feel that all o' we should just stop coming up here when the year come. Stop leaving we home and coming up here. If only for one year, we should stop. If only to prove a point, so we'll see what they'll do without we. Go on a kinda strike. I feel that way, that we should stop working on these fucking farms, living like slaves if you ask me, and that we should stay home when the year come and let the damn apples fall off o' the trees and rotten on the ground. Let them pick them damn apples themselves, and the pears and the damn tobacco. That's how I feel."

"But that won't make no sense," Rat Face answers. "I mean if we don't come, there got lots o' people lining up at the Labour Department back home just waiting to lap up these said same jobs. Lot o' people. Not only at home, but in all the other Caribbean islands and in Mexico. People who won't think twice to take we jobs, and then what we'll do: cut off we nose to spite we own self?"

"Sometimes you gotta stand up to prove a point," Timmy shoots back. "To prove you're a man, that all o' we still got balls, if you ask me. Just like the Minister was saying on the radio the other night, man. Black men like me and you got to stand and take our place in the world."

"Yeah, but going on strike? I don't know," Rat Face says. "As I keep saying, they got plenty o' people that not working that just can't wait to get these jobs. We can't go actin' powerful-foolish and not knowing what we starting. Remember that taxi driver Cuthbert back home at the airport? I always thinking o' people like he when I'm stretch out in my bed. Or even when I'm out in the field. Do you think he would think twice if somebody give he the chance to jump on a plane and come up here to replace any o' we? I don't think so. 'Cause every damn body back home think this is easy money — easy living. If we don't come back up here that won't mean one damn thing, they won't even miss we, if you ask me."

"That is why my runnin' shoes always ready, man," Smokie says. "And I got a strong feelin' this is the year them shoes in there under my bed will be takin' me to Toronto. I tired of all this bullshit, man."

His voice drowns out the others with its assurance and conviction. Johnny cocks his head and good ear to one side to hear better. At the same time, he continues his conversation with Tommy. It's obvious to me that Johnny doesn't like the tone or direction of the conversation in the next room. He always gets so jumpy when Smokie begins this foolish talk about running off the contract. I, too, get nervous. For here is a man letting his mouth just run away with him; he doesn't know the consequences of his words; does not know that from history very few people make it to the city; that fewer still live for any length of time in the city before they get picked up and packed back home.

Oh, how I wish I could speak directly to Smokie and get him off this foolish gig. Because this is the worst time to be making such statements, to be so inciteful. The men are most impressionable, accepting anything remotely promising a better life. They are angry and disappointed and could act rashly, striking out without thinking of the consequences. Smokie should know better or someone should tell him to just shut up.

There is a reason for the men going on and on with what we like to call so much mouth-talk, you know, just running their mouths by talking and talking, all the while knowing not one o' them is going to raise one finger to do anything, not as long as they can keep flapping their gums and airing their mouths. Pure mouth-talk is what we are hearing out there. And why are the men so upset? Because they are still digesting the news that the Canadian Immigration officials turned down Albert Jones' application.

Those were tense moments when word started filtering out of the bedroom where Albert was reading the letter. Some of the men were talking about the strange way Tommy looked and reacted to them. They knew something was wrong with Tommy, perhaps worse than what Tommy wanted them to know. That was why he didn't want to engage them in conversation, didn't want to frighten old friends with bad news. They understand why Tommy is silent. He doesn't want to be any more of a burden than he is already by making the men worry too much about him. And he doesn't want to lie to them by making his condition appear better than it is. So he says little, nothing really, to them. Most of the men understand this situation and know they would do the same.

The way I see it, the men were reacting, gathering within small knots of very close friends to just talk. This way they can begin to understand Tommy's reaction, to toughen themselves to accept the worst, while still hoping for the best. Then comes the second blow: the terse statement on the piece of white paper. The letter circulates hand to hand, with every man reading it, as if to confirm with his own eyes what he is hearing.

As they read the letter, the men circle the table, no longer in small groups, to discuss how the simple arrival of the three-paragraph letter could destroy their last lingering hopes for eventual escape from the farm, to a better life for them and their families. And unlike their discussion about Tommy, with this one they don't have to use careful language and gestures. They can speak as openly and frankly as they wish.

They have to deal with the rejection and hurt as a group. With Tommy, the sickness affects one man for sure and possibly others, but this rejection captures the fate and dashes the aspirations of virtually everyone sleeping under this roof. It is difficult for the men to acknowledge that they cannot live permanently in Canada. This is true even for those who have never openly expressed this hope, perhaps out of a belief that to verbalize their deepest wish in their hearts is to give it wings to fly away. They, too, now know there is no use having private thoughts, that they will not stand out as unusual, as Tommy does as a sick man — up until now such thoughts and even aspirations have been strictly private.

Now, all is clear and the dream dies bad. Although they have spent all of their working life in this country, they will still have to leave when they are no longer of any use to the country, when they are no longer needed by the farmer, by the bankers. And this is what they have lived such hard lives for; for what they have sacrificed, denied themselves, living in such isolation, picking apples, pears, tomatoes, whatever — all the stuff Canadians just love to eat while ignoring the presence of the providers.

Needless to say, the men are very unhappy and I can't say that I blame them. They all deal with their disappointment in different ways. Some resume practising for the dominoes tournament while arguing over what options are available to them. Others are just silent. Those are the dangerous ones, in my opinion, because nobody knows what they are thinking, what they will do.

Smokie, however, keeps arguing that if they cannot stay in the country legally, then there is nothing to lose by going outside the system. And to prove his commitment, he comes into the bedroom, takes the running shoes from under his bed, dusts them off with the palm of his hands and kisses them.

"Let's see who is man enough to put his foot in his own runnin' shoes to join me when I ready fuh run," he dares everyone as he rejoins the group. Only Preacher Man challenges him. The Bible says laws, even bad laws, are made to be obeyed, he warns. The eyes of most of the men glaze over instantly. Some roll to the heavens. This doesn't surprise me. Over the years, I have come to expect this reaction, but I am glad someone is speaking out, not leaving everything for Johnny to do. I have seen the same rolling of the eyes and the *cheupsing* whenever some firebrand levels the accusation that people like these in this room are kept in their subjugation by religion. I heard it during the nonviolence era of the Civil Rights movement and came across similar thoughts in stories from back on the Cape. And before that on the sugar and cotton plantations when a preacher turned up promising a better life as compensation for such long suffering. Sceptics in the crowd, and you don't have to look too far to find them, always react this way. Fortunately, few of them ever do anything, never raise a finger to act. And that's a good thing. That is why I am confident loudmouths like Smokie will do nothing more than talk, will never lace on those running shoes no matter how much big talk.

Here I must point out to those ready to cut my throat that the Prophet was as guilty as anyone for having this attitude. Yes, strange as it may sound, I think the Prophet was a great man, but that doesn't mean that he did everything the right way. Every great man has a fatal flaw, just remember Othello. The Prophet, being human, wanted to challenge and change everything overnight. That is where I believe he went wrong, why everything came tumbling down around us, why we still have this appalling legacy.

And believe you me, I've had time to think and reflect on these things, to find the weaknesses in his proposals. I definitely believe it would have been much easier if the Prophet had not tried to force things so quickly, but had acquiesced more gently and lobbied for change over time. That is what I have told Mother Nyame I would do if I were to come back as a leader. I would try to combine the vision of the Prophet with the patience of say, a Johnny. That is why I have so much confidence that Johnny will prove me right. I need Johnny for my case and my redemption. Mother Nyame did as much as show me that she feels I'm on the right track. Just don't get left behind is all she tells me. Just keep up to date and anticipating. Well, that is exactly what I do on a daily basis, so I don't think I have to worry too much about this admonition of sorts.

"As soon as I save a few dollars, just enough to keep me goin' until I can find a job and a place to sleep in Toronto, I gone,"

Smokie drones on. Thank God talk is cheap. That is all I can say if I want to remain generous to him. "I'd be done with this place, I tell yuh. I'd be burnin' up tracks for Toronto."

"I might even come with you too," Preacher Man says in that distinctively deep voice, but his words sure as hell surprise me. "Just as soon as I myself raise some money too. I'll join yuh like shite, Smokie. What we got to lose, eh?"

There is an air of seriousness and defiance in Preacher Man's voice that also frightens me. Obviously, it catches Johnny's attention too, because he sits up straight on the cot next to Tommy. Perhaps what surprises him most is the fact that this time nobody laughs at Preacher Man's about-face. Nobody cautions about winning the dominoes tournament first so that they can scout Toronto on the winning trip before running. Normally, that is what I'd expect the men to say.

After all, winning the tournament would provide such a perfect excuse for the men to get to Toronto and then to decide if they wanted to return to the farm or take their chances there and then. Indeed, some of them might just jump ship while on the trip and save themselves the hazard of running all the way to Toronto. And they are so close to winning the tournament. This is the week the Edgecliff men will hear whether they will get a free ride into the finals, if the Beatrice Farm workers will remain in the tournament now that their farm has gone bankrupt and they are getting ready to go back home.

"I ain't going back home, Johnny," Tommy says with finality in his voice. While not reminding me of a specific case, it is the same tone I have heard in the voice of a judge or two who had reflected long and hard on some matter and finally came to an unavoidable conclusion. The certainty in Tommy's voice causes Johnny to temporarily forget the conversation in the other room.

"What you talkin' 'bout?" he asks.

"I mean that I ain't going back home. Plain as that. I ain't getting on no plane and returning to no fucking Barbados. Not if there is any breath in my body."

"But you know what the Officer say. That it's best for you to go home," Johnny says.

"Fuck the Liaison Officer!" Tommy shouts. He gets up from the cot and paces the floor. "What he ever did for me or anybody up here? What anybody ever done for any o' we? I ain't going back home and walking the streets. I ain't going to be like Frankie, planting flowers at the goddamn airport and begging people for tips. Not if I can help it."

"But you got something to go back home to. You ain't like me. You got a big house and you got Barbara," Johnny says. "She's a good woman, even if you and she don't always see eye to eye. She'll take care of you until you catch yourself."

"*Godblindmuh,* Johnny, you ever try to live in the same house with Barbara?" Tommy blurts out. "I keep tell yuh, man, I can't live with she, man. No, man. I can't live with that woman. She must always be in charge. Of every goddamn thing. She ain't use to having no man around, to having me under her feet. She always got to be telling me this when I at home. Living in that house with she all the time ain't like living up here, man. At least here, the men don't keep bothering yuh all the time. If a fellow find out you're vex or something, he leave yuh alone to be with yuhself, so you can figure out things for yuhself without anybody confusing yuh all the time. Not Barbara, man. Remember how bossy she can be, like she was around the men last Christmas?"

"But you and she always get on so good," Johnny says. "Look at how the two o' you was getting on at the Christmas get-together. Such good food and she hugging you up and thing. Everybody keep saying how you and she look so lovey-dovey. That the two o' you can't wait 'til you get back home for good."

"You got it right," Tommy snaps. "You got it damn right. Get back home for good — six feet deep. That's what. But Barbara, she does control everything, as if I don't own the house too, I'm some little boy begging she for a lodging, the little boy in the yard, having to do whatever she want me to do. She's a' independent woman, don't need a man around she arse all the time. If two months is hell, can you imagine what a year would be like? It would drive me nuts, man. Nuts."

"But things would be different," Johnny tries to console him. "Barbara is a good woman. And with you needing to rest, she'd take good care of you. And the children too. You should look forward to seeing them."

"Don't talk 'bout no children, Johnny. Not unless you want me to tell you that this would be the first damn time in almost twenty years that I going back home with two long empty hands. With not even a pack of chewing gum, not even a mint sweetie, for them."

He stands over Johnny, raising the palms of his hand heavenwards, signifying their emptiness. "I don't have a damn dollar in my pocket; I owe everybody in this place a twenty dollars here and a twenty there. I ain't got a blind cent to carry back home, to spend on anything. And you want me go back home with my two long hands, after all these years? Be a burden on somebody? To be like Frankie? To do what: plant flowers?"

Tommy walks back to the cot and, in a rather rash move, flings himself on the bed. He closes his eyes. Johnny doesn't know if it is from the pain, from exerting himself too much with the outburst, or if he is thinking about back home, to what awaits his return.

This has been quite a revelation. Not only for me, but for Johnny as well. I mean, anybody would expect any couple to have one or two disagreements. But not anything like this, not even after, come to think of it, the broad hints Tommy dropped earlier. To put it bluntly, Johnny is simply flabbergasted. In all the years Tommy has been his best friend, he hadn't realized there was so much turbulence inside him. He never realized that, just like he and Maude, Tommy and Barbara — the happy couple with the three growing children — were all a charade. And this is the same Tommy who spends every waking moment reading them old, mouldy letters. How he fooled us! How, unlike women, men can keep secrets even from their best friends.

Johnny decides not to say anything. There is nothing he can say, really. He sits listlessly on his cot and automatically picks up one of the diaries from Panama. He begins reading, silently at first and then, without knowing it, out loud as he becomes more engrossed in the writings. As his voice rises, I can't help feeling that Johnny is really trying to drown out something he is hearing. Something in his head, or maybe the loud, laboured breathing from Tommy on the cot next to him.

"Could you read that again, Johnny?" Tommy asks.
"What?"
"What you just read there in the diary, about the explosion."
"You mean this," Johnny says, and starts to read.

The worst news since we arrived. I'm glad that I'm a water boy. Big explosion in the ammo dump killed sixty today. Some say it was an accident; but other people say that somebody might have done it on purpose. That some of the men wanted to kill themselves to rid themselves of this misery. Percy, Terrence, Hopeton and Ezekiah all dead. This was their first day back after they come down with the malaria. Funeral for them on Sunday. I think some of the men chose death. But I don't want to think my four friends would ever think about such a thing. But, from what I am hearing, I might be wrong. I could be wrong...

"That's okay," Tommy says. "That's enough. I hear enough."

"No. Listen to this. On the next page." Johnny continues reading.

> *Today, I came across the note that Percy, Terrence, Hopeton and Ezekiah left for me. It's true: the explosion was no accident. I destroyed the bloody letter rather than show it to Egbert, Hezekiah and Adam. It would only give them ideas too. I like to believe in the saying that where there is life there is hope. But under these conditions even someone like me can see where there is no hope, especially when you keep feeling so weak, so sick and can't work.*

Johnny closes the diary. He gets off the bed and stretches.

"You want anything from the kitchen?" Johnny asks.

"Nah. I don't think so. Don't turn off the light when you leave. I might go for a little walk later."

"Okay." Johnny walks toward the door. "Try and get some rest man, though. Don't worry about going home. Everything will be okay."

"If you say so, Johnny," Tommy says, as if now resigned to the inevitable return home. As if Johnny has persuaded him that there is nothing to fear. "Just make sure that they post these letter fuh me."

"Okay, Tommy." Johnny walks out of the bedroom. For the rest of his life he will relive this final conversation millions of time over and blame himself for not picking up the nuances in his best friend's voice. But the regret, like everything on the farm, would come too late and stay too long.

chapter twenty-two

From where they are working, Johnny can see the cabin. He keeps gazing over that way, not certain what he is looking for, but nonetheless expecting something, anything really, to happen. The hair on the back of his neck and arms is standing on end and his stomach has been queasy all morning.

From the time he guzzled down the coffee with, for the first time in years, a bit of milk in it, his stomach has been in a mess. Why he should choose to drink milk this morning, he still doesn't know. Just one of those spur-of-the-moment things. Now he can appreciate how Winston feels with such a breakfast riding his stomach. When every time he belches there is the reminder of the coffee and the plain slices of white bread. His bowels keep nudging him to free them.

Now it comes back to him why he drank the coffee with milk. He remembers Tommy refusing the cup, a move so uncharacteristic and unexpected that Johnny finds himself drinking the coffee before he realized what was happening. Every morning Tommy has a cup of coffee, with three heaping spoonfuls of sugar and half the cup filled with milk. Johnny never uses milk.

But when he brings the coffee to Tommy this morning, he refuses it. Tommy doesn't say why. Just that he doesn't want anything to eat or drink, at least not yet, that he can get something for himself later. So Johnny drinks the coffee, rather than confront Tommy over why all of a sudden he is being so finicky and aloof. And when he thinks of it, Johnny realizes that this is the first time in all these years he has taken a drink from Tommy's cup.

But his stomach has been paying the price ever since then. And it isn't only because of the coffee. Instinct tells him that something else is wrong. Something more ominous than the coffee and milk, something that his psychic body has been picking up. Perhaps the same way a wife or husband or a twin can always tell when something wrong is happening to a life-long partner. That is why he continues to glance over at the cabin in the distance. Why he gets nervous when he sees the first puff of smoke in the air, the black smoke belching in small spurts from the back of the cabin.

He calls Winston over and quietly asks him to run over to the cabin and to check on Tommy. He doesn't know what to expect. Only that something isn't right and he needs someone who can run fast. That his heart is fluttering too much. There is no reason for the puffs of smoke, unless George Stewart or one of the farmers is turning over the engine. But why would they do that and alert anyone for miles around as to where they are hiding the machinery?

Winston walks briskly toward the cabin. Johnny watches him enter the house. Seconds later he emerges. He walks around one side of the cabin and returns into view. Still walking briskly, he rounds the other side of the cabin, from where the puffs of smoke are rising. Later, they would find the engine still running, like a contented animal purring after having devoured its prey.

When Winston returns to view, he is running, desperately waving his long arms in the air. As he moves toward the orchard, his long loping legs barely touch the earth. He looks like a deer, muscular and majestic, fleeing some hunter. But he isn't running away from anyone. Winston is trying to get help. He is frantically waving his hands and obviously shouting, although in the distance no one can hear him. Johnny, however, must be hearing every word. He drops his knife and turns to the men.

"Like we got trouble!" he shouts. With that he too starts to run. At his age, his is more effort than speed. But he is at least moving faster than his quickest walk. "We gotta go and see what happen'd!" he shouts.

At that moment, and I have to believe him, Johnny swears that despite the distance, he could hear the final piercing screams, or at least feel something jarring in the pit of his stomach. The shout of pain as the machine crushes the life out of the body and leaves a crumbled mess of blood, flesh and bones on the brown sun- drenched grass. There is no human way Johnny should or could hear the screams, if indeed there were any. Not from so far away, out in the apple orchard with the rest of the crew. For there was no loud boom, the way his grandfather in Panama had been signalled when his best friends left him, no sounds of the cymbals to announce the arrival of the sweet chariot swinging low.

When Winston sees the men coming, he turns around and retraces his steps, disappearing behind the cabin. When the men arrive, they find him straining to lift the still purring machine off a listless Tommy. He succeeds in raising it off him, but Tommy doesn't move. The blood is still running out the side of his mouth, past his earlobes, onto the white collar of his shirt and the scorched grass. His opened eyes stare at the blue skies. The grass is already getting sticky with blood.

Effortlessly, the muscular men push over the machine. It crashes vengefully and heavily to the ground and rolls over several times before coming to rest against the cabin. Preacher Man reaches into his pocket for the old, tattered Gideon New Testament that he always carries on him. He reads silently, his hands trembling and his lips moving.

Johnny, among the last to arrive and panting heavily, bends over and feels for a pulse. He runs his hand along the side of Tommy's neck. There is nothing, no beat. He continues searching for some sign, however faint, his hands covered with blood. But Tommy just stares toward the heavens, serenely oblivious of the frantic and anguished activity around him. Finally, Johnny sits at Tommy's head, gently lifting it and placing it on his lap. Some blood trickles out of the dead man's mouth and soils his jeans. Johnny doesn't appear to notice. Obviously, he does not care what might be in the blood for *he's not ashamed of the blood of the lamb, for when I see the blood I shall pass over thee. The blood that is shed for thee.*

"Somebody," Johnny whispers faintly to the seemingly paralysed men. "Somebody... please go... go and get something to cover him, please. A blanket or something."

Winston dashes into the cabin and returns with a white sheet and a greyish blanket with brown and white stripes. He puts the blanket under Tommy's head and spreads the sheet over him.

"I'll go and tell the farmer to call somebody," Winston volunteers. "Johnny, you stay right there with Tommy. I'll tell the farmer to call the ambulance and the Liaison Officer."

He walks away. Slowly and purposefully this time, as if trying to formulate in his mind exactly what to tell George Stewart and his family. I can only imagine what that other storyteller is saying about Winston. I don't think I want to hear it. Johnny watches Winston going away and in anguish calls out to him, but, because of the direction of the wind, Winston doesn't hear and keeps on walking. Indeed, I wonder how that damn storyteller views this development, what the others listening to her make of this situation. For at that moment I detect what could very well be the passing of a baton.

Johnny turns his attention to the lifeless body in his arms. He gently presses the eyelids closed and keeps the pressure on them until he is sure they will never reopen, that, indeed, there is someone to lovingly close Tommy's eyes. Then he cups his hands around Tommy's mouth, pressing the pursed thick black lips together. The men form a circle around the two of them, breathing heavily but saying nothing.

Johnny looks up at the faces above him. He tries to say something, to console the men, but words fail him. He needs consoling himself and feels tired, angry and helpless. So he drops his chin to his chest and closes his eyes. And he remembers many of the things he and Tommy did together, how Tommy always made him laugh. He knows he will miss his best friend, more than he misses Grafton, and that life on the farm, life in general, will never be the same again. His mind flips back to Barbados, to the airport and the women's conversations. And he wonders how Barbara will take the news, and how Tommy's children will react, and the men in the cabin...they don't need this. Not a third strike against them. Not right now.

"Where is...?" Johnny begins. "Where is Winston? Is he back yet?" The pleading in his voice rends my heart. This is no way for a leader to behave, to cry out like this to someone who obviously is still so wet behind the ears. It is definitely not the same when leaders cry.

But in this weak moment, this one does. This is a time when Johnny wishes he were somewhere else, where he does not have the entire world on his shoulders, where he can pray for someone to take his load and carry it, if only for a short time, but long enough so he doesn't always have to be smiling and leading. Maybe when Winston comes back, I can hear him thinking, the young fellow will tell the men what to do. Maybe he is right, for Winston looks detached enough. Unemotional, even. I can only say that this might be so because he has not spent as much time as the other men with Tommy and his youth gives him such resilience. For Johnny knows that he can no longer think straight and that the men need someone to rally them until Johnny is whole again.

"Call Winston," Johnny whispers. "Somebody call Winston."

"He's gone to the farm house, Johnny," Timmy says, baffled by Johnny's statement.

"Call Winston," Johnny continues mumbling incoherently to himself. "Call Winston. Tommy, how can you do this? Tommy, how can you leave me now, like this? Winston, ask him why he do this to we?"

While you look on this scene, let me, Brer Anancy, storyteller grandmother, tell you something that strikes me at this very moment as profound. That makes me want to stand up and testify, to become a witness, to make a commentary, to tell it like it is all for the honour and the glory. For I, too, have known rivers that now run dry, streams and rivers that ran before the building of the pyramids, when we were young and bathed in the Euphrates. I, too, went to the mountain top and dreamt that dream, saw Hannibal cross the Alps, the Moors conquer Spain and were then, themselves, cast out. And I was the one taking notes when they grabbed Simeon from the crowd on that shortened day and made him carry someone else's cross.

Yes, I have been there. Seen it all, recorded them all. Sat by the rivers of Babylon, did I, and recorded the wailing and the false songs. And I heard the tapes from other storytellers of the times when the Brown Bomber shocked the world; when Robinson smacked the first ball across the white line, when a storyteller whispered into a receptive ear to write with fury and such elegance about the fire next time.

Believe me, I was there when they took the first of our people from Africa; I have seen countless faces of the eighty million or so that streamed through the House of Slaves, their feet in irons as they passed through the Door of No Return, with a last painful view of Mother Africa, to the Middle Passage, to the unknown in the Americas. When Caliban tried sailing back; when Othello tupped that great man's daughter; when they dragged Marcus, the Prophet, away so there could be no returning home for a people so many centuries in the wilderness. And yes, then there was the scene on the motel balcony in

Montgomery and then again at New York's Audubon Ballroom, when two leaders felt two bullets.

And I have recorded and told stories across the southern states of America and the Caribbean, talked about the good times and the bad times along the Mississippi and the Berbice rivers, witnessed and reported on the deaths of native sons and the murder of dreams, saw the young nations rise and fall in the Southern Hemisphere. I heard the three babies wailing uncontrollably when mothers and fathers of just a generation ago took to the boats looking for work in a London or Paris and I have seen the unfulfilled in the passing parade of the so many undone by death, a parade that Tommy and Grafton now join marching side by side in that eternal bond, a parade that includes all those hundreds of Empire loyalists who fled their chains to fight against the American republic but never got their rewards in this country.

Yes, I have seen it. Even when one man stood in the streets of Bridgetown and shouted *these days are funny nights* and the people were able to pick wisdom out of his foolish words and reinvigorate the fight and the riots spreading across the Caribbean for the vote. Ultimately, their actions would help spawn international commissions and the inevitable crumbling of a mighty colonial empire. When the beast Babylon would fall. And what I have not witnessed, I have heard about in the eternal stories carried on the wind. All the stories in the hands of Mother Nyame.

But it is moments like what we are seeing on this bankrupt farm far behind God's back that will always affect me most. When a leader becomes inarticulate, rejects his calling, these things remain with me. And this is why I am so afraid of diaries and all that stupidness from the past, because each time the leader falters the people perish. That is the story of our history, of the blues man singing *ain't got nobody in all this world,* of the calypsonian's mournful refrain, *woe is me, shame and scandal in me family*, or the gospel singer telling us to *sleep on, beloved, take thy rest*. For who will be our strong leader, the messianic one?

Indeed, I have seen the great rivers run dry without that leader coming. Worse, I have always had to report on them, to record each defeat, while hoping that, indeed, with every defeat the soul grows deep like the river and everlasting like time. Forgive me for not being objective, as I am supposed to be, but I just have to say my piece. Forgive me if, like Johnny, I am weak for a moment. Even though I have seen all these things, know all these things, I still cannot accept the sight of a leader reduced to tears and in front of his people.

Eventually, the ambulance carries away the body. When the men return to the cabin, Johnny finds the letters on Tommy's cot. Separate letters for Barbara and to each of his three children. On the pillow is Tommy's neat pile of letters, some faded, some yellowing, some with the envelopes still white and looking new — the letters stretching back to the first day that Tommy set foot on Edgecliff. It looks like the last thing Tommy did was to reread those letters; then he went out and did what he felt he had to do.

"Forgive me, Tommy," Johnny whispers, as if the dead man was still on the cot like old times. "I gotta do this for all of us." Slowly, he gathers up the four envelopes. "For you too, Tommy old boy. In life you never broke your vow. In death, you won't either. You will not be weak." And he rips the four letters for Barbara and the children into tiny pieces and stuffs them into his pocket. At that moment I saw defeat itself written on this brave man's face. And I heard my voice shake, just as it always does at the starting of a new story.

When Johnny looks up, Winston is standing inches away from him. This time, the younger man puts out his arms and hugs Johnny. He tenderly nudges Johnny into bed and pulls the blankets over him. "The doctor will see you when he comes,"

Winston says. "I'll make some ginger tea for you. Spend some more time alone with Tommy: talk to him. Cuss him, plead with him, cry with him. I understand. And I won't tell a soul 'bout them letters. I won't let anyone into this bedroom for the next little while either."

Winston walks out of room, closing the door to the bedroom behind him. The hinges creak loudly as he moves the door that has never been closed since the day it was fastened to the wall. The creaking reminds me so much of a musty mausoleum. Until this day there has never been any need for such privacy. Not until Winston decreed there must be. Now I have seen it all and I too feel like crying, but I can't. I mustn't. At least not yet, for while there is life, there is hope, even for me and my experiment.

―――――――

"What you're doing there, boss?" Winston joins the older man on the steps, just beyond the edge of the light from inside the barracks. "Like the guys kinda quiet tonight, eh?"

Johnny makes room for Winston to sit on the piece of plastic serving as protection from the wet and cold of the rain-soaked wooden steps. "And what kind of funny music they're playing on the boom-box inside there?"

"Joseph Niles and the Consolers," Johnny answers. His voice sounds as if it is coming from a distance, from a hollowness somewhere out in the darkness, beyond the heavy bank of clouds that drenched the fields all day. "You're probably too young to remember them, Joseph Niles and the Consolers. But I remember, back home, spending so many nights, when I was a little boy growing up, going to the church near where we used to live on Lodge Road, and hearing Joseph Niles and the Consolers singing. When Joseph Niles and the Consolers come to town, everybody used to stop doing whatever they was doing and come and listen. But you won't know what I'm talking 'bout, you're too young."

"I know 'bout Joseph Niles," Winston says. "I've heard my mother play his stuff at home. Just that I don't care too much for spiritual music. Why would anybody want to listen to that kinda music?"

"On a night like this, the men do," Johnny says. He nods his head in the direction of the door and the men inside. "That's all they want to hear on a night like this. You know why?"

Johnny doesn't have to explain the reason for the sad gospel music, doesn't have to add that the men's thoughts are with Tommy, that they are wondering how the funeral went back home, and how they wish they were on hand to lift the coffin and to lower it into the ground.

"I want to hear that kinda music, too," Johnny whispers. "It touch yuh in yuh bones. I think of so many things. I think of Tommy. What time is now…seven, eight o'clock back home. Perhaps, they've done bury him by now. In some hole back there in Barbados. And all like now, they're having one kind of a wake for him back at the house Barbara put up for him. And I keep thinking of what people are saying about Tommy as they drink the rum and eat the food tonight. What can they say, as he rest there in Westbury Cemetery in the black dirt this very night? Who really know anything about Tommy, who really know the man good enough to get up and say a few words about the dearly departed, words that are true and mean something about the man? And I can't think of nobody back there on that island that can really say anything 'bout Tommy. Nobody back there, not even Barbara, can say they really know Tommy. I would be the one to say a few things but…"

"What you're saying, Johnny? You hate talking before people," Winston says. "I mean, even here on the farm, you only like to talk to people one on one."

"There are times when you have to change. When things can't keep going on the same way all the time. I remember when I was a boy. The politicians used to come around and say they want to make the island independent and that it would be good for all o' we on the island."

"I think they still say the same thing to the foolish people at home," Winston says.

"They used to tell us how we won't have to keep sending our young men abroad, working their soul-case out, and then to bring them home just to bury them. Independence would be great. Everything would be fine. But look at Tommy. He's gone back home in a box. Look at people like me and a youngster like you. We'll just go home and be buried. Just like it says in the diaries my father and grandfather left for me. Of late, I have to keep asking myself if this is the way things got to be, if there's some way we can change these things from keep happening so despite what people like Joseph Niles does sing that the circle *will indeed* be unbroken in the good by and by."

The rain resumes falling. Winston picks up a stick and twirls it in a pool at the side of the steps. It isn't raining hard enough to force them to retreat into the house. In the distance, the wind stirs the trees, the same way it has for millennia, the sound of the wind predicting the heavy rains in its wake, somewhere out in the distance where thoughts and dreams merge and the rain is welcomed.

"I just wondering if it's raining in Barbados, too," Johnny said.

"Why?"

"For Tommy," he says. "It would be a good sign. Just as when you plant a seed in the earth, you hope the rains will come and water it. The old people back home used to say you're blessed if the rain fall during your funeral but..."

"The rain's getting harder," Winston says, "and the wind is

getting colder, too. Let we go inside and continue talking if you think that is what you want. By the way, Jessica says goodbye to you."

"I guess, you still spending all that time playing dominoes with she, eh?" Johnny says.

"Uh huh." Winston is smiling self-consciously.

"You sure it's *only* dominoes you two playing?" Johnny says, a brief spark of good spirits resurfacing. "I hope I don't have to speak to George about you. George can be funny, when he is ready."

"I'm okay, man. I was just over there with Jess. Just, you know, talking with her," Winston says. "She's gone to finish packing 'cause she's leaving in the morning for Toronto."

"I remember she and Grafton, that's where she learned to be so good at dominoes," Johnny says. "I think she could hold her own among any of the men in there." He signals with his head toward the cabin behind him. "I remember sometimes me and Grafton and Tommy used to go over to the farm house, you know when we was younger, and she used to be Grafton's partner. Used to give me and Tommy a good run for we money too. I really hope everything is okay for she when she's in Toronto."

"Tomorrow she says she might come over here to tell you goodbye sheself," Winston says. "But just in case she don't get the chance, she asked me to say bye for she. But let we go inside outta the rain and finish talking."

"What's a few raindrops?" Johnny says. "Maybe they will help the living too. I mean, we have Joseph Niles and his music. Just like the times back home, when we used to stand up in the rain, the church crammed so full it couldn't hold another body, to hear Joseph Niles singing. You were out in the rain, but you still feel warm inside. You feel you were a part of something. You were alive and growing. And you watch as Joseph Niles takes the microphone and leans over the balcony from the altar. And he is singing in that high-high voice, *this train don't carry no sinners, this train* and all the women in the congregation would take out their handkerchiefs and wave them in the air, and the church would start rocking, full of life, dancing, singing, so much so that nobody ain't even thinking 'bout no rain, and the people standing outside in the rain can't move from the very spot, as if their feet planted, for the music is alive and too sweet."

"Christ, Johnny. I never hear you talk that much before. What get into you, man?" Winston says. "I still think we should go in now and finish this talking inside." He throws the stick into the darkness and they hear the splash. The rain is falling harder, leaving big blotches on their shirts, slamming hard onto the plastic on the steps. "Let's go inside, Johnny."

"You go 'head, son," Johnny says. "A little rain won't hurt an old man like me, can't hurt me no more. I'll stay here a little bit longer and listen to the music. It will be just like back home."

"But this rain up here is different," Winston pleads. "It's colder, man. Like ice. Not like back home, when the warm air makes the rain warm. Up here, it's like taking an ice bath. You'd catch pneumonia this way."

"You go 'head," Johnny says. "I'll come later. I'll come in later. I just want to think and to be alone. If I die, they'll just have to take me back home in a box, just like Tommy."

This, dear friend, is my leader, the very one I keep telling Mother Nyame will never change. Shades of Prophet after the Atlanta jailing. Now I am wondering if I, too, should start crying, and for myself as well.

chapter twenty-three

Standing in the full glare of the headlights, his shadow spreading across the entire land and enveloping everything, Winston watches the men file dejectedly, lethargically, onto the school bus. They find seats and sit down heavily, their actions clearly showing they would rather be doing anything but participating in the finals of the dominoes tournament. My dear brothers and sisters, what you are seeing is just another example of how low morale has fallen — a taste for, and the size of, the task that awaits Johnny when he snaps out of his zombie-like haze, regains his spirits and becomes whole again.

As you watch them file onto the bus, I am sure you will find it striking, perhaps even unexplainable, what you are seeing and hearing. And yes, you are right: your ears don't deceive you; your eyes don't lie. There's a change, a big change around this place. Not the change our forefathers sing about, the one that's gonna come some day when the cleansing river washes away everything that hurts and defiles us.

But it is a change nevertheless. Just think that a mere few weeks ago, these very men would have been whooping it up. They would be shouting, screaming, banging on the sides of the bus, good-naturedly calling one another the foulest of names — doing all those things men always do over the centuries as they prepare for battle.

Who could blame them for behaving this way? For getting to the finals is momentous, something to scream about, to playfully bang heads and give high-fives. This is a notable success, a cause for celebration at achieving something that has eluded them every year, no matter how well they prepared. Instead, these men before us file onto the bus as if they are going to a funeral. As if they are going to bury a dream rather than to fulfil one of the oldest aspirations on this farm. And all I can attribute this to is the absence physically of Tommy and spiritually of my man Johnny.

Obviously, these men are mourning. That is understandable. But they have to realize that life must go on. As one great storyteller once said with such wisdom: Let the dead bury the frigging dead. And I wholeheartedly endorse this sentiment, even if at a time like this it does sound a bit callous and cold-hearted. But so much is at stake. Properly trained soldiers do not stop on the battlefield to cry for a fallen comrade. They march on, knowing the dead man's spirit is with them, that it will celebrate with them when they defeat the enemy. I see no difference here.

Uncharacteristically, Johnny is already sitting in the front of the bus, on the left-hand side, by the window. He looks just like any of the men, beaten, his head hanging low, his fingers locked in some defeatist gesture. I ask you, where is the leadership? And yes, I am getting a little tired of Johnny moping around, further creating a void that nobody but he can fill. Would Tommy have done what he did if Johnny didn't bring those damn diaries with him? I don't think so. Would someone else have planted such a tragic idea in his head? I think not. These questions only serve to prove my point. This is what you get for becoming too hung up on half-baked history, what happens when leaders take a misguided attitude. Combine the two, as we see in the situation with Johnny and Tommy, and the result is simply lethal.

Still, I must be truthful and admit that I don't like Johnny being so erratic and thoughtless. Most of all, I don't like these urgent calls from Mother Nyame and also, by the way, from a few close associates. Everybody is now asking if I am giving any thought to changing my mind about Johnny. Do I still want to bet the farm, so to speak, on a man who seems to change, to regress fetally, by the minute? What can I do? At this late date, I cannot change in midstream; I must stick with my game plan or just pack my Georgie bundle and head back to head office, another mission abandoned prematurely. Then what becomes of me?

So yes, I'm in a bind. If I don't stick with Johnny, then who? Winston, the only one showing any life or spunk on this damn farm? Really, sometimes I wish I were a poet. I would be able to take flights of fancy, to dream up situations and pretend things are not what they are. Change my mind as many times as I want. And you know everybody loves a poet. But my lot has to be that of a frigging chronicler of facts and, if Mother Nyame would have her way, a commentator.

When the last of the men boards the bus, Winston gives the thumbs-up signal to the driver and steps up from the first step into the aisle. He sits beside Johnny. The driver closes the creaking door with a bang and shifts into gear. The engine roars and sputters.

"I guess we all ready to roll now," Winston says to Johnny.

"Uh huh," the older man replies, no enthusiasm whatsoever in his darn voice. He shifts his weight and slides closer to the side of the bus, creating more room for the long-legged Winston to spread his knees, to stop them from bouncing against the plexi-glass safety protection at the front of the vehicle. As Johnny makes room, I can't help seeing the image of a man withdrawing into himself. He seems to want to become invisible. Instead of snapping out of this funk, by the minute he appears to be falling in even deeper.

The bus shakes heavily, rocks and then rumbles away from the front of the cabin. It drives slowly down the unpaved road that connects to the main highway leading to St. Michael's Anglican church hall in downtown Arkona. Johnny casts a quick glance throughout the bus, counting heads, as if he is still searching for that face that will always be missing. The face that is still imprinted on his memory. At least for this brief moment, he appears to be stirring into action, performing his mother-hen role, rather than just sitting there. My stomach is in knots. Something whispers in my ear not to be too optimistic. Johnny's looking around might be no more than a reflexive move, something unthinking and habitual. Like a body twitching before rigor mortis sets in. I can't agree with this assessment.

"I don't know why we're even going through with this thing here," Delbert says. He leans over the back of the seat, placing his head between Winston and Johnny, imposing some reality on this situation. "You think you might play tonight, Johnny? I mean with you not having a regular partner or anything like that..."

Johnny shrugs his shoulders, seemingly inviting Delbert to put an immediate end to that specific thought. Obviously unconcerned about anything else, he stares straight ahead.

"That is why I keep saying to myself I don't know if there is any sense in we even going through with this thing here tonight," Delbert adds. "If we lose tonight, it would only frustrate the men more, and you know how things is right now, Johnny. It would even hurt the men more by reminding them things might be a bit different if Tommy didn't go and..."

Johnny looks around the bus again and folds his arms across his chest, trying to remain aloof, alone in his thoughts. As if he is unwilling to even contemplate the effects of what could happen if things don't go well in the church basement. As if he is too weary to bother caring any more.

"We playing the hardest team in the competition and we need all the men we can if we want to win," Delbert continues, carefully watching Johnny's reaction. "And you know what the rules say: we gotta play ten separate teams in the finals. Nobody can be in more than one team. This way, and without Tommy, and you ain't got no partner, we can only muster nine teams. And I don't know if that is enough, if they'd bend the rule because Tommy's dead and we can't do nothing 'bout that."

"Don't worry your head, Delbert," Winston says, trying to sound confident, but intervening to take the pressure off the reluctant Johnny. "Nothing beats a try but a failure. And who says that you and the boys can't win the first six games straight off so that it won't matter if we got ten pairs or not."

"It ain't that easy," Delbert says resignedly. He leans back into his seat. "It ain't that easy. Rules are rules, man. Tell him Johnny. It ain't that easy."

Winston feels the breast pocket of his jean jacket. Inside, he discovers an unopened envelope. The letter is bent and crumpled, an indication that it must have been stuffed in there for some time. He cannot remember receiving the letter, let alone having placed it in his pocket. Just another sign, he tells himself, of how busy the last three weeks since Tommy's death have been for him. These days, he can't find the time to do anything for himself. Most nights he slumps into bed exhausted. He sleeps only a few hours so he can be up with the first men, so Johnny can get a few extra hours' sleep.

Winston turns the envelope over. From the postmark, he can tell it is from Toronto. Then he remembers. The letter came in the last batch four days earlier. He was on his way out the door to make arrangements for the school bus when George Stewart turned up with the bag of mail. Someone had said there was a letter for him. Since he was late for the appointment with the bus driver in the farm house, he had stuffed the letter into his jacket pocket, intending to read it later, and ran through the door.

But he never got the chance to read the letter, didn't even remember it, actually. There was too much to do in Tommy's absence. There was too much of a hole to fill. Tommy would have organized the transportation for the finals of the dominoes tournament. He would have registered the names. Perhaps more than Johnny, Tommy would have been the man to inspire the other workers that they could win it all. He would be the cheerleader, telling the men they would finally get that elusive trip to Toronto. And Tommy would have done his part by winning his games, he and Johnny teaming up to preserve their unbroken record of wins for the year. Now the men don't even have the spirit to want to win. Nothing seems to matter any more. They look dazed and listless, exactly the same way Winston found them when he returned from the farm house with George Stewart on the day of Tommy's death.

The bus is enveloped in darkness, with only the bright headlights leading the way. Outside, images move by in blurs; inside the men nervously settle back not knowing for what they should even hope. Johnny presses his head against the window pane and closes his eyes. Even Homer nods, as you know.

There is nothing here to report, not unless I want to do that other storyteller's job by concentrating on Winston. Right now, there is no need for me to take that tack. All I can hear is the voice of that other storyteller going on and on. What jaundiced eyes! How can she see the world so differently? How can she tell such perverted stories as if she is the alter ego and not just the chronicler of the boy she now officially refers to as the leader. I would kill anyone who even dared to call me Johnny's alter ego. But this other idiot doesn't seem to mind as she spews this propaganda about Winston. I mean, the things women can get away with! If anyone doubts me, why not give a listen to the report this Spinner of Tall Tales sent back on that fateful day. While there is a lull in the action in this bus, why don't you listen and judge for yourself. Here goes:

> *Looking like a natural leader assuming his role at this critical juncture, Winston arrives back at the scene*

after alerting Mr. and Mrs. Stewart. He finds the men standing around aimlessly in the circle, like a people now reduced to being directionless. None of them is talking. Nobody knows what to do or say. Johnny is still sitting on the grass with Tommy's head in his lap, the pool of darkening blood forming under his leg where the blood has trickled out of Tommy's mouth. George Stewart takes one look at the scene. "Oh my God," he exclaims in horror. "What next? What next this year?"

Winston realizes quickly that even George Stewart isn't going to be of much help. Maybe it is a good thing, Winston thinks, that he is in his first year on the farm and doesn't know Tommy that well, so that the death isn't as devastating to him as it is to everyone else, particularly Johnny, who for the first time since Winston met him is losing his composure.

So with everyone standing around not knowing what to do, Winston calmly and softly suggests that they should bring over the tractor and transport the body, still wrapped in the bedsheet and blanket, to the farm house to wait for the undertaker and the Liaison Officer. Fortunately, the secretary in Toronto had said the officer was visiting farms in the region and that she would page him to get him to come over to Edgecliff before returning to Toronto. Nobody says anything about the suggestion, neither approving nor disapproving.

Winston walks back to the orchard, hooks up the cart to the tractor and drives it over. He supervises the lifting of the body and asks four of the men to accompany him back to the house, to help lift the body off the cart. Again nobody says anything; they just comply.

Johnny stands at the edge of the crowd, George Stewart beside him, with the stain from the blood on the ground turning black, the men watching the tractor and the body depart.

"You should all go and get something to eat," Winston shouts to them as the tractor pulls off. "No sense going back into the field now." He has forgotten that Smokie has not cooked. In any case, nobody is likely to have much of an appetite. Not for food, not for arguing or even for playing dominoes. Nobody appears to care whether they will win the tournament. Getting to Toronto, or making money this year, don't matter any more. What a mess these men are in!

After the body is unloaded, Winston returns to the cabin to make sure everything is under control, that his mentor Johnny is resting to recover from the shock. Then he returns to the farmer's house to await the arrival of the coroner, the doctor, the undertaker and the Liaison Officer. By the time the Officer arrives, Winston has taken care of everything. Most things he does just instinctively. When he shows up, the Officer only has to sign the relevant government documents.

When Winston gets back to the cabin, he finds the men moping around inside. Half of them are standing around in the outer room, looking at the floor or ceiling, the rest are inside the bedroom around Tommy's cot. They are staring at the bed, at the trousers hanging from a nail in the wall, at the shoes under the cot, at the letters on the bed, as if they expect Tommy to appear in front of them and tell them it was all a bad dream. The Liaison Officer had suggested to Winston that he should gather up Tommy's personal belongings and put them in a box. No urgency to it, he had said.

Just bring them over and leave them with Mrs. Stewart and he'd have them sent to Barbados.

But Winston recognizes that the Liaison Officer is wrong. There is an acute urgency in getting Tommy's personal possessions out of the cabin so that the men can relax and not be reminded of him at every turn. Moving quickly, Winston goes into the kitchen and puts the biggest aluminum pot on the fire. In no time the water is boiling.

"I got some coffee in the kitchen," he says when he returns to the bedroom. "And them bottles o' rum I'd been keeping from the day I bought them at the duty-free place at the airport in Barbados, we can use them. Have a little wake for Tommy. Just like we'd do back home. And drink some coffee."

He places a hand around Johnny's shoulder and gently nudges him toward the door, but still making it appear as if Johnny, their leader, is approving of the wake and is showing the way. The men follow. Inside the kitchen, they form a circle around the pot of black coffee. Winston breaks the seal of the rum bottle with a quick jerk of his strong wrist. With the same action, he symbolically pours some of the contents on the floor at his feet.

"To our dear departed friend, Tommy," he says. *The spot from the rum spreads in the dust, the tipping of the alcohol a long and honorific tradition of our people, one Winston is so wise to honour, a way of ushering this dear man across the wide gulf and into the waiting arms of our ancestors.*

"May," *Johnny tries to say, taking the cue from this brilliant one, almost choking on the words,* "May... may he...rest...in peace."

> "Amen," the men chorus.
>
> "In Jesus' name," says Preacher Man, making the sign of the cross.
>
> The bottle and the coffee mugs circulate. First to Johnny. While the men drink in silence, Winston slips into the bedroom. He strips Tommy's cot. All the dead man's possession he piles into a big cardboard box which he places out of sight behind a cot against the wall. When the men return to the bedroom, there is no visible trace of Tommy. Only the empty cot, with its sagging bedsprings.
>
> Yet Winston knows he has done the easy part. For there is no way he can erase the memories. Only time, and maybe winning the dominoes tournament, could make this happen. That is why it is so vital that he organize the men for the last game, that he encourage them to believe in themselves.

Now let's skip ahead. But mind you, it will only get worse. I hope your stomach is good and bearing up with this nonsense. Let's pick up on what she says the next day, when the men are back in the field.

> Winston takes the box with Tommy's tacklings over to the farm house. Jessica must have seen him coming as she comes out the kitchen door as he arrives. She is dressed as if for some big occasion. Through the door, Winston can see Mary packing a suitcase with George Stewart standing over her. They appeared to be arguing.
>
> Jessica tries to engage him in conversation, but eventually abandons the effort. Angrily, she marches inside the house and lets the door slam on its own. For

a moment, Winston wonders if he has said something to upset her. He cannot remember, cannot understand her actions. He is too occupied anyway to linger long on that thought or away from the men. His mind is still with the men in the field.

Cut, cut, cut. Enough of that bullshit, I say. Let's get back to the real world, to the real story happening here. Anyone hearing that would automatically assume Johnny is absolutely in the palm of that Winston, when anybody in his right mind can see it's the other way around. At least, *I* can see that. And another thing, you might have noticed that the flow to that story is a little, shall we say, uneven. Obviously, the work of a greenhorn. Just compare my work to this amateur shit. I mean this young woman breaks so many rules, so many I don't want to identify them one by one, that I have to wonder if she remembers anything Mother Nyame taught us.

I hope what you just heard isn't an example of what those folks back at head office want; that would be frightening. Damned frightening. So, let us all sit back with our thoughts and listen to the drone of the bus. And let's hope that the other storyteller will do what any old hand would tell her, that is say something only when there is something worth saying, to tell stories only when they're worth telling. And to that I would add, don't crown the new king until the old one abdicates or dies.

chapter twenty-four

Listen carefully! From the one-sideishness of the laughter, from the happiness and dominance of the strange voices in this basement, it is obvious things aren't going too good for the team from Edgecliff. Can't you hear those unfamiliar voices screaming and so pompous? What a *pompassetting* people, as the people back home like to say. How show-offish can you get? Really!

Indeed, how fortunes rise and fall in one night, in one set of games! From the slamming of the dominoes and the loud screams of laughter from their side, it appears only a matter of time before the players from Cooleridge Farms draw even with Edgecliff. Then they'll win the tournament by default. What a bummer of a way to lose an entire tournament! To go down by default! It would be better not to have entered at all, the point Delbert keeps making, than to come so close to winning, only to go down in defeat. But that's life. That's all I can say — such is life.

Winston fills his disposable cup with 7-UP, that manly drink that causes hair to grow on the chest. I guess I can't help taking just one more dig at this youngster, this loafer, as he pours from the big bottle on the table at the far end of the basement. The drink is just one example of how Winston stands out in this room, perhaps the only one not playing on any team. Well, at least there is one person around who is purely a spectator.

With cup in hand, Winston pauses a moment to look around the crowded room filled with smoke, noticing the acrid smell from some of the men taking a few good tokes. The small table is laden with stacks of white cups still in the plastic wrapping, pots of coffee, sugar containers, a glass jar filled with multi-coloured plastic stir-sticks and, of course, a few bottles of rum.

Over by the door is a large white banner draped against the wall. It proclaims in large black letters: DOMINOES TOURNAMENT — SPONSORED BY THE CARIBBEAN MIGRANT WORKERS PROGRAM. *The first team to win six sets of games wins the tournament. Best of luck,* it says in smaller letters. Underneath the banner is a chalkboard with the names of the two teams. Under Edgecliff are five large strokes; four for Cooleridge.

But that score is deceptive, for it pains me to report that after such a good and impressive start, the momentum is now against Edgecliff. After winning the first three sets, our men lost the following two, then won the next two. They are now just one set away from winning. One elusive set away from going to Toronto.

Our men are in really deep shit, excuse my language, because they can't seem to hold a lead. They cannot afford to lose this set. And right now things are looking pretty bad because the thrust of this game is going against them. I mean it's just like what Brer Pig did say to Brer Sheep when she came back home from the pasture, all hungry and starved-out, to find Brer Pig relaxing in his pen with his belly full of slop. Brer Pig says, so you thought you were going to be in good grazing, eh? You think they'd tie you out all day in good grass? But, uh, sorry fuh yuh, no rass. It looks, my friend, like your grass brown, brown. Things certainly looking brown fuh yuh, man.

What a frigging bummer, for, as I said, these men can't afford to let things slip. It is now up to Delbert and Henry to win the tournament for Edgecliff simply by not losing. For after them, there are no other players left to take on what is definitely the strongest pair among the Cooleridge players. As you can expect, there aren't too many of our people smiling. The good guys are definitely going down for the count.

Apart from stirring occasionally for a drink, Winston has spent all evening sitting quietly off to one side watching the men play. If the earphones from his Walkman were strapped to his head, as they usually are, I would swear that his mind and thoughts are somewhere else, maybe back at the cabin playing the steel pan. That is how much he seems cut off from what is happening around him.

At the centre of this basement are several oblong tables, with the members of each team facing each other. Empty cups for coffee or stronger drink are on the table in front of them or under the wrought-iron chairs on which they are sitting. This is their battleground, tables for various skirmishes that collectively form the giant battle. So much is riding on this supposed diversion. The only thing everyone knows, that both teams equally understand, is this: When the sun returns tomorrow, it will be to smile on a winner and to curse and sting the vanquished.

Only one team will be marching off to the drudgery of working in the field with a spring in the steps of its members, with hope in their eyes and a long-anticipated reward awaiting them. The members of the other team will probably find it difficult enough just rolling out of bed. These, my brothers and sisters, are the cold hard facts of life.

Winston exchanges a quick glance with Johnny. Johnny is sitting across the room behind the Edgecliff representatives. Winston does not like the look on Johnny's face. It is a dead giveaway that Delbert and Henry are losing. But, even in the toughest of times, you should count your blessings. Johnny, the old giant he is, appears to be stirring. Winston is happy that Johnny seems to be coming out of his shell, if only slowly. But at least he is getting involved, trying to spur on the men, instead of sitting and moping because he doesn't have a partner and can't shoulder his load at the table. As the evening ages, Johnny gradually resumes his old role. He becomes more of his old self, encouraging the men to do their best, going from table to table rallying their spirits with his presence.

This takes the pressure off Winston, I suppose, so he can sit back and relax a bit, letting Johnny claim his usual leadership role. In any case, Winston knows that nobody would look to him for support or inspiration when it came to dominoes. He knows what it is like having your mother on the sidelines during a soccer game. She may scream and challenge you, may have the best of intentions, but they are just that: meaningless best intentions, hope and the hot air that is her breath. All the intentions in the world and a dollar won't buy a good bottle of rum, and the men know that. Winston knows that.

It's not the same as hearing encouragement from a man, from someone who actually plays the game, who knows of what he really speaks. There just isn't the same respect, the same authority in the words from the sidelines, as from a man who has tasted real battle.

I, too, like what I am seeing in Johnny. Just look at him huddling with the rest of the men in a corner, discussing strategy, although they know that in such a game as dominoes they cannot send signals to the players, that everything depends on the players at the table. Johnny is now at the centre of the discussion, where he should always be, despite what some storytellers are intimating even as we speak. Once again, I hope Mother Nyame is willing to concede that she might have been too quick on the trigger when it comes to my man Johnny. After all, he's human and entitled to a down day or two. I don't think we are anywhere near the end of his days. Not yet. Not by a long shot.

Winston sips his 7-UP. There is another of the frequent outbursts of celebration. One of the older Cooleridge players, standing to his full height and shouting, his hat falling from his head to reveal a shiny dome, is almost beside himself with happiness.

Not waiting for the others to play, he ferociously slams several dominoes onto the table, the noise echoing around the room and breaking the hearts of every one of us from Edgecliff.

Henry and Delbert throw their useless dominoes onto the table and exchange unhappy looks. The captain of Cooleridge gleefully adds another chalk mark to the four already on the table in front of his players. He writes so tauntingly slow that my blood rages at this insulting derision alone. But we have to keep our cool; he has the knife to our throats. Two lonely marks are on the table for Edgecliff and they do not offer much solace, if they offer any at all. That is why this big-guts man can *piss-parade* like this and get away with it.

"One more to go," the Cooleridge captain is boasting. He is about six-foot-four and big-eyed. His voice seems to rumble in his chest and then explode once it is out of his mouth. "One more and then it's Toronto here we come." He starts to sing and dance in the aisle between the tables. "Bring me a strong-arse rum there and let me wet my gizzards," he orders. "Let me feel the sting of a straight rum in muh rass, the same way the dominoes like they're stinging tonight. For this is celebration time, my man." His non-playing members are also dancing and singing, congratulating one another.

"Johnny," the opposition leader shouts across the room, pretending to be serious. "Who you'll be playing with tonight?" He takes a big swallow of the rum and wipes the back of his hand across his mouth. "'Cause lemme tell you something right now: You alone can't beat me and Bobby, yuh know. It's like what the Bible say: we keeping the best wine for the last. In this case, it's the best rum, not no foolish wine, in yuh arse tonight. The best for the last, me and Bobby, just in case your old-time partner Tommy come back from the grave."

"You don't got to take the man's name in vain," Mighty snaps, lurching at the man from Cooleridge. "Just because the man ain't here to defend heself. Like you never hear yuh don't talk ill 'bout the dead?"

"It's only joke me mekking, fellas," the Cooleridge man says in pretend humility, his supporters raising their voices in howls of laughter. "Don't get so touchous! Just that I know Johnny is a man that does work miracles and yuh can't put nothin' past he. So, I won't be too, too surprise' if he work another *do-flicky* right now, maybe a piece o' obeah in we arse, and next thing we know we see Tommy walking in here just like that. 'Cause believe, man, it will take a duppy to come back and beat we tonight."

By now the men from Cooleridge are in convulsions. The men from Edgecliff? Well, let's just say they are frowning and groaning, as loudly as if each Cooleridge player has a knife and is plunging it deep into them.

"You think you can do that, Johnny?" says the Cooleridge leader. Now he isn't even bothering to hide the laughter. "Bring back yuh partner from the grave?"

"You let the poor man rest in peace," Smokie shouts. "He ain't do you nothin' and if he'd alive he'd wipe up the floor with all o' you. Besides, what is a damn domino game, anyway."

"Yeah, it's only a bloody domino game," says Mighty, "so what's the big deal? It ain't like any o' you win the lottery or something so."

"Correction," the man says, the deep-effacing sarcasm bouncing off the walls. "You mean only a free trip to Toronto, right. That's what you mean, right?" The laughter grows louder as the bald man, his hat again falling to the ground, is on his feet slamming the dominoes on the table. Cooleridge's captain skips over to the chalkboard and puts the fifth mark under his team's name. "Toronto here we come," he sings again. Delbert and Henry throw their dominoes on the table, stand over them scowling, then dejectedly walk away.

"Five-five in sets," Delbert says. "Unless you got some real hardseed player we don't know nothing 'bout, Johnny, we may as well all go home now and try to get some sleep. Tomorrow is still work."

The Cooleridge men are whooping and dancing all sort of jigs, some like what the men see on television when someone scores a touchdown. Winston swallows the last of his 7-UP and crumples the cup in his hand.

"I think it's up to me an' you, Johnny," he says, taking off his jean jacket and slinging it over a table.

"Who, you?" Timmy says incredulously. "A man that can't even hold the dominoes good in he hands?"

"What choice we got?" Winston retorts. "If we lose, no big thing. We done lost anyway. If we win..."

Johnny glances across the room where the opponents are breaking open a bottle of rum. The captain starts to draw a final line through the five chalk marks, a sign that his team is claiming the sixth game by default.

"Not so fast, Brother Man," Johnny says. "We ain't done with yet. Come, my boy. I guess this is the only way you're going to get to Toronto to see Jessica, eh?" He and Winston march over to the table. My heart is fluttering. I want to shout to Johnny and ask him to at least let his men walk away with some pride. As a good general, he should know how to retreat with dignity. I wish he would spare us this humiliation, because what can he expect from putting Winston up against these men? Really! Even someone as hard-headed and full of pride as the Prophet would recognize the hopelessness and act to suit.

"Who that you bringing like a lamb to the slaughter?" the captain says, perhaps sensing the misgivings of even the Edgecliff group. He and Bobby, a shortish man with big arms and broad shoulders, take their positions at the table. Bobby begins shuffling the dominoes by placing the palms of his hands flat on the dominoes and mixing them up with brisk turns of his wrists.

The Cooleridge men look like gladiators, compared to the slimmer and smaller Edgecliff opponents. "Who is this lamb?"

"Never mind that," Johnny says. "Shuffle the damn dominoes."

The two teams gather around. The Edgecliff men are quiet, leaving the talking to Cooleridge. In any case, they don't know what to expect. For most of them the match is simply the prolonging of the inevitable.

Winston feels his heart flutter with excitement. Even though I know he is wondering what Jessica would say if she were to see him now, I get the feeling that this exercise is just one big lark for him, nothing too serious. I mean, it is almost insulting how cool he is, and when so much is at stake. After all, this is something these poor men sweated and fought for, gave their all, took the best taunts from Cooleridge, and now for Winston to do this, without one drop of emotion on his face. How callous can he be?

His only concern seems to be that he doesn't forget, or at least not too much, what he has read and practised with Jessica in the shed behind the farm house. The last time he had the book was four weeks ago, before Jessica took it back to the library and then left for Toronto. Worst of all, he hardly has time to think of what he is doing before Cooleridge wins the first three games of the final set, and in less than fifteen minutes. Even then, our old hero is unmoved, at least outwardly, so let's switch back to him.

Feeling the weight of the world on his shoulders, Johnny looks across the narrow table at his partner as he contemplates what to do. Winston's plays surprise him, obviously, but certainly Johnny knows not to let one or two lucky moves lull him into abandonment. Now Johnny, the old master and teacher of Winston's teacher, has to make the crucial decision. He will decide the outcome of this game, and possibly the set. And here I want you to pay close attention. Watch the looks on the face of a master, see how he thinks everything through so carefully. Not like someone who we will let remain nameless, but who at least can now hold seven dominoes in his hand and match his plays.

It's decision time for Johnny. Should he abandon any prospects of winning himself, by sacrificing his chances, in the hope that Winston's steady performance so far has not been a fluke? That is the nagging question: could it be that this youngster, who has played only once with the men in the cabin and was so poor that he was laughed at by all the men, is really the calm, calculating player now before him?

It is a complete transition and Johnny doesn't know what to make of this change. To grant Winston his due, I too must admit that he is nothing like the greenhorn who arrived on the farm just a few months ago. There has been a steadily increasing maturity about him, a seasoning that, I think, of late, is winning Johnny's respect and, perhaps, even his confidence. But at this moment, I wouldn't advise Johnny to take any chances. This is no time for flights of fancy, for the if-only scenarios. Trust your instincts, I would say to Johnny.

But back to the game. Johnny knows that it is he, not the untried novice, who is responsible for Edgecliff trailing three games to nil. He has underestimated Winston and has been trying to win all by himself, in essence attempting to play both his and Winston's hands. In the process, he has been playing too conservatively. I don't know how much you know about the strategy behind playing dominoes, but suffice it to say that you always have to anticipate what your partner will play next. This way you play in tandem, putting on the board the cards you and your partner have in abundance, while keeping off the board those that favour your opponents. At least, that is how I understand the game. We call it reading the game; knowing from what has been played what could and should be played and in what order. Tommy and Grafton used to be master readers. Johnny too. But tonight Johnny isn't his usual self. So that the turning point in the first three games coincided with Johnny's plays. Winston, it appears to me, just waited for Johnny to make the crucial moves that should have turned the games irrevocably in Edgecliff's favour.

Each time they lose, Winston simply throws his dominoes into the pack and silently begins shuffling. He says nothing as the Cooleridge team continues their victory celebration and the Edgecliff men grow more sombre. Beneath this display, Johnny can tell that Winston knows his senior partner is playing badly, that he does not have the confidence in him he would in any of the other tested players from Edgecliff or, perhaps, even in Jessica. As he would have in Tommy.

Now, Johnny realizes he is once again in that tight spot. The choice is between playing his double-five card or his five-three. If he goes the more conservative route and plays the double-five, it would be to cling to a fleeting hope that he could still come from behind and win the game, that he has a better hand, or is a greatly superior strategist, than his partner. But it would also show he simply doesn't trust the younger man to play well enough to win.

If he gambles and plays the five-three, he would be putting any chance of winning solely on Winston's shoulders. For undoubtedly his rivals would kill his double-five, shutting it out of the game permanently, making it impossible for him to win. Then, the only hopes of Edgecliff winning the game would rest with Winston having the last two threes — double-three and three-six.

Johnny sighs and feels the cold sweat running down his

back. He doesn't like handing over the leadership to anyone, let alone Winston. But what are their prospects otherwise? He recalls how the game is going, remembering that, from the beginning, Winston has favoured the threes, perhaps an indication that he might have the other threes. And Johnny knows that Bobby to his right has the sixth five, which he would undoubtedly play to shut out Johnny's double-five, killing it.

It is a big gamble. Johnny looks at the dominoes in his hand. The crowd is silent, sensing this defining moment. He looks across at Winston again, but once more Winston doesn't return the look. Instead, he unsmilingly examines the two dominoes in his hand. As if he doesn't want to put any pressure on the older man.

Finally, the conservatism in him comes to the fore. He just can't let go, can't willingly abdicate to this untried young man. Johnny takes up the double-five and raises his hand as if to play it. Then he hesitates. I have never seen Johnny dither like this. His hand remains transfixed in the air, as if some invisible wire from the ceiling is holding him back.

Slowly that large muscular hand starts to fall, with the card in the clenched palm. Something tells him he should gamble on Winston. But he cannot be sure. So he decides, once again, to silently read the cards that are already played, starting with the first one posed by Bobby and going over the game play-by-play until he arrives again at this crucial juncture. From the pattern of the plays, he should be able to tell what cards everyone around the table is holding.

When he finishes, he is no wiser or further ahead. He did not read the cards wrong before, Johnny thinks to himself. He still faces the same option: play his double-five in the hope that by some fluke he can win, or sacrifice his hand and hope Winston can win. The decision is up to him. Johnny mops his brow and glares at the dominoes in his hand.

"Man, play a fucking bone," Bobby says, growing impatient with the delay.

"Ah, shut up yuh arse," Delbert says. He is standing behind Winston and knows the dilemma facing Johnny. Have you noticed, too, how more of the Edgecliff men are moving over from Johnny's side of the table and are now lining up behind Winston? "Take all the fucking time yuh want, Johnny. We ain't got no babies to go home to and mind. We got all night, we don't have to *sleep* too soon. But just make sure that when you play, you play the right one, skipper."

"You better stop talking this game, yuh," the opposing captain says. "Anybody giving anybody hints 'round this table and we mark another game. Four-love in yuh ass, easy so. And once I got yuh four-love, that's like having a half Nelson 'round yuh neck. Ain't a fellow can come back and beat me from that position. So yuh better mind yuh talk, yuh."

Johnny places his three cards on the table. The opposing captain is right. If they lose this game, it would be almost impossible to stage a recovery. Not from four games down. He shouldn't be gambling at this late stage. Yet something tells Johnny that he really has no choice. He must trust Winston. Change the pattern of play and disrupt the rivals' thinking. More than that, something in him wants him to succumb, to stop fighting — to gamble, to break out of the shell, to stop being so conformist — to follow Winston.

With these thoughts going through his head, he can now feel the excitement for the game returning to him, a fire rekindling in his stomach. If only they can win this game, Johnny is thinking. They would be back in the set. It would be a new set all over. If I may say so, this reminds me of the first time Johnny played dominoes with Tommy almost twenty years earlier, the beginning of an almost unbeatable team.

Back then, and I hope you don't mind this digression while

Johnny thinks, Tommy had come to the game with a reputation, from playing in rum shops across the island at home and from playing in the tournaments in the United States when he cut canes in Miami. Johnny was more erratic in his play. Eventually, Tommy learned that it was best playing the game from behind Johnny, giving him the chance to make the play and, at times even gambling on him, even though Tommy was the better player.

For me, that is the beauty of playing dominoes. Partners have to be able to feel each other out, to know their partner's temperament, when to take chances and how well they can get along, almost like dancing, or like a couple living together. Someone has to know when to be the second fiddle; someone has to be the leader. Two equally erratic or equally conservative players are not suited as partners. Over the years, Tommy, the brash talker and bluffer, and Johnny, the quiet unassuming one, had smoothed out their acts. They became virtually unbeatable because they understood the psychology of the game and the men they were playing. They understood that even in a two-man team, each of them couldn't have equal billing. How do you like that for a commentary, eh?

"Cards all around," Johnny says, still playing for time. He leaves his three dominoes on the table. Bobby and the opposing captain place theirs face down as well. Bobby has three and the captain two. Once again, Johnny gets the confirmation that he is the laggard in the game.

"Oh," Delbert sighs loudly. "I thought you wasn't going to ask fuh cards before you play." Johnny tries not to display the surprise he must be a feeling. But you can knock me over. Do you hear the tone in Delbert's voice? This is the first time in years any of these men has publicly questioned Johnny's judgement.

"I done say no talkin'," the opposing captain repeats, fingering the stub of chalk in front of him. "Otherwise I goin' mark a game as a penalty. We're playing by rules. And I ain't talkin' no *rass-hole* more 'bout not talkin', you hear me?"

Winston places his two dominoes on the table and lets them stay there until everyone else picks up theirs.

Johnny smiles. He hopes that Winston knows what he is doing by leaving the dominoes on the table. If he does, Johnny thinks, Jessica must be a better player and even teacher than he remembers. If Winston wanted Johnny to play the double-five, he would quickly pick up his dominoes and hold them close to his chest as if cradling them as you would a baby: in effect signalling to Johnny to "sleep." To play his double-five rather than sacrificing it. But Winston seems not to be calling for this play. Sacrifice, he seems to be saying. As Johnny takes the gamble, remembering the many times they had laughed when Jessica would mix up her signals in the early days, he prays that he is reading his partner right.

"Five-trey," Johnny says, pressing the domino on the table. He does not slam it. I guess there can be no flamboyancy with such uncertainty, no royal fanfare to announce the arrival of anything new. Not making a sound on the table, he simply holds the domino between his index finger and thumb and pushes it toward the centre of the table. Winston notices the shaking of Johnny's hands, and he smiles for the first time.

Predictably, Bobby slams his five-six on the table, so hard that the dominoes, those already played and matched in a snaking line, jump into the air and scatter. "Call the undertaker," he exclaims loudly. "Take that double-five and plant it right beside you old-time partner Tommy, my friend. Somebody carrying around a duppy, a dead domino with them. And youngster, knock the damn board, you passed."

He looks steadfastly at Winston, as if expecting Winston to not only have the useless double-five but to have no play to either the three-end or the six-end.

Winston waits patiently until Bobby reassembles the dominoes. Then he plays the six-three, to make threes at both ends. When no one else can play, he drops the double-three, the final of the seven threes in the pack, on the table. Johnny sighs softly and his shoulders drop. Bobby swears. "You holding the last two treys?" he asks in disbelief, throwing his final domino into the pack.

The Edgecliff team quietly celebrates this first victory. I can feel the electrical charge in the air, the growing respect for Winston. From now on, Johnny will know how to play with his new partner, even if they do not win this set. He will play the same way that Tommy did with him. By letting Winston lead, while following cautiously and giving him the occasional nudge. The men, realizing this, crowd behind Winston; none is left standing behind Johnny. Even when he played with Tommy, there was always someone looking over Tommy's shoulders. I must admit I feel the rising excitement, too, and the realization that something important is happening. Maybe there is some truth, after all, in what that other storyteller has been saying. I sense we have just marched through a significant turning point.

Forty-five minutes later the set is over. The roar is deafening. George Stewart on the farm and Jessica in Toronto can probably hear the shouts. Edgecliff wins, six sets to four, with Winston winning the other five games in his set for Edgecliff. As Delbert and Henry lift the youngster onto their shoulders and run with him around the basement, Johnny tries to suppress a yearning to also join in the celebration, the discovery of a new hero. Another initiation — or is it an investiture, as that other storyteller is now saying — before his eyes.

Momentarily, Johnny notices that nobody bothers congratulating him, as if Winston has done it all by himself. But the tinge of jealousy does not go deep or last long. As he sees the big smiles break out on the faces around him, Johnny finally gives in to the emotion and pride building up inside his chest. He tells himself that Tommy, too, would have been beside himself with happiness to know that, after all these years, Edgecliff is finally going to Toronto. And Tommy wouldn't care one bit who won the final games. Only the victory counts.

"This one for you, Tommy," Johnny whispers. "Sleep easy, my brother."

Johnny joins the celebration, abandoning himself for the night, knowing that all would be well and that if it isn't, then Winston, with his luck so strong tonight, would probably find a solution. Now look at our men *pompassetting*. And, boy, do they know how to strut!

chapter twenty-five

Winston settles back into the darkened bus, watching the lights on the highway slip by effortlessly into the brightness behind us that is Toronto. Up ahead, as far as he can see, it is pitch-dark. Behind us is a city full of hopes and daring. Ahead is the great expanse of the rural life and dreams, that like the highway lights, peters out into townships and farms and hamlets, pointing inevitably to the nothingness of darkness.

We have been travelling for about an hour now. It seems so much longer since the bus pulled out of the motel parking lot. Only this very minute, with everyone getting comfortable, does the driver switch off the lights inside the bus.

Finally, the men are free to cut loose, to settle in for the four-hour drive. It allows them to sleep better, obviously. But it also provides the cover for them to think to themselves, to reflect on the challenges they do not have the courage to meet in the city, in the glow of the lights. So much like the last time we were making this trip from Toronto, at the start of the season, in a snowstorm with nobody really knowing what to do or expect. When this damn guy Winston was such an unknown. So, in the darkness of the bus, the only noticeable things now are the rumbling of the old engine up front and the loud snoring of some very tired and emotionally exhausted men.

This is definitely the point of no turning back and I too can breathe a bit easier. For life is settling into a comfortable pattern, as it should, as I would want and wish. Ahead of us is, perhaps, the toughest part of the schedule on this farm. From this point on, as Joseph Niles tells us in the song, this train won't carry no straggler, no loafer and definitely no complainers, this train, this train.

For most of the men, this is the first time they've closed their eyes in sleep since arriving in Toronto Friday night. The jazz festival consumed all their time on Saturday, Sunday and Monday. This left the men scrambling to the discount shops mere hours before the bus pulled into the lot. They had just enough time to spend the last of their money on the clothes, jewellery and candy — the things they cannot get cheaply in Arkona — all that valuable booty they will now store in the cabin until their return home at Christmas.

But Winston didn't spend time shopping, except on a pair of running shoes. He was out with Jessica most of the time and, anyway, he didn't have much money to spend. As we know, the first half of the season wasn't too good for him. As he contemplates returning to Edgecliff, Winston wonders if this type of life is for him. Is this how he really wants to spend the next twenty years of his life, how he wants to invest his youth, the only asset he has?

Something else is swimming freely in his brain. It is a statement from Jessica, a declaration that she so mysteriously left unexplained, obviously to haunt him, to make him question if he should even be taking this bus ride back. As women so often are, Jessica was plainly not above putting an ultimatum to Winston, if somewhat seductively and enigmatically. And, as usual, while massaging his heart through his ear, she was hitting him in the balls. Spitefully kicking just where it hurts most, where he not only can't forget but, because of the prolonged soreness, is damn-well forced to remember every bloody minute of the day.

She is playing hardball. Throughout the centuries, it's a call only a few men have managed to escape. Even the original Brer Anancy could not and finally succumbed at just about the same time someone else was passing around an apple. Winston should be glad for the escape this bus trip provides.

Fortunately, at least for the moment, Winston decides that his place is with the men on the farm. I like the way he is thinking, how they came to Canada as a team and should stick together as a team, at least until it is time to leave. This doesn't necessarily mean, he muses, that he will go back home to Barbados, or even try for a second stint on this Program. Only that he owes the men his loyalty. He must prove that he can survive and hold up the promise the men forced out of him that cold, wintry night so long ago. And in any case, I can tell you, he is as concerned as any of the men about the sudden call for them to return to Edgecliff. The officer simply said he wanted them back and right away. And with that went any plans these men may have had for a detour through the United States, let alone heading for and seeing the bright lights of New York City.

From where he is sitting, Winston can see the big boxes and suitcases stuffed with goods from Toronto. Every time the bus passes under a street lamp, the interior lights up temporarily. He can see the men sleeping with their heads leaning back over the seats, their mouths open, arms folded across their chests.

Along the aisle, the boxes are stacked erratically, very large boxes and very small ones, as the men press into service any portable container they can lay their hands on. Winston wonders what would happen if they had to make a speedy exit, if, for example, anything happened to the bus. Or if all the men, with one mind, were to suddenly realize there was no future back on the farm and that they had to get off this bus, had to disappear into the darkness in a desperate search for any kind of future. The boxes would most certainly make running away difficult. The same way that the realities of their immediate situation make it impossible for any of the men to run away from the only life they've ever known.

One good thing about the Toronto trip is that the men were able to do their Christmas shopping early. Of course, it left their bank accounts empty, meaning they will have to squeeze themselves financially for the rest of the year if they are to have any money to take back home.

Before the conversations petered out the men had talked about these things. Why they should return to the farm, instead of grabbing the chance of being in Toronto, the opportunity to run off the contract. Everyone who swore they wouldn't catch the returning bus has shown up and spent most of the last hour trying to justify this appearance. Winston understands why the men are reluctant to take the chance now. Toronto is an expensive city and it does not make any sense running with no specific destination, no safe house or promised job, with no money in their pockets. There is no longer an underground railroad these days. Certainly, not in Toronto. It is a strange, emotionally cold city, a great unknown. And this frightens the men. Justifiably, if I may say so.

Smokie is the first to raise the excuse of money. He still says that when he saves enough money back on the farm, he will be hitting the road. "At least, now that I've seen Toronto for myself, I know the lay of the land," he says. "I know where to go and where not to go. When you guys didn't see me over the last two-three days, guess what I was doin'?"

"What you was doin'?" someone rises to the challenge.

"Lookin' for the ins and outs of the city, nuh. You think I's a fool, that I'll say that I pickin' up myself from off the farm where, at least, I have some place to rest my head at night and that I runnin' when I ain't know where I goin'? You think I's a fool, that I born behind my mother back or something? No, man, I was checkin' out the place. I have it all up here," he points to his head. "Now I know the ins and outs of this place. Just watch me when I get a piece of change in my hand. The first chance, I gone."

"So if you plan to run, Smokie, why you went out and

get all them boxes full o' things for?" someone shouts in the darkness. "What you're going to do with them things if you run?"

Smokie patiently explains that all his purchases from Toronto could be sent home by parcel after he leaves. He will label the boxes with addresses as soon as he gets to the farm. And that's another reason, he says, for going back to the farm this time: he needs to work for even the money to post the gifts back home.

"The whores carry away all yuh money, eh," the same voice shouts from the darkness in the back of the bus. "You shoulda do like me and get a bottle of rum, get drunk and fall asleep. At least you'd have a few dollars in yuh pocket when yuh get back sober."

"I did that too, man, but it is the money that carryin' me back," Smokie says. "Really, man. I got to get a few dollars in my pocket before I do anything so."

The other men agree with him and say that he is describing perfectly their feelings about the situation and that now they really know what to expect in Toronto. At the first opportunity, they would be returning to stay permanently. Once they have a piece of change in their pockets. For to be poor in this city is hell, the men agree.

I can only smile at these excuses. They are so hollow and phony, the kind of bantering you can always expect in a group of men too chicken to do anything. It never changes, whether they are waiting at the airport to come back to Canada or on a bus travelling to Edgecliff. These men know the rules: they must put up a brave face. Even if they know they are liars, that actually they are afraid of even attempting to leave the arms of the predictable and familiar.

At the same time, I applaud their good judgement, for not feeling compelled to do something they do not believe in, for not feeling that they have to meet some stupid challenge just to prove themselves. For to be honest, I was holding my breath when they started to drift into the parking lot. I kept counting heads, looking to see who would be so foolish and selfish as to run off the contract and remain in Toronto, making life tougher for themselves and for all the men on the farm.

Strangely enough, I don't recall Johnny showing this kind of concern, not like the way he is always counting the heads at the Barbados airport every season. I guess he has a lot more confidence in the men than I. All the same, my worries were unfounded and I think this is due largely to Johnny never getting involved in such discussions. Even on this trip back, he will not join in any talk about running away. For some men, running away is the ultimate test of their manhood. I am happy to say Johnny isn't so insecure as to need this kind of test.

The talk of running still swimming in his head reminds Winston of the piece of paper in his pants pocket. It has Jessica's address on it and he keeps feeling it between his fingers, a lingering memento of the three priceless days they had spent together. But the paper also reminds him of something else, of the baffling statement Jessica made to him, a strange way of saying goodbye, as if there was more to tell.

Winston plays the goodbye scene over in his mind. He was leaving to rejoin the men at the motel, when Jessica reached into her purse and handed him the paper, a white sheet folded neatly in squares. As if teasing him, she said the address might be worth more than for sending letters. She also promised to write him. When he suggested that she should come back to the farm, ostensibly to visit her parents, her eyes dropped to the ground. Softly, she whispered that would not be necessary, that her parents, certainly her mother, might be coming to Toronto to join her.

She doesn't elaborate and Winston doesn't press her because he knows how painful it is for Jessica to talk about her parents and the rift with her father. Winston takes the paper and places it in his pocket. He grabs her and kisses her on the mouth. Jessica clings to him and he feels her sharp fingernails digging into his back. It isn't, as that other storyteller so poignantly pointed out, the first time she has done this to him over the past three days. (Of course, yours truly has to add *Jack Mandora, me ain't tek none*, 'cause here I am only going on someone else's reports, as I couldn't be everywhere at once and I decided to hang out with my man Johnny on this trip.) Now that he is leaving, she seems to be clinging even tighter, kissing him more passionately, as if she doesn't expect to see him again.

"You will like it in Toronto," she says.

"Yeah, but I don't know when next I'll get down here," he returns. "Guess I'll have to write a lot, eh."

"Just remember the address is for more than letters." She smiles and he kisses her again.

"I got to go," he says. "See you soon."

"And, Winston," she blurts out. "No matter what happens, what you decide when you get back, I will always remember you. Don't forget that, I will always remember you."

Winston still doesn't know what to make of the statement. It puzzles him, as if there is some code that he must decipher for it to make sense. It sounded like something you say to a lover you are dumping or to some unfortunate sick soul entering a hospital with little hope of coming back out alive. Indeed, it is unlikely that he will get back to Toronto before he goes home. The most he might be able to do is to ask Jessica to meet him at the airport before the flight home. But maybe he could come down to Toronto a day or two early and hang out with her. That is the most for which he can hope. Maybe that's what she meant. Obviously, with the most hectic part of the season approaching, he cannot see the possibility of even taking a weekend off, although he would be willing to go without pay, to visit her. There must be something else she was hinting at, he tells himself, deciding to put the puzzle out of his mind until whatever it was reveals itself. Maybe he will raise the matter with her when he gets back to the farm and writes his first letter.

Winston leans back against the hard seat. Maybe he is overreacting, reading too much into an awkward goodbye. He tells himself that the exhaustion from three days of almost no sleep must be catching up with him. And he reminds himself that the next day all of them, every man jack, will have to be out in the fields bright and early. August, everyone keeps telling him, is the month of eighteen-hour work days to get the fruits off the trees before they fall and spoil. This is the season that separates the men from the boys.

The drone of the engine helps Winston to fall off quickly. When he snaps awake, the bus is turning off the highway and heading for the farm house. The sudden bump of unpaved road awakens several of the other men. Some stretch and yawn, flexing the muscles and limbs that have fallen asleep in the uncomfortable positions. They are back on the farm and can't wait to crawl into their cots to rest up before taking on the second half of the season.

The presence of George Stewart on the front porch of the house so late in the night should be warning enough that something is wrong. But Johnny, and I must admit me too, thinks nothing of it. When the bus pulls up George is standing by the railing with coffee mug in hand. Evidently, he has been waiting a long time, for he is anxiously pacing the wooden flooring of the porch when the headlights first find him.

He looks like a lonely figure, some mystic seeking solace in the quiet of the night, in the stars above and in the gentle rustling of the wind through the trees and the grass. Until their arrival, his sole companion appears to have been the swarms of bugs busily circling the lone naked bulb at the side of the house, overhanging the porch. In a valiant but fruitless fight, the bulb is standing alone in an attempt to push back the night, to beat back the evils of the darkness closing in on a defenceless George Stewart. A darkness that already captured the farm at the fall of the sun.

"Christ, I thought I would have to spend the whole night waiting for you guys," he says as soon as the bus rolls to a stop and the driver opens the door. His voice sounds higher pitched than usual but perhaps he's trying to be heard above the wind and the noise from the bus engine.

"You guys must have had a whale of a time in Toronto that you didn't want to come back, eh?" he adds. The men snigger, thinking he knows of their guilty thoughts. "Anyway, I gotta talk to you two guys."

He points to the bus driver and to Johnny, who is standing on the first step of the bus. Now it is becoming clear why the bus driver came over to the farm house instead of unloading the men at the cabin before heading home.

"I think you might have to stay over for the night, Tony," George says to the bus driver. "That's why I asked you to drop by here before you left tonight. I'll have to use you in the morning, so I don't think it would make sense for you to drive all the way back into Arkona and then have to come back in a..." He checks his watch by holding his wrist up to the light. "In another three hours or so. But that is up to you."

"But Mr. Stewart," the bus driver shouts over the engine, "You know, in the morning, I gotta be picking up the children for summer school and camp. What are you talking about?"

"No children tomorrow. I've asked the company to make arrangements to free you up in the morning. But you gotta sleep over. So you can leave from here early," George explains. He takes a step toward the bus, trips over something, but quickly regains his balance. "You can sleep in the spare room that Mrs. Stewart's preparing for you. She'll explain everything to you."

He brings the coffee cup to his mouth and takes another gulp. Johnny starts to get back onto the bus, thinking that George Stewart is through with him.

"Come and have a drink with me, Johnny," George shouts. "And all you guys, you'll find some letters waiting for you in the cabin. From the Officer. It explains everything." His voice is definitely higher than usual and he seems to be swaying. "But Johnny, I want to have a good talk with you. The others can go on to the...the cabin; but I gotta have a few words with you right now, Johnny."

Johnny gets off the bus and the driver closes the door. Slowly he reverses the vehicle and turns it around at the edge of the field. The two men stand in silence watching the bright lights and the lumbering bus disappear into the distance. When the darkness finally swallows the bus, Johnny follows George Stewart over to the porch and walks up the steps.

"Come, have a drink with me," George offers.

"Can't sleep or something?" Johnny asks, trying to squash any hint of nervousness in his voice. "Not like you to be out here so late." He doesn't add that it also isn't like George to be drinking.

Without answering, George Stewart swaggers over to the side of the porch and takes up another cup and a bottle leaning against the house. With his back still to Johnny, he refreshes his own drink and, placing his mug between his legs, hands the extra cup and bottle to his intended drinking partner. It is one of the bottles of Barbadian rum Johnny brought up at the beginning of the season. Already more than a quarter of the bottle is gone.

Johnny knows instantly that something is desperately wrong. It would normally take George well over a year to finish a forty-ounce bottle. It is not like him to drink so heavily, Johnny thinks again as he pours a small helping into the cup. I dare say, it also isn't like Johnny to drink on the farm, especially on a night before he is to rise early.

"Johnny, it's damn well over," George blurts out, turning away and looking straight into the darkness. "It's over, Johnny. We've lost the fucking farm."

Before there is an answer, he takes another big mouthful of rum, stumbles a bit and leans against the railing. He is directly under the lone light and Johnny cannot see his face although he knows George is now looking at him. Johnny looks so shocked that I swear if you were to grab a knife this very minute and cut him, he wouldn't bleed. I feel the same hollowness in my stomach and my brain is just going whirl, whirl, whirl, like some reel out of control. George definitely knows how to deliver a whopper for bad news, and right off the bus.

"After all this time," he continues, "it has to end like this. The bank's foreclosing. I got the letter Thursday, delivered by the sheriff, but I couldn't spoil the weekend for you and the men in Toronto. Didn't have the heart to do it. But now that you're back, it means you and the men will be going back home in the morning. The Liaison Officer tried to find another farm that would take you and the men, but nobody's taking on any extras, not at such short notice, not with the banks cracking down on them to cut cost. In fact, there ain't nobody to take anybody. That's why I had to talk to you, Johnny, to ask you to tell the men for me. To tell them that I tried my best, but it's..."

He raises his empty palm to the heavens and sighs, unable to finish the sentence because of the lump in his throat. He takes another drink. "I'm sorry, Johnny. I'm fucking well sorry."

They both take large gulps of the rum. Johnny walks over to lean against the railing and props himself, almost shoulder to shoulder, beside George. He needs time to digest this news, to think of some way of telling the men that will reduce the disappointment. He wonders if he should go over and do it right away. The news in the letters must be alarming them. At the same time, he recognizes that he needs more information, to be able to answer their questions. Perhaps Winston will keep the place under control until he turns up and takes over. He can see the light coming from the direction of the cabin. The bus is returning. It looks like the driver is staying over. He parks the bus beside the tractor with the trailers for the tobacco and one of the apple-pickers. The bus that will have the airport in Toronto as its next stop.

"Jessica called back again this evening," George Stewart is saying. "She took the news pretty good when her mother told her Thursday night. Said she was liking Toronto, that me and Mary shouldn't feel too bad about coming out there."

"I did see she in Toronto," Johnny says, just in case Jessica had mentioned their meeting over the phone. "Looks like she's doing okay on she own."

"We, well her mother actually, asked her not to mention anything if she ran into you guys, 'cause she said she might be seeing that guy Winston when he got in. You know, Johnny, sometimes I wonder what she would be like if she'd been a boy. You know that I always wanted a boy, to carry on the farm, but Mary couldn't give me another child. Now I don't think it'll matter anyway." He takes another big sip. "Maybe the Lord knew what he was doing by not giving me that son. 'Cause what would I have to leave to him? And a man who can't leave something for a son may as well not have any."

In the silence they can hear each other breathing. Faint noises from the cabin are travelling through the air, although individual voices and words are indistinguishable. Johnny tries to imagine the reaction in the cabin.

"Remember when she was small?" George says.

"Who?"

"Jessica. How she used to follow you and the men around

the farm? She's always taken to you, even more so than to me. Maybe she realized I was angry she wasn't a boy. But she always took to you."

"She liked to hear me crack jokes, that's what," Johnny explains. "Even so, you must remember she's a' only child on a big farm. That must be tough for anybody, let alone a little child. That's why me and the boys used to tease she so much. And because all o' we did be away from we own children too. We like to watch she growing up and getting big, so we pretend we seeing we own too."

"Like the time with the ducks," George takes another mouthful of the drink. "The ducks that lost their mother and used to follow her around everywhere. You remember?" Johnny thinks he can make out a faint smile on George's face; at least the fondness is in his voice. "Then Mary killed one of the ducks. For Thanksgiving or something. Jessica cried a whole week. Only you could console her. She didn't eat meat for another month or two after that. I still don't think she eats duck."

Mary pushes open the door and pokes her head out. "Who's that you're talking to so long, George? Oh. Johnny. How was Toronto?"

"Great," he answers. "Saw Jessica too. She's fine. Me and she didn't talk too much, though."

"I guess George told you the bad news, eh? That we closing down and moving."

"We were just talking 'bout it," George says.

An awkward and heavy silence descends on the porch. Mary shuffles her feet and leans against the side of the door. The men continue to look into their cups, almost nervously examining the the contents over and over.

"And, Johnny," Mary says. "Maude says you haven't been writing home to her. Something wrong, Johnny? She says she writes you a letter about the house and the bank and that she's waiting for an answer from you. She's wondering if you did get the letter."

Johnny shuffles uneasily. "Guess I didn't read it," he says.

"Yes," she sighs, "and it's probably too late to answer her back. I guess you can settle anything that's the matter in person now."

"I guess so," Johnny says. The three of them stand on the porch looking into the darkness. Mary sighs again and pulls the cardigan around her shoulders, as if protecting herself against a winter's chill though it's the middle of summer. Finally, with no one having anything else to say, Mary decides it would be better if she left the men alone. She recognizes that at a moment like this men need other men to grieve, to say the things they wouldn't with a woman there.

"I'm turning in now," she says, pulling closed the door. "Goodnight, Johnny. I'll see you and the men before you go in the morning."

"Night, ma'am," Johnny says.

"Don't stay out too long now, George," Mary says. There is an added touch of caring in Mary's voice, a concern for George Stewart that isn't always so apparent. "Tomorrow, remember, we got to decide on a few things of our own before we clear out of here."

She closes the door and turns off the lights inside the house. Everything is in darkness, except for that lone bulb struggling against the night. With the lights going out, the finality of it all suddenly hits Johnny in the stomach, punching him much harder than the hot rum. Christ, he thinks. It's over. No more returning to Edgecliff. Maybe no more returning to Canada for him. From now on a lifetime with Maude. Christ.

"Have another drink, Johnny," George says. "I'm having one myself. When everybody was gone from the farm, me and Mary had a good long chat. I think she understands me a little bit better now." He takes another drink and adds dryly, "and I her too, I hope."

Johnny doesn't move or say anything. I can just hear the wheels of his mind grinding. And I know how, suddenly, he is feeling so bloody tired and weary. How he wishes that Winston were with the two of them to at least stand by him and make Johnny feel comfortable and assured.

"Have a drink, Johnny," George insists. "I can't think of having a last drink with a nicer guy than you. You know, I really appreciate everything you ever did for me and the family, man."

"I did get pay to do it," Johnny says, trying vainly to make light of the moment. He is wondering what Winston is telling the men in the cabin, what plans they are cooking. Until now, Johnny hadn't realized how he had come to rely on this youngster, perhaps even more than he did with Grafton and Tommy, and they were two hard-backed men of his age, not mere boys. Maybe when they're back in Barbados, he can find out where in The Pine Winston lives and visit him, or even invite him over to his house.

"You know what I mean," George is continuing. "Like the time when I took a year off from studying and came back from the Agricultural College at Guelph. And I had all this book learning in my head. And I wanted to buy combines and plant more tobacco and the old man was a bit cautious and said he'd only agree if you backed me. You told the old man, and he always used to listen to you on farming matters, that I was young and needed a chance. To prove things for myself. And then when I started fucking things up, you helped cover for me and made me look good, even though I took all the credit."

"I don't think we fooled your father, anyway," Johnny says, relishing the memory. "Old Man Stewart always did know what was going on. You couldn't fool him. And it's he that did teach me anything I'd know 'bout farming up here in Canada."

"No offence though, Johnny," George says almost in a whisper. "But...but I think he, I think he wished that you'd been his son in place of me. That you were the better farmer and manager. What you think?"

Johnny purposely doesn't answer. Instead, he hides behind the drink in his hand and the big mouthful. Christ, he thinks, it's all over for everybody. The men in the cabin must be going crazy with worry, and after such an enjoyable time in Toronto. Poor Winston probably has his hands full. In his mind, Johnny can hear Timmy railing and ranting. Timmy would be the hardest for Winston to handle, he thinks. Indeed, any of the men could be hard, for you can never tell what will happen when a dream dies and someone, could be anyone, snaps. I share Johnny's concern; unless they are like Johnny, the men's behaviour will be totally unpredictable.

"Then Pops dies and they call me back from studying," George says. "And you, Johnny, didn't even say a word."

For the next two hours the conversation ebbs and flows with the two men dredging up shared experiences from over the years. By then the first bottle of rum is empty and George stumbles into the house for another. On the way in he crashes into something. Johnny hears a resounding clap like glasses shattering on the floor. Mary doesn't show up as Johnny expects. Somehow, Johnny figured that she would have come running at the first sound, but maybe she too has changed, he thinks. Moments later, George emerges unscathed. By this time the two men are pretty drunk and the alcohol has loosened their tongues considerably, although George doesn't mention what that ruckus was about.

"One of," George says, trying to wrap his tongue around the words, "one of the hardest thing for me is wondering what will become of you, Johnny. But then I say, I say to myself that you will be, will be probably better off than me. You'll be back home.

In the warm weather. With the people you love, and I'll, I'll be up here shovelling snow for some asshole."

"It's not that easy," Johnny says. "When you realize I've been coming up here for twenty-five years now. That I don't know nobody at home. Everything's changed."

"But that's nothing, man," George says.

"That's why Tommy kill himself. We can't just always try to go back and try to fit in. Twenty-five years is a long time, man. A long time."

Johnny takes a swig and looks out into the darkness, his back to George, standing to his full height. The bulb behind him throws a shadow that abruptly falls off the edge of the patio.

"Take the last time I was at home." Johnny is talking slowly, reflectively. "I was having a few drinks in the rum shop in the village 'til it was time to go home. I left the shop, thinking I was going in one direction, only to find myself in the middle of a pasture, going another way. The whole place's changed on me and I'm lost. I double back and the next thing I know these men are trying to rob me. They take every cent from me and leave me in the gutter, blood running down my face from a big cut over my left eye. The same eye I got a good lick in a couple of days earlier, so that the eye now swell up black and blue. Since then, my eye's never been the same. I still got the scar."

"But you know what I mean, you'd be among your people," George emphasizes.

"I'd be like Frankie too," Johnny says, taking another drink.

"Who?"

"Frankie Devonish. Used to be on the contract cutting canes in Miami. Spent some time up here in Canada too, until he get too old for the Program. Now all he can do is work as a gardener at the airport."

"But you know what I mean. You're building the house at home and you have the wife and three children. We've talked about those things, haven't we? You can spend more time with them."

"The kids? Maybe they won't want to spend any time with me," Johnny says. I can almost swear that Johnny is also arguing with himself. "I have to keep remembering the two boys are young men now and Melissa, my little Melissa, might be the only one interested in seeing me. The last time I was at home, me and the two boys couldn't get along. We couldn't even talk for five minutes to one other. And that...that is why we had the fight. Why I end'd up putting my hand on them and they had to run out of the house."

The two men look at each other. They have gone through many experiences and trials together. Now they are at the end of the line. Now they are drunk together, in this final moment reduced to the same commonness. George Stewart takes up the bottle and hefts it in his hand.

"It didn't have to end like this," he whimpers. "We need farms. The people of this county, of the world, need food. And the farms need people like you and the men, Johnny. People like you are so important, we just can't cast them away. And everybody can't go running to the city or looking for office work. Some of us have to stick around."

In anger, he takes the empty bottle and with all his strength throws it as far as he can into the night. First there is the whistling sound of the bottle hurtling through the air. A long moment of silence. Then the sound of the bottle crashing to the ground out in the darkness, that bottle from Barbados breaking into billions of little pieces. Johnny remembers Cuthbert and his saying "billions of dollars, billions of dollars," and the thought of being near Cuthbert and of Maude makes something in Johnny revolt. For a moment he feels like vomiting. The sound of the crash lasts only a few seconds, but in the calm of the night, the breaking sound is not only amplified but seems to last forever.

Indeed, Johnny thought he heard only the sound of glass breaking. But speaking for myself, it was a broader noise I heard, that of so many dreams crashing and burning.

"I guess I should go and see how the men're doing," Johnny says after a long while.

"Yeah. You gotta leave here at seven o'clock to get to the airport on time," George says. He raises his wrist to the light. "And that's...ah, who cares how long that is?"

"Good...goodnight, George."

"Goodnight, Johnny. And I love you, man. Like a brother, man."

"Bye, George. I'm sorry, man. Real sorry."

Around him the men are busy packing. At first Johnny tries to answer their questions, but in the end he gives up. There is simply no pleasant way of dealing with the bad news. And with the rum in his head, he is not in any mood for long conversations, for trying to explain things that even he doesn't understand. All he knows is that come seven o'clock the next morning, drunk or sober, whether or not anything he says makes any sense to them, they will get onto the school bus and start the trek back home. That is the only certainty. Back to an uncertain life, not knowing if they will ever return to Canada, not knowing what they will do for the rest of their lives. All of them will be going back with one thing in common: empty pockets, flat broke, without even the unpaid wages George Stewart owes them from earlier in the season.

Johnny sits on his cot and picks up the last of his grandfather's diaries. It is the same one he was reading the night before Tommy killed himself. Since then, Johnny has had neither the urge nor the time to continue reading. Even now you might detect a smouldering anger in this man, sparked I think, by the mere sight of this particular diary. I don't like what is happening. Johnny is too cool on the outside, but he is boiling inside. The effects of the rum and now seeing that damn mouldy diary! I don't like it. Something has to give. Not with Johnny smelling stink o' rum and in such a state.

Distrustfully, Johnny looks at the rest of the diaries and thinks too of the letters Tommy kept all these years. What history and stories they tell! What if the people back home were to read them? To read the history of three generations of men in isolation, an experiment no doubt in how well men like these can hold up. Then people would know the truth, and understand why these men cannot just go home and pick up the pieces. The truth of how these men are strangers and how, because they are now trained to act one way, they know no other life, have no other skills. They will always be misfits. There is no rehabilitation, no guidance and, therefore, no future. It is the same story whether the men are returning as homies to the Projects, as a member of the 'hood or to just pick a lime under the village street light. Maybe, Johnny muses, they should all open up and let people know the truth.

Let me break in here and say the following: I am becoming even more concerned about Johnny and this line of thinking. Man, he's too angry. He's not thinking straight. His face, his eyes, every part of him show the difference. I can imagine someone like Albert Jones feeling this way, 'cause his case done salt. Jonesie, poor soul, has to be really disappointed now knowing for sure that Canadians want him for one thing only and that they don't care one fig about him or his dreams. Just pick the damn apples and tobacco and stop dreaming. And while you're at it, they have now confirmed to him, keep out of sight so nobody won't bloody well notice yuh, so everybody's conscience can rest at night. For if you can't do the job, can't help to keep flying into our face and reminding us of what we choose to ignore, we'll get somebody else who will. Good help might be hard to get, but it's always available at the right price. I appreciate the reality behind this thinking; I can also understand that some people, dreamers really, are simply incapable of accepting the raw edge of the knife, the truth. Yes, truth does cut, and deep too. So I can sympathize with someone like Jonesie, over how his house came tumbling down with such sudden and total destruction. But not Johnny. I expect, and demand, better of him. Jonesie and Johnny might be men, but they are not equals. Everybody knows it's, to put it mildly, pie in the sky, mere smoke illusions, to expect these apple-pickers and tobacco harvesters to think they would really be accepted into this country, welcomed beyond their confinement to a farm like this. So let's be real. Let's build our dreams, like our houses, on solid ground. Let's understand the facts of life and accept them. I hope a good dose of sleep is enough to cure Johnny of any virus that might now be loose in this place.

But I'm rambling. Look at how Johnny shakes his head at the implications of what he is proposing. Pride and a sense of commitment would never let these men reveal their secret, to talk to the uninitiated about their bond as men in solidarity. They will take the indignity and teasing that is ahead of them when they return home with no money. Stoically, they will take the insults with pretend bravado, never really explaining what has happened. Just like the soldier returning home on a stretcher, hurting not only from the pain of amputation but also from knowing he hasn't completed his mission, knowing that the only reason soldiers exist is to finish the job. So, Mr. Bugle Boy from Company C will smile and pretend he believes it when people say it is the sacrifice that matters, not only the result. Yeah, it's an honour to contribute and there is no greater achievement than to be chosen as a fighter, he'll tell any youngster in the audience.

What bullshit! Every soldier knows this. What hypocrisy! Nobody rewards losers. Nobody likes them.

Maybe, Johnny is thinking, the people back home should read these diaries and letters and open their eyes. Indeed, perhaps he too needs his own eyes opened, and should complete his own readings when he is back home, when it is hot in the afternoon and he has nothing else to do. That would give him the excuse for not going into the village shop and buying friends by offering round after round of drinks, for not spending money he doesn't have, as he does every time he returns. Instead, he will have to try explaining to Maude why they will have to go slower building the house, why he won't have the money to repay the bank, why their house, like Brer Dove's, may never have a roof.

He could plan to spend his time back home this way: reading, avoiding people and visiting Tommy's and Grafton's graves, and the graves of every goddamn man that died on the Program, whether in Canada, the United States, Panama or wherever. He can invite his family, and Winston, to accompany him on these visits. Maybe this will give him the chance to get to know his boys and Melissa better, to try to come to some understanding with Maude and to slowly prepare himself for a new life, whatever life is available to him. Maybe he can help to keep the men busy by seeing if they would agree to go to the graves of these fallen heroes to beautify them. Perhaps, he thinks, Frankie could give a helping hand here. He might know where they could get flowers for the graves. Maybe flowers identified with the country where the dead men worked. Monuments. So that with time, maybe, simply by looking at a certain floral arrangement anyone could instantly identify the grave and the country where the men laboured.

Something like this, Johnny thinks, would show that people remember these men. And with time, if he approaches the Liaison Officer to get the ball rolling, the government might even take over the project. The same way the government pays Frankie to plant the flowers at the airport supposedly in recognition of the Program's contribution to the island. This could be his project back home, at least until he decides about his own future. To tell the truth, I don't mind Johnny thinking this way and becoming all sentimental and mushy. At least it shows that he isn't defeated yet, that he can occupy his mind by thinking of things to keep himself busy and the men focused when they get back home. Johnny, true to form, recognizes that his leadership will be even more in demand when these men return and become like fish out of water, needing someone to guide them. At least Johnny is one step ahead of them. And I like this preparedness.

Jutting out from the side of the diary is a letter serving as a page mark. Johnny cannot remember receiving or even placing the letter in the diary. He cracks open the book and looks at the writing on the envelope. This is the same letter that Mary Stewart had asked about. It is the letter he received the day Tommy committed suicide but which he was too busy to read, which he forgot about in the aftermath of Tommy's death. He sits on the bed and, obviously still steaming in his calm controlled way, rips open the letter.

"I'm not going home," Winston is saying. There it is. I was wondering how long it would take before someone got around to the question of running. Well, here go these Buffalo soldiers, or is it someone claiming the legacy now more than two hundred years old, riding on the shoulders of those Black Loyalists from the Ethiopian Regiment? Loyalists who, if I may emphasize, were among the first Africans to run away *en masse* from any farm on this continent. But what did they get for their efforts? The same thing these latter-day diplomats now talking about running will inevitably get. Nothing but heartache and grief. Must I spell out everything for yuh?

It doesn't really surprise me that it is Winston, though I expected Smokie, talking this garbage. What startles me even more is that I sense Winston has hit a chord in Johnny. It is almost as if Johnny has lost his sense of reasoning. There he is, with Winston's words resonating in his ears, thinking that he can't blame Winston for thinking of running. If he had his life to live all over, if he had Winston's youth, he would probably take the risk too. It wouldn't surprise him if some of the other men didn't also choose the uncertain future of living in Toronto over the uncertainty of going back home and having to wait until the Liaison Officer put them on a new Program. People like him and maybe Smokie and Delbert and Henry, Preacher Man and Timmy, Mighty and definitely Albert Jones are probably too old now to even be considered for another farm. Not with so many young people lining up for the few jobs. And because he applied unsuccessfully for permanent immigrant status, Albert Jones would definitely not be coming back to Canada, not even if it were possible to place all the men on other farms.

Needless to say, I find this kind of thinking frightening and even dangerous. What has happened to the idea of getting the men to take care of the graves back home? It sounded like a good recommendation to me. Something to do while you're in quasi-retirement or, as some people would say, between assignments. But just as soon as Winston opened his mouth, that suggestion disappeared from Johnny's mind. I can't take this roller-coaster ride, you know man, can't take Johnny acting so unstable in thoughts, if not in deeds. Must be the influence of Bacchus, I tell yuh. 'Cause this could only be *bacchanal* in we arse, and without any music at that, so you can't even dance if you want.

Now tell me something though, what is it in Winston that causes him to have such an impact, such an effect, on a man like Johnny? I can remember when Johnny was a free-thinker. When he was stable as a rock and just as predictable. That Johnny is hiding tonight, or at least playing peek-a-boo; the man in front of me has changed his personality, has pulled the mask off. As if he is the the real trickster, the real Brer Anancy. Remember? *Anancy is a spider, Anancy is a man.* I certainly wouldn't want to be associated with this kind of thinking in any way. And I don't think the true Johnny would either. But there.

"I don't see any reason for going back home," Winston says. Unlike the other men, he is not packing a suitcase. The ones he brought up from Barbados six months earlier are still in the corner. Instead, he is stuffing a few clothes into a blue and white imitation leather travelling bag, a kind of Georgie bundle, just like in the Dick Whittleton story. I am mighty suspicious of this boy, but then again, I freely admit to not knowing what to make of this Winston these days. He's still too erratic for my liking, showing promise in some areas, but totally immature in others.

Some of the men are taking care to note what he is doing. This Winston, as we know, can be real trouble self. I wish Johnny would calm him down, bring to bear, as he did during the domino tournament, the firm hand of surety and experience offsetting his brazen youth, a winning combination. Instead he is seemingly giving tacit approval to Winston's ranting by saying nothing, by almost encouraging him in his thoughts. No, I am not heartless. I can understand why even people like Johnny are a bit concerned about the future. But this is no time to panic, no time to act rashly. No time to go running. This is the moment for a steady hand, a predictability, a calming influence. Cool heads must prevail and we must respect the law. So, you tell me, what the hell is happening to Johnny and Winston? I would like to know. And why doesn't this fool put away those running shoes and stop giving his mouth such liberty?

"Anybody's coming with me?" Winston asks, obviously trying to make an already bad situation worse. Who does he really think would be so foolish as to follow him into a hell hole? A mere boy who hasn't even lost his mother's features yet, let alone earned his spurs. I don't understand this at all. Maybe I should listen to that other storyteller and see if she is making any sense of what we are seeing. If she can, then obviously she is a better man than I, because I can't make head nor tails of this situation. Maybe I'm too old to understand, not like she and this Winston. Still, I suspect, if she is truthful she will admit to being no further ahead than I.

"I plan to cut out at the first sight of light," the fool is advising, obviously feeling so proud of himself, this idle braggadocio. Take my word, and you know how much I hate predicting, but come later this morning, I expect Johnny or someone else will have to do some hard shaking to wake up Winston to get him to pack his bags so he won't be the one holding back the bus. Then we will see how much of a mood he is in for running. "Anybody joining me?"

"Why you got to keep askin', man?" Smokie asks angrily. "You like you can't take a hint or something. Look at me good: you see me touch them running shoes there yet?" he asks, pointing to the blue and white shoes at the head of his cot. "Well, let me spell it out for yuh. If you don't see me touch them shoes to pack them away, then you know I could only be planning one thing. You don't have to keep askin' no foolish questions. 'Cause I really believe the way things are turnin' out that we're goin' to surprise a lot of people later today when they see only a handful o' we, if so many, turn up at the airport. Right, guys?"

The statement gets general approval all around. It appears all the men are willing to take the chance of their life. Although there isn't much conviction in their reply, just as I would expect, I dare say. Remember, these are the same men that swore on their mother's graves they were going to run off in Toronto. Now, ask yourself, just for a reality check, how many of them had the balls to do anything? I want you to remember this point when you hear these men talk, for talk is cheap. Anybody can run his mouth. It costs nothing but hot air. Do like Johnny and ignore all this idle talk.

On the other hand, notice how Johnny is concentrating on the letter in his hand, a deep frown encasing his face. You'll never find a man like Johnny wasting time talking about the improbable. Tell me truthfully, who in his right mind would go running in the darkness, into that great unknown and without one penny in his pocket? 'Cause you must remember every last one of these men is broke, their pockets lined with emptiness, as dry as a biscuit.

"Well, I'm going to try and catch an hour or two o' sleep," Winston says, stretching out on the bed. "I got a few things to send home for my mother and brothers and sisters and I hope somebody could take them for me."

"Why don't you give them to Johnny?" Albert suggests. "In fact, all o' we should give Johnny our things. He might be the only one o' we left to go back. Christ, I still can't believe how they turned me down at the Immigration Department. Think I'd trust anybody any more? Not me. I gotta look out for me own self. Make a way for me and my starve-out children at home."

They look across the room at Johnny, sitting on the edge of the bed, reading Maude's letter and scowling. This is why, deep in my heart, I am not too worried about all this running talk. Ultimately, the men will turn to Johnny for guidance. In the end, they will recognize genuine leadership and common sense. Nothing like what that other storyteller is claiming; for as I, Brer Anancy, know and tell yuh, she ain't even coming close, her expectations don't have even the remotest possibility of seeing the light of day. Still, you should hear her carrying on. You'd think it was Christmas morning.

Johnny is glad that he did not read this letter earlier. No good news here. Melissa, his little girl, has moved out of the home and is living with a man. Maude says she regrets to have to send this sad news, knowing how much Melissa is the apple of Johnny's eye. But Melissa, who of late had taken to acting real womanish, not behaving at all like a young lady, has left home because she couldn't get along with Cuthbert. And, according to the letter, the young man that Melissa has gone and set herself up with, he and her two brothers have all signed up to work on the Program, probably in the United States. As to the house, the bank wants to know why Maude has fallen so far behind in payments and she might have to ask Cuthbert to take over the payments as the government isn't coming through with the insurance and she doesn't think she can wait any longer. With this arrangement, Johnny can repay Cuthbert later. Otherwise, they might lose the house. She says that Cuthbert is suggesting that, so as to make the money stretch, it is better to put a flat-top galvanized-zinc roof on the house, rather than the regular gable roof with shingles, the falling ceiling, that was in the design plan. Maude says she is going ahead right away with all other plans, except for the suggestion about changing the roof, unless Johnny tells her what is going on with him and how soon she can start expecting some help from him. Still, she was holding out for as long as she could about changing the roof, bearing in mind that they are dealing with the crowning glory of the house, and the intended man of the house, by rights, should always have the roof of his choice over his head.

Johnny closes his eyes. He can feel the blood pounding in his head. How could Melissa be so foolish as to do this to herself? And she's so young, he groans to himself. How could she ruin her life? It is all because he was never at home to give her any guidance, Johnny thinks. Now he would never get a chance to make it up to her. Now she will be emulating her mother, and her grandmother and great-grandmother. Johnny hefts the diary in his other hand as if testing its full weight.

He glances at the letter again. Maybe it is the rum in his head, but he can see no reason why a young person would want this type of life. More than that, he can not see why his own children would want this experience. He has to do something to let his boys know that there is no real life working on a farm in somebody else's country. He has to, in perhaps the only fatherly gesture he will ever make in his life, steer them toward something else, anything but this never-ending battle against such incredible odds.

If you continue to look at Johnny's face, you'll see his frustration from not knowing how to communicate with these younger men. Which makes you wonder. How can he in good conscience tell his sons the truth about the Program and yet not betray the secrets of all the men that ever worked on it? Suppose, when the men get back home, they decide not to break under the stress, but continue to live up to their bond to one another and live by their oath. And if Johnny were to tell his own family the truth, what would he tell Barbara and her family if they found out that he tore up Tommy's letters to them, letters that would have, perhaps, made the pain of the suicide a bit easier to handle? So you can understand all this unnecessary worry Johnny is bringing on himself, when he should be concentrating on one thing only — how to sleep off this stupid alcoholic haze that is beginning to make even the ugliest picture attractive to him.

Johnny looks across at Winston stretched out in his jeans. It is a long harsh look, as if he is seeing this young man for the first time. Johnny pulls the blanket over himself and falls fast asleep, his thoughts still not completed. As you might guess, I don't blame him for seeking this down time. In a few hours, he will need all his strength. Like a shepherd, he will have to gather the men around and help them to put on a brave face. They will go home as proud as they left, and the first night back, as has been the tradition for all of this century, they will spend the night doling out the gifts packed in those boxes from Toronto.

Johnny will ensure that everyone gets something to carry back home. I've seen him do it before. Nobody will return with two long, empty hands. Before they finally pack away everything, Johnny will somehow get the men to divvy up the few things they have, so that everybody gets a little something. Then, when they are back home, and life begins to move into a groove, he will think about the implication of the letter from Maude and whether he should have a talk with the boys, if he should tell them the truth or let them discover life for themselves.

And then, maybe after he has rested a month or so, he and all the men, perhaps individually, sometimes in small groups, will go back to the Ministry of Labour and try to get re-assigned to another farm. For, after all, farm work is the only thing they can do. And when the sun is hot and scorching their arses, when the heat waves shimmer off the road and the galvanized tin roofs, whether flat-top or gable, when the sun moves in for the kill, they will need to escape again.

I know, because Brer Anancy knows these endings. Mother Nyame has been after me for the longest time to project my thoughts into the future. That is what I am now doing, and what better time to do it than on the last night on this farm? For in a few short months I swear that these men will be ready to return to the life they talk so fondly of running from. Until then, Johnny will have to make sure these men stay focused. That they stick to what they know best.

Now let me get some sleep too. For tomorrow has all the makings of a very interesting day. As that man said many decades ago, these nights are funny days. Which means that for once I am in complete agreement with that other storyteller: it's definitely a new day breaking. Apparently, she really expects this fool Winston to do something. Someday, I am sure, me and she will sit down and have a good talk, this time face to face. Just the two of us. And I will gently point out to this Miss Never-get-it-right all the mistakes she has made on this farm, all the important signals she missed, how youth can never bamboozle experience.

But such a discussion will have to wait for another day. Right now I need sleep. As Mother Nyame instructs us all to say at the end of the day, *Now I lay me down to sleep...*

———

There is that stirring. Listen! The first rays of the new day's sun are breaking. Winston gets out of bed and in the semi-darkness puts on his shoes. As I did hint, it shouldn't really surprise this ignoramus that everyone is sleeping or, more likely for men used to rising early every morning, pretending to be asleep. None of the men has the heart or the guts to run with him. None of them so foolish. I hope he learns a lesson from them and don't bring down trouble on the men's heads.

And who can blame them for sleeping so strongly, if they really are, for nobody likes taking unnecessary risks. If these men did, they would have run before. Winston knows he has to do it alone. I also hope he knows what a big risk he is taking, for my history tells me no one has ever made it to Toronto running alone. Still, I shed no tears for him. Let him sleep on the bed he made up. If he steps one foot out of here saying he's running, I don't expect him to get as far as the highway before the police and the immigration people snatch him up. Remember them two idiots at the airport? How long did it take for them to get caught? Why should it be any different this time? And let me admit something else right now: if that guy Winston is foolish enough to run, he'll be doing me one big favour — getting rid of that storyteller. She would have to go traipsing after him, while me and Johnny could go about our business, hopefully singing, free at last, free at last, thank God Almighty, free at last. As for me, I will snuggle down in hopes of getting a few more winks before the bus comes.

Gently, Winston puts his pathetic-looking Georgie bundle over his shoulder. He walks quietly to the door of the bedroom, takes one last look and murmurs a soft goodbye to his sleeping friends. Boy, it looks like he's really running for true; he means business. So do the other men, if you know what I mean. People he has never heard snoring are busy sawing logs in their sleep, obviously hoping that he doesn't challenge them by calling any of them by name. Ah, what a shame, heh, heh, heh. Look another Brer Jackass in action. Slowly, he turns to walk away, loping off proudly and upright from the darkness into the light. It will be lonely for him out there. Through the door, a ray of light penetrates the darkness, bouncing off the flooring of the bedroom.

"Wait for me, son," a familiar voice, a bit disguised by sleep, says softly from the darkness. "I coming too."

Winston looks back and in this one ray of sunshine sees a large black hand reach out and grab the pair of running shoes from under Smokie's cot. Right then, I almost die. For when I try to get up to join them in this fruitless run, I find that I can't move. Nobody is holding me down physically, but somehow I feel literally pinned to the bed, my legs kicking in the air. Like some damn *duppy* riding me in my sleep, like all my strength oozing out of me and I can't wake up or shout to end this nightmare.

And it is definitely a nightmare from which I cannot awake. I want to leave, because my duty has not ended. It can't end this way. No way, man. I have to report this emergency and not get left behind. I can't appear guilty of the greatest sin for a storyteller, the iniquity of not anticipating. And I got to leave because I can't take the excitement in the voice of that other storyteller and because I know this story has crossed a crucible.

But I can't move, can't wake up, even though my eyes are wide open. All I can hear are those words of Mother Nyame cautioning me. *Make sure you don't get left behind, Brother Man. Remember, you got to keep up with the times. Anticipate the changes and be ready. Don't just take anything for granted. Just don't get left behind, my friend.*

When I clear my head, I swear I see Mother Nyame at the foot of my bed and she isn't smiling. Then, quick, quick so, she too is gone, leaving an unbearable quiet, except for all those pretend snores. For I still can't move or run. I am paralysed. Worse still, there is something even more frightening. For the first time in a long while, I can't hear the reports of any of my fellow storytellers. Once again, Mother Nyame is pulling the plug on me.

Gradually, the reality of the situation comes home to me. I must acknowledge that my days as a reporter are over, perhaps for good. I will get my movements back, but my voice and where I can go from here on, I am not so sure. Everything I stood for, argue for, is in pieces. What can I now say about any leader, when a youth like this can drag anyone around by the nose, to get a big hard-backed man to do things he would never have thought of. What more can I say? Nothing.

For at this moment I realize that even though I am Brer Anancy, the spider, I am now no different from the men around me. And all this is happening because of that man that let me down so much, the same one that is now running to some damnation with Winston, and that man's name shall never ever cross my lips again. Still, because I am Brer Anancy, I am always entitled to one last trick.

I will erase that person's name from any report in the hand

of Mother Nyame. So that centuries from now, African people will end this story with these words:

> *And because Brer Anancy was so vex, he decided to rub the names of those tricksters out of history. And that is why even to this day everybody talks about the Black man with no name. So that for forever and a day, the Black man will always be running from something, not running to anything to help him. That's why the Black man will always run from rain but run to fire. It's Brer 'Nancy that mek it happen. Jack Mandora. So jump on wire, the wire won't bend; that's the way this story end. Lord have mercy on muh, nuh!*

The silver and white jet touches down at the Barbados airport, kicking up a puff of dust behind it. As my friends the birds scamper for safety, I feel like shouting out to them not to go too far. For my sake. But with my luck, they too will just run away.

With the engines roaring as the plane heads down the runway, rapidly decreasing its speed, I brace myself for an ending to this story that isn't happy. I still can't believe this tragedy. I was unceremoniously stuffed into somebody's bag and kept there in the darkness for this trip back, so I cannot even tell if they caught those two fools and put them on this plane too. In my heart, I fear something bad is happening, but with Mother Nyame keeping the news from me I have no way of knowing. Losers are simply nobodies. Alas! I can now speak from personal experience on that score. Nobody celebrates an army coming back home in rags, even its generals no longer committed to the cause that started the war.

Everything that is happening reminds me so much of the last days with the Prophet, when we were so cut off and isolated. The only thing different is that this time I am not nearly as crazy, even if I am as equally uninformed. Except for the very obvious knowledge that I have definitely screwed up real bad in truth and for the second time.

Try as I might, I can't locate the channel for that other storyteller, the one accompanying that youngster and probably braying about her ability to spot leadership skills and potential, just because that beguiling youngster pulled off the coup of getting a fool twice his age to take a gamble and run with him.

I can't believe I could be so wrong, or that everything I've stood for is now in tatters; for it is true when people say you can spend a lifetime with a man and still not know him. Not that it eases the pain any, but for a consolation all I can tell myself is that these things always happen when a woman is involved. Men just go screwy over them, no discipline can keep them in line. They will endure anything, take anything. Damn dogs. In this case the youngster ran for the love of a woman. For a woman some of his comrades do not think is of the right colour or background. A woman at whom the Prophet would have sneered. And the idiot for an older man runs to be with the youngster, turning nature as we know it on its head.

All I can say is that this is just like here at home, when the dogs come from miles around for the bitch in heat. How they gather under the cellar of the house, yapping and barking, fighting and making so much noise people can't sleep, so that occasionally someone has to throw a bucket of water on them. But what do they care about getting wet? That is just part of the risk, part of the terrain, just like getting caught goes with running. These dogs would walk and run for miles, just for a little piece. What a story we have here in the making, one that, thank God, I will not now be called upon to complete. Besides, I have bigger potatoes of my own to stew. I am definitely not looking forward to meeting Mother Nyame and begging for yet another chance.

Through the window, I can see the relatives and friends awaiting us. They are pressing against the airport glass to look for the returning men. The expectation and tension must be high among them. I know it is with me. Judging from the larger than usual crowd, word must have spread fast around the island. Of how when the government officials called the families with the unexpected news of the men's return, they also had some more titillating information, about the two that went missing, the two with no names.

The officials could only tell the families that nobody would know who the missing men were until the bus arrived at the airport and the men checked in. Judging from the bits of conversations I picked up here and there, apparently, in a last act of defiance, still obviously clinging to this much-discredited bond, the men steadfastly refused to divulge the names of the runners. As it turns out, the Officer was meeting with the immigration people and could not make it to the airport to see the men off. When he telephoned once more asking for names, nobody broke the promise, everyone remained silent. Nobody was willing to step forward and be a leader. Even George Stewart wasn't cooperating. Except I noticed that at the very last moment, when the plane started moving, there was one big excitement, the men clapping and whooping it up, and I knew all that had to mean only one thing — the arrival of those two fools. They had to have been caught, otherwise how would you explain the wild elation when the plane doors closed? Obviously it was joy at having them back in the fold safe and sound, no more wandering off like lost sheep in search of a master, for these men are proud to have come as a team and to be returning as a team, jubilation to be followed by just silence, an uncomfortable quiet, for the entire journey. It has to be that that experiment ended in failure. Now I'll find out for sure as we disembark. Still, I must be careful to keep my distance from that man with no name. You know I don't like to bear grudges but, still, it'll be a long time before I forgive him.

Even from the plane I can sense the tension between family and friends. Impatiently, I wait in the bag of my trustee and observe, just in case Mother Nyame asks me for a debriefing. Once again, this airport has captured the interest of the entire island, allowing people to put off, if only for a short while, their interminable daily battles, a chance to gossip and talk. Even the sun in its glory appears nosey, and while it blazes away from a cloudless sky, I cannot help feeling it too is suspending hostilities until it finds out what will now happen to this person with no name. From my spot, I can see Frankie over by the far end of the terminal watering the gardens, but also looking steadfastly at the door of the plane.

Slowly, the doors of the plane swing open and the first of the men, mixing with the regular tourists, appear on the steps. Batches on batches of passengers are coming out in a rush. Then there is a trickle, as the attention turns to the long queues at customs. Family members identify some of the men in the long lines and wave to them.

I am going to crawl through a hole in this bag. No, I'm not running away too, so don't start making jokes. I am freeing myself so that I can wait inside the plane for as long as possible. For I cannot face the outside without knowing the full story. Only then will I know all my options. I prefer to go out when it is quiet, when I will be exposed to my friends the birds in case I need them. For like all those people waiting outside, I don't know what to expect. To acknowledge this development in my life is like eating humble pie. And it doesn't taste good, not even with a generous dollop of Caribbean pepper sauce to spice it up. It will take me some time to accept that, once again, my reports have been useless, that my bosses were right to send another storyteller to shadow me. Lord knows I don't want to accept this judgement and the resulting sentence. My fate, dear friends, is now in the hands of a man with no name. How is that for irony? How would *you* like to be in my position?

No more bodies are emerging from the plane. This is my chance. I look to see if the coast is clear. I can see Maude and Cuthbert exchanging bewildered glances. They can't believe their eyes. My heart is pounding so fast it feels like it will explode. Frankie goes over and joins them. I can see a mischievous look on his face, and I don't like it. Please, dear Lord.

"Christ," I hear Frankie say, "I can't believe that of all the people *he* would be the one to run, to be slammin' tar all like now." And then he says it again, louder, more purposefully this time. "Of all people, not *he*. Yuh lie, man. Not in a million years. I'd never expect he to do a thing like that."

I can hear that annoying laughter in Frankie's voice, a vindicated mirth reaching me over the noise of the waves bashing Brer Donkey's bones, as if that old fart Frankie is finally saying to Cuthbert, and to Maude also, it's payback time. As if he too hears the cooing of doves and knows that one more house will have to go without a roof.

But yes, my brothers and sisters, that man with no name ain't going to be the last off the plane today. Finally, the flight attendants are coming down the stairs and the doors are closing behind them, so I'd better get out. Maude and Cuthbert turn to leave. Sad to say that man with no name ain't coming home. He's too busy, as Frankie says, slammin' tar, running like some idiot into an uncertain future, like Brer Donkey trying to find a back door. Do you think it's the rum that changed him so? Regardless, all I can say is that it is all over now, especially for this storyteller. I salted.

The only thing I can hope for as I come out of this plane is a shadow and then a swift ending. Quickly, so I will not have to endure much more. I hope the darkness covers me, not as a respite from the battle with the sun, but in the same way fate intervened when I believed I was alighting from one of the vessels of the Black Star Line. For if, as some diarists claim, we simply repeat the same stories over and over only in different forms, then let this ending be the same. If Mother Nyame has any mercy, she would instruct Brer Bird, preferably one of those long-neck gaulins — not Brer Dove for I can't take his prophesies any more — to swoop down and remove me, her faithful and now humble servant Brer Anancy, from this misery, so I can immediately begin my atonement and my re-education. So that, perhaps, one day she will lift my curse.

And if you can hear me Brer Bird, wherever you are, I beg you, please come quick, quick, quick.

A riddle, a riddle, a ree...

A NOTE ABOUT THE AUTHOR

Cecil Foster is the author of several works of fiction and non-fiction, including the critically acclaimed *No Man in the House* and *Sleep On, Beloved*. His latest work, *A Place Called Heaven*, a study on racism and the Black experience in Canada, recently won the Gordon Montador Award for Best Canadian Non-Fiction Book on Social Issues. Mr. Foster has also written for leading Canadian magazines such as *Maclean's*, *Report on Business*, *Chatelaine* and *Toronto Life*. A frequent radio and television commentator, he has worked for *The Toronto Star*, *The Globe and Mail* and was a Senior Editor at the *Financial Post*. The former host of "Urban Talk" on Radio CFRB in Toronto, Mr. Foster also did stints in the newsrooms of CBC Radio and Television and for CTV News. He lives in Toronto.